Noir:
Three Novels of Suspense

Also by Richard Matheson

NOIR:
THREE NOVELS OF SUSPENSE

RICHARD MATHESON

A Tom Doherty Associates Book
New York

NOIR: THREE NOVELS OF SUSPENSE

First published in 1997 by G&G Books, Delavan, Wisconsin.

Copyright © 1997 by Richard Matheson

Introduction copyright © 1997 by Matthew R. Bradley
Someone Is Bleeding copyright © 1953 Richard Matheson; renewed in 1981 by Richard Matheson
Fury on Sunday copyright © 1953 by Richard Matheson
Ride the Nightmare copyright © 1959 by Richard Matheson; renewed in 1987 by Richard Matheson

A Forge Book
Published by Tom Doherty Associates, LLC
175 Fifth Avenue
New York, NY 10010

www.tor.com

Forge® is a registered trademark of Tom Doherty Associates, LLC.

ISBN 0-765-31139-9 (hc)
EAN 978-0-765-31139-9 (hc)
ISBN 0-765-31140-2 (pbk)
EAN 978-0-765-31140-5 (pbk)

First Forge Edition: October 2005

Printed in the United States of America

0 9 8 7 6 5 4 3 2 1

INTRODUCTION

by Matthew R. Bradley

For those who know Richard Matheson only through his celebrated *Twilight Zone* scripts, the Edgar Allan Poe films he wrote for director Roger Corman, and the memorable TV-movies *Duel* (1971) and *The Night Stalker* (1972), it may come as something of a revelation that he has written widely outside the realms of horror, science fiction, and fantasy. His impressively diverse body of work also includes five Westerns, a work of mainstream fiction based on his World War II experiences in the 87th Division of the U.S. Infantry in Germany, an Emmy Award-nominated telefilm about the effects of alcoholism, and biopics of the Marquis de Sade and Oz creator L. Frank Baum. To Matheson, the quality of the storytelling has always mattered more than any pigeonhole into which that story might be placed, and as he remarked with only slight exaggeration in *Richard Matheson: He Is Legend*, the seminal "illustrated bio-bibliography" compiled in 1984 by Mark Rathbun and Graeme Flanagan, "I only do things once—and then move on."

For Matheson aficionados, the hardcover publication of these novels is a literary event, for all three were issued as paperback originals in the 1950s and, incredibly for a writer of such stature, have never been reprinted in the U.S. "A lot of these things that were published back then were just sort of forgotten, then later on people look on them with awe as *noir* classics," Matheson observes. His first two published novels, both *Someone Is Bleeding* and *Fury on Sunday* were issued by Lion Books in 1953 at 25¢ apiece, rising to a princely 35¢ when Ballantine released *Ride the Nightmare* (1959). Any of these would command hundreds of dollars today, and with the recent release in its uncut form of *Earthbound* (so heavily edited on its 1982 publication by Playboy Press that he substituted his pen name of Logan Swanson), they are Matheson's most sought-after works.

It may seem odd that Matheson, who had established himself in the SF community at the age of twenty-three with his very first published short story, "Born of Man and Woman" (*The Magazine of Fantasy & Science Fiction*, Summer 1950), would graduate to writing novels—albeit brief ones of 159 and 128 pages, respectively—outside that community. Indeed, the bulk of his published work up until that point had been of a fantastic nature, and included such classic stories as "Third from the Sun" (*Galaxy*, October 1950), "'Drink My Red Blood...'" (aka "Blood Son"; *Imagination*, April 1951), "Witch War" (*Startling Stories*, July 1951), and "Dress of White Silk" (*Fantasy & Science Fiction*, October 1951). As Matheson told Mark Rathbun in an interview for *He Is Legend*, "I backed into that field completely. They said that ["Born of Man and Woman"] was a mutation story, about which I knew nothing—I'd never heard of such a thing. But then, in the early '50s, they had an enormous amount of science fiction magazines, so being practical, I decided I'd try it."

Born of Norwegian parents in Allendale, New Jersey, on February 20, 1926, Matheson was raised in Brooklyn, graduated from Brooklyn Technical School in 1943 before entering the military, and came to California in 1951. While staying with pulp writer William Campbell Gault, he told Rathbun, "I joined this group called The Fictioneers, and almost all of them were mystery writers, so I started writing mysteries. If they'd all been science fiction and fantasy writers, I probably would have tried that type of novel first. And the mystery phase didn't last long, of course—I just did a couple and that was about it." His occasional contributions to the genre in later years included sales to *Alfred Hitchcock's Mystery Magazine* ("The Children of Noah" and "I'll Make It Look Good" [aka "A Visit to Santa Claus," as Swanson], March 1957) and *Ellery Queen's Mystery Magazine* ("What Was in the Box" [aka "Big Surprise"], April 1959; "Needle in the Heart" [aka "Therese"], October 1969; "Till Death Do Us Part," September 1970; "Leo Rising," May 1972).

As Gault—to whom Matheson paid playful homage in his humorous story "Miss Stardust" (*Startling Stories*, Spring 1955)—recalled in an affectionate essay printed in *He Is Legend*, "Dick Matheson (in those days) had the same agent I then had. Both of us have changed since. I had enjoyed his short stories, and when he came out to California, I met him at the bus station in Santa Monica. I forget how long he lived with us, not long. I got him a job at the Pacific Palisades Post Office where I had worked, but he soon tired of that and got a much better paying job at Douglas Aircraft in Santa Monica. He tried at that time to get some studio acceptance as a writer without luck. So he moved back to New York. Naturally, as soon as he was three thousand miles away, the studios wanted him. You know the hackneyed adage: 'Don't call me; I'll call you.' It was the start in that area of his many-sided successes. I remember *Someone Is Bleeding* because it was dedicated to me [as "Bill Gault, a guy you can call your friend without crossing your fingers"].

"As for the Fictioneers," added Gault, "if they had been alive neither Henry James, Mark Twain nor even (if here in America and resurrected) the Bard himself would have been accepted into that group. The major qualification for membership was that one had to be a pulp writer or a *former* pulp writer. Many of the members had gone on to the slick magazines by then but the old camaraderie of the pulp gang persisted, a great and (generally) nonpretentious group of fairly hard drinkers, though Dick was not one of the heavy imbibers, nor [Ray] Bradbury, nor the late Chuck Beaumont. [William R.] Cox was a member, as were Henry Kuttner [a fellow science fiction writer to whom Matheson dedicated his third novel, *I Am Legend*], Les Savage, Frank Bonham, W.T. Ballard, Frederic Brown, Dean Owens, Mel Colton, Chick Coombs and Wilbur [S.] Peacock. But that was in another country and many of the nonwenches are dead....Dick has never shown any pretension. He is as natural as rain and just as refreshing, a true talent."

Matheson notes that although his fellow Fictioneers indirectly influenced the subject matter of his first novel, none of them provided a specific stylistic influence: "I hadn't read any of them. As I said, I was living with Bill Gault for a very short time. I think he was just writing his first novel, *Don't Cry for Me* [1952], that won the Mystery Writers of America [Edgar Allan Poe] Award, and then he went on to write twenty or thirty others. But I think the only mystery novels I'd read were twenty or twenty-five of John Dickson Carr's books. Not only were his mysteries absolutely impossible to solve—even though he was totally fair, unlike Agatha Christie—but he wrote wonderfully. He was a marvelous author, and his historical novels are great. Then as Carter Dickson, he wrote the Sir Henry Merrivale books. They were great, too. And he had supernatural overtones to many of his mysteries. As I said, I think I'd read about twenty of them at the time, but obviously there was no hint of me trying to imitate him with the locked-room mysteries or anything.

"Actually, my first novel was written when I was sixteen years old. It was called *The Stars Stood Still*. It was a true story that Mary Baker Eddy mentioned in *Science and Health* or one of her books, about a teenaged girl who had fallen down a flight of stairs and never aged; in her fifties she still looked like she was seventeen. So I wrote a terrible novel, maybe 170 pages long, something like that. Then I started writing another one, a variation on *The Island of Dr. Moreau* called *Island of the Animals*, and wrote quite a bit of that. And then, long before I wrote *Someone Is Bleeding*, I wrote this novel in New York with the pretentiuous title of *Hunger and Thirst*, like a great Russian epic, a young man's attempt to be really arty. It was about a young guy who's down and out and robs a pawn shop, and the owner shoots him in the back. He manages to get back to his furnished room and falls on the bed. Something snaps in his back, and he's paralyzed and spends the next, I don't know, however long it takes, dying of hunger and thirst.

"While he's doing it he thinks about his entire past, going back to his childhood, the war—there's a war section I later revised for *The Beardless Warriors* [1960]—high school, college, everything. The book was about 800 pages long. My agent at that time hated it, and I was crushed. I showed it to Henry Kuttner and he wrote me a letter, and the first line was, 'Your agent's a damned fool.' But it was just something a young guy writes when he's full of himself and wants to do something big. It never sold, but it was a big whopper of a novel, so obviously I knew how to put a long piece together. When I was going to do my second one, equally obviously I wasn't going to make the same mistake and do another Leo Tolstoy-type novel."

■ ■ ■ ■

Of these three novels, *Someone Is Bleeding* comes closest to the traditional definition of a mystery with its focus on "who done it?," evoking the work of Cornell Woolrich in its depiction of a man drawn ever deeper into an increasing spiral of uncertainty and danger. "I don't even know whether I'd read Cornell Woolrich at that time," Matheson says, "but Tony Boucher referred, I think in his review, that it was very much like Cornell Woolrich, the mid-day terrors, things like that. Obviously, the one man up against the wall was his major theme, too, as it certainly was mine and always has been." *Fury on Sunday* and *Ride the Nightmare*, on the other hand, concentrate on pure suspense as they place their protagonists in jeopardy from implacable antagonists who are driven by lust, greed, insanity, and/or a desire for revenge, each relentlessly ratcheting up the tension as it explores the ramifications of its premise and builds to a suitably violent climax.

While these novels have sometimes been labeled as *noir* or hard-boiled fiction, and Matheson himself has occasionally referred to them as mysteries, he notes, "They're suspense. The only thing that has any scintilla of mystery is *Someone Is Bleeding. Noir's* all right, it just means 'dark.' But hard-boiled, I mean, maybe these private eye things, you know, where the guy is getting sapped every other chapter and falling down on the ground and down a black tunnel and then coming to, or he's punching people out—I never wrote that, I never came anywhere near hard-boiled. But *noir* is fine, sure. They have a darker cast on storytelling."

Someone Is Bleeding is among a half-dozen of Matheson's seventeen published novels written in the first person, including the romantic fantasies *Bid Time Return* (aka *Somewhere in Time*, 1975) and *What Dreams May Come* (1978) and the Westerns *Journal of the Gun Years* (1991) and *The Memoirs of Wild Bill Hickok* (1996). "I alternated between them," he observes. "You start out when you're writing doing it in first person, then I guess you decide that it's more professional, more cool, to do it in third person. You're one step removed and maybe you can describe things more objectively. Later on you say, 'Hell, I *like* first person.' But I have this thing about suspense novels, that if these terrible things are going to happen to the hero and he's writing in the first person, you know that no matter what happens to him in the book he must have gotten through it because he's telling the story. Unless you do it day by day, and that's no good either, because you can't have him write about any part of it 'til after it happens, and then it's not as suspenseful, either."

David Newton, the narrator and protagonist of *Someone Is Bleeding*, resembles Matheson in several ways: both are young writers who have come to California from New York just a few years after graduating from the University of Missouri Journalism School, and David is also working on a novel— "except," Matheson adds, "that he was obviously making a living out of his writing and I needed a job! I was working at Douglas Aircraft. I don't know what he made his money on." Given his reported lack of success with the studios, it is perhaps not surprising that Matheson takes a few potshots at the film industry, especially during a party scene in which David meets an aspiring, amply-endowed actress and pretends to be a producer at Metro whose greatest picture was called *Vanilla Vomit*. Matheson laughs that in re-reading the novel, "I thought, 'Jeez, I've gotta change that. It's ridiculous. It makes him look like an idiot.' I never really tried to get into screenwriting. I just had the typical smart-ass attitude toward the Hollywood scene."

David also shares his creator's status as a veteran of World War II, in which Matheson saw action and later received a medical discharge after sustaining a combat-related injury, and during the novel's climactic chase runs "through a woods so deep it reminded me of the Hurtgen Forest, another place where I'd faced death." Of the novel he based on his wartime experiences, Matheson told Rathbun, "The reviews I have on *The Beardless Warriors* said the combat sections were so vividly described that it was almost painful to read.

But you cannot overdescribe the horrors of war. It's not just like describing violence in a crime story where you can say, 'Well, that's not necessary—that's gratuitous.' [No description of violence] in war [can be] gratuitous. I was part of every one of the characters in *The Beardless Warriors*... I liked the book, and I think it's pretty well done. It's one of the few things that I can re-read and think, 'Well, gee, that's not bad.' Of course, they made [an inferior] movie out of it [*The Young Warriors*], and that's a shame.

"The theme of almost all my earlier stories was someone alienated by some strange occurrence from his normal way of life," he elaborated, which to some degree applies to his crime fiction as well as his fantasy. "Actually, whatever theme I had would be just what my inner psyche was doing at that time. I never had any conscious theme, and when people started pointing [mine] out to me, I was surprised to hear it... But that's true of any writer—you could go through the works of Bob Bloch, Harlan Ellison and Ray Bradbury—go back through everything they've written, and see where their mind was at the time. I wrote *The Beardless Warriors* because I had been there. In *Someone Is Bleeding*, the first chapter is exactly how I met my wife, Ruth. In *What Dreams May Come*, the whole novel is filled with scenes from our past. I think every writer does it. They may disguise it or they may do it more openly, but you can't get away from it; you're always going to write about your own life. I mean, the wives of my characters were called Ruth [a] lot of times."

As Matheson noted, the most overtly autobiographical element in *Someone Is Bleeding* is that first encounter on a sparsely populated California beach between David and blonde, brown-eyed, and pretty Peggy Ann Lister on a brisk weekday in June, "sky a little overhung, the Palisades greyish behind the mist... A long stretch of beach with just her and me." However, one can only assume that any resemblance to Matheson's relationship with the then newly-divorced Ruth Ann Woodson, to whom he has been happily married since 1952, ends there, for as the reader soon learns, Peggy Ann Lister is clearly someone around whom it is not safe for a man to be—or even to *be* a man, all of whom except for David she summarily dismisses as "pigs."

David's narration also allows Matheson to include a considerable amount of foreshadowing, such as when he first hears Peggy describe a man as a "pig": "A significant remark. Not to me at the time. But later I understood... How could a face like that give you premonitions? It just didn't. And that was too bad." From here on in, these three novels share the distinctive elements of crime fiction at its toughest: booze, guns, knives, chases, aberrant psychology, blackmail, icepick murders, *femmes fatales*, sinister psychos, brutish thugs, drunks, nymphos, homicide dicks, and a generous helping of sweat.

Fittingly, the rare film version of Matheson's *noir* debut would be written and directed by Georges Lautner under the novel's French title, *Les Seins de Glace* (*Icy Breasts*, 1974); Gallimard had also published F.M. Watkins's translation of *Fury on Sunday* in 1971 as *Jour de Fureur* (*Day of Fury*). "My recollection is that the film doesn't follow the book all that closely, and of course it takes place in France, so it has a different environment," notes Matheson. "I'd like to get the film rights back because I think in today's market it might do well out here. The hero [Claude Brasseur] was some guy I never heard of, nor the woman [Mireille Darc]. I know Alain Delon played the lawyer. That was the right thing—Alain Delon looked too sophisticated to play this naive writer. It's been ages since I saw it, so I don't really remember it. Now that we're talking about it, I seem to have a vague recollection that someone sent me a copy, but if they did, I still don't remember it. It must be a very memorable film if I've seen it in the last few years and I still don't remember it!"

■ ▥ ▤ ▢

"Four Seething Hours with a Depraved Man," promised the lurid jacket copy on Matheson's stunning sophomore effort, *Fury on Sunday*. "Boy, that's right," he notes, "but there are more people. It's 'four seething hours,' so to speak, but it's one of the few novels I ever wrote where I jumped from viewpoint to viewpoint, which I almost never do. *Hell House* [1971] is the only other one that I can recall that I ever did that in. I wrote *Fury on Sunday* in three days. We lived in an apartment right near the beach I used for *Someone Is Bleeding*. I had a little typewriter, my old Standard Corona that I got when I was twelve years old from my sister at Christmas, and I sat in a closet and banged the thing out in three days. That's why some of the writing is quite interesting, because it's really stream of consciousness. They almost made it for TV two or three years ago. We were ready—Allen Epstein, a producer who did several things that I wrote for television; James Sadwith, who did *Sinatra* [1992] was going to direct it; and I had the script. We went to HBO and they said no. Maybe someday."

The story centers on Vincent Raden, a concert pianist in his mid-twenties who escapes from a Manhattan insane asylum and, over the next four hours, tracks down the people in his former orbit with an eye towards punishing those he believes have wronged him.

"I've always liked to do that," Matheson says of the novel's compressed time-span. "One of the first things I ever did for television, even before *The Twilight Zone*, was for the Western series *Lawman*. It was called 'Thirty Minutes,' and it took place in a half hour. I like to do that, and I thought, 'the shorter the period of time I can make it, the better,' so I just set *Fury on Sunday* over one night. I don't enjoy suspense novels where weeks go by. Although it had some flaws in it, the best suspense picture I ever saw was Andrew L. Stone's *The Last Voyage* [1960]. It started out behind the titles and went right through to the very end, never flagging, and that to me is really good suspense. In *Zulu* [1964], the time span was a little longer, but still it progressed and progressed. A wonderful movie."

Vince is one of Matheson's most terrifying creations, his fingers constantly in motion as they pick out various passages of classical music on a nonexistent keyboard, and his emotional state equally changeable as he veers between cold calculation and a hot-tempered desire for vengeance. He echoes the unnamed narrator of Poe's "The Tell-Tale Heart" in his misplaced insistence on his own sanity: "They thought him mad. That was their mistake. Did the truly mad plot escape the way he did, with detail and care? No, not the mad. They gibbered and beat fists on plaster walls and kicked at the door... But they never planned like this." Asked how he conceived of this psychotic pianist, Matheson replied, "When you write something in three days, you don't 'conceive' of anything, you just open your brain and it all floods out. It's just the concept, it all depends on the concept, that's all. So this was the concept, that this maniac gets loose and terrorizes these people."

While such aspects of sexual dysfunction as frigidity and nymphomania that appear in *Someone Is Bleeding* and *Fury on Sunday* may have been considered somewhat shocking at the time of their original publication, Matheson takes pains to point out that, "When I do something, it's inherent in the story. I don't put it in for its own sake. Of course, when you're a younger writer you always have a tendency to put more sex in your stories, because your hormones are raging anyway, so it creeps—sometimes explodes—into your work. But even so, I don't think I ever just dragged it in by the hair just to have it in there. Even then I had this feeling that you've got to be true to the concept. I never wrote really sexual stuff until I did *Hell House*, and because it was supposed to be such an evil place, I felt, well, I had to do it, otherwise it's going to sound ridiculous to call it the most evil haunted house in the world and, you know, they're cheating at Monopoly or something."

It was a much more accomplished Matheson who returned to crime fiction with *Ride the Nightmare* after publishing three other novels, including the two for which he is best known—*I Am Legend* (1954) and *The Shrinking Man* (1956)—and the first to draw on his lifelong interest in what he calls the "supernormal," *A Stir of Echoes* (1958). He had also produced two critically praised collections, *Born of Man and Woman* (1954) and *The Shores of Space* (1957), and become a screenwriter, cannily making the sale of film rights to *The Shrinking Man* dependent on his adapting it into director Jack Arnold's masterpiece, *The Incredible Shrinking Man* (1957). "I think probably writing for films helps you," he notes, "not in your actual word use or descriptions, because sometimes I think your writing becomes thinner; a lot of novels today are like screenplays in past tense. But what it does enhance, if you pick up on it, is an ability to make a story move fast, because you can't waste time in a film, and you shouldn't waste time in a novel, at least a genre novel."

Spanning the hours between Wednesday night and Thursday afternoon, *Ride the Nightmare* begins with an anonymous phone call to the Santa Monica home of Chris Martin, a call that will lead to the revelation of a dark secret from his past and a suspenseful struggle to hold onto his family in the present. "He had done the only thing possible. That was what made it all a nightmare. Everything seemed so inevitable....Nothing could have happened in any other way. It was as if they were trapped in some inexorable plan which had determined their past and their present and would also determine their future."

Ride the Nightmare is one of Matheson's few works to have been dramatized more than once, the first time as an episode of *The Alfred Hitchcock Hour* directed by Bernard Girard and broadcast on November 29, 1962. "It was all right," recalls Matheson, who adapted the novel himself. "It was only an hour long, which means with twelve minutes off [for commercials] it was only forty-eight minutes, which was a little short for a novel. It had Hugh O'Brian and [John] Cassavetes's wife, Gena Rowlands. As I recall—I haven't seen it since then—I guess it was done reasonably well. I think Norman Lloyd [a former actor who had played the title role in Hitchcock's *Saboteur*, 1942] produced it." Matheson's only other contribution to the series was an adaptation of Julian Symons's *The Thirty-First of February*, which aired on January 4, 1963, under the Swanson pseudonym, he relates, "because they changed it so much. I didn't like what they did to the script. I've seen it, and it just doesn't add up the way I think my script did. It's an interesting novel."

The French-Italian *Cold Sweat* (aka *The Man with Two Shadows*, 1971) typified the kind of polyglot production in which the late Terence Young specialized after directing the James Bond films *Dr. No* (1962), *From Russia with Love* (1963), and *Thunderball* (1965). It featured an American leading man, Charles Bronson, who starred in Young's next two films, *Red Sun* (1971) and *The Valachi Papers* (1972); a British villain, James Mason, who had appeared in the director's *Mayerling* (1968); and a Norwegian leading lady, Liv Ullmann, best known for her work with Swedish *auteur* Ingmar Bergman in films such as *Persona* (1966). Ironically, while *Cold Sweat*— a phrase that does appear in the novel—is one of the few adaptations of Matheson's work outside the fantasy genre, screenwriter Shimon Wincelberg (who shared script credit with Albert Simonin) was a veteran of many science fiction series and, under his frequent pen name of S. Bar David, contributed to the original *Star Trek*, for which Matheson himself wrote the fifth episode, "The Enemy Within."

Despite changing the location to the Riviera, the film begins fairly faithfully with Bronson as Joe Martin, an American expatriate who runs a fishing boat in the south of France, Ullmann as his wife, and Mason, affecting a jaw-dropping Southern accent, as his nemesis, Ross. The primary departure from the novel is the inclusion of a new character, Ross's pot-smoking, guitar-toting girlfriend, Moira, presumably as a vehicle for British actress Jill Ireland, Bronson's frequent co-star and real-life wife from 1968 until her death of cancer in 1990. Once again, Matheson laments, "They changed the story. They tried to open it up and make it big—he's got a boat, and it's in the Riviera. I mean, it should have been great, with James Mason as the villain and Liv Ullmann playing his wife, my Lord. It should have turned out better. But most of my stuff is small-scale. Whenever they try to open it up and make it big-scale, it takes away from it. You set it in the Riviera instead of Latigo Canyon in Los Angeles, it puts too much of a weight on it."

The vagaries of the cinema aside, Matheson is pleased to have the novels available once again. "I love it," he says. "I mean, if nothing else, it's nice to have them in permanent print. It gave me a chance to re-read them, which I would never have done otherwise, and find some pleasure in what I did. It's like, 'Yeah, this stuff's not half bad.' There's a scene [in *Ride the Nightmare*] which sort of has a British quality to it, where [Chris] is in agony in the bank waiting to take some money out, and this woman comes up who he's been working with on a musical charity, and wants him to talk all about it, and he's dying inside. That's the sort of the thing the British do, and that's nice suspense." Fortunately, a whole new generation of readers will now be able to savor that suspense in the pages that follow.

SOMEONE

IS

BLEEDING

CHAPTER ONE

IT WAS A pretty brisk day, as I recall. Sky a little overhung, the Palisades greyish behind the mist. I suppose that's why the beach wasn't too crowded. Then again, it was a weekday and school hadn't let out yet. June. Put them together and what have you got?

A long stretch of beach with just her and me.

I'd been reading. But it got tiresome so I put the book down and sat there, arms around my knees, looking around.

She had on a one-piece bathing suit. Her figure was slight but well-placed. I guessed she was about five-five. She was gazing intently at the waves. Her short-chopped blonde hair was stirring slightly in the breeze.

"Pardon me but could..." I said.

She wasn't turning. She kept looking at the shifting blue ocean. I looked over her figure again. Very well-placed. A model's figure. The kind you see in *Mademoiselle*.

"Have you the time?" I asked.

She turned then.

Eyes. That was my first impression. The biggest and the brownest eyes I'd ever seen, great big eyes seeming to search for something. A frank look, a bold one, meaning a bold curiosity. But no smile. Deadpan. Did you ever have a child watch you from the seat in front of you in a bus or a trolley car?

That's what it was like.

Then she lifted her arm and looked at her watch. "One-thirty," she said.

"Thank you," I answered.

She turned away. Her eyes moved to the sea again. I felt the uneasiness of the unconsolidated beachhead.

I rested on my elbows and looked at her profile. Delicately upturned nose. Lovely mouth. And those eyes.

After watching a while to catch her eyes again, I gave up. I was no professional at pickups. I got up slowly and walked down to the water. I felt her eyes following me.

I didn't leap in like athletes do. I stalled, I edged, I shivered. I evolved quick arguments for forgetting the whole thing.

Then I slid forward with a shudder and swam out a little way. Body heat took up the chills, my blood started moving.

On my back, looking up at the sky I wondered if I should speak to her. Whether it was worth it.

Then, when I came dripping back, she asked me if the water were cold.

I jumped at the opening.

"Pretty cold," I said. "I'll give you ten dollars if you go in."

She shook her head with a smile.

"Not me," she said.

I dried myself.

"Does the weather get cold out here?" I asked her. Weather talk, I thought. Always an ample wedge.

"It gets cold at night," she said.

The eyes intent on me again. I almost felt restive. They *were* searching. But for what?

I edged a little closer to her blanket.

"Well, I've just come from New York," I said, "and I came to get warm."

"Oh," she said, "is it cold there?"

Weather talk. Enough to start on. We eased into other things. California. New York. People. Cars. Dogs. Children.

"Do you like good music?" she asked me.

"What's good music?" I asked.

"Classical music."

"Sure," I said, "I love it."

The eyes looking harder. Was that the basis of the search?

"Gee," she said.

She sat hugging her knees. The filtering sunlight touched her white shoulders. She couldn't have been more than seventeen, I thought.

I was smiling. "Why gee?" I asked her.

"Because men never like good music," she said. "My..."

She stopped. Her eyes lowered.

"What's the Hollywood Bowl like?" I asked her, not wanting to let conversation run down.

She was looking again, shaking her head.

"I don't know," she said, "I sure wish I could go, though."

Too easy, I thought. Where is the hedging, the sly evasions, the mental sparring of a he and she? The moxie?

No moxie in Peggy.

That was her name.

"What's yours?" she asked.

"David," I said, "David Newton."

And so we talked. I'm trying to remember the significant things she said. They came out once in a while in between straight data about her mother, dead, her father, a retired navy man, her profession, none, and her spirit, obviously stepped on somewhere.

She saw my book and asked what it was. I told her, and we got started on the subject of historical novels.

"They're dirt," she said, "nothing but sex."

Something in her eyes. A hardness. I said why read them if they offend her.

"I'm looking for a decent one," she said.

"I'll write one," I said.

Obvious move. Impress the little girl. I am a writer, what do you think about that, young lady?

She didn't catch it.

We kept skating around with words. Talking about home and background, school and other things. I told her I'd graduated from the University of Missouri Journalism School three years before. She told me about traveling around with her mother, father and brother until her mother died, then she and Phillip, her brother, not being able to follow the old man from one base to another anymore. So they stayed in San Francisco with a friend of her mother's.

"She was a swell woman," Peggy Lister said. "But her husband…"

"What about him?"

"He was a pig," she said.

A significant remark. Not to me at the time. But later I understood.

Now, though, I just listened halfway, devoting the other half of my attention to looking at her almost childlike face. At the way her hair was parted on the right, the boyish wave of blonde hair over the left part of her forehead. The full lips, delicately red. And those eyes.

How could a face like that give you premonitions? It just didn't. And that was too bad.

We were in the middle of a discussion on jazz when she stood up.

"I have to go," she said.

I felt myself start. I'd almost forgotten we'd just met.

She began to put on her jeans and blouse.

"Well, I have to get back to my novel too," I said standing up. Trying again.

"Oh, that," she said, frowning.

"No, one I'm writing, not reading," I said, giving up subtleties.

We scuffled across the warm sands.

"Gee," she said, "you like good music and you write." She shook her head. I got the impression she was confused.

"Is it so strange?" I asked.

"Men aren't sensitive enough to do things like that."

We reached a corner on Arizona and she started to turn off. I fiddled around, asking for her phone number and she fiddled back, finally giving it to me with a brooding reluctance. I memorized the number.

We said good-bye and I watched her walking down toward Santa Monica Boulevard. She moved with a relaxed, effortless grace.

I turned away. I went home and worked on the book with a renewed vigor.

That afternoon I sent a card to a friend in New York. *Met me a cute gal,* it read. *Glad you aren't here.*

That evening I remembered something. I remembered that I'd forgotten to write down her telephone number and now it was gone from my mind.

I went to the beach every day for a week but I saw no Peggy Ann.

I gave up three days and wrote heavily. Then, on the fourth day, I got up late, couldn't get up the fortitude to sit in front of my typewriter, ended up by putting on my bathing suit and leaving for the beach.

And, down there, happened to glance up while I was walking across the sands and saw her. My heart beat harder. I realized I'd been looking for her. Again.

She didn't see me. She was sitting on her blanket rubbing cocoa butter over her legs when I came up with my blanket and clothes.

"Hello," I said.

"Hello, Davie," she said.

It made me feel strange. No one since my mother had called me that, Davie. There was something about it.

"I was going to call you," I said, "but I forgot your number and your name wasn't in the directory."

"Oh," she said. "No, I live with another couple and the phone is under their name."

She seemed a little evasive that day. She avoided my eyes, kept looking down at the sand. Then, when she tried, without success, to put the cocoa butter on her back, I offered my services.

She sat stiffly as I rubbed my hand over her sun-warmed back. I noticed how she kept biting her lower lip. Worriedly.

"I..." she started to say once and then stopped. She sat quietly. Finally she drew in a deep breath.

"I have something to tell you," she said.

I felt myself tremble slightly. She sounded so serious.

"Go ahead," I told her.

"I'm divorced," she said.

I waited.

"Yes?" I said.

Her throat moved. "That's all," she said, "I...I just thought you might not want to go out with me when you knew...I..."

"Why not?"

She started to say something, then shrugged her shoulders helplessly.

"I don't know," she said, "I just thought."

She looked so young, so timorous.

"Don't be silly, Peggy," I said, quietly.

She turned in surprise.

"What did you call me?" she asked.

"Peggy," I said. "That's your name isn't it?"

"Yes, but..." She smiled at me. "I didn't think you'd remember."

She shook her head in wonder. "I'm so surprised," she said.

It was one of those things about Peggy. The littlest thing could delight her. Like when I brought her an ice cream cone later that morning.

It might have been a diamond ring.

Peggy lived on Twenty-sixth Street off Wilshire.

It was Sunday night and I was walking up the quiet tree-lined block looking for her house. It was to be our first date.

I was thinking that it was amazing how quiet it got right off Wilshire. Like a country street. That's what a lot of Los Angeles and suburbs are, I'd decided. A hick town with feathers. Gaudy but rustic.

There were two things in front of the house. An old Dodge. A man watering the lawn. The car was a 1936 model. The man about a 1910 model, pudgy and pasty-faced, wearing most unfetching shorts.

"Peggy Lister live here?" I asked him.

He looked at me with watery blue eyes. His expression was dead. He held the hose loosely in his hands. His head jerked a little.

"She lives here," he said.

I felt his eyes on me as I stood on the porch. Then Peggy opened the door.

With heels on she was tall, about five ten, I guess. She wore a sweater and skirt, a brown sport jacket. Her shoes were brown and white, carefully polished. Her hair had been set and combed out painstakingly. She looked wonderful.

"Hello, Davie," she said. "Won't you come in?"

I came in. Those big brown eyes surveyed me.

"You look nice, Davie," she said.

"You look terrific."

Again. Surprise. A half-quizzical smile which seemed to say—oh, you're just fooling me.

Just then an older woman came out of an adjoining room.

"Mrs. Grady, this is David Newton," Peggy said.

I smiled politely, said hello.

"Going out?" asked Mrs. Grady.

"We're going to get acquainted," Peggy said.

Mrs. Grady gave us a nod. Then she leaned over and called out the window.

"Supper's on, Albert."

We went to the front door and passed Albert. He gave me a sullen look. And her a look. A look that made me start. Because there was almost a possessiveness in it. It gave me an odd feeling.

"Who is that guy anyway?" I asked as we started down the street.

"Mr. Grady," she said.

"That look he gave you," I said.

"I know."

That expression was on her face again. Not quite identifiable. Mostly disgust. But there was something else in it, too. I wasn't sure but it might have been fear, I thought. The fear of a child who has come upon something it does not quite understand yet instinctively shrinks from.

I decided to change the subject.

"Where would you like to go?" I asked.

"I don't care," she said, brightening. "Where would you?"

"A movie?" I suggested, without really thinking.

"Well..." she said.

"What am I talking about?" I said. "I don't want to go to a movie. I want to talk to you."

She smiled at me.

"I'd like to talk, Davie," she said.

We went down to Wilshire to the Red Coach Inn for a few drinks. It's a cute little place, intimate, booths, a man playing casual organ music.

She ordered a Vodka Collins and I ordered a Tom. Then she turned to me and, casually, said.

"I think I should tell you I'm madly in love with you."

I took it for a gag, of course.

"Splendid," I said. "That's grand."

But her face wasn't smiling. It made me feel a little restless. Sometimes you couldn't tell what Peggy meant.

We drank a little. It was quiet.

"Would you like to come to a party with me?" she said. On the spur of the moment it seemed.

"Why...sure," I said.

"Good," she said.

"Where is it?"

"At my lawyer's house," she said.

"You have a lawyer?"

"He handled my divorce," she said.

I nodded. I asked her where the house was. She said Malibu.

"Oh," I said, "how will we get there? I plan to get a car but I haven't yet."

"We can get a ride," she said confidently.

Then the confidence seemed to slip. She fingered her glass nervously.

"Davie," she said.

"What?"

"Will you...will you promise me something?"

I hesitated. Then I asked what.

"Well, I..."

She looked irritated at her own fluster. "These parties are so..."

Again she halted.

"You're a gentleman," she said.

I waited. "I am?" I said.

"I mean," she went on, "you know how these parties are. Actors and actresses and...well, usually they get all drunk and the men start to..."

"You want me to promise not to touch you."

"Yes."

I didn't like to say it. She looked delicious then, in that soft light. But I nodded. "All right," I said.

She smiled gratefully.

After a few drinks we started down Wilshire again, headed for the ocean.

"I wish I did have a car," I said.

"It's all right," Peggy said.

We walked and talked. Peggy told me about her mother. Her mother had died when Peggy was twelve.

"Tell me about your marriage," I asked once.

"There's nothing to tell," she said and that was all I could get out of her.

When we walked past my room I asked her if she'd like to come in and read some of my published stories. Strange it didn't seem wrong with Peggy. With any other girl I would have felt obvious, but with Peggy I couldn't even conceive of anything under the table. She had too much...what's the word? Class, I guess you'd have to call it.

Peggy sat on my bed and looked at my stories. I sat across the room by my typing table. I watched her draw up her shapely legs and rest one of them under her, then drawing the slip and skirt down. Watched her as she took off her jacket, as she leaned against the wall reading, watched her large brown eyes reading my words. Living in them. She was right there.

She looked up after reading the first one.

"My goodness," she said, awed. "I had no idea."

"Of what?" I asked.

"Of how...deep you are."

I chuckled self-consciously. "I've done better," I said.

She shook her head wonderingly. "You're so sensitive," she said. "Men aren't sensitive, but you are."

"Some men are, Peggy," I said.

"No," she said. And she really believed it. "They're pigs. They don't care anything about beauty."

Was that her marriage talking? I wondered. What had it really been like to put that look of bitter conviction on that sweet face?

All I could do was shrug. Feeling a little helpless before her complete and dismaying assurance.

"I don't know, Peggy." I shouldn't have said it.

"I do," she answered.

And there was hurt there too. She couldn't hide it. I didn't want to spoil the evening. I tried to let it go.

But Peggy wasn't finished.

"I've seen it time and again," she said. "My uncle left my aunt with three children to support. The husband of the woman my brother and I stayed with was a drunkard. Phillip and I used to lie in bed on Saturday and Sunday nights and listen to the man beat his wife with his fists."

"Peggy, those are only two examples. In my own family I can give you four examples of happy marriages."

She shook her head. She read some more. And her jaws were held tightly. I sat there looking at her sadly. Wondering if there were anything I could do to ease that terrible tension in her.

The night seemed to disappear, Houdini-like. The first thing I knew we were walking back on the block off Wilshire. It was a nice, starry night. The street was dark and quiet. Peggy took my arm as we walked.

"I do like you," she said. "You talk my language."

We talked of different things. Nothing important.

"I should work," she said, a little ashamed. "It's not very honorable to live on…my alimony. But…" She looked at me as if almost pleading. "I don't know how to do anything, and I dread the idea of working in a ten cent store or something. I did that when I was married. It's…awful."

I patted her hand.

A little later. "Where does your ex-husband live, Peggy?"

"Do we…have to talk about it, Davie? Please."

"I'm sorry," I said.

It was when we were walking past the little park between 24th and 25th Streets.

"Would you like to sit in the park a while?" she asked me.

"Sure," I answered.

So we sat on the grass looking over the mirror-like pond. Watching the moon saucer that floated on the water surface. Listening to a basso frog giving out a roundelay for his lady love.

We didn't talk. I listened to her breathing. I glanced at her and saw her looking intently at the pond. Felt her hand on the ground and covered it with mine. And, naturally, without forcing it, found my head resting against hers. Her cheek was firm, soft. The cologne she wore was a delicious, delicate fragrance.

And, then, in a moment, casually, I drew back her hair and kissed the back of her neck. Long.

She didn't move. She shivered. Didn't struggle. But her hands tightened on the grass and pulled some out. I wondered what her lowered face was like.

I took off my lips. Her breath stopped, then caught again. In time with mine? I wondered.

Her throat moved. "Wow," she said.

I guess I laughed aloud. Of all the words in the world, it was the last I expected.

Peggy looked hurt, then offended. I quickly apologized.

"The word seemed so odd right then," I explained.

"Oh," She smiled, a little awkwardly. "No one ever kissed me like that," she said.

I looked at her in amazement. "What? *No* one?"

She shook her head.

"But...your husband?"

Her lips tightened.

"No," she said. She shuddered and her hands tightened into hard fists. *"No,"* she said again.

"I'm sorry," I said.

She shook her head. "It's not your fault," she said. "You just don't...realize. What it was like."

I put my arm around her.

"Peggy," I said, softly.

When we reached the front of her house I took her in my arms and kissed her. Her warm lips responded to me.

I left her three times. Then, each time, turned to look back. And saw her standing by the picket fence that glowed whitely in the moonlight. And she was looking after me. The way a frightened and lonely child looks after its departing parent.

I kept going back. Holding her. Feeling her press her face against my shoulder. Whisper. "Davie. Davie."

And trying to understand that childlike look, that hungry, wistful look in her eyes.

It was while I was walking away the third time that the big car passed me, I didn't notice it. At least not any more than I'd notice any car that passed me on a dark street in the early morning. We'd sat talking till way after midnight.

But at Wilshire I stopped to go back again.

And found the car parked in front of her house. Right behind Albert's old Dodge. I saw a man at the wheel wearing a chauffeur's cap. He was slumped down, staring at the windshield.

Another man was at the door. He had on a top coat, a homburg.

At first I thought, Oh my God, it's her husband and he's a millionaire. I felt like creeping away.

Then I saw her framed in the doorway and I suddenly knew I couldn't leave and I had to know who this man was. I walked past the Cadillac, a sleek, black job. I glanced at her room which faced the street. But the shades were drawn. I turned into the alley and walked up to the side window of her room. I stood there in the darkness, holding my breath. The window was open. I could hear her voice.

"You shouldn't come here like this," she was saying, "at this time of night. What will the landlady say?"

"Never mind that," said the man. "I was talking about something else."

"I said no and I mean it."

Silence a moment. The man's voice again.

"And who's the new one?"

She didn't answer. I felt my brow knitting. Because the man's voice was familiar.

"Some poor fool who..." he started.

"Oh leave me alone, will you?" she burst out.

"Peggy."

The voice was low and it warned. "Don't keep trying my patience. Even I have a limit. Even I, Peggy."

I heard her skirt rustle, then a long silence. I tried to hear. I tried to look under the shade. Nothing to see or hear. I imagined. I'm good at that.

"Jim," she said, "Jim...no."

Another connection. Not quite secure. The voice. The name.

Then I heard the back screen door shutting and I walked down the alley. As I turned onto the sidewalk I saw a dark figure coming up the alley. Albert. I recognized the form. I didn't know whether he was just out for the air or whether he was going to listen at the window too.

It didn't matter to me.

I'd had enough. I stalked past the black Cadillac and walked quickly toward Wilshire. In my mind I kept seeing her in the man's arms, being kissed, minutes after I had kissed her. Kissing him the way she kissed me. Peggy, the new, the bright, Peggy, the deceiving one.

I think I felt sick. I just wanted to get far away. When it comes down to it, I'm not very confident about my overweening charms. Right then the only thing I wanted was escape.

Good-bye Peggy Ann.

There was someone scratching on my screen.

I raised up on one elbow and looked at the window. She was looking in. She knocked at the door then. I hesitated. Then I relaxed.

"Come in," I said.

She was carrying her bathing suit and a towel in one hand. A grease-spotted paper bag in the other.

I looked at her clinically.

"I brought doughnuts for breakfast," she said.

Still no answer from me. She caught the look. Peggy was always quick at that. She knew the moment your feelings toward her chilled. Her face fell.

"What's the matter?" she asked.

I didn't answer. Her face was disconcerted. The face I was beginning to love. I tried to fight that but it was just about impossible.

She turned away sadly. "I'll go," she said.

I didn't feel anything until her hand touched the doorknob. Then it seemed as if someone were wrenching at my insides.

"Peggy."

She turned to look at me. Her face blank.

I patted the bed. "Come here," I said.

She stood there, looking hurt. She tried to flint her features, failed, tried again. I patted the bed a second time.

"Sit down, Peggy," I said.

She sat down gingerly.

"I haven't done anything," she said.

"I came back last night," I said.

At first she didn't understand. Then her face tightened.

"You saw Jim," she said.

"Is he your husband?"

"He's my lawyer," she said.

Last connection. The voice, the name, the profession.

"What's his last name?" I asked.

"Vaughan," she said.

"My God."

She looked at me in surprise. "What is it?"

"I know him," I said.

"You do?"

"We went to college together."

"Oh." Her voice was faint.

I shook my head. "My God," I repeated. "Jim Vaughan. Of all the crazy coincidences."

I turned to her.

"Is Jim in love with you?" I asked.

"I…" She looked helpless.

"Is he?"

"I don't know."

"Isn't he married anymore?" I asked.

"They're going to be divorced," she said.

Audrey divorced. I saw her face at college, in my mind. Adoring Jim Vaughan. Divorced.

"Is Jim's brother here too?" I asked.

"Yes."

"My God, it's so fantastic." I saw that look again and let it go for the moment though there were still many questions I wanted to ask. Jim and I had known each other very well at the University of Missouri. "It's his party we're…supposed to go to?" I asked.

She looked at the floor. "I suppose you're not going now," she said.

"I don't know," I said. "I'd like to see him again. But if he's in love with you it would be a…little strained."

"If you don't want to," she said.

"Don't you think he'd mind?"

She didn't answer.

"Peggy, come on."

"I had no idea you knew him. But...what difference does it make? I asked you to go with me."

I remembered something.

"Poor little fool," I said. "Why that snotty son of a bitch. He's as smug as ever. Sure, I'll go. I just want to see his face when he sees me walk in with you."

I was putting the polishing touches to my bowtie when the car horn honked outside.

I found the black Cadillac waiting.

Peggy was inside, the door open.

"Hi," she said. "Come on in."

I got in. The door shut and the car pulled away from the curb. Good God, I was thinking, this ices the cake.

Peggy smiled at me.

"What's the scoop?" I asked, quietly so the driver couldn't hear.

"What do you mean?"

"You didn't say we were going in Jim's own car."

"What's the difference?"

I started to answer. Then I chuckled. "Jim will do nip-ups."

"Why?"

She actually didn't know. Not my Peggy Ann Lister, divorced and very wonderful.

I patted her hand.

"Here is the picture, my dear," I said. "You taking Jim's rival to Jim's party in Jim's car. You get it?"

She looked blank. "You're no rival," she said.

It was my turn to look blank. Maybe she was naive, I thought.

I took a closer look at the driver. Affluence, I was thinking. Jim has done well for himself. A Caddy, a chauffeur, a house at Malibu.

But the chauffeur didn't fit. Not quite. Rich men's chauffeurs have non-committal features. They match the upholstery.

Not Walter Steig. That was his name. Steig stood out like a keg of beer among wine glasses. Big and stolid. His face and neck were reddish. He looked like a left-over from the Third Reich. Big and brutish with closely cropped hair of grayish-steel color. Rimless glasses and a stiff, unrevealing expression.

The first time I saw Steig I don't think I believed him. He was a living cliché.

He turned the car onto Pacific Coast Highway and speeded up the ocean. Malibu, I thought, Jim *has* done well. A beach house probably. Fireplaces and French windows and opulence. Jim Vaughan.

I looked at Peggy.

"I'm sorry," I said. "I didn't mean to be rude. It's just that I can't help being surprised that you know Jim. That he's so well off. When I knew him he was...as poor as I am now."

That was poor.

She smiled back. My love was wearing a dark blue dress that clung fittingly to her boyish figure. Her blonde hair was brushed out again, haloing her head with light curls. Her skin was flawless. No makeup other than lipstick.

Everything seemed fine.

Why, then, did I start to feel premonitions? No, it wasn't her face, that was silly. I guess it was the memory of the look Jim had given me that last time I saw him. On graduation day. It was a look that killed and Jim was one of those people who try never to let such looks be seen on their faces.

And that chauffeur. Again the disparity hit me. That burly German just didn't go with Jim's overt refinement, with his cultivated taste for the inoffensive, the best in company.

I wondered why.

I tried to let it go. Talk to Peggy and not jump the gun. And I pretty well succeeded except for a stray conjecture here and there.

The Malibu house was a lush two-story affair that rambled all over a hillside and ended up like a luxurious animal crouched on a cliff, peering down at the pounding surf way down below across the highway. I imagined that the living-room windows were tightly fastened because the back porch was air.

I felt nervous as we stood on the front porch waiting for the door to open. Years had passed. And now I was entering Jim's life again. With the only tongue that could ever scathe him. And, more important, with another of his women on my arm. Stab in the back number two, I was thinking. A maid opened the door and we entered the high-ceilinged hallway.

It was quite a place. Thick broadloom, everything smart and rich. Jim's taste, all right. I could see that.

35

"Well…"

And heard him. I turned and saw him standing, one foot below the other on the step that led to the raised living-room.

Staring at me.

Prophetic, I thought, that the last time I had seen him and this first time again, the expression I saw was devoid of all concealment. With not enough time to combat shock, it was Jim Vaughan in the raw looking at me. The look had surprise in it. Surprise, and, no hiding it, although he did his best thereafter, distinct and obvious displeasure.

"David!"

The pose was back. His hand holding mine was firm. The smile, the look was one of pleasure.

"If this isn't a coincidence," he was saying.

"How are you, Jim?" I said.

No need to ask. He was in fine shape. From his well trimmed head of red hair, down through his well-shaven, well-fed face, through his maroon dinner jacket, and down to his shiny, dark maroon shoes. Jim was all right. I almost felt like a tramp in my old jacket, one he'd seen at college no less. And that feeling was a new one for me. When I was with Jim especially.

I'd always felt at least equal, if not superior.

"What are you doing out here?" he was asking me.

His arm around Peggy's waist. Obviously. She looked a little pained but she didn't move away. The move made me feel strange. As if with one calm, assured gesture, Jim was removing her from my sphere.

"Writing," I said.

"Oh yes, of course," he said, as if he didn't know it. "You wrote."

His tendency towards smugness that I'd taken delight in puncturing at school had now blossomed into a full-fledged snobbishness. This, I suspected, was progress to Jim.

Then came a move which sort of put down the groundwork for the coming months

"Peggy, I've got someone you must meet," Jim said.

That was the opener. There were other words, quickly spotted. But the kicker was me standing alone in the hallway. A few seconds after I'd met a guy who'd been a good friend years before, I'd been dismissed that easily. Jim Vaughan discarding the past like a scab.

He'd said, "We'll have to have a long talk," but I knew it was only words.

I saw him wedge Peggy into a mass of people standing up near a large fireplace which was crackling with orange flames. Peggy looked toward me once, apologetically. But it didn't much ease my irritation.

I went up the small staircase and into the huge living-room. Just as expected. Lush. High-beamed ceiling, thick, wall-to-wall carpeting, huge, solid color furniture, copper lamps. Jim had it.

I looked around. At first I thought there would surely be someone I had known from college. He couldn't have discarded them all, he knew so many. If nothing else, there would be Audrey. She and I had been minor buddies at college. She wasn't too pretty a girl. She made up for it though. So well you hardly ever knew she wasn't particularly attractive. Something inside. Not many people have it.

No Audrey. I kept walking around adding unto myself a drink and a plate of well-catered canapes, a high-class antipasto. I stood, back to a wall-high picture window and surveyed the room full of affluent strangers. I got philosophical. I always do when I'm around people who all have more money than I do.

It was about that time that I saw Dennis.

He was sitting on a couch with a pretty young thing. He was glowering alternately into his drink and at the mass of people wherein stood Jim and Peggy.

I went over, sat down. I hadn't known Dennis at college except by sight. Flitting about the campus like a scholastic phantom, carrying books and a woman. Always a woman.

"Hi," I said.

The young thing showed teeth. Dennis looked at me with his dark eyes. Stuck in a lean face that seemed more than anything else to reflect one big, endless resentment. Of anything. Of everything.

He didn't answer. Once a spider looked at me like he did.

"You don't remember me," I said.

"No, I don't," he agreed.

"I'm Dave Newton," I said. "I was a friend of Jim's at Missouri."

Recognition. But no pleasure.

"Oh, yeah," he said.

I can't get on very well with people who won't talk.

"You've got quite a home here," I said.

"*Jim* has quite a home."

There it was. Plain as the nose on his sullen face, The resentment. I'd heard Dennis talk once at college. That was one day when I'd come up to him and Jim on the campus. Dennis had walked away saying, "Sure, *have* it your way. You always do anyway."

And Jim had said to me, faintly amused, "*That* is brother Dennis. The brat of the family."

Now, in the present, I saw that Dennis was still the brat of the family.

"Yeah," I said, for want of anything better.

Young thing coughed. Dennis didn't stir.

"I'm Jean Smith," came a gushing introduction. "Dennis is just *awful* about introductions."

I smiled and nodded. I forgot about her.

"Where's Audrey?" I asked Dennis.

He looked at me coldly a moment. I guess he didn't see what he was looking for. He turned away.

"She's sick," he said.

"That's too bad."

"Yeah, isn't it?" he said and was up and moving for the bar.

"Are you in pictures?"

That was the young one. The busty one, revealing her deepest interest, her religion. To gain stardom at all costs, chastity to soul.

"Sure," I said disgustedly, "I work at Metro."

"Oh, *really!*"

Big eyes popping. Brassiere straining.

I was looking at Peggy. She was smiling at some big man who was holding her hand and obviously shooting her a line.

"You're an actor, I bet," the young thing simpered.

I paid little attention. "Producer," I said.

"Oh?"

The poor girl was losing breath. She was dying to do something impressive. Chant Ophelia's song going downstream, or peel clothes or do something noble.

"What have you produced?" she asked.

I took out a cigarette after she took one. I lit it and blew out a cloud. David Newton, producer and liar.

"I just did a remake of *Lassie Come Home* with Gene Kelly."

"Oh?"

"Musical. Technicolor," I said. I watched Peggy look around cautiously, looking for me. Around her waist still, Jim's arm.

"Technicolor," said the young thing.

"Couple of million," I said. "Prestige picture."

"Yes, I see."

I looked at Miss Nothing. I sighed.

"My greatest picture though..." I stopped, overcome.

"What? What?"

"Vanilla Vomit," I said.

"I beg your pardon?"

"That was the title."

"Vanilla...?"

"Vomit."

"I don't believe I..."

She was still looking very blank as I moved for the big group. I was getting tired of this. It was obvious that Jim had no intention of sharing Peggy. She was private property.

"It was superb." Jim was doing some soaping up. Lamar Brandeis, real producer. Influential man. I stood behind Peggy Lister.

"Peggy, let's dance," I said.

Jim's smile was antiseptic. Toothpaste ad smile.

"Not right now, Dave," he said. "We're rather busy." Then I was left to stand there, unintroduced, the ghost of Hamlet's father at Malibu. I felt a heat churning up in my stomach. I've got a temper. I'll be the last to deny that.

Peggy kept looking at me when she could, trying to smile. But Jim kept closing up the group so that his back was to me. I looked at the back of his neck. Jim Vaughan, I thought, my old buddy. You dirty, smug, son of a bitch.

Why didn't she come to me, excuse herself? I figured that she was afraid to. She was a timid girl really. She could be taken advantage of.

I listened to the talk awhile. Then when my arm muscles felt like rigid glass I just moved around and grabbed Peggy's hand.

"Come here, Peggy," I said aloud. "There's someone you must meet."

I could feel their stares on me as I pulled her away.

"That wasn't very polite," she said.

I took her over to the small open portion of the floor where a few couples were dancing to record music.

"It wasn't polite to bring me here and ditch me, either," I said.

"I didn't do anything," she said. "He took me over."

"No, you never do anything," I said. "Peggy Lister, victim of fate."

She tried to draw away. I tightened my hold. "You're going to dance with me," I said.

She was quiet then. Her mouth was a resigned line, parenthesized. She held herself stiffly.

"My old friend Jim Vaughan," I said.

No answer.

"Peggy."

"What?"

"Do you want to meet the person I was going to introduce you to?"

No answer.

"Do you?"

"Who *is* it?" she asked, with false patience.

"Me," I said. "I'm all alone."

Her eyes on me. And softness coming back. I felt her hand on my shoulder tighten.

"Davie," she said softly.

"How do you do," I answered.

Later. About. Jim taking her. Then me dancing with her. And both of us standing by, around eleven, while Dennis danced with her. Both of us trying to put on an air of Auld Lang Syne.

"I suppose Peggy has told you about our marriage plans," Jim said. Casually. Jim loved to flick off bombshells.

"No," I said, keeping it casual even though it killed me. "She didn't say anything."

"Well, it's understood," he said. The dampener. And was that a little threatening in his voice?

"Does Audrey understand?" I asked.

The twitching that presages a well-reserved smile.

"She understands," said Jim Vaughan.

"The way Linda understood," I said.

Another twitch, without a smile this time. I knew he remembered as I did the time at college when I'd started to date Linda. Linda, who everybody but myself considered Jim's un-ringed fiancee. And Jim had taken me into the Black and Gold Inn one afternoon and given me the low-down. Told me, just as casually, that he and Linda were going to be married. Although Linda didn't know it. Although Linda later on left him cold.

"That was a childish thing," Jim was saying now. "I'm past child-ish things."

I nodded. "I see," I said. Then I said, "I hate to say it Jim but I'm in love with Peggy."

No sign. No hint. He gazed at me like an exterminator, sighting on his prey.

I smiled thinly. "I know it isn't very guest-like for me to tell you," I said, "Especially after what happened with Linda but...well, there it is."

He looked at me as if making some sort of decision. His grayish-blue eyes examined me carefully through the lenses of his glasses. His thickish lips pursed slightly as he deliberated.

He decided.

"Come in here, David," he said. Father about to tell his son that the birds do more than fly and the bees buzz.

He led the way to the library. He ushered me in. The door closed off the sound of the party. He locked the door. We stood together in the quietude, surrounded by the literature of the ages, all dusty.

"Sit down, David," he said.

I sat. I didn't know what to say. I decided to let him play the scene his own way.

"What has Peggy told you about herself?" he asked.

I sat quietly a moment, trying to figure out what his angle was. Jim was always trying for an angle. It might be hidden at first but it was always there. I knew that from school. He'd lead up, lead up, then sock you over the head with his coup de grace.

"Her family," I said. "Her life." I paused for effect. "Her divorce," I said, as casually as possible, figuring that it was the angle he was working on.

James Vaughan, late of Missouri farm town, now of California society, raised his eyebrows. Most effectively. All right, let's have it, Jim, I wanted to say, you can spare the histrionics. I know you.

"That's what she told you," he said. "That she was divorced?"

"That's right."

A sinking sensation in my stomach. What in hell *was* he driving at?

He looked at me, still deliberately. Until the thoughts of what he might be hiding started to make my skin crawl.

"What is it, for Christ's sake?" I asked.

He put one hand into his coat pocket.

"I don't know whether you'll believe what I tell you," he said.

"What?"

"Peggy isn't divorced," he said.

"She's still married?"

"No," he said, "not now."

"What about her husband?" I asked, perfect straight man for horror.

He hesitated. Then he said, "Murdered."

I felt the cold sickness explode in me because I knew his coup de grace before he said it.

"Peggy murdered him."

CHAPTER TWO

I SAT THERE and I felt as if the walls were tottering, ready to fall in on me. Everything out of proportion and coldness in me and him looking down.

"You're lying," I said, weakly, very weakly.

"Am I?"

And I couldn't convince myself that he was.

"All the facts can be found in newspaper files," he said, "if you don't believe me. I have some of the clippings here if you'd like to see them."

I thought, I'll throw him, I'll ask to see the clippings. Then I was afraid to try. The thought of holding them in my hands, reading them, sickened me. I kept seeing that angelic smile in my mind. That smile. Those eyes, those lustrous, frank eyes. The way she stroked my hair. Her soft lips on mine. The long, happy days together.

Murder?

"Don't you think it would be better if you left?" I heard him saying.

I want to see Peggy, I thought. I visualized it though.

A writer's curse. I heard myself asking, inanely it seemed, "Peggy, did you murder your husband?"

"I'll have Steig take you home," he said.

I looked up at him. His face was without expression. Certainly there was no sympathy there.

"I should see her," I said.

But without conviction. I didn't want to see her. I was afraid to see her. Afraid of seeing her lower her eyes and refuse to answer me. And all I could think of was Peggy lying to me.

I couldn't face it. I'm a coward, I guess, in lots of ways.

"I think it would be foolish to see her," Jim said.

I found myself standing. For moments at a time I forgot where I was, even who I was. Just pain standing there, overwhelmed with misery.

"Listen," I heard him say, "I know Peggy. For years I thought what you think of her now. That she was simple, uncomplicated." He shook his head. "She's not," he said, walking me to the door. I wanted to get away. I was sick.

"She's hopelessly erratic," he said. "If you spoke to her now about it, she might cry. She also might explode in your face and tell you it wasn't murder, really, and besides, it isn't any of your business. Her mind shifts from one emotion to another. You must have seen that yourself, David."

I don't know whether I did or not. But the words were in my brain, and, in the state of shock I was in, I took them straight.

"Peggy is a dangerous girl," he said.

David Newton, sheep. Led from the house. Luckily or unluckily, depending how you look at it, I didn't see Peggy. I think she was in the big room again, dancing with Dennis. Or looking for me. A me that was being led, dazed and shocked, to the big black Cadillac. Slumping back on the cold seat. Vaughan leaning in.

"If you don't believe what I've told you," he said crushing some more, "I want you to check. Don't take my word for it."

Then the door slammed and Steig pulled the black car around the pear-shaped drive and onto the road that led precipitously down to the highway.

I sat in the car staring at the floor. And listening to the wind whistle by the car as it roared along the ocean at eighty miles an hour. Under a cold moon.

I wrote sporadically. I went to the beach, way up the beach, far from the spot where we'd met. I went to the movies. I read. And, from all activities, absorbed nothing. I was still half anesthetized. I hadn't known her long, a few weeks. But she'd gotten to me.

I thought about her after the first few days of deliberately avoiding any thoughts at all about her.

I remembered taking her to the little bar downstairs in one of the hotels along Ocean Drive. I forget the name of it. I remember the soft lighting, the heavy wood paneling, circling the dance floor with Peggy in my arms, listening to the music of the three-piece combination. Sitting at the tables and having a couple of drinks together. Her eyes over the glass, looking at me. A soft look. Adoring and unquestioning.

I remembered the first time I'd told her how I felt about her.

I remembered other things. It had been such a short time really. Yet so long, it seemed. Years of walking through the silent streets of

Santa Monica looking at the pretty houses, making unspoken plans. Walking together through Will Rogers State Park in the Santa Monica Hills. Finding fresh mountain lion tracks and running back to the parking place, breathlessly excited and laughing. And walking all the way back to Santa Monica. Walking everywhere, hand in hand, never needing to speak.

Murder?

I went to the library and looked through old papers. I didn't find anything. And when I thought some more, I remembered Linda and that look Jim had given me on graduation day.

I went back to my love. Days after. In sorrow and repentance. And found her on the back lawn, trying to read. But just staring at the same page.

And she was cold at first because she'd been hurt. I didn't let it stop me. I was apologetic. I smiled at her and said again and again and again:

"I'm sorry, Peggy. I'm sorry."

"Murdered!" she said to me. "Is that what he told you?"

I nodded, grimly.

She shook her head. "How could he?" she said. And I felt some slight relish in seeing indications of the chinks in Jim Vaughan's self-forged armor.

"Why, though?" she said. "I didn't murder him."

"Where is your husband?" I asked.

"He's dead," she told me. "He died in San Francisco. A year ago."

We sat in the back yard, talking. And she kept shaking her head and saying she couldn't understand how Jim could say such a thing about her.

"It *is* strange," I said. "I never saw Jim involve himself in such an obvious lie before."

"I don't know," she said.

She looked away. "I didn't murder him," she said, softly.

"I know," I said.

"You didn't know it before," she said. "You believed what he said."

"It came as such a shock," I said. "Think of how you'd feel if, out of a clear blue sky, someone told you I'd murdered my mother or my wife."

"I'd check before I believed."

"What would you think if I told you I was divorced, made you think my wife was still alive?"

She didn't answer.

"Let's forget about it," I said, leaning over to kiss her cheek. "I have missed you," I said.

"But you stayed away."

I couldn't answer. I just felt rage. At Jim for lying so blatantly to me. At myself for believing him. Mostly the latter. For a guy who considers himself superior, I thought, I'd been awfully easy to delude.

It was around that time that I noticed Albert.

He was looking out of his window at Peggy. I forgot to mention it, but Peggy only had on shorts and a tight halter.

I called it to Peggy's attention. Her mouth grew hard again.

"Oh." She bit her lip. "I have to get out of here," she said. "Do you think I could find an apartment...or something?"

"Has he...tried anything?"

"No. Not with his wife around. But I'm afraid."

"We'd better get you out of here."

"And he pretends to be so pious," she said angrily, "just like all men. Pretending to be moral when all the time they're just pigs."

I didn't want to get started on that again. Besides, I thought, she was probably right in Albert's case.

Albert turned away from the window when I made it obvious from my look that I felt a severe desire to plant my foot in his pudgy face. His white, sickly face. Mushroom shade.

"You sure he hasn't tried anything?" I said.

"No," she answered, "but I know he'd...like to. The other day Mrs. Grady called me to the phone. I had on my shortie nightgown. I was too sleepy to think about putting on my robe. And Albert came out in the hall and saw me."

She shuddered.

"The way he looked at me made me sick," she said. "Like a...like an *animal.*"

"I'd like to break his neck," I heard myself saying. Manly pose. I really couldn't break anybody's neck, I was sure. I get melancholy just dressing a chicken for Sunday dinner.

"I don't want any more trouble," Peggy said. "I'll just leave."

"Trouble?" I asked. And, sometimes, wished I'd cultivated a deceiving voice like Jim's. Too often, practically always, my voice is a mirror of my feelings.

She looked at me dispassionately.

"You're still thinking about it, aren't you?" she said.

"About what?" I pretended.

"You're thinking about what Jim told you."

I must have looked flustered.

"I'll tell you what I mean," she said. "Maybe you'll be sorry I told you."

Her sensitive face was cold, hurt.

"When I was eight years old," she told me, "I was attacked by a boy. He was seventeen. He dragged me in a closet and tore all my clothes off."

She swallowed and avoided my eyes.

"When my father found out," she said, "he tried to kill the boy."

I reached for her hand instinctively but she drew back.

"Was it...?" I started. "How far did...he go?"

Her voice was like an axe blow.

"All the way," she said. "I was unconscious."

Peggy, Peggy.

"I can't help the way I feel," she said, "about men. It's in my flesh. If you weren't...if you hadn't been so different, I'd have run from you too."

"And Jim...?"

"Jim took care of me," she said. "He was always good to me. And he never asked anything in return."

We sat there in silence awhile. Finally our eyes met. We looked at each other. I smiled. She tried to smile but it didn't work.

"Be nice to me, Davie," she said. "Don't be suspicious."

"I won't," I promised. "Peggy, I won't."

Then I said, as cheerfully as possible, "Come on, let's find you an apartment."

I found a car that same day at a used-car lot, and afterwards we found a place for Peggy.

It was a small place. Two rooms, bath and kitchenette for $55 a month.

It wasn't going to be empty for about two days so we went back to her old place. I invited her out to dinner. Then to a show or maybe down to the amusement pier at Venice. She accepted happily.

"Let's start all over," she said impulsively during the afternoon. "Let's forget the past. It doesn't matter now, does it?"

I hugged her. "No, baby," I said, "of course it doesn't."

When we went in the house Albert and his wife were sitting there in the front room. That they'd been arguing was obvious from the forced way they broke off conversation. There were splashes of red up Albert's white cheeks.

They looked up at us. The old, sullen resentment in Albert's expression. The prissy, forced amiability in Mrs. Grady's face.

"Mrs. Grady," Peggy said, "I expect to be moving out in two days."

"Oh?" said Mrs. Grady. With that tone that can only be attained by landladies about to lose a tenant.

Albert looked at her. He looked down at her bust. I felt myself tighten in anger. The look on his face made me want to drive my fist against it.

"Is there something wrong here?" Mrs. Grady asked, a trifle peevishly. "Perhaps..."

"No, no," Peggy said, "it's fine. I just want an apartment, that's all."

"Well," said Mrs. Grady. "Well."

"I just happened to stumble across it today," Peggy said, "or else I would have given you more notice."

"I'm sure," Albert said, his fat lips pursed irritably.

More tightening in me. Peggy moved for her room.

"Excuse me," she said.

I followed without thinking.

"Gratitude," Albert said. And when I was going into her room he said something else. Something about little trash.

I felt myself lurching to a halt. I threw a glance over my shoulder. Then I felt Peggy's restraining hand on my arm.

In her room she looked at me.

"I guess you should have waited outside," she said.

"What's the difference?" I said, loud for all to hear. "Change your clothes and let's get out of here."

She put up a screen and went behind it. I saw her halter and shorts flutter over the top and I tried to avoid thinking of Peggy standing there tanned and nude. I tried to concentrate on my rage at

Albert. But your mind is hardly your own when it's distracted by such merciless visions.

She came out in a little while. During which time I sat listening to the angry voices of Mr. and Mrs. Grady, lovable duo. And I heard the word "trash" used again. Albert wasn't hiding it.

"We'd better go," I said, "or I swear I'm liable to punch that slob in the nose."

Silence outside. I hoped they heard.

"I wish you could leave tonight," I said.

"I...so do I," she said. And in her voice I heard the mixture of revulsion and contempt and, yes, fear.

They were talking when we went out into the front room again. But they shut up. They looked up at Peggy, who wore a light blue cotton dress and had a blue ribbon in her hair.

"I'm afraid I won't be able to refund your money," said Mrs. Grady, revealing the depth of her soul.

"I..." Peggy started.

"She's got no claim to it, mother," Albert snapped bitterly, "no claim 'soever."

"I don't expect it back," Peggy said.

"I'm *sure* you don't." That was Albert.

"Shut your mouth, Albert," I said. Surprised at myself how easily it came.

"Uh!"

In unison. Mr. and Mrs. Grady were both outraged at my impertinence.

"Come on," I said and Peggy and I left. Hearing a muffled, "She'll be sorry for this," from Albert as we closed the front door behind us.

"You shouldn't have said that," Peggy said as we got into the car. Then she laughed and it was nice to hear her laugh again.

"Did you see the look on his face," she said. "It was priceless."

We laughed for three blocks.

I parked the car on one of the streets that lead down to the Venice pier. And we walked down together, hand in hand.

Unaware that we were being followed.

We tried to hit a swinging gong at a shooting gallery. We nibbled on buttered popcorn and threw baseballs at stacked wooden bottles. We went down in the diving bell and watched tiger sharks circle the shell holding us, watched manta rays and heard the man say over and over, "They fly, ladies and gentlemen—they fly!" We rode the little scooter cars and bumped each other and Peggy laughed and her cheeks were bright with color.

I don't remember everything. I just remember the walking, hand in hand, the warm happiness of knowing she was with me. Remember her screams of mock fear as the roller coaster plummeted us down through the night and then up again, straight at the stars.

I remember *Funland*.

It's a strange concession. One of those things. Nothing really but a big black maze. You 'wander through it, down inclines, turning corners, searching for an exit—all in a blackness that's complete and abysmal. This sounds pointless, I guess. Until you take a girl. A lot of loafers hang around there. They wait for unescorted girls to go in.

I don't know what it was that made me nervous from the start. Maybe it was Peggy. She seemed to be driving herself, daring herself not to be afraid. Her laughter was forced and her hand in mine shook and was wet with perspiration. She kept tugging.

"Come on, Davie, let's find our way out."

"What did we come in for?"

"To find our way out."

"Progress," I said.

The place was like a coal mine. I couldn't see a thing. It had a dank, rotting odor too, that place. The smell of uncleaned spaces and water-logged wood and the vague, left-over smell of thousands of phantom bodies who had come in to get out.

And there were sounds. Giggles. Little shrieks of deliberate fright. Or were they deliberate? Peggy's breath was fast, erratic. Her laughter was too breathless.

"Babe, what did we come in here for?" I said.

"Come on, it's fun, it's fun."

"Some fun."

She kept pulling me, and I held on tight, moving through the blackness that was filled with clumping and shuffling of feet. And more shrieks and giggles. And the sound of our breathing. Unnaturally loud.

"This is scary," Peggy said, "isn't it?"

We touched walls, bumped down inclines, pressed together in the dark.

"Excuse me," I said. It sounded inane.

"All right," came the phantom reply. In a voice that had more fright than elation in it now.

"How do you get out of here?" I said, trying to get rid of the rising uneasiness in me.

"You just wander and finally you come out," she said.

Silence. Except for feet shuffling and her breathing and my breathing. Shuffling along in the dark. With the rising sense that we weren't alone. I don't mean the other people in the black maze. I mean somebody *with* us.

The next thing I remember, the last thing for a while, was a sudden blinding beam of light behind us. A rushing sound behind me. And me whirling around into the eye-closing light. Then feeling two big hands grab my throat, strong arms spinning me, now in blackness again. A heavy knee driving into my back, and something hard crashing down on my skull.

And though it was dark, for me it got darker. I felt myself hit the floor and start falling into night.

But not before, on my knees and almost gone, I heard Peggy scream out in mortal terror.

Somebody was slapping my face.

I twisted my head away and groaned. Sounds trickled back into my brain. I opened my eyes.

I was still on the pier, half-stretched out on the walk, propped up against a wooden fence. A crowd was watching me with that alien and heartless curiosity that crowds have for stretched-out victims of any kind. I heard a voice saying, "It's nothing folks, he just fainted. Don't congregate, please. Don't get the police on me, thank you kindly, I appreciate it. Nothing at all folks, just fainted that's all, he just fainted."

"Peggy!"

I struggled up, suddenly remembering her. The pain in my skull almost put me out again. I fell back on one elbow.

"Take it easy, boy," said the man with the cigar in his mouth, the loud sport shirt, "Just fainted, folks. Don't congregate, please don't congregate."

He looked at me. "How's the head?" he asked.

"Where *is* she?" I asked. I grabbed his arm, fighting off the dizziness. "She's not still in there, is she?"

"Now, now," he said, "take it easy."

"Is she!"

"No, no, no, no, nobody's in there now. It's cleared out. Stop yelling please. You want the police to come down?"

"Did you see her leave?" I asked.

"I didn't," said the man, still looking around. "Somebody said they did."

"Alone, was she alone?" I slumped against the fence, dizzily.

"I don't know, I'm not sure. *Please,* folks, don't congregate like this. Be a good egg, folks. Give me a break and don't congregate like this."

I pushed up then and started through the crowd, holding myself tight to keep the pain from knocking me on my face again.

I kept seeing her in there. In pitch blackness. With her fear of men. And someone attacking her in blackness. It would drive her out of her mind.

Then another thought.

Jim.

Steig trailing us. Jumping me. Taking Peggy away. It seemed terribly logical to me then.

I started running up the pier for the car and planning to drive to Jim's place to find her. Strange there seemed no doubt in me that she actually was there. Only in a white rage could I be so certain.

I rushed past endless gaudy concessions, the barker voices shrouding me with blatancy, calling me to break balloons, and throw pennies and pitch hoops around knife handles and telling me what they were going to do if only I'd stop. I got a stitch in my side but kept running, gasping for breath.

Then, suddenly, I thought, I'll phone him. He would more than likely deny it but then again he might not. He might flaunt it. It was worth the try.

In the airless booth my head started throbbing. I gritted my teeth, panting. I looked up Jim's number, sweat rolling down my face. I called the operator and had the call put through.

His voice, assured, dripping with aplomb.

"This is David," I said. "Is..."

"David who?"

"Newton!" I said angrily. "Is Peggy there?"

"Peggy? Why do you ask?"

"Is she there?"

"You sound hysterical," he said.

"Did you have me attacked tonight?" I asked furiously, not thinking at all. "Did you have Steig take Peggy?"

"What are you talking about?"

I suddenly felt my insides falling. If it weren't Steig, then who was it?

"Speak up, David. What are you talking about? What's happened to Peggy?"

I hung up. I pushed out of the booth. I walked a few feet. Then I broke into a weaving run again. I felt a wild fear in me. What had happened to her? Where was she? Oh good God, where was she?!

I moved off the pier and wove up the dark street past bars with tinkling pianos and a mission with a tinkling piano and tone deaf converts singing for their supper.

"Peggy," I gasped.

And found her in my car.

She was sitting slumped over on the right hand side. The first impression I got was one of stark shock. She was shaking violently and continuously. Just staring blankly at the windshield and shaking. She had her right arm pressed over her breasts. The fingers of her left hand in her lap were bent and rigid.

"Peggy!"

I slid in beside her and she snapped her head over. Her stare at me was wild with fear. I put my arm around her shaking shoulders.

"What happened, Peggy?"

No answer. She shook. She looked at me, then at the windshield again. Her pupils were black planets swimming in a milky universe. I'd never seen eyes so big. Or so terror-stricken.

"Baby, it's me. Davie."

She started to bite her lower lip. I could almost feel the rising emotion in her. She literally shook it out of herself.

It suddenly tore from her lips. She threw her hands over her face. Then she drew them away just as suddenly and held them before her eyes in tight claws of blood-drained flesh. She clicked her teeth, clenched them together and tried to hold back the moaning.

But her breath caught. And a body-wracking sob burst from her throat. She dragged her hands across her breasts. And I saw that the front of her dress had been ripped open and one of her brassiere straps had been snapped.

"I'm dirty," she said, "dirty!"

I had to grab her hands to keep her from ripping open her own flesh. I was amazed at the strength in her arms and wrists. Impelled by savage shock, she was almost as strong as a man, it seemed.

"Stop it! Peggy, stop it!"

Sitting there in Venice, California, in a black Ford coupe trying to calm the hysterics of a young woman afraid of sex who had been attacked.

Some people stopped and watched with callous curiosity while Peggy shook and groaned and gnashed her teeth and tried to claw away the flesh that had been touched by some vicious attacker.

"Peggy, please, please…"

I wanted to start the car and get away from those staring people. But I couldn't let her tear at her own flesh.

A long shuddering breath filled her. And she started to cry. Heartbroken crying, without strength or hope. I held her against me and stroked her hair.

"All right, baby," I said, "cry, cry."

"Dirty," she moaned, "I'm dirty."

"No," I said. "No, you're not."

"I'm dirty," she said, "dirty."

As soon as I could, I started the car and drove away from the curious people. I drove along the ocean for a while and then stopped at a drive-in. By that time she'd stopped crying and was sitting quietly, way on the other end of the seat, staring at her hands.

I'd put my jacket over her to cover the torn dress and slip. I ordered coffee and made her drink it. She coughed on it but she drank it.

It seemed to calm her a little. I stayed away from her. She wanted it that way, I knew. She almost pushed against the other door, crouching as if prepared to leap out should I make the remotest suggestion of an advance.

"Tell me what happened, Peggy?"

She shook her head.

"It'll help you if you can tell me."

Finally she did. And the visualization of what she said made me shiver.

"Someone grabbed me," she said. "I screamed for you but…but you didn't answer."

"I was unconscious, Peggy."

For the first time she looked at me with something besides fear.

"You were hit?" she asked.

I bent over and told her to touch the dried blood on my head.

"Oh," she said in momentary concern, "Davie…"

Then she drew back.

"Go on," I said.

"Some…some *man* put his hands on me. He clawed at me. He tore at my dress. I scratched him. I think I must have scratched his eyes out. Oh, God I hope I did. I hope he's *blind!*"

"Peggy, stop."

I saw the look of revulsion on her face. Because she had suddenly picked up her hands to look at them.

She made a gagging sound. Then she started rubbing her fingers over her skirt. I saw what it was.

Skin under her nails. The skin of the man who had tried to rape her.

I got a pen knife from the glove compartment and cleaned her nails while she kept her head turned away, her eyes tightly shut. Her hands trembled in mine.

"I think I'm…going to be sick," she said.

I felt sick myself, flicking those particles of someone's skin on the floor. Someone who had terrorized the girl I loved. It was almost as if he were present with us. I thought vaguely of taking those particles to the police but then I just let them fall. I couldn't stand putting them in an envelope.

"Peggy," I said, "do you think it was Steig?"

She couldn't speak for a moment. Then she said she didn't know.

"If I'd had a gun," she said, "a knife, a razor, *anything*. Oh God I'd have…"

I felt the muscles of my stomach tighten. Until I told myself that she'd been driven half-mad with fear. And I pushed away the thought I was trying so hard to avoid. And came up with another one that had preyed on me since I was conscious again.

"Peggy."

"What?"

"Did he…?"

She closed her eyes.

"If he had," she said, "you wouldn't have found me here. I'd be in the ocean."

My stomach kept throbbing as I drove up Wilshire. The thought of her being alone after this experience distressed me terribly.

Worse than alone, alone with Albert. What if he made an advance this night?

And then I thought, what if it were Albert who had attacked her in the first place?

I didn't know how to put the thought to her. I didn't want to alarm her needlessly. She seemed set on going back to her room. If I made the idea horrible, and she went anyway...

Thoughts. No end to them. And no resolution.

As I turned up 26th I saw Albert's Dodge in front of the house. And another car too. Jim's Cadillac.

I pulled up to the curb. Jim got out of his car and came quickly over to mine. He opened the door on Peggy's side.

"What is it, Peggy?" he asked.

She shook her head.

"Come here," he said.

By the time I got out of the car, he'd led her to his Cadillac and tried to make her get in it.

"I don't want to go!" I heard her say, her voice edging on hysteria again.

"Stop it, Peggy," Jim said. "I just want to talk to you."

Then she was in. And I came up to the car. I looked in and saw their dark forms. I heard Jim's muffled voice.

Steig got out of the car and walked around to where I stood.

"This is private," he said. Guttural. Thick German accent.

"Miss Lister is..." I started to say and found that one of his beefy hands had clamped on my arm. The strength of his grip pressed pain into the flesh.

"Let go of me," I said, gasping.

"You go," he said.

He started to lead me to my car. I couldn't do a thing. He was too big, too strong.

"God damn you!" I said, suddenly raging. "Get your fat hand off me!"

I wanted to call for Peggy but I didn't. She was in no state to come to my aid. Besides, I felt like a fool being led around like a baby this way. Struggling with teeth-gritting frustration. I was shoved against my car.

Steig stood by the door he had just slammed shut.

"You get out of here," he said.

"Listen, you ignorant Kraut," I said, more angry than sensible.

His face hardened, the pig eyes blazed at me. "You get out of here before I break your little neck with my hands."

He glanced at the Cadillac. Then, under his breath, he said something that covered my flesh with ice water. "If you did not know Mr. Vaughan," he said, "you would be *dead*. For snooping."

I gaped at him, my hands shaking. I saw his brute white face in the light of a street lamp. And I was afraid. No one had ever threatened my life personally. And it comes as a shock to a man to suddenly learn that another individual wants to kill him.

"Get out," Steig said.

My fingers shook as I slid the ignition key in. They shook on the gear shift. My legs trembled on the clutch and the accelerator. My heart pounded violently as I pulled up the street, afraid to look back.

I got out.

I jolted up on the bed with a gasp.

There was a dark figure standing over the bed.

My heart lurched. *"No!"* I gasped, throwing one arm up toward off the expected blow.

"Davie, what is it?"

I fell back on the pillow, panting. My throat clicked. I lay there heaving with breaths.

"Davie?"

"You s-scared me," I said. "I'm...I was dreaming."

"Oh. I'm...sorry. It's Albert," she said quietly.

"What...?"

Then the light was on. She was over at the sink, back. She pressed a wet cloth on my skull. To my surprise I saw her wearing a different outfit. She had a dark pair of slacks on and a tight black turtleneck sweater. She'd taken a shower too. I could tell from the fresh smell of her, from the dampness on the lower part of her hair where it had come out of the shower cap. Her only makeup was a little lipstick.

She looked very calm.

"What *about* him?" I said.

"When I went in the house tonight," she said.

"Yes?"

"I...I went to brush my teeth and I met Albert in the hall."

She paused.

"*Well...?*" I asked.

"*His face was all scraped off,*" she said.

"Albert," I said.

She turned the cloth over with her gentle, unshaking fingers.

"What did you do?" I asked. I wanted to tell her what Steig had said to me but I couldn't get to it. Things were happening that fast.

She stroked my hair gently. "I left," she said.

"You took a shower first?"

"No," she said, "I took that before. It was after the shower that I met Albert in the hall."

"You came right here?"

"I stopped to call Jim."

"He didn't stay with you?" I asked, inanely.

She looked slightly surprised. "Of course he didn't," she said, "he just wanted to find out what had happened tonight. He said you called him."

"Yes."

"Why?"

"I thought maybe you were at his house. I thought maybe it was Steig who had..."

We drove back to her place in the morning.

"Well, I'll just *tell* Jim," she was saying. 'He'll get rid of Steig if I tell him."

"Are you sure?"

"Of course, Davie," she said, "you're his friend, aren't you?"

"I doubt it."

"Davie."

Then I said, "I still think you should move out today. Stay with me one more night. But, my God, don't spend another night there with Albert."

"I won't," she said.

She shook her head then. And her throat moved nervously.

"We'll just pick up your things," I said, "You don't even have to go in the house."

As we drove up to the house and I parked behind the Dodge, Peggy's face got suddenly pale.

"Baby, it's all right," I said.

I got out. She got out too.

"Baby, stay here," I said. "You don't have to go in."

"No," she said, "I'll come in."

"Well...all right."

We went up the walk together. I felt in myself that if Albert were there and he said a word to me, I'd knock him down and step on his face. The victimizing by Steig the night before had given me a tight, vicious temper.

The front door was open. We went into the living room.

"Is Mrs. Grady home?" I whispered.

"I guess so," she said.

We went into the hall. She went into her room and I followed. Then as she turned to close the door I heard her voice sink to a whisper.

"Davie..."

I looked in the direction she was looking. Down at where Albert's room was. My heart jumped.

There was a body sprawled on the floor.

I broke into a run and pushed open the half-open door. I heard Peggy behind me.

Mrs. Grady was crumpled on the floor. Her white face was pointed at the ceiling. In her right hand she clutched something. I couldn't see what it was but the tip was red...

Then my eyes moved suddenly to the bed.

Albert was there. He was staring at us, his eyes were wide open.

Albert was no more. And that was when I recognized the instrument in Mrs. Grady's hand.

An icepick.

It had been driven into Albert's brain.

CHAPTER THREE

LIEUTENANT JONES, Homicide, was a broad man with horn-rimmed glasses. His mood was surly.

Mrs. Grady was giving her version of what had happened.

"I went in to call him for breakfast," she said. "I found him in there with that—that *thing* in his..."

"Why did you take it out?"

She shook her head. Then suddenly she twisted her head and pointed a shaky finger at Peggy.

"*She* did it!" she said wildly. "I know it, I *know* she did it!"

I sat beside Peggy on the big flowered couch, afraid to look at her.

"That will do," Jones said.

"*Do!* My husband is dead. He's killed! Do you understand that? Are you going to let her get away with it?"

"I know he was killed, Mrs. Grady," Jones said. "We're trying to find out who did it as soon as possible. If you'll just help us and not throw around accusations."

I sat there numbly staring at him. Listening to the murmur of voices in Albert's room, the muffled pop of flash bulbs, the shuffling of feet.

I kept visualizing Albert lying in there, the icepick hole in his head—and the other. It was almost unbearable to think about the other. Whoever had driven the icepick into Albert's brain had also taken Albert's straight razor and made an enormous bloody slit around Albert's neck. It was long, nearly the whole circumference of the neck. And it was deep. It was almost as if...

As if...and I wanted to be sick.

"Miss Lister?" Jones said.

"Y-yes?"

"You were out last night?"

"Yes."

"What's that you said about having trouble with him?"

The way he spoke made me start. As if he were trying to rip away all incidentals and get to the core of everything.

"He was..." Peggy started. She lowered her eyes. "He..."

"Albert tried to rape her last night," I said.

"Lies, lies!" cried Mrs. Grady. "He was a dear, clean man, a dear, clean man."

"You'll have to stop this," Jones said to her, "or I'll have to ask you to leave this room."

She slumped back in silence again, blubbering helplessly, her toothpick shoulders twitching with violent sobs.

I was sitting there, suddenly wishing I'd kept my mouth shut. Because all I could think was that I'd given Peggy a perfect motive. Like a fool I'd practically accused her.

Jones looked at Peggy.

"Is this true?" he said.

She tried to answer but couldn't. She nodded her head once, jerkily.

Jones looked back at me. "Well," he said, "what about it?"

I told him about the scrapes on Albert's face. I told him about *Funland* and the attack on me and Peggy. My words were punctuated by moans and muffled denials from Mrs. Grady. I didn't know whether she really doubted me or not. After all, I kept thinking, the icepick had been in her hand. And she certainly had a motive.

"Did you see him?" Jones asked.

"You mean last night?"

"I mean last night."

"No, I…"

"Why not?"

"It was pitch black."

"I see," Jones said. But he really said, in effect, thirty days, next case. It occurred to me that he might even think I did it. The jealous lover. I lowered my eyes.

Jones worked on Peggy again. "You two were together then?" he said.

She swallowed. "Yes."

"And you went to…" Jones consulted the pad in his hand, "to Newton's apartment later."

Peggy looked flustered. "I…"

"What time did you go there?"

"She came to my room about…" I started.

"Will you kindly let Miss…" He consulted the pad again. "Miss Lister answer her own questions?"

"About two," Peggy said.

"Why did you go there?" Jones asked.

"Because I saw the scrapes on Albert's face. I didn't want to…"

"Lies…lies!" Mrs. Grady again. *"Murderess!"*

Her voice broke off with a choking gasp as two men carried a stretcher into the room, a blanketed body on it.

"Couldn't you go the back way?" Jones asked sharply.

"Alley's too·narrow," said a bored cop.

Mrs. Grady was up. Her face was strained and wild.

"I'm going with him," she said, "I'm going with my darling."

"That won't do any good," Jones said quietly.

"I'm *going,* I tell you." Her voice was cracked, her eyes almost glittered.

Jones let her go. He said a few words to one of the cops. While he was talking, I turned to Peggy. "Don't tell him how you feel about men," I whispered.

"What?"

I glanced at Jones. "I *said,*" I whispered out of the side of my mouth, "don't tell this man how you feel about men. It would only…"

She was looking at me curiously.

"What were you saying to her?" Jones asked me.

"Nothing," I said instinctively.

Jones looked at me coldly. "No talking," he said. Then he sat down as the door shut behind Mrs. Grady and her dead husband.

"How sure are you that the dead man is the one who tried to rape you?" Jones asked Peggy.

"I know how I scratched the face of the man who…And Albert had scratches all over his face too. You saw him…"

"I know." Jones said. "did you see anyone else last night?"

"My…lawyer," Peggy said.

"When?"

"When…when we came home from Venice."

"You told him about the attack?"

"Yes."

"Did ·you suspect the dead man of being the one who had attacked you at the time you were speaking to your lawyer?"

"Not then. I told him later that it was Mr. Grady who had done it."

"You saw him later?"

"I called him before I went to…to Mr. Newton's room." Her eyes were lowered in embarrassment.

Mr. Newton, I thought. Murder, the strange impersonalizer.

Then the doorbell rang. Jones got up and opened it.

Jim. He came in and talked to Jones for a few minutes, and then Peggy went to the station with Jones and Jim. I wasn't invited. As they got into the police car, Jim told Steig to follow them. I felt a tremor in my stomach as the big German eyed me before getting in the Cadillac. I tried to imagine him with an icepick in one hand and a razor in the other.

It was easy.

I tried to catch Peggy's eye as the police car moved away from the curb. But she avoided my look. I guessed because I'd as much as told her I suspected her.

I watched the two cars go down the street. And I felt sick and empty.

That afternoon, back at my room, I was trying to nap when I heard footsteps on the porch and, looking out the window, saw that it was Jim.

"Come in," I said when he knocked. He came in and the first thing I asked him was how Peggy was

"As well as can be expected," he said, always cryptic.

"What the hell does that mean?"

He took his hat off and looked at me dispassionately.

"If you're going to tell me that Peggy killed Albert, save your breath. I know she didn't," I said.

"And how do you know?"

"I...I know."

"Hardly a legal defense David," he said. "You always did talk before thinking."

"And you," I said, "always did destroy what stood in your way."

A flicker. Gone then. He sighed.

"What's the use?" he said. He reached into his inside jacket pocket and drew out a rich leather billfold.

He was holding something out to me.

"Well, take it," he said. He paused for effect. "Are you afraid?"

I reached out a visibly shaking hand and took it. Thinking, imagining...refusing to accept.

"No," I muttered.

"Read it."

The clipping was five years old. San Francisco dateline. Picture of a man I'd never seen. And next to him a picture of Peggy.

The headline:

G.I. Student Stabbed
Pregnant Wife Confesses

I sat slumped on the bed staring at the floor. The clipping still hung from my nerveless fingers. Jim still sat in the chair looking at me. His expression was vaguely sympathetic now. He'd made his point. He didn't have to belabor any more.

"I met Peggy's father when I was in the Navy during the war," Jim said. "I was his aide for about a year while he served on the court martial board.

"When the war was over he invited me to his home several times for dinner. That was before I went home to Missouri. I stayed on the coast about three months after I was discharged.

"Lister wasn't trying to be social. He was trying to make me join the regular Navy, it turned out. It was at the captain's house that I first met Peggy."

He paused and I heard him clear his throat in the silence of the room. I lay there, still apathetic.

"There was no particular attraction," Jim said, "and when I went back to Missouri, I forgot about her and her about me. She married George."

Was that bitterness in his voice? I couldn't be certain. I didn't explore.

"It was what you might call a shotgun wedding," Jim said, and that *was* bitterness in his voice. "Peggy was forced into it by her father. She'd stayed out late one night and Captain Lister accused her of being intimate with George. He said his name was in disgrace. And poor Peggy, too naive to know any better, too shy to argue, married George."

He smiled without pleasure. I guess he was showing me a little more of his feelings because he figured that his battle had been won.

"George didn't mind," he said. "It was all right with him. And maybe Peggy didn't mind at first either. She hated her father. She still does. I don't even know all the reasons. They stretch back through the years. At any rate all she thought of at first was leaving her home and how glad she was to do it. Leave the tyranny of her father's control. If he was anything at home like the unfeeling flint he was on the court martial board, Peggy's life with him must have been intolerable. Then I saw her one day years later. I'd set up an office in San Francisco. And one day Peggy came in."

He drew a deep breath.

"I didn't recognize her, David," he said. "She was almost...gaunt. Her face was lined. There were dark hollows around her eyes. She looked as though she'd been violently ill for years."

He paused.

"She *had* been," he said. "She'd been married to George."

I turned my head on the pillow and looked at him, He was looking at the wall, hands still clasped in his lap.

"I won't go into details," he said. "Her problems were partly sexual, of course."

His voice became contemptuous.

"Her husband was completely indifferent to Peggy's timorousness, her hypersensitive system. And it was killing her. In addition to the fact that her husband was going to college on the G.I. Bill and they were just about living on that income alone. It was actually poverty. And to a girl like Peggy, who'd had every material advantage anyway, this was an even greater torture."

He shifted on the chair.

"She said she wanted a divorce," he said. "She said some doctor had told her that divorce was essential if she wanted to remain sane. The poor physical relationship, the extreme poverty was destroying not only her health but her mind. She was pregnant, too. We never got her the divorce," he said. "I started to get the papers together, but it was too late."

He stared at his hands.

"A few days later Peggy went out of her mind and stabbed her husband to death in their one-room apartment. It was a measure of her torture. Because she's a very gentle girl, as you know."

I knew.

"She came to me then," Jim said. "I took her to the police. I put up her bail, I defended her. I got her acquitted on a temporary insanity plea, and during this time she miscarried. I tried to help her forget. I gave her money to live on because she didn't have any profession and I didn't want her to work in dime stores as she had during her marriage."

"She told me...alimony." I heard myself saying, not to him. The thought just had sound that's all.

He shook his head.

"And you doubted what I told you," he said. "You surely see now what I meant. The lie about her husband's death, the failure to tell you about her pregnancy. The lie about her income. *Peggy.*"

I don't know what time it was. Because I was back in the past. Shadows of years flickered across my mind.

Jim, me, sitting in his office at college. He used to be assistant to the head of the Law School.

Jim talking. "I don't think you really know about Linda," he said, his face very serious.

"What about her?" I said.

"She's been sleeping with me for a year now."

The crusher. My first blind-eyed attraction for Linda's sharp intelligence, her long red hair, her svelte form— shattered.

Later on, of course, I found out it was a complete lie. Jim hadn't even kissed her.

And that brought me back. But not completely. I'd seen that clipping. She'd killed her husband. But the rest? I wasn't sure.

So, Jim or no Jim, facts or no facts, I was back in the car. Driving at near violation speed up Wilshire. And going in the front door without knocking. Pretending to ignore the shudder I got going back into that house.

She was packing, her face very sad.

"Peggy."

I stood in the doorway. Knowing that if everything Jim said was true, our love had to end. Because it would have been founded on lies. And the only thing that could console me was that Jim never did say once that Peggy *had* killed Albert.

She kept packing after she looked at me. She moved around the room, her motions crisp and tight. I watched her for a moment. And I just couldn't, for the life of me, visualize murder in those hands.

I went in and sat on the bed by the suitcase.

"Peggy."

No answer.

"I want to tell you why I didn't come back this afternoon."

"It doesn't matter."

"Doesn't it?"

"No."

"I saw Jim this afternoon."

"I see."

Coldly. As if she were a woman who didn't care for anything in the world. Instead of a shy, timorous girl afraid of the world and its multiple terrors.

I reached out and grabbed her wrist. She didn't honor me with a struggle. She just stared straight ahead.

"He showed me a newspaper clipping, Peggy," I told her.

Her eyes moved down at me.

"It was the story of how you killed your husband," I said.

She shuddered and her wrist went limp.

"Jim also told me you were living on his money, not on alimony," I said.

I wanted desperately for her to snap out angry words at me and make me know they were all lies. But she couldn't. She didn't speak. Then she said, softly:

"Let me go."

"When you tell me why you lied to me. About so many things."

"I didn't want to tell you," she said.

"Why?"

She bit her lower lip and kept her face averted.

"Peggy, I want some truth! Do you hear me?"

She cut off a sob.

"What sort of a girl are you," I said, "who can speak of love and yet lie incessantly to the person you say you love? What kind of self- ish girl are…"

"Selfish!"

She jerked away her hand violently.

"Selfish!" she said, "yes, I'm selfish! Very selfish! I was brought up by a father who hated me. Who did everything he could to make my life miserable. I was shuttled around from city to city, never hav- ing a home. Only hotels and motels and dingy little apartment houses near naval bases. I had boys try to rape me. I had older men try to proposition me. And to top it all off, I married an animal who dragged me through poverty and gave me nothing but filth in return. Filth, do you hear! A man who made me pregnant, then tried to force me to get an abortion! A man who had no regard for me. I was a piece of flesh to him. And I killed him and I'd kill him again for the things he did to me! And now…when I find something good for the first time…when I try to hold on to the only beautiful thing I ever had in my whole life…you call me *selfish!* Yes I'm s-s-selfish…"

Her back was turned from me. She shook violently, crying and trying not to cry. But unable to keep all the pent-up misery of years from flooding out.

I got up quietly. I stood behind her. I put my hands up to hold her shoulders. Then I drew them back. I didn't know. I felt terribly contrite. Everything seemed to fall into a pattern. Jim had colored an already ugly picture with even uglier hues. For his own purpose.

She cried for a long time. We sat on the bed and I kept drying her eyes with my handkerchief. Later I asked her about her marriage. She told me substantially what Jim had said.

"And the money?" I said.

"Money?"

"Jim's."

She looked at me unhappily. "Why...what's wrong with that? If he wants to give it to me?"

"Baby. you're being kept!"

"He never *touched* me, Davie."

"It's the idea, Peggy."

She looked at me, a little frightened.

"Peg?"

"Yes, darling?"

"Did you...?"

"What?"

I didn't speak. Finally I said, "If you did it, Peg, I'll understand, and I'll stick by you. I'll—"

"Love my memory?" she said.

"No, I—"

"I didn't kill Albert," she said.

I grabbed at it. I clung to it and it was like a tonic, the first moment of limp ease after a raging fever has abated.

"I believe you," I said.

We moved her into the new place that afternoon, and I tried to get her to tell the police about Jim. But she refused with her little girl logic. Then I suggested that at least we ought to confront Jim himself with his lies, and she refused to do that, too. It wasn't loyal, she said.

So I went alone to see Jim. I didn't find him, but I did find somebody else.

Audrey.

Audrey flung her arms around my neck. She had a silk pair of lounging pajamas on. Black and sheer and nothing else. I could feel the uncupped softness of her breasts mold against me.

"Give us a kiss, Dave."

The thin face, that sweet smile. Her soft lips pressed against mine. And I got a sense of tension in her. The way she clung to me. It wasn't right.

Suspicion vindicated by the distinct odor of whiskey on her breath.

That was a shock. Audrey had never drunk at college. She'd just follow Jim around, a disciple to his calloused presence. Treasuring the few scraps of affection he gave her.

"Gee, Dave, it's good to see you," she said.

"It's good to see you too, Audrey."

She drew back, her small hands still gripping my shoulders.

"Let me see," she said. "Oh, yes. You're heavier. Affluence? Or beer?"

I chuckled and leaned over to kiss her cheek.

"Audrey, Audrey," I said, "what transmutation is this? I remember saddle shoes and bright-eyed naiveté. Now I find a new hairdo, sexy pajamas and...well..."

"And liquor?" she said.

I tried to slough it off.

"Come on in," she said, "come on in and talk to me. I'm lonely."

"Is Jim home?" I asked as she led me into the living room, big and empty now.

"He's on business," she said.

I got that too. Too chipper, too much a toss-off. She had found the phrase too easy. And from it I knew there'd been a lot of nights when Audrey had stayed home while Jim went out on "business." The old American synonym for cheating. Yes, it all added up. College had been the preamble.

I sat down and Audrey got a couple of drinks, Big ones, and straight. She drained hers swiftly and filled her glass again.

We talked for a long while. It wasn't too pleasant.

"Sometimes I could scream," she said later on.

I thought of Peggy. "Sometimes I could, too," I said.

Then I stood up. "I'd better go," I said. Before I forget myself, I didn't add. I went over to her.

"Good-bye, Aud..."

I stopped when she looked me in the eye. Her breath was tortured. It shook her body. Something seemed to be bubbling up in her.

"I could scream," she said.

"Scream," I said.

Suddenly she grabbed my arms and pressed her open mouth against my chest. I heard the muffled sound of her screaming at the top of her lungs into my flesh. It lasted until her breath went. Then she raised her darkly flushed face and looked at me, gasping.

"There," she said, hardly able to speak. "Mostly it's a pillow. Thanks for the nice cushion."

She turned away. I followed her from the room. We stood together by the front door.

"Will you give me a good-bye kiss?" she asked.

She raised on her toes and slid her arms around my neck. She brushed her warm lips over mine. Then she smiled and stroked my cheek.

"You're sweet," she said. "I wish…" She shrugged. "Oh, what's the difference, anyway?"

"Good-bye, Audrey."

"Good-bye, dear."

I went out the door and down to my car. I got in and sat there a long time staring at the windshield, wishing I'd stayed with Peggy.

Then, as I stepped on the starter, light streamed across the porch and leaped on the car.

"Dave!"

I looked over and saw Audrey come running across the porch and down the steps. She had on a long black raincoat with a hood over her head. I saw a maid at the door watching her go. Then the maid shrugged and shut the door.

Audrey ran around the car, opened the door and slid in.

"How about giving a gal a ride into town?"

"All right," I said, caught off guard.

Back on Pacific Coast Highway, I asked her where she was going.

"Santa Monica," she said.

"You're not quite dressed for evening activity," I said.

"Nobody will notice," she said, "where I'm going."

"Where's that?"

"Just drop me off downtown," she parried. "I'm not going any place in particular. I'll probably go to a movie."

"Oh."

I drove in silence a while. Audrey sat staring out at the ribbon of road unraveling under my headlights. Her face was expressionless.

"You can let me off here," Audrey said at Wilshire and 3rd.

"I'll take you downtown," I said.

"You don't have to."

I slowed down at Santa Monica Boulevard and 3rd.

"This is fine," Audrey said.

I kept moving. Down to Broadway. I stopped the car and she turned to look at me.

"I'm not clever, am I?" she said.

Broadway is where all the bars are.

"Come with me," I said. "Meet my girl."

"Oh, you have a girl."

"Come on. Shut the door."

"No."

"You'll like Peggy," I said.

And from the look on her face I suddenly realized that it was Audrey's husband who wanted to marry Peggy. And I knew that, contrary to Jim, Audrey didn't "understand" it.

Audrey shuddered and pushed out of the car.

"Bye," she said hurriedly and slammed the door.

She was already turning the corner. I started the car and pulled around. I saw her going into The Bamboo Grill.

I drove to Peggy's and found the note on the door.

Davie: Jim came. He said we had to discuss my legal case. I told him I was waiting for you but he said it's very important. After all Davie, I have to have a lawyer and I don't know anyone else and he doesn't charge me. I'm sorry but I think I should go. Please call me in the morning. Peg.

Legal case. Fat chance that's what they were discussing. He was pouring more lies into her. I was burned up. I'd told her I was coming right back. She might have waited. After all the tension we'd had between each other—this.

I stood beside my car, glowering, wanting to hit back. I was sick of it all. I wanted to write a note telling her it was all over. Something that would hurt. But I knew I had no right to do that.

I didn't want to go home, though.

Audrey. Downtown, alone, my old pal Audrey.

I got into my car and drove back to The Bamboo Grill. She wasn't there, and she wasn't in the next four bars I tried, either. But I had a drink in each of them.

In the fifth bar, I decided to hell with it. I grabbed a booth and ordered another bourbon and water. I drank half of it. And then she appeared. From the cosmos. From the universe. From the ladies' room.

And, even slightly potted and disarrayed, Audrey was out of place there.

She almost passed my table.

"Buy you a drink, girlie?" I said.

She turned to cut me off, then smiled as she saw me.

"Davie!"

She slid in across from me. She still had on the rain coat.

"Where did you come from?" she asked.

"From the cosmos, from the universe," I said.

"I came from the john."

"Won't you allow me to purchase you a magnum of chantilly?"

"That's lace, isn't it?"

"Who knows? If it's lace, we'll drink it anyway."

We drank a lot. The time seemed to pass. And I found myself sitting beside her instead of across from her. The strong sensation of drunkenness on me. The loss of balance. The sense that you're hyper-brilliant, that your brain, though cased in numbing wool, is glittering like a jewel.

And, around midnight, I remember putting my mouth on hers. And feeling all the animal heat in me dredging up. And not caring. She made no attempt to stop my hands from touching her. Her body was warm and soft and willing.

I don't know what time it was. But somehow we were in the car driving up Broadway. Then over to Wilshire on Lincoln. I remember that. We parked. We were out of the car and into my room. In the darkness, weaving as in a dream. I took off her raincoat, letting all the things I believe in be washed away by the tides of coarse desire flooding through me.

It was dark. She was naked in the cool darkness, waiting for me.

And then a car came past the house in the alley, slowly moving out. And the light played on Audrey's face. She was lying down on the bed and I had my knee on the mattress beside her.

In the light I saw her face. It was blank. That headlight was like a spotlight of revelation on those expressionless features.

Her cheeks were shimmering with tears.

"Audrey."

My voice was broken. Something cold billowed up in my body, freezing everything as violently as it had come. I got off the bed and stumbled to my closet. I stood there, trembling, putting on my robe. I stayed there a long time, fumbling with the sash.

Then I went over to the bed. I reached down and pulled the blankets over her nude body. Without a word I bent over and kissed her forehead.

I was afraid to say anything. I was about to straighten up when she put her arms around my neck.

"I'm sorry," she whispered, "I tried to believe it was right. But..."

I almost fell out of the chair in shock when the knocking came on the door. A loud knocking, hard.

I leaped up, wincing at the stiffness in my back and neck. My heart was pounding. My head ached a little.

Suddenly I remembered Audrey with a gasp. My eyes ran over to the dark outline of her body in my bed. Lying there naked, asleep.

I didn't know what to do. I just stood there shivering, staring stupidly at the bed, then at the door. I felt myself jump as Audrey stirred restlessly. She moaned a little and turned on her side. I think I was paralyzed. All I could do was visualize Peggy standing out there. My claims of innocence would mean nothing to her.

I started for the door.

"What is it?" Audrey asked in sleepy fright. She was propped up on one elbow.

"Shhh!" I said anxiously.

Then I leaped back as the door was shoved open violently and I saw a figure in the doorway, lit by the hall light. A tall figure, square, powerful.

Steig.

He came in and flicked on the light switch.

I don't know what I felt in those first moments. Shame, fear, anger. But I exploded in his face.

"Get out of here!" I almost yelled. Wondering suddenly if the other tenants in the house were awake by now.

My words were hacked off as Steig drove a violent right into my stomach which doubled me over.

All the night seemed to flood in on me. I was bent over, gasping for air. The floor ran like water to my eyes.

Another blow on the side of my head. Like a cast iron mallet it felt. It drove me into the table and sent me and the whole business crashing over onto the floor.

I was helpless. I've read of men who fight back after being struck like that. But how can you fight back when you can't breathe or see?

I felt one of his beefy hands grab my upper right arm.

"Stop it!" Audrey screamed, "Stop it, Steig!"

I was dragged up. Then a rock exploded in my face and I felt hot blood spurting out of my nose and sharp pain in my head.

"You stay off!" Steig snarled. *"Stay off!"*

I think he might have beaten me to death if Audrey hadn't jumped up and grabbed his arm. She was Vaughan's wife, Mr. Vaughan's wife. He couldn't afford to harm her.

He had to let me go. His way of letting go was shoving me across the room. I crashed into the partition that separated the room from the kitchenette. Then I slid down and crumpled into a heap on the rug.

"Let me go!" I heard Audrey screaming.

I couldn't help. I was gone. Falling through a black pit that hurt. And hurt. And hurt.

CHAPTER FOUR

I FELT LOUSY for a couple of days after that. Nothing seemed right.

Jones stopped around to tell me it was dangerous business getting mixed up with Jim's crowd. He was a little late with that information, and I just grunted.

I told him I wanted to prefer charges against Steig but he said that was just a lot of trouble for nothing.

Nothing?

Yes, he said. How could I prove anything?

I pointed out that Audrey had been a witness, and Jones pointed out, not very gently, that Audrey herself was always being hauled in on drunk charges and that her testimony wasn't worth anything. He also told me that Steig was bad business, as if I didn't already know, and that he used to be a professional killer back in Chicago in the days before Jim got hold of him.

After Jones left, I drove to Peggy's and found Jones just coming out of her apartment house. He grinned smugly at me.

Peggy was inside. So was Dennis. And another miserable afternoon began. Dennis was in a nasty mood and he made it plain that he was after Peggy and that he didn't want me seeing her any more. That led to one thing and another and, finally, a brawl. I took out on Dennis all the anger Steig had built up inside me, and when the fight was over, Dennis was battered and bloody.

While he was picking himself up off the floor, Peggy announced that she thought it would be "nice" if I drove Dennis home.

Very nice.

I drove Dennis home. He didn't open his mouth once during the drive, but as soon as he got inside the house at Malibu he began squabbling with Jim. Jim sent him upstairs and invited me into his den for another father-to-son chat.

I sat there stupidly while he told me that Peggy was his. Only his. I was to lay off from now on, and if I didn't, well…

"I'm going to have Peggy," he said. "I'm going to take her away from your dull influence. And if I have to lie to do it, I'll lie, justifying the means by the end. You can rectify one lie. I'll tell another. You can keep refuting one lie after the other but my words will go on and gradually they'll forge ahead of you. I'll build such a structure of lies around you that Peggy won't know what to believe. I've done it and done it quite successfully with other men who were foolish enough to think they'd win Peggy. I have more strength than you. And more will. And I'll beat you. There's no step I won't take."

"Even unto murder," I said.

And watched his face.

No tremor, no twitch. The man *was* a master at deception. He smiled casually.

"That's for you to prove, isn't it?" he said.

He smiled and I had to face it. It was the cold, unyielding smile of the professional killer.

"I'll get Audrey to tell me all about your..." I started.

At last. A rise.

"You'll leave Audrey out of this," he said tensely.

"I'll leave nothing out of this," I said as slowly and as hostilely as I could, "because you'll leave nothing out; you just said so. Because your war is no gentleman's war."

"You'll leave Audrey out of this."

More strenuously spoken. The composure was going slightly. And it gave me a distinct pleasure to see it peeling away.

"Someone is bleeding," I said.

I drove home slowly. I thought all the way of the look of white, shaking rage I'd finally managed to wreak out of Jim. Of his threats which he obviously had the means to carry out. Of my poor, ineffectual rebuttals. Of whether I could do anything I'd threatened.

There was one thing necessary, I realized.

Pinning the murder on him. The rest didn't matter anyway. Why hurt Audrey? Why hurt Dennis? They weren't responsible for anything. No, a murder indictment against Jim and Steig. Two birds with one subpoena.

And I thought of what I'd said to him.

Someone is bleeding, I'd said.

Sure. Someone is always bleeding. Bleeding over politics. Bleeding over religion. Over where the next meal is coming from. Lots of things.

And over women? Good God. Hemophilia.

And the next day, Peggy came and told me that Jim wanted to take us to dinner and to a concert at the Bowl. Us?

Sure, she said. Us. Peggy and me. "Why this change in Jim?"

"I told him I didn't intend to stop seeing you."

"Is that what he wanted?"

"Yes."

He was working on her already. Already? He'd probably been working on her since she'd come in that time to tell him she wanted a divorce. It wasn't hard to desire Peggy. And for a man like Jim who took what he wanted...I wondered how many men he had frightened away from her.

"I told him I had no intention of not seeing you," she repeated. "I said if he wanted it, I'd find another lawyer." I imagined Jim's reaction to that.

"Is that all?" I said.

"So he said all right, to see you if I wanted."

"That was sweet of him," I said.

"Yes," she said, "he told me..."

"What?"

She seemed flustered. "It's not important."

"Tell me."

"No, Davie, it isn't..."

"*Tell* me."

"Well." She looked upset. "He said...you...he said he'd show you up. It's silly."

"Silly."

I put on my jacket.

"He'd show you I wasn't worth anything," I said.

"Let's not talk about it," she said. "Let's talk about something else. You know what they're playing tonight? Sibelius' Second Symphony. Isn't that wonderful?"

I took her arm with a heavy, dejected breath.

"I'm sure the three of us will love it," I said.

One of the first things Jim said at dinner was, "David, I want to apologize quite sincerely for the terrible mistake Steig made the other night. I guess he jumped to conclusions that were unwarranted."

He shrugged like the genial apologizer he wasn't.

"Steig has been disciplined," Jim said like a stern schoolmaster.

"What did you do," I asked, "take away his pet spiders?"

He smiled. Perfect combination smile. Clever admixture of amusement and aloofness. A look that said to Peggy—there, you see, my dear, I told you that this lout was beyond all appeal to decent behavior.

I drank heavily at dinner. I don't know what was the matter with me. I guess I'm spoiled. I just wouldn't take that evening straight. I couldn't beat Jim in his own territory at a game he made the rules for. I felt clamped and a hapless jerk from the start.

As a result I just drank and sniped like a kid all night.

Jim's tactics weren't too obscure for me to guess, however, drunk as I was. A simple maneuver. An overweening niceness toward me, a mannerly well-behaved attitude toward Peggy. And, behind all this, a machete mind hacking away at Peggy's opinion of me. How?

By showing off.

Simple. Little boys do it. They stand on their heads and get red-faced and impress little pig-tailed inquisitors. And as they grow older they keep it up. But more subtly. No more standing on heads. There are other ways.

He took us to Ciro's for dinner. He ordered for the three of us like a father. I started to argue but he made me feel like a clod for doing it. He said he knew what they did best there. I didn't want to make a scene yet and I let him have his continuously jovial and throat-cutting way.

He was charming the pants off us. Off Peggy, anyway. With his knowledge of wines and exotic dishes. And, naturally, with his ordering of the most expensive dishes on the menu—and that's expensive.

And all the while treating me like a misbehaving little son who he'd been compelled to drag along because no one would baby-sit with the little bastard.

Giving out with little cleverly coated stabs.

Like, "You look very nice tonight, David. I always did like that suit at college."

Or, "Have you been here many times, David?"

Or...why go on. Only one thing to say. Peggy was impressed by all of it. Impressed despite her so-called love for me. In spite of the fact that she saw how Jim was trying to relegate me.

While I drank, I kept thinking of Audrey, driven to the same expedient but, now, permanently. I saw her in her room pining for this big hulk of egotism or driving into town looking for bars wherein to find amber solace. Her body twisting itself into knots over a man who didn't care if she was alive or dead.

And Dennis with his temper and his nervous stomach living from tantrum to tantrum, wanting Peggy for no other reason than his brother also wanted her. All these human beings in search of something.

At the Bowl, it turned out that Jim had bought the most expensive seats. Right in front of the stage. We'd be able to smell what Mitropoulos had for supper. The best seats. Jim thought so, anyway.

But when we sat down, Peggy looked around restlessly. She looked at the people around us. She stared up at the hill, the banks of seats climbing.

She turned around and tried to pretend she was satisfied where we were. But then some loudmouths sat behind us and started giggling and blathering about the show they'd seen that afternoon. Jim gave them a Vaughan look but for some appalling reason it didn't seem to impress them.

A man started blowing cigar smoke around. Peggy coughed. She looked unhappy. She kept turning around and looking up the hill at the sky.

'What is it?" Jim asked her.

"I…I feel so cramped down here. Could we…Jim, could we go up there?"

"What, in the 65 cent seats?"

"We stand aghast," I said.

They paid no attention to me. She asked again. Jim couldn't see any way out of it. Pampering her was his choicest weapon. So he shrugged and picked up his coat, looking like a martyr going up in flames.

We climbed up the hill. Peggy first, me next. Jim behind us like a tired old man following his nutty children.

"Oh *this* is the place," Peggy said when we sat down half-way to the moon.

And, of course, she was right. Down there it was absurd, like sitting in a hole in the ground. Paying more to jam yourselves down with a thousand others when the sky and the night were calling.

Afterwards we went to the Mocambo. All I remember is people laughing and cigarette smoke and dancing once with Peggy and her not looking me in the eye.

I drank. The room spun around me. I didn't taste the drinks any more. They were just containers of liquid. And Peggy drank some and so did Jim.

Then we were up again. Large denomination bills fluttering out of Jim's wallet like flocks from a sanctuary. And me, God help me, staggering, almost falling. Jim's hand at my elbow, guiding.

"Let go!" Me, rambunctious. The tough guy. Sing me an old refrain. *"Oh what an ass was Davie!"*

Out in the street. The reaction at last. Sudden quietude in me. A desire to be rid of everyone and everything for good.

"Good night," I said, casually and walked away from them as Jim was helping her into the car.

"Davie."

Her voice was more irritated than concerned. I paid no attention. I walked quickly up Sunset. The wrong way, I later discovered.

They didn't follow. I suppose Jim talked her out of it. She was just angry enough to let him.

I was peeved at that. I had sort of envisioned a car cruising alongside of me with Jim and Peggy sticking their heads out of the window entreating—Davie, come back, oh *do* come back.

Me just sneering, the gallant one, despised of all.

No such luck. They let me walk. Oh, I'm sure Peggy worried but, by the time she started, I guess I was gone. She must have worried how I was to get home. Jim must have been delighted. It must have warmed the chilly crypt of his heart, I kept thinking.

I don't know how long I wandered. The night went on and on and so did I. Everything whirled around, it was just dumb luck I wasn't flattened by a car. I bumped into a couple of people who looked mildly revolted. I tried to get into somebody else's 1940 Ford which I thought was mine.

I don't remember everything. But I remember sitting in a diner and drinking coffee and discussing religion with the cook. I remember sitting on a curb and petting a very patient collie dog who must have been repelled by my breath and my soporific mumbling. I remember standing in front of a ten-cent store and staring at hairpins. I remember lying on my back on somebody's lawn and looking up at the stars and singing a soft version of *Nagasaki* to myself with lyric variations pertaining to the atom bomb.

Then, finally, in some erratic fashion I found my way down to Wilshire Boulevard and got myself on a red bus. I rode down to Western and picked up my car where I'd left it. I drove back to the room.

Key in door lock. Opening of door. Drunken weaving to lamp, turning on of lamp.

Breath sucked out. An icy hand crushing my heart.

On my bed, Dennis.

In his brain, an icepick.

CHAPTER FIVE

I DON'T KNOW how long I stood there looking at him.

I kept shivering. I kept waiting for my stomach to throw up its contents. Which it soon did. I bent over the sink and heard myself muttering, "No, no, no, no, no, no, no..."

Then I sat at the table in the tiny kitchenette and stared at my hands. Afraid to turn around, afraid his open eyes were looking at me. I could feel them. I stared at my shaking hands and I was as sober as a judge.

Dennis dead.

Who? The thought finally managed to emanate after the initial shock had faded a little. Who had done this? Another icepick.

It had to be Steig. Peggy was out with Jim. But Steig had been driving us around. I didn't get it.

But how long had Peggy been home? I jumped up and ran out of the room. I got into my car and started the motor. Then I stopped it and ran back in again. I tried not to look at those glassy, staring eyes and that great patch of blood on my pillow. I drew the light blue bedspread over his body, his face. Then I turned out the light and went into the hall and back to my car.

A mistake. But who ever makes the right move when he's all twisted inside? Who ever makes a right move when his nerves are frayed? I drove up Wilshire fast after a U turn. And halfway to 15th Street I heard a voice on a loudspeaker.

"Black Ford, pull over to curb."

I didn't know what it was at first. Then a red light flashed on and a car pulled alongside.

"Pull over," ordered the voice.

My heart jolted and I went numb. I drew over to the curb and stopped the motor, trying to keep my hands from shaking.

The cop came over to my car. Another one went around to the other side and opened up the door.

"Why were your lights off?" the cop on my side spoke.

For a moment I was almost relieved. I had some crazy idea that Jim had told the police. I was certain he was behind the killing. Dennis was expendable.

"What?" I said, hearing the cop speak.

"I said your license," the cop said irritably.

"Oh. I'm sorry."

I handed him the wallet. He told me to take the license out. I did. He pulled it away from me. The other cop finished looking into my glove compartment.

"No gun," he said.

"Gun?" I said.

They didn't talk to me. The first cop looked over my license. He looked in at my registration card wrapped around the steering column.

"Why didn't you have your lights on?" said the cop. A little more restrained now.

"I've...I've just had an argument with my girl," I said. "I was upset. I'm sorry."

I thought of the dead man in my room. I thought of how that policeman would be very interested to know I had a dead man in my room. A murdered man.

"Your license is okay," he said. He still seemed to be deliberating. And I was thinking that if he gave me a ticket I'd have the incident recorded. Recorded that one David Newton was found speeding away from a murdered man in his room. The thought made my insides turn over.

"I'll just give you a warning this time," the cop said.

I swallowed. "Thank you," I said.

When they were back in their car, I started the motor. I almost drove off again without turning on my lights. Then, pulling away from the curb I suddenly remembered and almost lunged for the knob. My heads beamed out onto Wilshire.

I turned off at 15th and drove down to Peggy's. I saw a light in her living room as I ran across the lawn.

She was alone, sitting in her bathrobe reading a book. I forgot about the night that had gone before. All I could think of was Dennis.

I knocked.

"Baby, how long have you been here?" I asked hurriedly as she opened the door.

"What do you...?"

"Peggy, how long?" I asked, grabbing her shoulders.

She jerked back and her right hand slapped against my cheek.

"Get your hands off me!" she said angrily.

She stood there trembling, her chest rising and falling with sharp breaths.

"Dennis is in my room," I said.

"What has that got to do with…"

"He's dead," I said.

She stared at me.

"What?"

"He has an icepick in his head," I said slowly and watched the look come over her face. A lost look. Her mouth fell open. She stepped back and bumped against the couch. She sank down on it and looked at the far wall.

"He's…?"

I didn't say anything.

"Dennis?"

"Yes, Dennis," I said, "how long have you been home?"

"I…I don't know. A few hours, I guess."

"Think!"

"It was…I remember looking at my watch. We were…just turning the corner at Wilshire, I think. Yes, we…"

"What time?"

"12:30. No, 12:45."

I looked at my watch. It was past four.

"Did Jim stay here?" I asked.

"For a while," she said.

"How long?"

"Oh…twenty minutes."

Then she was in my arms, crying. Her fingers held tightly to me.

"Davie, Davie, what's the matter with everything?"

"All right," I said, "I know you didn't do it."

She drew back as if she'd been struck.

"Me!" she said. "You thought I'd killed him!"

She pulled away from me.

"Get out of here," she said. "Oh, get out of here!"

"Peggy, listen to me."

"No, I won't listen to you," she said. "I've had enough of you. All you've done is act suspicious and hateful!"

She looked at me angrily, hands clenched.

"Listen, Peggy," I said, "your pride is rather unimportant now. In the past week, two men have been murdered. That's a little more important than vanity, isn't it?"

She turned away. "I don't know," she said. "I know I'm tired of everything. I'm tired of it. I'll never find any happiness."

"I'll leave you alone then," I said. "You can go to sleep. But I advise you to call Jim. You'd better find out if he's arranged an alibi for you."

She looked at me but I left. I got in my car and drove back to the room. I was going to walk up to the gas station and call Jones.

I didn't notice the big car as I parked and got out. I didn't notice anything, I was so upset.

But there were two plainclothesmen waiting. And Jones said, "I'm glad you had the sense to come back."

The body was gone. Jones and I were sitting in the room.

"And that's your story," he said.

"Easily checked," I said. "Ask Peggy Lister. Ask Jim Vaughan. I was with them."

"There's a long time you weren't with them."

"I saw other people then."

"We'll find out about Vaughan first," he said.

"Do you really think I'm lying?"

He shrugged. "The pick is from your drawer," he said.

"Are you...do you actually think I did it?"

He shrugged again. "You'll do for now," he said.

"Are you serious?" I said. "For God's sake, why should I come back here if I did it!"

"Come on."

"I told you I was going to call you!"

"Are you coming?"

"Listen..."

"Let it go, boy," he said. "Get some toilet articles and let's get out of here."

That's how I spent my first night in jail. Lying on a cot in a cell. Staring at the walls. Listening to a drunk singing college songs.

In the morning I was taken to Jones' office.

He sat there working on some papers while I waited nervously. I watched his lean, blue-veined hands shuffling through papers. I looked at his thin face, the dark eyes.

Finally the eyes were on me.

"So you were with Vaughan," he said.

"That's what I said. Have you spoken to him?"

"Yes," he said, "we have."

"Well...?"

He kept looking at me and not answering and all of a sudden the bottom started dropping out.

"Oh, *no!*" I said.

He looked at me without speaking. He nodded.

"This is crazy!" I said. "You mean that he actually said he wasn't with me last night?"

"He actually said that."

"Well, he's lying! Damn it! Isn't that obvious?"

He shook his head.

My hands started to shake. "Have you asked Peggy?" I said.

"Yes."

It hit me right in the stomach. I felt as if I were going out of my mind.

"Let me get this," I said. "Peggy said I wasn't with them last night?"

"How long are you going to insist on that?" Jones asked.

"Have you heard of people lying?"

"Yes, I've heard of it," he said, looking at me.

"Peggy," I said, *"Peggy*. To lie about me. I just don't get it. I just...don't."

"Tell me what happened last night," he said.

"I told you."

"Tell me again."

I told him. When I finished, he looked at me studiedly.

"That's it, huh?"

"Yes, that's it. I have no reason to lie."

"Except to save your life," he said.

"Listen, Jones," I said, "You're falling right in with that redheaded bastard who's trying to shove me around the way he's been shoving people around all his life."

He looked at me a long time until it made me nervous.

"I don't know," he finally said, "whether you're telling the truth or not. I'm inclined to believe you. I don't think you could make up as many verifiable lies on the spur of the moment and then duplicate yourself. But—unless either one of those two will change their story, there's not much I can do. Your story *could* be a lie."

"The concert program," I said.

"In the paper," he said, "a telephone call to the Bowl."

"What about the waiters at Ciro's? At the Mocambo? What about that cook in the diner?"

"What about the collie dog?" he said. "You have as much chance of him identifying you as anyone else."

"Let me go," I said, "I'll kick it out of them."

"Sure," he said. "That's a swell idea."

I was taken back to my cell.

I spent the morning reading the paper. The story was on the front page. There was no picture of me, just one of the house, a front view. I knew the landlady wouldn't exactly love me after this. Her house would have a reputation now.

I tried to go over the whole thing in my mind but it didn't add up to a thing. I couldn't understand Peggy lying about me. What was she? How could she do that? And I tried to avoid the idea that kept growing bigger and bigger. Dennis was dead, so he wasn't the killer. Mrs. Grady was obviously out of the picture because she had no place in Dennis's life. That left Audrey or Jim or Steig or...

About noon, a cop opened my cell door and gestured with his head.

"Get your stuff," he said.

I found Steig out in front. I was going to get irate first and refuse the bail. I decided otherwise.

As we started down the steps, Steig said, "Mr. Vaughan wants to see you."

"I don't want to see him," I said.

"You go with me," he said, assured.

I felt that rising heat again. You can just hold temper in so long.

"Listen, tough man," I said, too burned up to be afraid, "I'm not going with you. If you want to try and make me, go ahead. I'd just as soon kick your groin in as look at you."

"I have a gun in my pocket," he said.

I looked down, saw the snub end of the barrel pointed at me.

Where I got the guts to do what I did, I don't know. Maybe there's a streak of insanity in the family.

"Then shoot me in the back," I said, "right here in front of the police station. I'd like to see you get away with it."

Then I turned on my heel and started away.

Luckily, Steig couldn't imagine shooting me in front of the police station either.

I walked all the way to Wilshire with him trailing me in the car. But I stayed in crowded sections and he didn't try to get me. Maybe he was a little off balance, too. I don't suppose he'd been treated like that for some time.

I found Peggy in her living room. I went in without knocking. She jumped a little as I entered.

"All right," I said, "let's have it."

She stood up and I grabbed her wrist.

"Well?"

"You're hurting me!"

"You're hurting me, too!" I snapped back. "Does it mean anything to you that I might be executed for murder?"

I've seen confused faces in my time. But the look on Peggy's face had them all beaten.

"Who told you? Vaughan? Told you what? That they couldn't pin anything on me?"

"Well, I'm the only suspect," I said. "Who the hell do you think they're going to suspect—Dracula?"

"I don't understand, Davie..."

"Obviously," I said. "Listen, Peggy, maybe you don't realize what's been going on. There have been two murders, two of them!"

"But you didn't..."

"I know it and you know and Jim knows. But if neither of you tells the truth about it, who's going to take my word?"

"I..." She ran a hand over her cheek.

"What did he tell you?" I asked. "Come on, let's have it. Did he actually tell you I wouldn't be involved?"

"Yes. He told me they...couldn't prove a thing against you. So he said we shouldn't get involved. I mean, I shouldn't get involved."

"A dead man in my room with an icepick from my kitchen drawer," I said, "and I wouldn't be suspected? Come on Peggy, what's the matter with you? You're so naive, it's near criminal."

"I know. But he..." She shook her head. "He said we shouldn't!"

"And you just...*took* his word."

"Well..."

"Peggy, when are you going to start using your head?"

She looked up defiantly a moment. Then her shoulders slumped. She lowered her eyes.

"What did he really tell you?" I asked.

Her voice was defeated.

"He said he'd re-open my old case. He said I'd be executed for it."

"You can't be tried twice for the same crime!"

"He said..."

"He said, he said! What is he—a Svengali? Haven't you got a brain in your head?"

"He has my life in his hands," she said.

The thought was sickening.

"He has *not*," I said. "He has no control over you. Are you going to set his welfare above mine?"

"Davie..."

"What kind of love do you have for me anyway? Fair weather love? The kind that..."

"Please, Davie."

"Listen," I said incredulously, "this is serious business."

"I was *afraid...*"

"Afraid," I said. "I'm afraid too, Peggy. Jim said he'd get me one way or the other. Steig said he'd kill me. What am I supposed to do because of that—crawl into a hole and die?"

"Steig said that?" Something new to worry about.

"Yes. *Yes*, Peggy Ann. And I say that Steig killed Dennis on Jim's orders."

"But...they were with us last night."

"We met him at Western," I said. "It took us almost an hour to drive there. Then we had to drive all the way back to Hollywood. Was there any real sense in that?"

"He had a case over there and..."

I didn't say anything. I looked at her somberly.

"He wouldn't kill his own *brother*."

"Jim would kill his own *mother* if it served his purpose."

"No."

"It serves his purpose to get me out of the way. And he'll do it too, if you keep lying about me."

She looked at me blankly, then nodded once.

"All right," she said quietly. "This afternoon I'll go to Lieutenant Jones and tell him you were with us."

I took an easy breath. They were short and far between those days. I knew I should start worrying about what Jones would do when she changed her story in midstream. A girl who was proven to have murdered once and suspected of having done it again.

But sometimes I'm selfish, too. Or thoughtless.

"Thank you," I said. "I'll go now."

I was beginning to sense the end of our relationship. I couldn't see how it could last through all this. Even if I loved her. Let's face it. It *isn't* enough when everything else is lacking.

I turned at the door.

"Don't forget to tell Jones that it was Jim's suggestion for you to say I wasn't with you. Put the onus where it belongs."

"I'll...do what I can."

I left. I told her I'd come back soon. And, in my mind I knew that I loved her but I didn't understand her. If only there was a way to find out what she'd gone through, what had been her life before I came. If there were someone who she had known before. Maybe her father or her brother. If I could talk to them.

A thought. Why couldn't I?

I was thinking about that when I found Steig waiting for me again.

"This time, you try to get away and I'll break your neck," he said viciously.

I tampered with the immediate instinct to take a flying kick at his groin before he could make a move. I decided against it. I wanted to see Jim anyway. At least that's what I told myself to avoid a battle which I would, rather obviously, come out second best in. In this case that might be dead, too. Yeah, I wanted to see Jim.

This didn't take long. He was sitting in the back seat of the car. He nodded once as I sat down beside him. He was dressed immaculately as usual. Grey, subdued sharkskin, homburg just right, tie just right. A man to excite admiration and respect. Until the shell was pierced anyway.

"So I wasn't with you last night," I said before he could talk. "I dreamed it all."

"Don't be a fool," he said. "You must realize why I lied about it."

"I'm not a fool," I said. "You did it to incriminate me. When did Steig kill Dennis? Before you met us or after I left you?"

"You *are* a fool," he said, "if you can't see that I did the only thing possible."

I was going to let him know that Peggy planned to spike his lie but I changed my mind. I didn't want to have him trying to stop her before she had a chance to do it.

Instead I said, "Your brother must have meant a lot to you."

He surveyed me icily.

"You really think I had my brother murdered, don't you?" he said.

"I know it," I said. "Real life murder isn't as complex as one in a two-and-a-half dollar mystery. There aren't so many suspects in this case that I have to read two hundred pages to know who killed Dennis."

I knew that Steig was listening. I saw those big shoulders hunch back, then forward. As if he were flexing, readying himself. It made me a little nervous.

"You're a blind idiot," Jim said. "I'll tell you why I lied about you. Because I knew there wouldn't be any evidence against you that meant a thing."

"Just a corpse in my room with my icepick in his head."

"Do you think you'd be out on bail if Jones really suspected you?"

I didn't know.

"I knew you'd be free," he said. "But the real murderer wouldn't be."

"You," I said, "Steig."

"Peggy," he said.

That skin crawling again. I'd tell myself, he's lying, he's lying, he's lying. Three times, because once wasn't enough. But every time I did, he said something more and I got sicker and weaker in conviction. He seemed so sure and I am chronically incapable of believing that intelligent people can keep lying. Even if they threaten to. And Peggy had stabbed her husband to death. That was authenticated.

"You're lying," I said, but only to talk.

"You know I'm not," he said. "You know that there's every possibility in the world that Peggy went to your room last night and killed Dennis."

"No."

"Why not?"

"I...I know Peggy."

"You don't know Peggy."

"She didn't do it."

"She killed Dennis."

"Can you prove that?" I said.

"Prove it?" he said. "I'm trying to make it impossible to prove. I don't want anyone to have a chance to prove it."

I must have looked blank.

"I'm telling you," he said, "Peggy killed my brother. And I'm trying to save her."

"Why did she kill him in my room?" I asked, suspiciously, but weakening.

"He told her to come there. He threatened her."

"With what?"

"With exposing her as Grady's murderer."

"Oh, you're crazy," I said.

He paid no attention. He seemed to sense me weakening. He went on.

"She's insane," he said. "You may not choose to believe that, but it doesn't alter the fact. She's killed *three* men now. God knows why."

"But you still want her," I said, searching vainly for confidence in Peggy.

"I guess you wouldn't understand that." he said. "You who live by the morals of a petty world."

We sat in silence a moment.

"All right," I said, looking for a peg to hang my mind on. "Where does that leave us?"

I couldn't go on. I couldn't concentrate. I was sick thinking that maybe everything Jim had ever told me was the truth. How long can blind love sustain you when someone keeps hacking away at it with a very tangible axe? And the thought that my relationship with Peggy had been an endless fabrication of lies made me ill.

"I've told you," he said, "they can't do anything about it. And as long as you don't try to involve her, I'll leave you alone."

"I still don't believe you," I said. "I saw the shock on her face when…"

"One night Peggy and Dennis went out together," he said. "At three o'clock in the morning, Dennis came in the house with his arm streaming blood. He had to have five stitches."

"It's…"

"And the next day Peggy came to see him and she cried and said she didn't mean it."

"It's your story," I said.

"It's the facts," he said. "Use your head, David. When are you going to stop plunging into things you can't cope with?"

"Look..." I said.

"You look," he said. "Open your eyes. You're not up to this."

That's what Audrey had said too. Maybe they were right. Maybe I wasn't up to it. I knew it would be a relief to get away from it all.

"Peggy is..." Jim started, "I don't know what word will express it. Deranged, perhaps. I know it's not a nice word but I have to use it. There's a Hyde beneath her. I don't know what brings it out, but it's there. Love won't help her. Psychiatry may. I don't know. But she's dangerous, very dangerous."

"Why do you love her, then?" I asked.

"I happen to love Peggy," he said, "with a love I don't think your type of narrow-minded idealist understands. Because it's a love that asks nothing."

"Maybe it asks nothing," I said, "because it gets nothing."

"Now we're being petty," he said.

He said it with the old familiar expression of intellectual scorn on his full face. And it was a shock to realize for a second that this man and I had gone to college together and called each other friends.

I got out of the car and looked at him. He made no effort to detain me and waved Steig back into the car.

"There's only one thing to say," I said. "Your entire story is a lie from beginning to end."

But as I walked back to my room, I knew I'd been reaching. Peggy *had* murdered once. These clippings were genuine. Even Jones had told me that.

Which helped not at all. Because there came visions to my mind. Of Peggy holding an icepick, a razor. Standing over Albert, standing over Dennis. Plunge of the arm, sound of steel point driving into flesh and tissue. A look on Peggy's face. One I'd seen that night on the pier when she'd been attacked. A shocked and wild look.

A look not human.

Funerals are not nice.

They are creations of society which are intended to provide people with a last chance to show respects but which turn instead into miniature Grand Guignols. For my money, they're morbid and tasteless. You just can't effect anything tasty with a corpse They're too dead.

Dennis's funeral was no exception. I don't know what brought me to it. Peggy told me about it. She wasn't going with Jim so I took her.

And I did feel sort of sorry for Dennis. A little ashamed, too, at having suspected him of murder. He'd just been an ill-fated kid with no chance at all. Victimized all of his short life by brother James.

A few relatives were there. Not many. Most of them, I suspected, were in Missouri. Even the ones that came looked like country cousins. Their clothes weren't on a par with Jim and Audrey's. Yes, Jim had his wife with him. It was his concession to appearance. After all, this was in the paper and no breath of scandal must besmirch the moment.

Some people there I didn't understand. They were men mostly. And there was something about them. Something faintly tawdry in spite of the clothes they wore. An aura of inherent cheapness and vulgarity.

They didn't look too sad either. One of them even snickered during the service. Jim didn't hear it. But Steig did and I saw him put his big hand on the man's shoulder and the man went white.

The relatives played their expected role. They looked sad. They clucked pityingly. They commented. Once I thought it was a joke, that line about how "natural" the corpse looks. Well, it's not a joke. I heard it about five times that afternoon.

And there was poor Dennis, unable to complain, lying up there in front and taking it straight. That ugly little hole in his temple all covered up and prettied. Dennis finally at peace. The hard way.

Peggy didn't speak to me much. She kept her head lowered during much of the service. I don't think she looked at Dennis once. Her dark gloved hands were clasped tight in her lap. The thought in my mind that she might have caused all this was enough to make my hands tremble spasmodically all afternoon.

I watched Audrey in the front row. I'd been surprised to see her at first. I didn't think Jim would want her there. Maybe he didn't. Maybe she went in spite of his wishes. But there she was at his side, thinner-looking than ever in her black dress, looking at Dennis fixedly.

When the dismal charade was over and we had all guessed that Dennis was dead, we filed out in the sunlight and found Wilshire Boulevard much the same and all the people thereon alive and moving.

The assemblage milled respectably in front of the parlor. They made gentle, strained smiles and spoke in muted, strained tones.

"Horrible thing, James, horrible."

Jim nodding gravely, lips pressed together. To keep back a smile? I didn't know.

"The dear boy looked so natural."

Chicken claw hands plucking at pearls. A relative ghoul passing comment on the dead.

I didn't concentrate on staying by Peggy and somehow, Jim managed to get her beside him. So I moved over to where Audrey stood with an aunt.

As I approached, the woman said a few extra words of vain condolence and then passed into the void.

Audrey looked at me, dry-eyed and dead sober, it appeared. There was a certain classic loveliness about her. Dressed in black, her dark hair pulled back tight, her eyes as funereal as her outfit, her skin pale and clear.

She tried to smile at me but couldn't. "It was nice of you to come," she said.

I took her hand and squeezed it.

"I'm sorry for him," I said. "That's why I came."

As I stood close to her now, I noticed her breath. She wasn't sober. Sorrow had just given her the capacity to hold it in. She was as taut as a drum. I got the impression that it wouldn't take much to unhinge her.

"I'll be going," I said.

She held onto my hand.

"Don't leave me," she whispered. "Don't leave me with these...jackals. Relatives waiting for scraps. And those...those tramps."

I didn't know what she meant. But I stayed as her fingers dug pleadingly into my arm.

"Have you your car?" she asked.

"Yes, but..."

"Take me somewhere," she begged, "anywhere, David. I've got to have a drink or I'll go out of my mind."

"But I'm with Peggy."

"Does she look as if she'll have to walk home?" she asked bitterly.

"Well," I said, "I should..."

■ ■ ■ ■

The bar was cool, dark and empty. We sat in a back booth. Outside July shimmered hot fingers over the streets.

Audrey had a long one, a stiff one. I watched her throat move convulsively as she poured it down. When she'd finished it off, she put down the glass and leaned back against the booth. The tenseness gave a little at the edges. Alcoholic relaxation eased her nerves temporarily. And two big tears forced themselves from under her closed lids and ran down across her white cheeks.

"Poor baby," she said, "poor helpless baby."

Audrey needed someone to talk to. I listened.

"He never had a chance," she said. "Money, sure he had money. Is that what they call a chance nowadays?"

She looked at me and the anger slipped from her thin features. She started working on her second drink. She put the glass down and pressed her right hand to her breasts as it she wanted to rub the liquored heat into her flesh. She reached up and dragged off the black veiled hat with a sob.

"I *hate* funerals," she said miserably. "They stink. You hear me! They *stink!*"

"I hear you."

She leaned her head onto her right palm and then ran shaking fingers through her hair.

"Poor baby," she said.

She lost breath for a moment as a sob clutched her throat. Then she drank some more.

Her eyes on me. Red. Lost eyes.

"You know what he said to me a few nights ago?"

"Jim?" I asked.

"Dennis. Jim never talks to me." Another sob. "Dennis said— *You're* my family, Aud. The only family I have."

"Yeah," I said quietly.

"Imagine it," she said. "Just his sister by marriage, but to him, I was his family. And he...he kissed me on the cheek. And he hugged me."

Her teeth clamped together. Her lips pressed tightly, drained white under the lipstick.

"If I find out who did it," she said, "if I find out for sure that she did this I'll…"

"What?" I said.

Her eyes dropped. She shook her head and picked up her glass.

"You'll do what?"

"Nothing," she said.

"I'll tell you who killed Dennis. Steig killed him."

She shook her head. "I don't know."

"You don't want to know," I said. "You'd rather believe it was Peggy."

"Buy me another drink?"

"No, I won't buy you another drink. I'm taking you home. I'm never buying you another drink again. Drink yourself to death on your own money. I've lost sympathy."

She didn't say a word all the way to Malibu. She got out of the car and I drove away. I imagine that she went to her room and locked herself in. There, she probably took off all her clothes and went to bed with a bottle of whiskey and drank it until she was senseless. Happy college days gone. Betty Coed in a drunken stupor.

Later that afternoon I stopped by Peggy's apartment. Apparently Jim had to entertain a few visiting firemen he happened to be related to. And, naturally, since Audrey wasn't around he'd have enough trouble explaining that without having Peggy around to arouse comment too. As a matter of fact I found out later that Jim was burned up because I'd taken Audrey away. Lord know why. She certainly was in no shape to play hostess to ferret-eyed relatives.

Peggy was sitting in the living room listening to the radio. I recognized the introduction the orchestra was playing. In a moment Lanza would start heaving his lungs out and using up his incredible gift a little more.

The door was open to let the breeze in so I went in and sat beside her. She smiled a little and patted my hand as I sat down.

"How long have you been here?" I asked her.

"I don't know," she said. "I haven't been keeping track. Where were you?"

"I took Audrey home," I said.

"Oh. Jim took me home. That is, he had Steig take me home."

"I imagined he would."

Casual conversation with *Che gelida manina* in the background. And my mind tearing at me to ask her once and for all if...

But how can you ask a girl you love to tell you—yes or no—whether she's murdered?

"I'm sorry you went," I said, unable to ask.

"Went?"

"To the funeral. They're depressing. And you have enough troubles."

She smiled mirthlessly.

"I'm used to funerals," she said. "My mother. An uncle. An aunt. A cousin. Dennis."

She shrugged.

"Everybody dies," she said.

I looked at her closely. At her finely etched profile, the light from the dying sun on her cheeks.

Then she started to talk. More to herself than to me, I think. Just her thoughts spoken aloud.

"He looked nice lying there," she said. "He wasn't a...a man anymore. I mean there was nothing ugly about him."

Was that a smile? It was gone too quickly for me to be sure.

"You know what he looked like?" she asked.

She began to examine her white hands.

"He looked like a gentleman," she said.

CHAPTER SIX

IT TOOK ABOUT an hour to drive to Pasadena. I followed winding Sunset all the way to its end, then turned off into the speedway that led to Pasadena. The car worked fine. I hit eighty once. A good thing the car was in working shape. I was in no mood for more troubles. I had enough.

Driving gave me time to think.

About my novel, which was getting nowhere at an exceedingly rapid clip. About my life, which was getting more and more complex and unenjoyable. About Peggy, who seemed more an enigma by the day.

That's why I was going to Pasadena to see her father.

I wanted to meet him, talk to him. There had to be some beginning to all this. Some cause for all this unbalanced effect.

The house was a small bungalow near the California Institute of Technology.

The place was fastidiously kept. I don't know whether the captain or his son or hired help did it. It was probably hired help. Whatever the case, the lawn was cropped close, the house was neatly painted and everything was square and neat and clean. You could almost guess that a very appearance-conscious man lived there. A man to whom exterior presentation was half the essence of personality, if not a good deal more than half.

I stood on the porch waiting for someone to answer the bell, looking at the porch railing scrubbed clean recently, the smell of soap and lye still in the air. The welcome mat was dusted and swept but no more welcoming for that.

It was a young man in his teens who answered the door. He was pale, he wore glasses. I knew him, though. It was Peggy's face. I noticed the black coat sweater over his white shirt, the small, tight knot on the tie.

"Yes?" he said.

Myopia. A lot worse than mine. Braces on his teeth. Nothing to glean a Mr. America vote.

"Are you Phillip Lister?" I asked.

"Yes," he said, "that's right."

"I'm a friend of Peggy's," I said. "I don't know whether she's mentioned me."

He looked confused.

"No...she didn't."

I extended my hand, feeling awkward, feeling a slight sense of anger with Peggy. Was she ashamed of me? The inevitable question popped into my overly male brain.

"I'm David Newton."

"How do you do?" His handshake was weak. "Won't you...come in?"

The same hesitating way of speaking as Peggy. As if he weren't sure that what he was about to say was the right thing.

I was in the hallway. It was as fastidious as the outside. Scrupulously arranged. It was more like the waiting room of a doctor than a home. Lister probably ran his house like they said he ran his ship before the war. With a tyrannical insistence on the immaculate.

"Won't you sit down?" Phillip asked me. He was a little taller than Peggy, about five ten I guessed. He was quite lean. And overstudied, it was obvious. I could just picture him in the early morning hours poring over complex engineering volumes.

I sat on the couch. He sat on the edge of a chair. Like a timid man in a furniture store, afraid to damage anything because it isn't his property.

I noticed the room, too. Everything in its place. A sterile cleanliness. The fireplace obviously unused and swept clean, the andirons polished to a bright luster, the unneeded screen dusted and standing in precisely the right spot. On top of the fireplace, polished candlesticks, empty. Over them, pictures, all hanging at the right angle. Pictures of Navy men and ships; Captain Lister's only concession to nostalgia, I imagined. A discharge prominently displayed. Or did an officer get retirement papers? I didn't know. Maybe it was a citation.

Phillip was clearing his throat.

"How is Peggy?" he asked.

"Fine," I said.

"She...she was here about a week or so ago."

"So she said," I said, nodding.

"Mmm-hmmm," he said, nodding too. He swallowed. "What is she doing now? Has she found a job yet?"

"Uh...no, no, not yet. Still in the process, I guess." He smiled. It faded.

"Have you known Peggy long?" he asked.

"About a month," I said.

He looked surprised. Then he hid it.

"Oh?" he said. "Are you from California?"

I got the impression that he'd spend the whole day chatting about nothing before he'd ask me what I'd come for.

"I'm from New York," I said. "Say, is..."

"I was going there once," he said.

"Oh, I..."

"But Father..." He paused, smiling falsely. "I changed my mind."

"Is your father home?" I asked.

He looked at me blankly.

"Uh, he's...he's upstairs. He's taking his nap."

"I see."

"Did you want to see him?"

"Yes."

He stirred restlessly. "Oh," he said, "I...can I help you in any way?"

I hesitated. Then I said, "Maybe you can. I want to find out about Peggy."

"Oh."

The glasses, the coat sweater, the lean, bowed form. Student. Driven son. I threw off the thoughts about him.

"Can you tell me about Peggy's marriage?" I asked.

"Her marriage?"

He looked at me carefully.

"Tell me," he said, "is Peggy really involved in all these...these terrible...things?" He finished weakly as if the word "murder" were more than he could speak.

"I'm afraid she is," I said.

"Oh. Poor Peggy." He bit his lip. "She must be terribly upset. She wouldn't tell us much when she was here. And Father..."

He broke off, ill at ease.

"Did Peggy kill her husband?" I asked abruptly.

He flinched. As if someone had cracked a whip over his head. He looked over into the hall. I got the idea he was looking to see if his father were around.

"She..."

"Did she?"

He nodded jerkily.

I closed my eyes for a moment. It was true. I couldn't even take the pleasure of doubting it vaguely any more.

"Do you know why?" I asked.

I shouldn't have asked. I should have realized how it would hurt him. But curiosity was conquering any sense of consideration I had.

"Well," he said, "I really don't…"

"I'm not just prying for its own sake," I said. "Peggy is suspected of these other two murders and…"

Silence from both of us. It clung to us. He was shocked, looking at me with disbelieving eyes. And I was shocked too by my own words.

Peggy is suspected.

I knew then, finally, objectively, that she could have committed either crime. And the knowledge was like a wedge between us. And more knowledge would be like hammer blows on the wedge, hurting us, separating us. I was almost afraid to learn anymore, to admit anymore to myself.

"Peggy?" Phillip said. "Peggy is suspected?"

"Yes. You see she…"

"Who rang, Phillip?"

Stentorian voice. Our eyes shifted quickly to the hall. There in the doorway, straight and bleak.

Aaron Lister.

He was tall. There was some resemblance to Peggy. In the frame. In the touch of masculine strength in Peggy's face. That strength that hinted of flint-like resolution. He was her father, all right.

His eyes were on me as he spoke to Phillip.

"Father, this is…" Phillip looked at me for help.

"David Newton," I said.

I was standing up as he came walking in. Captain Bligh on the maindeck, I thought. Ready to squelch mutiny or flog a dead man. His face was unmoving and rocklike, like one of those faces carved out of that mountain out west.

"Newton," he said. He seemed to taste the word to see if it were poisonous.

Then his eyes moved over me in examination. I might have been before his court martial board, a twenty year A.W.O.L.

"Mr. Newton is a friend of Peggy's," Phillip said nervously.

Lister didn't speak. He walked over to the fireplace and turned. Still not a flicker on his face. This guy even makes Vaughan look transparent, I thought. World, oh world, full of people afraid to show themselves as they are.

"You wished to see me?" he said and it wasn't a question. It apparently never occurred to him that anyone might come there to see Phillip.

"Yes," I said, "I did."

"May I ask why?"

Phrased politely. But behind it, the unspoken words—Speak, man, or I'll have you thrown to the dogs.

I looked at him, wondered why I always felt that momentary sense of uneasy timorousness when I came across these people who were bent on dominating all relationships. Was it because I wasn't ever pushing hard? Because I just took life easy and was thrown off stride by these intent ones? These people to whom life is a challenge and a never-flagging combat? I don't know. But I felt a little nervous at first. Until I realized, as I ultimately did in all such cases, that they were born the same way as I was and were no better. No Olympian horn had sounded the nascence of Aaron Lister. Just a squawling like mine. Ten fingers, ten toes, et cetera. I looked at bleak Captain Lister without a qualm then. The regal manner was just show to me.

"I'm interested in your daughter," I said.

"Are you?" Amusement? Contempt?

"I plan to marry her," I said. I felt a slight twinge in the knowledge that I wasn't sure whether I said it because I meant it or because I wanted to get a rise out of the captain.

His cheeks seemed to twitch. His whole body seemed to be galvanized, then stiffened as if his spine had transformed itself into a long iron rod. His poker face changed an iota.

"I believe my daughter is expecting to marry another gentleman," he said. Final words, the clap of doom.

"I don't think so," I said.

There went my plan. He wouldn't talk to me now. Why did I always bristle before smug minds?

"Your opinion is immaterial to me," said Captain Lister.

That was that, it appeared. Thirty days, next case.

Dead silence. Lister apparently expected me to retire, bowing. Phillip cleared his throat.

"Mr. Lister," I said.

"Captain Lister," he corrected.

I licked my lips.

"Captain Lister," I said.

"I have nothing to say," he said.

"Captain Lister, I want to know about your daughter. This is very important. She's involved in murder and..."

"I have no interest in it," he said, deceptively mild. "I do not care what my daughter is implicated in."

"Well, for God's sake, can't you...!"

I stopped. I could see I wasn't going to get anything out of him. I might as well try to melt an iceberg with a match.

"That's all, I believe," Aaron Lister said. Still on the board. He'd die on that court martial board. I could see him instructing his pallbearers.

"Captain Lister," I said, "you have no idea what a shock it is to see a father who doesn't give a damn about his own child."

He closed his eyes.

"Lister!"

"Mr. Newton!" he exploded. "My daughter is no longer a part of my family!"

I looked at him. I shook my head. Then I turned on my heel.

"Good day," I said.

"Good day," he answered.

I slammed the door in a fury and started down the walk. So. That was her father. A starchy, heartless ramrod. I could just visualize Peggy's bringing-up by him. The unbending discipline, the harsh cowing of her young personality. Like taking a bird and holding its wings so that all it could do was flutter in mute impotence.

Then I heard the door open. I turned.

"Mr. Newt..."

"Phillip!"

The voice rang out inside. Phillip looked at me. Then he tried to smile but it didn't come off. He shut the door quietly and I stood there looking at the white door, the polished brass knocker, the entrance to emptiness.

I couldn't concentrate as I drove back. I was too distracted. Peggy had been brought up by *that*. Her impressionable brain assailed with hardness and cruelties. Her entire youth sterile of love after her mother's death. No wonder she was hungry for it. She'd been starving for it all her unhappy life.

I wanted to run to her, to make it up. I drove to her apartment when I got to Santa Monica. She wasn't there.

I waited a while but she didn't come back. I tried to think she wasn't with Jim. She couldn't be. Not now, after what she'd told me. Could she trust him after he threatened her? If she could...

I tried to think it out as I drove to Malibu to see if Jim were out.

Yes, it made sense. I finally decided that. She'd never had anyone she could really count on. Jim had been the rock she needed. She had never known real love. Was it surprising then that she misinterpreted and decided that Jim loved her the way she needed? How could she really know that being given things and having favors done for her wasn't being loved? No one had ever taught her differently.

A maid opened the door at Malibu.

"Mr. Vaughan in?" I asked her.

"No, he isn't," she said.

"Oh." I stood there looking at her.

"Who is it, Jane?" I heard a voice calling from the head of the stairs. Audrey.

I leaned in and looked up.

"Hi!" she said, smiling. "Come on in. All right, Jane."

The maid nodded, closed the door and disappeared down the hallway.

"Come on in the living room," Audrey said, coming up to me. "I'll make you a drink."

"Where's Jim?"

"He's down at the police station."

"Oh."

We went up the stairs and into the high-ceilinged living room. I remembered the first night I'd gone there, met Jim again for the first time since graduation. Since then—murder, murder and here I was again.

"What'd you want to see Jim about?" she asked, pouring drinks.

I shook my head.

"That's right," Audrey said, "we went through that routine once, didn't we? We'll skip it this time. Soda?"

"A little."

"None for me, thank you," Audrey piped to herself. "I like to drink it straight if you don't mind I don't mind at all well that's nice of you thank you you're welcome."

She was drunk again. Good and...

I went over to the big picture window and looked out. Way down below, across the highway, I could see rocks and blue-green ocean dashing out its white brains on them. Foam flashed and drops sparkled in the crystalline air. The breeze coming through the windows was crisp and tangy with the smell of the sea. To live in a house like this, the thought came. It had everything.

Except happiness.

"Quite a view," I said.

"Quite a jump," she said.

"Planning on it?" I said.

She pursed her lips.

"Who knows?" she said, sinking down on the couch. She patted the cushion beside her.

"Sit here," she said. "Tell mama all about everything."

I sat down. She grinned at me.

"You're feeling pretty chipper today, aren't you?" I said.

"No," she said blithely, "just pretending."

"Okay," I said, "I'll pretend too. Is it easy?"

"It is if your brain falls out," she said.

"Uh-huh. Oh...I...guess I should apologize for the nasty way I spoke to you last time I saw you."

"When was that?"

"The day...I took you home."

"Oh." She shrugged. "Anything you said, I'm sure I deserved."

I smiled at her. I took a sip of my drink.

"The police station, you said? What's going on?"

"Questions and answers, I suppose," she said. "Jones probably has the culprit."

"If he has," I said, "you have no husband."

She looked at me without anger.

"I haven't got one anyway," she said.

"When are you going to leave him, Audrey?"

"When are you going to leave that girl?"

"I'm not."

She shrugged. "That's my answer," she said. She held up the glass and looked at the liquor. She shook her head.

"It looks so innocent," she said. "Just some colored water. But what it does. Lawsy."

I didn't say anything. We had nothing to discuss really, but I didn't want to leave. I was tired of driving, tired of looking for answers. I wanted to relax. You can't pile-drive twenty-four hours a day.

"You look pretty," I said.

She smiled.

"Sweater girl," I said.

"That's me."

"You have a nice figure, Audrey."

"Mercí." She drank. She licked her lower lip. "Well here we are, Davie boy."

"Here we are," I said.

"You in love with a murderess, me in love with…"

"Cut it out."

"Sorry."

"Audrey."

"Wha'?"

"Did Dennis…have his arm cut open by Peggy?"

She looked at me. "Yes," she said. "He had to have stitches taken, it was so bad."

"What did he do?"

"You mean to deserve a cutting-up?" she said. "He probably looked cross-eyed at her."

"Oh, stop it. You know he must have done something serious. He probably made a pass at her."

"Is that bad? A man should make a pass at me. I wouldn't cut his arm open."

"*She* would. You don't know what she's been through."

"I don't care, Davie. I don't care."

"All right. Forget it.

"Audrey," I said then, trying to get somewhere in all this crazy tangle, "who were those men at the funeral? The ones you called tramps?"

She looked at me over her glass.

"I don't know whether I should tell you," she said.

"Listen," I said, "I know about Jim. I know he didn't win his money at a raffle."

She raised her eyebrows.

"Law is profitable," she said.

"Come on, Audrey. You know what I mean."

"You won't..."

"Repeat it? I won't use it against him. I wouldn't hurt you even if you are in love with the wrong guy."

"Who's the right guy?"

"I don't know."

"Kiss me, Dave?"

I leaned over and her warm mouth opened a little under mine. I could taste her breath.

She sighed as I straightened up.

"Gee, it's nice to be kissed," she said. "It's been so long. You kiss nice, Dave."

"Tell me about Jim, Audrey."

She looked away from me. Then she settled herself in the couch. She poured a little from the bottle into her drink. She smiled. Then it went. She couldn't relate it in a joking way. That was clear.

"It's not too complicated," she said. "Jim has dozens of ties with the crime syndicate out here on the coast. He started out as just a lawyer. But he found out soon enough that a beginner couldn't make out in law. At least he couldn't make out the way Jim wanted to make out. So he took on a couple of shady characters as clients. He defended them. He saved one from the gas chamber and got the other one acquitted. He got money for that. And a rep, too. They started coming to him. One thing led to another."

"Did you know about it?" I said.

"Not at first," she said, "but he couldn't keep it a secret. Those men kept coming to the house. You can't keep them away. When I found out, I almost left him. But I can't, you know that. I tried to talk him out of doing it. You can imagine what good it did."

"Did Dennis ever threaten to expose him?"

She didn't answer.

"Audrey, did he?"

"Well..."

"He did, didn't he?"

"He...Dennis was always a hothead. He'd threatened lots of things."

"And you wonder why Jim had him killed," I said.

"David, I don't want you to say it anymore."

"Listen," I said, "do you know what Steig is?"

No answer.

"Audrey, he used to be a Chicago gunman. A paid killer!"

I thought she'd gone into a coma the way she stared at me.

"Jones told me that," I said. "He showed me the card on Steig, too. He's suspected of murdering about a *dozen* men. That's your husband's chauffeur, Audrey."

"Is that true, Dave? You're not lying?"

"I swear to God it's the truth, Audrey."

Her head slumped forward and her eyes closed.

"God help him," she whispered. "God help my poor Jim."

I stared at her. At a woman who could love him still.

"Audrey, how can you..."

"Don't. Don't, Dave. I love him. That's it. I don't question your love even if I question the girl you love."

"I'm not sure I love her," I said.

She looked at me bleakly.

"I hope you don't," she said, "I hope at least somebody gets out of this in one piece."

I put my arm around her but she didn't respond in any way. She stared at her lap. She put the drink on the table.

"I guess you'd better go," she said.

I took my arm back and looked at her. Poor Audrey. Not a sodden alcoholic. A girl, confused and betrayed in her love. Lost in a morass of frustrations and unanswered yearnings. One thing I know and will always know. When love starts turning itself in, the results are horrible to see.

"I wish there was something for you to hold on to," I said. "I wish I could be that something."

She smiled momentarily and patted my hand. Then she got up.

"Thanks," she said.

I followed her across the thick rug, feeling a dragging sense of inevitability in me. That Audrey would live and die here in this house. In her terrible despair as long as Jim lived. And if he died, maybe even then.

Someone was bleeding.

Later I went home and sat around my room. I tried to work on the novel but it was impossible. I kept writing the same sentence over and over again. I read the paper and saw that nothing had developed on the case. Nothing that the papers had anyway. No fingerprints on the second icepick either.

Finally I threw down the paper and went to call up Peggy. I didn't get an answer. I drove over to her place. She wasn't home. I got disgusted and went out to have supper. I ate at the Broken Drum, a little place on Wilshire whose motto is—You Can't Beat It. The pun is bad but the food is good.

I went back to my room and tried to write. I couldn't. I kept thinking about Peggy being with Jim. It disgusted me. Yet I think I almost felt glad. It gave me an excuse for being disgusted with her. In spite of everything I felt I had a desire to get away. I was on a fence and it seemed as if Peggy was pushing me over the other way.

I tried to read. I couldn't do that either. I listened to the radio. That wasn't any good either, so I turned it off and went to the movies.

"Hi!" she said brightly, standing by the screen window. I jumped up and unlocked the door. She came in and we embraced. I'm like Audrey, I thought. I can talk too, but when it comes down to it, I can't do anything but love her when she's near.

"Did I wake you up, Davie?"

"Nope."

"What are you going to do?"

I was going to tell her that I *had* to work on my book. But I knew if I did she'd go away and I didn't want her to go away. She looked so fresh and clean. Come to think of it, the only time I could deliberate about leaving her was when we were apart. When she was close to me, I didn't have a chance.

"Nothing in particular," I said.

"Wanna take a hike?" she said.

"I...guess so."

Her face fell.

"Wouldn't you?" she said.

"Sure, babe."

"If you don't want to, tell me, Davie."

"Baby, I'm a little sleepy, that's all. Go make us some breakfast while I take a shower."

She smiled and rubbed her warm cheek against mine

"Davie," she whispered happily. And even though the words in my mind were *Here we go again,* I didn't care.

"Shall we go to Griffith Park?" I said, dressing after my shower.

"Ooh, yes!"

I smiled to myself. Just a big kid, really. Give her the love she needed and the world was her oyster.

"Shall I make sandwiches?" she asked.

"Sure. I'll go get the stuff."

"Okay. After you eat. Breakfast is almost ready." While we ate she looked up.

"Jim says I might not even have to go through a trial," she said excitedly. "Isn't that wonderful?" I smiled and patted her hand.

"That *is,* " I said. "I'm glad, Peggy."

"I'm so happy," she said. "I've dreaded it. I couldn't sleep at night thinking about it."

I nodded. "That's wonderful, Peggy," I said.

It was a beautiful day as the car buzzed along Sunset. A day to make a guy forget there is violence in the world. To make a guy forget that double murder had been a part of his life. To make him forget everything except that he was going on a picnic with his girl. It's amazing how little can change a fellow's attitude. Sun in the sky, a car driving along at a fast clip, breeze on you, the car radio playing *Der Rosenkavalier Waltzes* and her hand holding my arm.

I glanced over at her. She had a bright red ribbon in her hair, a tight red sweater, a pair of jeans, loafers. I noticed she kept pulling the sweater as loose as she could but it insisted on clinging to her curves.

"You look good enough to eat," I said.

She leaned over and pressed her forehead against my arm. She sighed happily.

"I'm so lucky," she said.

I kissed her hair. And felt the first sense of peace in weeks. It was almost as if we were escaping. To a sunlit day, away from every dismaying thing.

"It's been a long time," she said and her hands tightened on my arm.

We drove about fifty minutes to reach the park. We talked about inconsequential subjects mostly. I didn't tell her I'd been to see her father. I wasn't sure how she'd take it and I didn't want to spoil anything.

The park was as Peggy said, just like going out into the hills. Wild overgrown hills, not at all like the Prospect Park in my home town, Brooklyn.

Griffith Park was a park. In size alone it made Prospect Park look like a corner lot. And for sheer beauty and clean wilderness it far surpassed the Brooklyn spot. Deer run loose in Griffith Park. Only teen-age gangs run loose in Prospect.

When we got out of the car and locked it up and got the two brown paper bags with our lunch, I looked around. Far up a winding path, on the crest of a hill stood a white-domed building. It looked like a fortress The country around it looked like Scottish wilds. It was fascinating.

We left the path after a little while and plunged into the thick brush. Overhead the sun grew very hot. The blunt waves of heat seemed to cling to the ground as we climbed. Peggy pulled up the sleeves of her sweater and kept plucking at the wool to loosen it from her flesh. The sun on my head didn't help toward cool detachment. Great drops of sweat rolled over my temples and cheeks. I watched her ahead of me as she climbed. If I could touch her, I thought.

And thought something else.

Was it possible that, unconsciously, Peggy dressed and behaved in a manner calculated to draw desire out of the men she was with? Ostensibly she feared men and their aggression. Why, then, did the very thing she claimed to fear always happen to her? That boy, her husband, Albert, and all the men she had driven half-mad with desire for her. Include me. What was it about her? Was that shy withdrawal part of her calculation? Was it all intended to gather to herself what she claimed to fear but actually desired intensely? They talk about accident-prone men. Well maybe there are rape-prone women, too.

I shook my head under the hot sun and felt dizzy. Partly with heat. Mostly with the confusion that a human mind can evoke when it begins to exist on different levels.

She stopped and sat down in the shade of a tree. I plopped down beside her.

"Phew, it's hot," she said.

"Am I out of shape," I said.

"We both are," she answered.

"Typing doesn't give me much muscle," I said.

"Neither does loafing."

"Your brother said you were getting a job. Are y...?"

"My brother?"

Give me a scissors and I'll snip off my tongue.

She was looking at me intently.

"When did you see my brother?" she asked.

At first I hesitated. Then I told her. Her face hovered undecided between acceptance and anger.

"Why did you have to go *there?*" she asked.

"I wanted to meet your father," I told her. "I wanted to find out what sort of man had raised you."

She looked at me a little sullenly. I noticed the halo of sunshine around her golden hair, the way the breeze flicked the delicate hairs against her forehead.

"Well, did you find out?" she asked.

"Yes."

"You couldn't have asked me to take you, could you?"

"When did you ever offer to? I've asked you four or five times if I could go with you."

"I don't like to be investigated, Davie."

"I wasn't investigating."

"What do you call it?"

"Listen, Peggy, isn't it…"

"Oh, don't start," she said. "I've had enough lectures this week."

She leaned back against the gnarled tree trunk with a sigh. She stared at her lap, then closed her eyes as if to shut me out.

"Everybody wants to investigate me," she said.

I reached out and took her hand but she drew it back.

"Peggy, I'm sorry if I…offended you. But I think I have a little right to know something about you. Apparently you don't care to tell me anything about yourself. I have to find out some way."

"You don't believe what I've told you, do you?"

"You've told me practically nothing."

"Maybe I thought it was better."

"Maybe I didn't," I said.

She opened her eyes.

"What would you like to know?" she asked, bitterly, "how I killed Albert? How I took an icepick and…"

"That's enough, Peggy."

"Let me tell you all about it," she said.

"You *did* kill your husband, Peggy."

"Yes, and I'd kill him again! You hear that, I'd kill him again! He was a pig, an *animal!*"

"And would you go through everything else again. The trial, the accusations, Jim?"

"Why do you always keep harping on Jim? He's always been good to me."

"Good! He threatens to have you executed for a crime you've already been acquitted on! Is that what you call being good to you?"

"Maybe he's…"

"What?"

"I don't know."

"I guess not. Well, Jim hasn't been exactly good to me."

"He's your friend."

"Does a friend have you beaten senseless?"

"That was a mistake and you know it," she said. "He thought you were with his wife."

"He doesn't give a damn about his wife!"

"She's an alcoholic and a nymphomaniac, why should he?"

"What? Is that what the son of a bitch told you? God damn it, Peggy, when the hell are you going to get some sense in your head. Oh, stop looking so goddamn petulant! That man has been shooting lies into you until you're poisoned! He's the one who *made* Audrey into an alcoholic. And you're as much of a nymphomaniac as she is! She's so faithful to him, it's pathetic."

"Jim told me…"

I slammed a palm against my forehead.

"Jesus! Jim told you, Jim told you! Horse manure! Let me tell you what he told me. He said he'd do anything to win you. He said he'd lie and cheat and connive and consider it all justified if he won your affections. He said he'd lie about me. He said I could keep refuting his lies but he'd keep lying until you didn't know whether you were coming or going. He said you killed *three* men! He said you were deranged! Is that the man you want to marry?"

Her face was pale as she looked at me. She shuddered with caught breaths. And I kept thinking of how many troubles would be avoided if people would only tell each other the truth.

"Is all this true?" she said, her voice shaking.

"Uh!"

I lurched to my feet and started sliding, stumbling down the hill in a blind rage.

"Davie!"

I stopped but didn't turn. I heard her shoes on the hill. Then she came heavily against me and moved around to face me.

"Don't leave me!" she said. Almost angrily, as if I were betraying her.

I held her in my arms without spirit.

"Why can't we get away from all this?" she said unhappily. "Why does it follow us wherever we go?"

"Murder has a way of following people."

We stood there a few silent moments, then went back to the tree and sat down on its roots. I took two apples out of one of the bags and we ate without speaking.

"I can't believe it," she said after a while.

I looked at her sharply.

"Davie, I don't...mean I don't believe you. I mean that it's so incredible to me. Why hasn't he ever told me about his wife, told me the truth?"

"Because he only tells lies or that segment of the truth which serves his advantage. Like the way he told me how you cut open Dennis's arm but neglected to tell me also that Dennis threatened to expose his crooked practice to the police."

"He told you..."

"Peggy, don't deny this. It's been verified."

"I...I cut him. He tried to...to make love to me."

"Why should that frighten you so?"

"Davie, if you went through what I did, you couldn't stand having anyone's hands on your body. Can't you *see* that?"

"I...suppose."

"He...touched me. He tried to make me take my blouse off. I..." She shuddered. "I don't know what happens when...men try that. It just makes me..." She couldn't find the words but could only express it by the clenched fist she held shakingly before her.

"All right, Peggy," I said, "I've understood that a long time. You've never seen me try it, although God knows I've wanted to."

She looked at me sadly.

"Oh Davie," she said, "I'm sorry. I don't mean to tease you. You know I don't. It's Just that..."

"All right."

"What did you say about Jim's practice?"

"You mean you don't know that either?" I said wearily.

"No, I..."

"He's connected with the crime syndicate here, Peggy. He's a criminal."

"Oh, *no...* "

"Is there anything else you need?" I asked. "He's lied to you, he's cheated you, he's threatened you. He's a criminal, he's had two men killed, he's turned his own wife into a drunk. Is there anything else you need?"

She glanced at me, then back. She sat there silently, looking at the ground.

"I'm so...confused," she said.

"It's been his most effective weapon against you," I said. "Confusion."

"It's so hard to believe. All at once."

"Take your time," I said. "He'll be the same for years to come."

"Jim," she said, shaking her head.

After a while, we got up and climbed the rest of the way. At the peak of the hill we stood panting and looking down at Los Angeles, which was spread like a carpet at our feet. The climb had been exhausting. At least it had worn away our tempers.

"You should see it at night from here," Peggy said.

"I bet it's nice."

"It is."

She turned to me. She looked into my eyes, then lowered them. She looked up again, and her hand stole into mine.

"Davie."

"Yes."

"I'm...sorry. I mean. I'm sorry. That I keep...fighting the only thing that ever meant anything to me."

She looked up and smiled.

And I don't know what happened. Words came over me suddenly. I don't know from where. But suddenly they were in my mouth and I was speaking them.

"Peggy, marry me."

She looked startled.

"Marry?" she said.

"Why not? Don't you love me?"

"Davie. *Davie*, you know I do." Her eyes on mine, the way they were that first night. "Oh, Davie."

"Will you?"

"You want to marry me?"

"Yes, Peggy."

"You love me enough to marry me after all this?"

"Peggy!"

The moment seemed huge. Maybe it was the moment that over-whelmed me more than a love for Peggy. High on a hill as if we stood above the world. The hot sun on our heads, the wind on us, the white-domed castle waiting for its prince and princess.

"I love you enough for that," I said.

"I want to tell you," she said, "I want you to know."

I felt myself shiver.

"Know what?"

"I'm going to tell you...about myself. Then when...when it's over you can decide. If you want me or not. If you even want to see me again after today."

"Peggy, stop..."

"Don't say anything," she said. "Listen.

"I killed my husband," she said. "You already know that. But you don't know why. Not really," she said, as I was about to speak. "You can't know how it was."

She clasped her hands in front of her. She didn't look at me. She looked out at the darkening hills

"My mother was dead a long time," she said. "And the woman I stayed with when my father was away had too many troubles to spend any time with me. No one ever told me about... *men*. I didn't know *anything*. Oh God, I was so ignorant. Once I...once I thought you could have a baby if a man kissed you. I was afraid to let any boy kiss me. Once a boy kissed me at a party in grade school. I was *paralyzed*. I was so afraid. I thought they all hated me and were making me have a baby. I was in torture for *three* months, Davie. Until a girl I knew found out and told me the facts."

I heard her throat move and I knew how much it must have embarrassed and hurt her to tell me these things. I could feel it. I was probably the only one she'd ever told in her whole life.

"I was forced to get married," she went on. "You know about that. I was barely seventeen but I got married. Graduated from high school one day and the next day I got married. Because my father accused me of..."

"I know," I said.

"Married without knowing the slightest thing about sex," she said. "My wedding night was a nightmare. You can't know how hideous it was. He was like an animal. I know you don't like me to use the word but it's the only one that describes him. He chased me around the hotel room. Maybe that sounds funny but..." Her voice broke. "It wasn't funny. I was so afraid I couldn't even think. All I could do was run and the more I ran and the more I cried, the more excited he got. He trapped me in a corner and he...*ripped* my nightgown off my body. Into shreds! I hit him, I scratched him, but it didn't do any good. It just excited him.

"I was raped by my own husband."

She sat there in silence, a shiver wracking her frame Breath quivered in her throat.

"It was like that all the time," she continued, "all through my married life. Me with no knowledge of anything, just fright. And him...*brutalizing* me. Night after night until I thought I'd go out of my mind and commit suicide. You don't know what it's like to lie awake at night and plan on committing suicide. I kept trying to *make* myself do it. But I didn't have the courage. So instead I just went deeper and deeper until I...I lost my head."

She drew in a quick breath and bit her lower lip to keep it from trembling.

"I was pregnant," she said. "I was *sick*. I couldn't hold down any food. Nights I used to just stay in the bathroom on my knees on the cold tile floor...just *waiting* to throw up.

"But that didn't matter to him. No, he wanted his flesh, his...his *toy!* I killed him and I swear I'd do it again, I *would*, I *would!*"

"I understand," I said. But did I?

"No," she said, "I haven't told you yet."

She hesitated a moment. Then she said, "Once I went to a movie and...and *the person* I was with put his arm around me and tried to put his hand inside my blouse."

"Peggy."

"No, you have to know sooner or later, Davie. This isn't just another story I'm telling you.

"That same person...attacked me later in the car."

"Peggy, don't. Stop torturing yourself."

"Do you know who it was?"

"Peggy."

"Do you?"

Her hands were shaking uncontrollably in her lap.

"Peggy, *please.*"

"It was *him!*" she said, her voice shaking with the memory. "Him! *My own father!*"

CHAPTER SEVEN

AS WE ENTERED he looked up from the couch. He was dressed informally in a brown suede jacket with a lightly patterned sport shirt under it.

"I've been looking for you all day, Peg," he said firmly. He didn't even glance me.

"Jim," I said.

"Will you get dressed as quickly as possible," he said to Peggy. "We're to go to a barbecue at Lamar Brandeis' beach house. We're late already."

I held my temper. The axe would fall on him soon enough. I glanced at Peggy.

"Jim, I…" she started.

"Peggy, I wish you'd hurry."

She took a deep breath.

"I can't, Jim," she said.

His eyebrows drew together and I felt inclined to utter a mocking "Bravo" at this splendid bit of facial business. But facetiousness didn't have much of a hold on me. I was thinking of what he might do to me or have done to me when he found out. More particularly of what he might order Steig to do.

Jim was looking at her gravely.

"And why, may I ask?" he said, still ignoring me.

She couldn't finish. She seemed halted by those eyes. Those grey-blue eyes on her, probing, demanding, almost hypnotizing.

"Peggy is staying here," I said.

"No one is speaking to you!"

Anger at last! And anger in Peggy's sight. I almost reveled at it. Something ugly that had been veiled too long from her eyes. Now at last, revealing itself.

"Listen, you pompous ass," I started.

"Davie," she pleaded. I stopped and her eyes moved over to Jim. Her throat moved. She bit her lip.

"Jim…"

"Well, *what* is it, Peggy?"

"Jim, Davie and I are going to be married." She spoke quietly; half in defiance, half with the still remaining timidity.

Jim Vaughan's body twitched. Something almost gave. Like a great wall about to topple. He stared at her, speechless for the first time I could remember since I'd met him, so many years ago. Someone had finally hit Jim Vaughan where it hurt.

And, suddenly, it came to me that Jim was in the same boat as Peggy and Audrey. And all of us to some degree. He was starving for real love and he'd never received it. And now it was tearing him apart at last because the shell he'd made to hide himself was cracking.

"It's not true," he said.

She nodded once. "Yes. It is."

Something seemed to drain from his body. He pumped it back with will power. He managed a thin smile.

"Oh?" he said. "And have you told him how you murdered Albert? Is he willing to..."

"Your lies won't work anymore," I told him.

"Lies?" he said.

"I know who murdered Albert. And Dennis. I know about your argument with Dennis. I know that he threatened to expose your...your *practice*. And I know about that call Peggy made to you the night that Albert was killed."

I didn't know the last thing but I suspected its truth.

"I know a lot of things Jim," I finished, "a lot of them."

He turned and walked to the door. There he turned again. He looked at us, his face a stone mask. His eyes settled on me like the benediction of a cobra.

"Then maybe you also know," he said "how you'll live long enough to marry Peggy."

Peggy gasped.

"Jim! You wouldn't..."

For a moment, Jim's face was stripped of everything. The animal, the hating, frustrated animal showed for that moment. And it was ugly.

"I'll do anything for you," he said. "I've lied, I've cheated for you. Yes, I've *murdered* for you! And now..."

His words went on. But they were lost in the sudden explosion of joy in me.

He had confessed! Peggy was free. Sick in mind and afraid—but free. And it seemed as if breath began for the first time since I'd been struck on the head that night that seemed so long ago. That had been about two weeks before.

I put my arm around Peggy.

"Don't argue with him," I said. "You don't have to argue. Look at him, Peggy. He's beaten."

Those were my words but my stomach was throbbing because I knew that from that moment on, my life was in danger. All possible friendship between us was kicked away for good.

His face was cold and murderous.

"I've despised you for a long time," he said, "And now, by God, I'll see to it you bother me no longer."

I tensed myself instinctively, almost expecting him to reach into his pocket and take out a gun. Or an icepick, my imagination said.

I should have known better. That was not his way. Once I'd seen Jim refuse to sweep a floor in his fraternity house room. And he would always have someone else do his dirty work. And murder was dirty work.

He just opened the door.

"Good night," he said as casually as his shaken system would allow.

Then he closed the door quietly and we heard him walking down the path, unhurried, carrying through to the last his pretense that the illusion of his casualness might even deceive himself. We stood there motionless and silent until the sound of his footsteps had disappeared. Then we heard a car door slam and the big Cadillac drew Jim Vaughan away into the night.

Her hands were shaking.

"I never knew he was like that," she said, frightened. "I never even suspected he was like that."

"I know you didn't, Peggy."

"What are we going to do?"

In answer, I went to the phone and dialed.

"Lieutenant Jones," I said when they answered.

I felt her hand grow limp in mine.

"Yes?"

It was Jones. I told him what Jim had said.

"I'll have him picked up," Jones said, "and you'd better come by in the morning. With Miss Lister."

"I will," I said.

"All right. You say he just left 15th Street?"

"Yes."

"All right. Good-bye."

I hung up and looked at Peggy.

"All over, baby," I said.

How wrong can a guy get?

I left about ten. First I stood at the door and looked through the small peephole. Then I opened it and looked up and down the path to see if there was anyone around. There wasn't. I turned and kissed her.

"Goodnight, baby," I said.

"Goodnight, Davie," she said. "Please be careful."

"Don't worry," I told her, "he's probably been picked up already."

She looked worried still.

"Do you really think so?" she asked.

I nodded. I hoped so, anyway. I hated to think of him and Steig running loose. I also didn't care for the idea of Audrey alone, her life ended. But I didn't let myself think about that.

"Maybe you should go down to the station and see," Peggy said.

"That's a good idea. Very good."

"Be careful, Davie. If I lost you…"

"Shhh. No more now. Smile."

She smiled.

"You *will* be careful," she said

"Honey," I said, "I *like* living. You'll find that out when we're married."

That angelic smile.

"Married," she said, almost sighing the word, "to a man I can trust. Oh, I'm so…you have no idea how relieved I feel. I can forget everything that ever happened."

I kissed her cheek.

"Breakfast at nine," I said. "Bacon and eggs."

"I'll have it ready," she said cheerfully.

I approached the car cautiously. All sorts of ideas filled my head. Steig was behind a bush or a tree with a rifle, a pistol, an axe, an…I wouldn't let myself think the word. Or Steig was in his car waiting to run me down, to drive me to the curb, fire a gun into my brain…

I moved along the house, my heart pounding violently. I thought of going back to the house but I felt too ashamed. I'd just said good-bye. I knew she'd welcome me back. I could sleep on the couch. But I'd feel silly. And there was nothing definite to be afraid of, anyway. Just imaginations. And I was curious to know whether the police had picked up Jim and Steig. If they hadn't, my imaginations would come to life.

No black Cadillac in sight. Only my little black Ford. I ran to it and jumped in fast after cursing at my shaking fingers that wouldn't let me find the lock with the key.

I slid in and pulled the door shut and locked it. I looked around anxiously as I searched for the ignition with my key. No black figures dashing at the car. I would have been helpless if there had been. I swallowed and slid in the key.

Another fear. Bomb in the motor. I knew it was far-fetched but my mind would not discount it. I looked up and down the street, feeling the tug of rising fear in me. I got out and pulled up the hood, threw the flashlight beam around it. No infernal machine. I felt like an ass. Then I jumped around nervously and looked back up the street. I got back in the car.

I started the motor. Illegal U-turn before I thought. I could have gone over to Santa Monica Boulevard. I turned left at Wilshire and headed toward the ocean. At Lincoln I made another left turn and started for the police station.

I don't know when I first became conscious of the car following me.

But when nervousness kept me looking into the rear view mirror, I saw it.

Big and black and Steig at the wheel.

My hands clamped spasmodically on the wheel and my legs shook. There wasn't much doubt now what he was after. He kept pulling closer, closer, gunning that big motor.

I stepped on the accelerator harder. In my mind I saw visions of him pulling alongside, a gun in his hand. My foot pushed down harder still and my small Ford spurted ahead. I forged away a little distance. Steig put on the gas and moved up on me.

I pushed harder, hit fifty, then sixty. Still he gained. I felt sweat breaking out on me. I roared past a red light, another. I kept hoping that a policeman would pick me up. There weren't any, though. I passed a car, saw Steig pass it too, the big car sweeping out into the opposite lane and then back. He moved up on me.

Suddenly I pushed down hard on the horn, hoping that the noise would attract a police car. The shrill blasts filled the early morning stillness. Still no police. Still the Cadillac moving closer as we both sped toward Venice.

At Olympic he was almost on top of me. My heart was tearing at my chest like a crazy prisoner in his cell. The old Chicago way. Pull alongside, empty gun into driver's head. The rub-out.

Steig moved the Cadillac around me. He was almost beside me. I glanced over my shoulder and saw his face, white as tallow. My hand slipped off the horn. I saw his right arm raised. He was pointing something at me...

I jammed on the brakes and almost flew through the windshield as my tires shrieked in friction on the pavement and the car skidded to a dead halt. Steig went speeding past and across the intersection. I dragged the Ford around, almost panic stricken and started down Olympic for the ocean. I didn't know what to do. I knew the police station was down this way but I didn't know how I was going to get to it. All I could think of was I had to get away from Steig because he wanted to kill me.

I was half-way down the block when the black car came around the corner and started after me. I was suddenly very grateful that my car had been owned by a hot-rodder. The way it sprang forward at my touch, the speed it was giving me was the only thing I had then between life and a bullet in my head.

Then I cried out loud in horror as I roared past the Fourth Street intersection without thinking. There was no way to get to the police station now. I was headed for the coast highway! And on a straightaway I could never outdistance the Cadillac.

Then, as I started down, I saw the light behind me change and saw that Steig had to stop violently as a big trailer truck started across the intersection. It gained me another half block. Then the view behind disappeared and I fled into the dark tunnel under Second Street.

I turned the dark curve and was on the Pacific Coast Highway. I shoved the accelerator all the way to the floor and the Ford almost leaped ahead. The pistons pounded crazily under the hood, it felt as if the car was going to take off. The roar of the motor was tremendous coming out of the double exhaust pipes. The black ocean flew by, the high bluffs of Santa Monica above me. I raced along at ninety and way behind I saw glaring heads as the big Cadillac pulled out of the tunnel.

As I roared past the light on the hill that led to the Santa Monica business district I saw that Steig was gaining on me. No Ford could outdistance that car, souped up or not. At least not a Ford more than a decade old. Sweat ran down over my eyebrows, along my temples. The thing seemed insane but here it *was*. I came to California for the weather, the phrase occurred inanely. I came for the weather and about two months later a man was chasing me in a car because he wanted to shoot me.

I couldn't keep going on the highway. He'd catch up to me too easily. My only chance was eluding him somehow.

At Channel Road, I wheeled around the corner and bulleted up the canyon, past the Golden Bull, alongside of the flashflood channel. I'd passed the first intersection when Steig turned too. I moved up to the second intersection and made a sharp left turn.

There were two streets branching off. Without thinking I steered my speeding car into the right one, too afraid even to think that it might not be a through street. My Ford powered up a gradual hill and spurted down the grade on the other side. The bright heads of the Cadillac swung around and were boring on me.

My hands were slick on the wheel now. I had to keep taking off one at a time to rub them, almost frenziedly, on my trouser leg. I had no idea where I was going. Finding a policeman was hopelessly out of the question now.

The only thing that could possibly save me now was Henry Ford's 1940 model. I was almost praying that it held together. If anything went now, I was dead.

My eyes were straining to see if there was anything ahead. I was too upset to think of getting my glasses from the glove compartment.

I almost turned left, then saw at the last possible second a sign reading—*This Is Not a Through Street*. I jerked the car around, bumped over a curb and back into the street, gasping for breath. I roared up a hill, past the silent Country Club, past the tennis court that stood empty and white in the moonlight. The headlights behind me, the throaty growl of the Cadillac's motor. Steig with a gun.

Down a hill. Two intersections. I chose the right by dumb luck. I found myself speeding around a twisting road, over a wooden bridge and through a woods so deep it reminded me of the Hurtgen Forest, another place where I'd faced death. But then I was on foot, fighting war. Now I was in a car and a civilian and at war with no one. But a man was following me and he was going to kill me if he could because he'd been ordered to kill me and there are men who will kill on order. And the man who had ordered him had been my friend once.

A sign. *Sunset Boulevard.* And an arrow pointing. I jerked the wheel around and fired up the hill to Sunset. Now Steig was very close. He knew how to handle that car of his.

There was a hill on the right side I saw as I sped up Sunset toward the Pacific Palisades. I don't know why I turned onto it. One of those snap decisions made more by reflex than by mind. I just wheeled around and went roaring up the steep incline, watching those heads behind me whip around in the dark and start after me again like blinding monster eyes.

Now I was headed into the hills. I hadn't a chance in the world of finding anyone to help me. It would deserted up here, probably not a house for miles.

And, for the first time since I'd started being chased, I began to realize how afraid I was. So afraid my body was starting to go numb. A person goes through life and never sees violence except in a war. But this was personal violence. I couldn't understand it and it frightened me. Steig didn't even know me but he hated me. And because another man had told him to kill me, he was going at it as if his life depended on it.

A winding road, up and up. I kept the car in second and the pedal on the floor. The phrase occurred to me out of nowhere. I hoped that man had been telling the truth. The creeping indicator indicated that he might have. The motor roared under the dark sky as it kept pulling me up the hill rapidly and I kept spinning the wheel wildly to keep on the road.

A gate across the road!

I jerked the wheel instinctively and the Ford climbed up a small embankment beside the gate. The wheels ground through soft earth and came down again on the other side of the gate, back on the road. I threw the car into second again and picked up speed; then into high. It was a lucky break. Steig couldn't get the heavier Cadillac through the soft ground easily. I saw his lights spin around behind me as the car skidded, dug into earth.

I moved on through an open gateway into a wide concrete stretch. There was a dark house looming out of the ground on my left. And, suddenly, I realized that I was back in Will Rogers State Park where Peggy and I had hiked that time. The house was that of the late humorist. The park was closed, there wouldn't be a soul anywhere close by. My heart jolted as Steig came powering through the gateway after having regained the road.

There were two ways to go. I remembered that the one ahead led to the park entrance. I had come in by the road that is used for the exit. If I went straight ahead, I'd go down that road and come to a closed gate. But there was no way around *that* one.

All in the space of seconds I knew that and I spun the Ford left and headed for a narrow bridge that led to the other road. My fender raked across the wooden railing as I crossed the bridge. I jammed my accelerator to the floor as I gunned up the tree-lined road. That led to...I didn't know.

Stables. Bleak and dark and deathly still under the moonlight. I sped up the road passing training yards, dark buildings. I kept going, praying that there was an exit, my eyes straining ahead to see if there was an exit. There wasn't. I left the paving and the car ploughed over the grass through low bushes, around a flimsy fence. My speed kept going down as the soft earth impeded the wheels.

And, finally, the wheels dug in too far and the whole car spun around crazily, almost tipping over. The wheels started grinding away at the earth.

Without a thought or a plan, I flung open the door and plunged out into the night and started racing across the ground, headed for the thickly overgrown hill on my left.

I jumped out of the Cadillac's bright headbeams. I ran and heard the big car stop and grind itself into the earth. I heard a door slam and other feet running. I reached the foot of the hill and started up.

Steig moved fast for a big man. He was close behind and there was no way I could be quiet. I made a loud noise as I thrashed through bushes and tore through thick undergrowth, slashing my skin, ripping my trousers and shirt sleeves on the brittle twigs.

Not a sound from Steig. He might have been a brainless robot built for only one purpose. He came running up after me, his big feet thudding on the ground, his big body ploughing through all the shrubbery that blocked his way.

Something scurried away under my feet and I leapt to the side, running. My heart jolted harder still as I remembered the mountain lion tracks Peggy and I had seen that day.

Now my breath was going. A stitch started knifing my side. My face and body ran with sweat. But I couldn't stop. I thought of falling to the dark ground and hugging it, hoping that Steig would bypass me. But it was too much of a chance. He'd hear the sound of my running stop. And he might even stumble right over me. He wasn't fooling. He'd just fill my body with bullets.

I kept going. But the going was tough. And getting tougher. The shrubbery was getting so thick I kept banging into branches and being knocked aside. It's a wonder I didn't put out my eyes on the sharp sabers of branches. One needle-pointed twig raked across my forehead as I plunged on and the laceration drove lances of pain into my head.

I reached the top of the hill. For a moment I must have been outlined against the sky. Because, suddenly, the night was torn by a loud explosion that echoed. And I heard something whistle by me.

I drove myself over the peak and found a hard, flat path. I started racing down it like a fool, clearly visible. In the bright moonlight. I don't know what I had in mind. Maybe getting distance between Steig and me. My legs trembled as I ran, they felt as if they were ready to collapse.

Another shot. It kicked up dirt by me and sent me plunging to the right. I couldn't see where.

My footing was gone. I found myself sliding and clawing down a steep embankment covered with shrubbery. My hands tried to find something to stop my rapid and helpless descent but I got only friction burns. My body kept rubbing and banging against earth and rocks and bushes.

At the bottom of the drop, I turned a complete somersault and landed on my side with a violent impact.

Only fear got me up. My breath was gone. It felt as if it had been ripped from my lungs. My side ached sharply. Every limb ached. Only a force of survival could have kept me moving. I started across the ground, in a hollow so deep that a hill kept most of it in dark shadow.

I heard something overhead and I stopped dead. I thought that if I were silent he might think the fall had killed me.

I looked up and, on the crest of the embankment, saw his big form outlined. He was looking down. I held my breath.

He stooped down for support and started climbing down.

I turned and ran. Shrubbery whipped past me, clawing at me like maniacal arms. Branches flailed at my face and body. My chest ached. I breathed through a wide open mouth.

Then Steig lost his grip. I stopped and whirled. I couldn't see but I heard him clawing his way down the embankment and landing heavily. Silence. I waited. Was it possible he'd been knocked out? I waited, trying to hear something beside my own breathless, whistling gasps.

He was moving again.

I turned with a whimper and started running again. He was still coming. Slower but still coming. He must have been deranged. It was all I could think of. No man could be so intent on killing and be in his right mind. His thick, Teutonic brain was devoid of everything but murderous hate.

I ran into the embankment. And, gasping, looked up to see that I was trapped, blocked by an almost perpendicular wall of earth and bush. No way out but back or sideways. I had no idea how small the hollow was. And if I ran sideways I'd be running out into the spotlight of the moon. I felt a panic-stricken cry tear at my throat. *Help!* I wanted to scream it. But who was there to hear? At least I didn't lose my mind that badly.

I heard Steig stumbling through the brush. It was like one of those crazy dreams where no matter how ingenuously you hide yourself, your pursuer finds you without any trouble. As if he knew where you were at every moment. That's what I felt about Steig.

In a brainless fright, I spun around and started to pull myself up the sheer incline. Some of the bushes I held on to slipped out and I grabbed out for more. I half-climbed, half-pulled myself up by my aching arms. I was closer now. I dug my feet into the earth and lurched up the embankment for a way.

I stopped dead and hung there against the earth trying to be absolutely quiet as Steig came bursting through the shrubbery and stood at the bottom of the rise.

I clenched my teeth. The breaths caught and almost choked me. My heart was hammering violently. Was it possible he didn't see me? I didn't know then that he'd lost his glasses in his fall and couldn't see much of anything.

Then dirt trickled down from under my feet and it silted through the air, down on Steig. I twisted my neck to look down. I could see the dark, shapeless hulk of him down there. He was looking up, I was sure. It was an insane picture. A half sightless killer ready to fire bullets into my body and me clinging to the side of a hill no more than twenty-five feet above him. Wondering if he could see me. Thinking, momentarily, that Jim had won his victory.

Steig started to climb up.

It was no use going on, I knew that. The hill got steeper and steeper as it went up until it was vertical with the trees and bushes growing out sideways. I couldn't take it. I was too exhausted. I'd slip and fall. He'd be able to see me.

My mind felt all jumbled and thick as I tried to think of some way to defend myself. I had to have a weapon. A stick, a rock, anything. My eyes fled around, squinting.

I saw one. A big rock. It was perched precariously to my right. My hand touched it, then I had to pull it back quickly to get support.

I reached for the rock again. I lost balance and had to throw myself against the dirt, slapping for support. The dislodged dirt slid down on Steig. He didn't say anything but kept climbing methodically. I could hear his breathing now, thick, whistling breaths. He was an animal with a quest. Insensitive and mute, he climbed up to kill me. Crawling fear covered my flesh.

I edged over quickly and my fingers touched the cool stone surface. I almost jarred it loose. My heart leaped at the sensation of complete terror in me. I felt as if my hands would freeze, my whole body be struck with paralysis and I would just be stricken there until he came up to me, put the barrel of the gun against my body and pulled the trigger.

The breathing. Closer. Coming up at me. My lips drew back in an uncontrolled gasp of horror. There was no time. *No time!* My mind howled the words. He had heard me, I knew he'd heard me. In a matter of seconds he would be able to see me despite shadow, despite impaired sight. He was almost to the point where his hands touched my feet.

I lurched over, slipped and caught onto a heavy root with one hand, to the rock with the other. I pressed my body against the rock and looked down. My feet slipped and I hung down loosely a moment before I found a foot support. I tested the support with frantic haste. I had to have both hands free.

I froze rigid. Steig was just below me. He'd stopped climbing. He was reaching into his pocket as he squinted up. It was so still I could hear his fumbling hands on his trouser leg.

I grabbed onto the rock and tried to turn. The scuttling sound made him throw up his arm. An explosion surrounded me and I felt a hot flame gouge through the flesh on my right shoulder.

It must have been the pain that did it. Because I suddenly forgot about balance. I just grabbed onto the rock and started falling down toward Steig.

He threw up his gun again with a guttural cry as my dark body came heaving down on him.

He had no chance to fire. I held the rock before me and drove it violently into his face and we both went flopping down the hill like broken dolls. I grabbed out for support as we fell and managed to grab onto a bush and cling there as his body went all the way down and landed with a single hollow thud.

Silence.

I hung on a long time, my chest shuddering as I breathed. Then, finally, when I'd stopped the terrible shaking a little, I eased myself down the hill to where he was.

I stood over the body.

His face was in moonlight which made it even whiter. It was crushed in.

The sight of it made me gag and turn away. I stood with my back to him, shuddering uncontrollably. Steig's left arm was twisted out of shape too. He'd been climbing that hill after me with a broken arm.

I don't know how I found my way back to the car. I was sick and I was exhausted. My legs trembled under me. I shivered from the cold wind. I kept wiping the sweat off my face and neck as I stumbled through the wilderness.

I got lost for a while but finally I spotted the headlights still shining and heard the rumbling of the Cadillac's motor. Mine had stalled.

I climbed into the Ford and slumped down on the seat. I pulled the door shut and turned out the light and turned off the ignition switch. Then I lay down on the cool seat cover, pressing my cheek against it, gasping for breath. I turned on my back with my legs bent up.

I must have fallen asleep or into an exhausted coma for more than an hour. I jerked up quickly, eyes staring around me and I didn't remember what had happened for a good minute. Then I straightened up with a groan. My body was sore and aching. Every bone felt bruised, every inch of skin either torn or scratched.

It took a while to back out of the soft earth. I went backwards around the fence, into the stable area again. I left the Cadillac still running, its lights on. I swung my car around and headed back for town.

I went up Sunset and then down Chatauqua to the coast highway. I stopped at a bar and called Jones and told him about Steig and told him I was going back to my room. He asked me to come in but I hung up. I was too tired. I went back to the car. I just wanted to go to bed and forget everything.

I drove slowly up the canyon and down Seventh Street. I turned left at Wilshire and parked across the street from my room. I unlocked the door and stumbled across the room in darkness.

In the light of the bulb I saw my face in the medicine cabinet mirror. It was puffy and scratched. I gritted my teeth in pain. I drew open my torn shirt and looked at the thin line of blood-caked flesh where the bullet had gouged. I drew in a pained breath. Then I stared at the mirror and felt a burst of insane rage in me. I felt rage at Steig and wanted to kill him again. I wished I had Jim alone too. The same rock in my hand.

"Son of a bitch!" I snarled at the mirror, at the world. "Dirty, lousy son of a bitch!"

"So he failed," said Jim Vaughan.

CHAPTER EIGHT

I WHIRLED AND stared at my bed.

He was sitting there in the shadows, hat and top coat on.

"Where is he?" he asked.

I started for him, then stopped as he leveled the gun at me.

"Don't come any closer, David," he said, "or I'll take the pleasure of putting a slug in your belly."

I gaped at him. Sickness hit me again. I'd just escaped from death. Was I to be asked to face it again? I don't know whether I was afraid or outraged at the turn of events. I think it was more outrage. Fear had been so much in me that there wasn't any left. I had to concentrate to realize that I might die now too.

"Well?" he asked.

"He's dead," I said. "I killed him."

Surprise on his face·a moment. The slightest of consternation. Then a flicker of amusement. Even now Jim could force upon himself the pose of detached bystander.

"Dead," he said. "So, at long last, you are also guilty of murder."

"Murder," I said. "You speak of murder."

"Indeed," he said, smiling deceptively, "I'm quite versed on the subject."

He was drunk. I hadn't realized it at first. That smile, the slightly, almost imperceptibly disheveled appearance. The tie knot slightly off center, the hair slightly uncombed, the hat at the minutest wrong angle. All added up. I remembered how Jim had been at college the few times he'd been drunk. He'd been quite unpredictable. And this time he had a gun in his hand. And hate for me.

And I remembered something else, too. Me refusing to go down to the station to see Jones. He must have known that Jim would be after me. Now it was too late.

"I know you're versed on the subject," I said, my mind tripping over itself in the attempt to find an escape, "well versed."

He gave me a look of dispassionate criticism.

"So the poor, bungling kraut finally found his peace," he said. "And to think it was at *your* hands. The hands of a dull, indefinite pacifist. The young American idealist, the writer of novels, the seeker of truths..."

He kept rattling on. There was a reddish tint in his cheeks. And a light in his eyes that wasn't there normally. I let him rattle. I hoped he'd rattle himself to sleep.

I moved for my chair.

"Careful, careful," he warned, breaking off his bantering continuity.

"I'm not trying anything," I said, disgustedly. "Do I look like I'm in any condition to try anything?"

"You look like something three cats dragged in," he said. He lowered the gun.

I wondered what he was planning. He might have been confused; it was just possible. I don't think he knew what to do. He wanted me dead but the idea of personally committing murder had never occurred to him, I'm sure. That fell in the province of menial labor. But he might change his mind.

Except for one thing. My mind seized on it. Steig had done those killings. I was sure of that. And now Steig was dead. And there was no one who could prove Jim was involved. He was clear. I think even he realized that.

"So poor, benighted Steig, Kaiser Wilhelm's beloved warrior, Chicago's beloved killer and navigator of getaway cars, is dead. We bow our heads for Walter Steig, victim of society's perverseness."

His face grew cold, the humor drained from him in an instant.

"I never trusted the fool. He was a lunk-head."

Amusement back.

"It must have been the climate that got him," he said.

He stopped talking and looked at me. He raised the gun.

"I should shoot you," he said, "now, while the opportunity is here."

A car motor. Headlights coming to the curb. I saw them out of the corner of my eye. My heart thudding. Was it Jones? And, if it was, would he come thudding up or the porch?

It was fortunate that Jim was drunk. Otherwise he surely would have heard the car door slamming, the footsteps on the porch, the shadowy figure that stopped outside of the screen window.

"Now that you're going to kill me," I said, "you can tell me about your murdering of Albert and Dennis."

He looked at me with that thin, supercilious smile on his lips. The light reflected off his polished, rimless glasses.

"You had them killed, didn't you?" I said, hoping that there was no sign of eagerness in my voice.

His face sobered.

"Of course I did," he said. "They both stood in my way."

"Albert?" I said.

"He attacked her," he said.

"And Dennis?"

It seemed too good to be true. A confession in the hearing of a police lieutenant.

"Why go on?" he said. He raised his gun and pointed it at me.

"And now a third victim?" I said.

Jim didn't point the gun at me. He just let it hang loosely in his hand.

"Who knows?" he said.

"You can put down that gun now," Jones said from the window.

Vaughan twitched a little. But he didn't turn. He seemed to listen a moment as if waiting for Jones to say something else. Then that smile came to his lips again.

He seemed too drunk, too emotionally exhausted to feel fright.

"Trapped," he said.

Then Jones took Jim Vaughan away.

I rushed over to Peggy and told her and we decided to drive down to Tijuana the next day. When she saw my bruised, swollen face and the torn gully in the flesh of my shoulder she cried terribly and couldn't help me bandage it.

We packed her clothes and then I went back to my room and packed some things for myself. My shoulder throbbed and I felt exhausted but I was at peace.

I slept that night. I turned out the light without dread. The end of it, I figured, closing my eyes.

No.

Because the next day after I'd gone to a doctor, after I'd picked up a wedding ring, after I'd bought a bottle of champagne to open that night, I found a note slipped under my door.

I opened it.

At first I couldn't believe it. It seemed too cruel a joke.

The letterhead was *Santa Monica Police* and the message said that...

I drove as fast as I could up Wilshire. I wheeled around the corner of 15th and jerked to a stop in front of Peggy's house.

I ran in the open door.

She whirled in fright as I entered. Her fingers clenched on the dress she was holding.

"Davie! What is it?"

"Are you finished packing?" I asked quickly. "We have to get out of here right away."

"Why?"

I handed her the note. She looked at it. Then looked up at me, her eyes frightened.

"Jim?" she said.

The note said that Jones hadn't shown up yet.

My car raced down Lincoln. Every time I hit a red light I thought it was a plot. My eyes stayed fastened to the road ahead. I wasn't going to the police. I didn't want to stay in town. I wanted to get out fast.

I remember looking out the rear view mirror.

But I didn't notice anything. Because, without thinking, I was only looking for a black Cadillac.

Tijuana. A five hour drive. Dirty and almost wordless, with me looking at the rear view mirror. With Peggy sitting close by me and glancing at me in fear every once in a while.

We stood side by side in the little place and I slipped the ring on Peggy's finger. It felt wrong though. As if I were being forced into it. As if we really weren't sure but had to go through with it. Inevitable. There was nothing casual, nothing leisurely or pleasant. The nerve-wracking aspect of a man following to kill me. And if I felt uneasiness at the haste of the wedding, Peggy felt it twice as much.

"What is it?" I asked.

For the last ten miles she'd been staring ahead glumly at the highway. She shook her head.

"What *is* it?" I asked again.

She tried to smile and press my hand reassuringly.

"Nothing," she said.

"Tell me."

She shrugged.

"Oh…"

"I guess I know," I said. "The wedding. The way we're rushing. It isn't what we'd hoped for. It doesn't seem like a wedding at all."

"I…" she started. "I guess it's because it reminds me of my first wedding. The same rushing and…I was even more scared then."

"Scared?"

"Of him. Of…my…of George."

"What are you afraid of now?"

"Not of you," she said, but it didn't sound convincing. "Jim, I guess."

That didn't sound convincing either. I tried to get her mind on something else. I thought I knew what she was afraid of.

"As soon as we hear one way or the other about Jim," I said, "we'll have a real church wedding. We'll go back to New York and have all my family at it."

She turned, a smile flickering on her tired face. We'd been driving all morning and afternoon.

"Honest?" she said.

"Honest."

She leaned against me wearily and was at peace for a moment. She held my arm.

Then a horn honked behind us and she sat up with a gasp and looked back. The car passed us and disappeared up the dusty highway. Peggy drew in a heavy breath.

"We'll be out of it soon," I said.

But I was beginning to get the feeling that neither of us would ever get out of it. It seemed to be going on endlessly. Months of it. Would it go on for years?

Night was falling over the highway and I was sleepy and tired. And starving, too. We hadn't eaten much all day and my stomach was about empty.

I signed the motel registry with as pleasant a smile at Peggy as I could manage.

Mr. and Mrs. David Newton, Los Angeles.

For a moment I had the crazy notion that the man was going to ask us for identification because we looked so young. But the man didn't. He looked bored and slid us the keys. To Cabin K.

We walked along the gravel path under the sky that was hidden by dust clouds. And we tried to pretend we were happy.

But every sound made us start nervously and I was almost getting angry at Peggy, with a whole society for getting me into this. There were no thoughts of wedding night pleasures. I felt grimy and disgusted with life. It took a strong effort to be pleasant for her sake.

Cabin K. All wrong. A slanty little structure, painted green and white and the paint was probably an inch thick. The shutters hung lopsided and the window curtains looked as if they hadn't been laundered since V-J day. And then with lye.

I stood before the door and looked at her. She shook her head once and I didn't go near her. It would have been a tragic mockery to carry her over that dismal threshold. I just opened the door and stepped aside.

She looked inside. Something held her back. She shuddered once.

"Davie."

"Don t be afraid," I said. "Have I ever harmed you?"

The pleasantness slipped as she still hesitated.

"Come *on*, Peggy," I said. "I'm too tired to make a pass at anyone."

She stood inside looking around the room as I put the bags on the bed. The room was terrible. For anybody. Especially for us. We were newlyweds and the room was dingy and uninviting. No touch of sweet romance. No windows with boughs stirring outside. A dusty floor, a touch of stale whiskey in the air.

I looked at her. And the expression on her face made me forget my own irritation and worries. I took her hand.

"Peg," I said, "I'm sorry. I wish it was a castle. But it's all we can get now. We *have* to sleep."

"I know," she said. Without enthusiasm.

While she was in the bathroom I went down to the manager's office.

"Hey, can I get some food?" I asked.

"Afraid not," he said. "All I got's candy. And that popcorn machine over there."

"How about some ice?"

"Only got a little, mister," he said. "Ice's hard to get around here."

"Look," I said, "we've just been married. And I have a bottle of champagne in my bag. Can't you let us have a little ice? Maybe a pailful or something?"

He looked at me studiedly. Then he got compassion. He got a pail and put a chunk of ice in it.

"Fifty cents," he said.

I paid him and held back the temper.

"What about glasses?" I said irritably.

"Glasses in the cabin."

"I can't get this chunk of ice in the glasses," I said.

He reached under the counter...

"Voila!" I cried to her as she came out of the bathroom. I'd chopped up the ice into small pieces and decided to chill the bottle instead of putting the ice chips in the glasses. I'd stuck the bottle into the pail. But the ice only covered about two inches on the bottom of the pail. The champagne would never chill.

"Oh!" Peggy said. "Champagne!"

She tried to smile and keep smiling. But even Peggy with her imagination couldn't overcome all this dinginess. Couldn't picture us as being anywhere but where we were—a dreary cabin K on the highway.

She sat on the bed as I opened the bottle. I noticed her glance at the pail, at the object beside it. Then she turned her eyes away and smiled at me again.

She was wearing a long dressing robe over her body. She sat on the bed and watched me. But she wasn't relaxed. Her poise was strained, her lips forced into a smile.

I put down the unopened bottle and sat beside her and put my arms around her.

"Honey, be happy," I said. "It's not paradise, I know. But we're away at last. And we're free of the past."

Her arms clung to me.

"Oh, Davie," she said, "don't let anything happen to me. Don't let anything spoil it."

"I won't," I said, cheerfully.

Then I stood up and opened the bottle.

"Ooops!"

The white foaming champagne spurted out of the bottle mouth and ran onto the floor. I leveled the bottle quickly and poured it into the glasses. Then I put down the bottle on the bedside table next to the pail. I put some pieces of ice into the glasses.

"I shouldn't dilute it," I said, "but if I don't, the champagne will be too warm."

"It's all right," she said.

I handed her a glass. I held my own out to her.

"My love," I toasted.

She smiled. We sat side by side and drank. I was thirsty. The cool tingling of the champagne tasted good. I polished off the glass in two swallows.

"Popcorn, m'lady?" I asked.

She took a few pieces. I tried some. It was stale.

"I wish we could get a steak dinner," I said, "but there's nothing around here. I promise as soon as we get back to Santa Monica or...wherever we're going," I added as her face grew concerned, "I'll buy you a nice, juicy sirloin."

"You'll make my mouth water," she said.

I felt a little lightheaded. I blinked at her and grinned.

"Mrs. Newton," I said.

She smiled dutifully and I poured two more glasses. One and a half really. Peggy had only drunk about half a glass.

I felt the warmth coursing my body and I had a little more popcorn. It made me thirsty. I put the bag aside because it spoiled the taste of the champagne.

The stuff worked fast. I felt as if I were floating. I put my head down on her lap and felt the bed rolling gently under me. I reached out casually and stroked her soft, swelling breast.

She tried to smile but she couldn't.

"Baby," I said.

I raised up and kissed her on the mouth. I felt something rising in me. A familiar sensation. Everything had been building it up through the months. And now hunger and lightheadedness were added to it. A cabin isolated And my brain saying speciously—she's your wife now, you can do anything to her you want. The immediate philosophy of the deluded male.

I squirmed on the bed and poured some more to drink.

"Peggy?"

'No thanks," she said. "Maybe we should...find someplace to eat."

"There isn't any place around here," I said.

"Maybe up the road."

"Honey, not now. I'm tired. I don't want to drive again."

"But..."

Her chest rose and fell with a shudder. She swallowed. But not champagne.

"Do you think Jim is...?"

I had my mouth over her to stop her talking about it.

"Now, never mind him," I said. "This is our wedding night."

"Davie."

Her fingers in my hair were shaking.

I ran a hand over her leg.

"Davie," she said.

I started to unbutton her robe.

"Why are you doing that?" she asked, like a timorous little girl.

"Because..."

Her hands held mine.

"No, Davie." Gently pleading.

"Peggy, stop it," I said. "What are you afraid of? Have I ever hurt you?"

"No, but..."

"Well, stop it, then."

"I'm sorry. I just..."

I opened another button. She was staring at me, her face white and tense. She looked like some maiden about to be sacrificed to a horrible god.

"Peggy!" I said angrily.

She had her dress on under the robe.

"Davie, please don't be angry. Don't you see I'm..."

"See! See *what?*"

"Davie..."

"What do you think marriage is, a *business* relationship?" I snapped pettishly. "Oh...for God's sake..."

"Davie."

I didn't look at her. I had another drink. She drank another glass. We sat there in silence and we both drank. She seemed to be trying to get drunk. Relentlessly trying to lose herself so she could please me. But it seemed she couldn't do it, as if this fear in her were imbedded in her very flesh.

I don't remember every moment. But I do remember that she took off her robe after I acted sullen. She took her dress off and lay beside me in her slip. Her motions were nervous and shaky. She kept drinking. Her lips shook. She tried to smile.

"You won't...do...anything, will you?" she asked, quietly.

I didn't answer. My breath was heavier. I could see the lines of her body through the silk now. A beautiful body. My lips pressed against the warm flesh of her shoulder. I remembered that night we'd gone to Ciro's and Peggy had worn the low dress. I thought of all the times I'd wanted her. I thought of Audrey screaming into my chest. I wanted to scream too. Hunger seemed to have been converted into an ugly drive in me. I couldn't keep my hands off her. My mind kept trying to stop me but I kept kicking it aside.

I caressed her. She shuddered.

"Davie." A frightened little voice.

"Stop that," I said.

I heard her throat move. I kissed her throat. She drew away. I pulled her close in what I thought was a gentle way.

She drew away again and stood up.

"I think I'll take a bath," she said.

It sounded so obvious to me. It irritated me. I stood up quickly and stood before her. I slid my hands around her.

"No," I said.

"I'm...Davie, can't you..."

Her eyes like a frightened bird's. Trapped, helpless.

"Peggy, I'm your husband." Thick voice, uncomprehending voice.

"I know, I know but...you said you'd..."

"I just want to touch you."

"Davie, please."

"I just want to *touch* you."

"Da*vie.*"

"All I want to do is...touch you."

I was lost in a fog. I kept running my hands over her. She kept backing away. I followed. I was out of my mind. I grabbed her. She squirmed out of my embrace.

"No," she said. More firmly now. A little fire in her eyes.

I grabbed her.

"I told you to stop it!" I said angrily and the unspent fury of the last months surged up into my voice.

She tore away from me.

"You're not going to touch me!"

"No?"

I moved toward her and she backed away. I thought about her husband. I threw the thought aside. Almost, her fright drove me on harder. I could almost understand a man wanting to take Peggy by force. She seemed the sort of woman.

She backed into the bedside table.

"Davie…no!"

I clutched her shoulders.

Suddenly her eyes expanded, her lips drew back as she sucked in a terrified breath. I could almost hear the scream tearing up through her throat.

That was when something managed to lance its way through the thick coating of mindless desire in me. I saw myself. I saw her. And I was doing to her what they'd all done. I was no better than any of them. And the shame of it made me turn away with tears in my eyes and a shaking hand over my eyes.

"I'm…I'm…I'm…sorry," I muttered brokenly. A sudden rushing sound. A biting pain in my right shoulder right below where the bandage ended. I jumped around with a gasp.

She was holding the icepick in her hand and staring at me, her eyes like white dotted marbles in her head, her lips pressed together into a hideous white gash.

My mouth fell open. I stared at her dumbly.

I don't know how long we stood there without a sound. She was like a tensed animal, the icepick raised in her hand, her dark pupils boring into me.

I moved back a step then. The words seemed to come from my mouth by themselves.

"You're *crazy,*" I said.

She still looked at me, something tight holding her together.

Then she noticed the big drops of blood running over my hand and dripping on the floor. She leaned forward a little, the berserk look fading from her face. The features relaxed. Her arm dropped.

"Davie?" she said.

"Get away from me."

"Davie."

"You *heard* me."

"Davie, I didn't stab you."

I backed away some more.

"Davie, it wasn't you."

"Get *away.*"

"I didn't stab at you. Davie, not at you!"

"I said get away!"

I backed off in horror. And then the idea came and the breath was sucked out of me.

"You killed Albert, didn't you?" I said.

She stopped. She looked at me blankly.

"You *killed* him, didn't you?" I said hoarsely.

"Davie, I..."

"Didn't you?"

"Davie..."

"You did, didn't you!"

"What difference does it make?"

"Oh my God!" I cried. "You kill a man and you ask what difference it makes!"

"You said you could forget everything," she said.

"Forget that you murdered a man!"

"He wasn't a man, he was an animal!"

"He was a man, a *man!* And you killed him!"

Her throat moved. She started to tremble. She raised her hand. She saw the icepick and then threw it away with revulsion and it rolled over the floor.

"I didn't," she said weakly.

"You did!"

"Yes, I...I killed...h-h-him. But..."

I felt myself drained in an instant. As if by some invisible vampire of the strength. I staggered back, hardly feeling the pain in my shoulder at all.

"You lied to me," I said dizzily. "All this time you lied to me."

"No, Davie, no," she said miserably.

She was trying to wipe away the past. It was what she always meant. That we should forget everything, even that she had killed.

"You said what happened before didn't matter. You said it didn't," she said.

"What are you?" I said. "An animal yourself? You kill a man and then you say forget it."

"I was out of my mind. I couldn't help it. I...didn't mean to."

"Why did you lie? Why did you lie to me?"

"Davie, don't." Tears were flooding down her cheeks. "I was upset. I couldn't lose you. You're all I have now. Don't desert me. I need you. I *need* you."

"And you let me think that Jim killed them," I said.

"He had Dennis killed," she said, "I didn't do that. What's the difference if he dies for one crime or two. Didn't he *say* he killed Albert?"

He'd lied for her. I knew it suddenly. I hadn't gotten any confession from him. He'd heard Jones out there and he'd lied once more to save Peggy.

I couldn't get it. I just couldn't understand it. All I could think was one thing.

"And we're married," I said. "We're *married.*"

Something hard gripped her features.

"Oh, that's awful, isn't it?" she said, her voice breaking. "That's just horrible, isn't it?"

"I don't think you feel guilty at all," I said, "I think you feel *justified* for everything you did. You think you had a *right to* kill Albert, don't you?"

"I *did* have a right! He was a pig! He tore at my clothes and he tried to make me filthy with his own dirt! I *had* to kill him! I had to, can't you see that!"

"No, I can't! I can't see it!"

Something seemed to start in her. Way down. Like a flood of hot lava surging up to the mouth of a volcano. It shook her body as it came up. It made her arms tremble at her sides, made the fingers clamp into boney fists.

It exploded in my face.

"You're like *all* of them!" she yelled. "Like every damn one of them! *Defending* each other! *Plotting* with each other against us! Driving us into a pit! A *pit! Hurting* us, *brutalizing* us, *destroying* us, making us into tools for your filthy hands! Twisting our hopes into knots! And tearing our hearts out! You don't care, oh, you don't care! You're all the same, *all* of you! You don't care about us! You don't care if we have minds, you don't care if we're sensitive, you don't care if we're afraid, you just *take* us! You just rip the beauty out of our lives and give us ugliness instead! And then you tell everybody what wonderful men you are, how *happy* you've made us! All of you—*pigs!* Get away from me you pig, *you pig, YOU PIG!*"

Her blood-drained fists were crushed against her white cheeks and saliva ran from her twitching mouth. I stood there, paralyzed, looking in blank horror at a girl I'd never seen.

I didn't even hear the door open. The first thing I knew was Peggy turning. And then I looked.

Jim.

He came across the room quickly. I couldn't move. I watched him take off his top coat and put it over her shoulders. She tried to throw it off but, without a moment's hesitation, he slapped her across the face. Hard. The red flared up on her cheek and she gasped and backed away.

"You're coming with me," he said. "Don't argue with me. You'd better if you don't want to be turned in. You don't want to be executed for murder, do you?"

Her eyes on him were wide and staring. Eyes like an insane cat.

"I'm all you have now," he said. "Your dear *David* wouldn't lift a finger to save you now!"

His words seemed to whip her into submission. The wildness was gone. The deepest Peggy came into control. The weak Peggy, the Peggy who always needed guidance and discipline. Who could never think for herself. She looked at him like a frightened child at its parent.

"Jim, you…" she started, "you won't…let them do…"

"Come on, Peggy," he said. "How long do you think I can protect you from the world?"

She didn't answer. She just stood by him and let him lead her to the door. I stood there bleeding and not feeling it. Staring after them helplessly. Detached from reality.

"You won't let them, will you Jim"? she begged.

He looked at her pathetic face. He heard the lost fright in her voice. And, for the first time in his life, he showed in my sight that there was more than machinery in him.

He drew her against him and pressed his lips to her hair.

"Peggy," he said, "oh, *Peggy.*"

Only an instant. Then he raised his head and his face was hard.

"They won't get you," he said. "Not while I live."

I might have been invisible standing there. The blood dripping from my finger tips onto the floor. Me watching a world slip away from me. A rootless, detached feeling. As if something I'd called my heart had been torn away leaving me hollow, a shell.

I noticed that there was somebody outside the door.

"Is there anything wrong in here?" the voice asked. "I heard shouting."

Jim Vaughan spoke calmly, distinctly.

"This is my wife," he said. "I'm taking her away from that man in there."

Muttering. "I knew it, I *knew* it."

Then, at the door, Jim turned. He had his arm protectingly around Peggy's shoulders. And for some reason, all the smugness and the meanness and the cynical detachment seemed to have gone from him.

He looked at me. And it seemed as if he felt as helpless as I did. He had tried to save her again and again. Doing everything he could, even confessing for her crime. Now, if they were fugitives, it would be Jim they sought for murder.

And, despite all that, she had not changed.

And I knew later—not then because I could do nothing but stand there mutely—that Jim loved her. In a way that I and my sort of person cannot understand, much less appreciate. In the old way. The unquestioning way. Defying the traditions of society rather than losing it. Loving in a way that even allowed a man to kill for his love. Right out of the middle ages. Yet, something strangely and perversely noble there.

At least there seemed a sort of quiet unassuming nobility to Jim as he stood there by the silent Peggy. The frightened and weak Peggy who would never in her life be able to face the world without help even if she feared that help above all else.

"Just for the record," Jim said to me, "I had both Albert and Dennis killed. *Both.* Do you hear me?"

I knew he hadn't. He'd had Dennis killed. But Albert had died at another's hands. The hands of a girl I had loved and who, even now, was my wife. But I was too dazed to think of that.

Jim turned to her then. His eyes were on her only and his mind and heart held her alone.

"Come away, my dear," he said.

And led her out of my life forever.

The police came soon. I hadn't left. They picked me up on a morals charge. Later they called Santa Monica and fortunately Jones was still alive. He gave them the facts and they released me and started after Peggy and Jim. But they didn't catch them.

And one day I saw Jones and he told me they'd caught the man who'd attacked Peggy at *Funland*.

"I don't understand," I said, "Albert…"

"Grady didn't do it," Jones said.

"But…the scratches," I said, in a last confusion about my Peggy Ann, "She said she'd scratched the man who'd tried to rape her. And Albert's face was covered with scratches."

"That's right," he said, "they both were scratched."

I looked at him a moment and then I lowered my head. And I whispered, "God help her."

That's about all. I finished my novel and sold it and made $1700 on it. I talked Audrey into going back to her family in Pennsylvania. I met some people and laughed again and pretended that everything was status quo again.

I read the papers.

Maybe you read the story, too. It was about a month ago. When they found Jim and Peggy in a Kansas City hotel room. And when they took away the thing that Peggy was fondling in her lap she said they mustn't.

She said they had to let her keep his head because she loved the man.

THE END

FURY

ON

SUNDAY

There was moonlight on his face and he was playing a funeral march. But there wasn't any piano. There was just the cot he was lying on, low and narrow, without any bedding except a coarse brown blanket wrapped tightly around the mattress. He lay on the blanket, fully clothed, his head resting on a thin pillow. The wide shaft of moonlight flooding across his body lit up the whiteness of his lean hands while they played Chopin on his legs. There was silence in the ward but he heard the music in his head.

He was a young man, about 26 years old, with tangled black hair and dark eyes. His face was the work of a sculptor who had forgotten to stop at the right place; who had, in attempting perfection, overdone the job, cutting everything to paper thinness—ears and nostrils that seemed liable to tear, and lips and chin like brittle glass that might shatter at the slightest blow. And all white—alabaster, ivory white.

He lay straight on the mattress, the gray-flannel trousered legs stretched out so taut that the heels of his ankle-high shoes pressed against the railing at the foot of the bed. His chest, covered by a shirt of grey flannel, rose and fell slowly and evenly.

Breathe correctly, Vincent. You must have the breath control of a distance runner.

The eyes that had been staring at the high ceiling now closed tightly. The hands were transformed to white spiders that jumped on his legs, gouging and scraping out music.

Not triple f, Vincent, double f, for the love of God!

The dirge crashed in his ears and the chords echoed down the endless passage of clouded darkness that was his brain.

Now the slow reflective passage came to life beneath his fingers, consoling. He opened his eyes again to stare at the ceiling.

He was waiting for Harry. Harry was the male nurse who handled the ward, an ape of a man with plastered-down hair and fat hands with black hair on their backs. Lying there, Vince thought about those hands while his own rippled gently over the keyboard that wasn't.

159

Harry's hands weren't piano hands, Vince knew. Harry had ape hands that were coming soon to pluck him from the darkness. He could almost see Harry moving down the outside hall for the door that led to the ward. He could almost see the door opening and Harry standing there, waiting for him.

His hands punched down and a crescendo of despair mounted in his brain. He didn't want to think of Harry so he pushed aside the thought of his moist searching hands, the vacuous smile. He jammed his eyes shut and propelled himself back to Town Hall. The audience was rapt. They held their breaths while he ended the funeral march, paused dramatically, then drove himself into the incredible fury of the last sonata movement.

Now he was really there. He had driven away all memories. There was no Ruth in his life. No Bob. No Stan or Jane. No Saul. He was alone with his music; the music that had always been his only comfort. He was bent over the keyboard, brow glistening with sweat, hands a blur of white movement on the keys, drawing out crystal sound from the stillness. Faster and faster. The sound of the music welled up in his brain.

Then the little man who had stabbed his wife sixteen times with a carving knife began to cough.

Vince's hands snapped into fists that trembled in the moonlight. His teeth clicked together and his body shuddered on the bed. The need for violence pushed out from his insides until he felt as if it would force out the walls of his body. It came on him like this, his temper. It came pounding up from his guts, eager for destruction.

Vince rolled onto his stomach and clamped his teeth on the pillow.

Vincent, you simply must control your temper!

A hissing breath escaped his lips. The memory of forgotten words only made it worse. He tossed onto his back and pushed up to a tense position, eyes wide open, planning to rush down to the little man's bed and squeeze the coughing from his lungs.

Then the man stopped coughing and went back to sleep. Vince caught himself, waited a moment, then fell back on the pillow. After a moment, he smiled in the moonlight.

Not now. Not when his chance was here at last. He'd waited too long to throw it away on a moment's vengeance. His breathing slowed down and he cleared his throat softly. I can control myself.

I'm sane. That's the difference between a sane man and an insane man. When you're sane you have control. He smiled again.

Then he rolled on his side and looked toward the door that Harry would open soon. The door that led out to freedom. To revenge.

Madhouse, he thought, and his fingers tinkled a witty improvisation on his legs. They thought him mad. That was their mistake. Did the truly mad plot escape the way he did, with detail and care? No, not the mad. They gibbered and beat fists on the plaster walls and kicked at the door until Harry came. But they never planned like this. He kept his eyes on the door, his hands drawing at each other as he waited. In his mind he went over the plan again. It was very simple. Once he had escaped he would leave the building and take the subway down to 18th Street. Walk a few short blocks in the early morning when the streets were deserted. Ring the bell, go upstairs and wait outside the door. Then when Bob came to the door...

His knuckles cracked as he drew his hands into fists.

But what if Ruth came to the door first? His brow knitted at the sudden problem. Then he nodded curtly to himself. Never mind that. She'd understand why he was there. She wouldn't stop him. After all, wasn't she as much a prisoner as he was? Maybe she wasn't behind locked doors but she was a prisoner anyway. Held in a more vicious kind of chains, the chains of emotional terror.

Poor Ruth. She'd suffered long enough. Well, he'd take care of her. After Bob was dead they could go away somewhere together. He could get a job doing something. He had strong hands. Maybe he could play the piano in a bar at night when no one could see his face. But that didn't matter. It wasn't important that he played the piano anymore. He made a soft, scoffing sound. What was piano music to compare with his love for Ruth?

Yes, that was the plan. The long wait was ended. Escape, revenge, escape, revenge, es...

He was up like a hungry cat at the slight clicking in the door lock. He crouched in the shadows by the bedside, licking the sweat drops from his upper lip.

The door opened.

Harry stood there, square and white. Vince remained motionless, hearing in his brain thumping piano music beneath the liquid voice of the male nurse. The voice that always made Vince feel as if hands were massaging syrup into his brain. *You like Harry, don't you Vin-*

cie boy? Harry likes you. You're a nice little boy and Harry will take care of you.

Vince took a deep breath and stood up. He started to walk down the aisle between the beds. Harry stood motionless, waiting. Vince's stomach muscles were tense at the sight of him. His fingers bent over into tight arcs at his sides. He moved stealthily through the ward of the sleeping mad. He didn't want any of them to wake up and start a disturbance. Everything had to go right.

He walked by the next window and the moonlight bathed him in its whiteness.

Then he started violently as a low chuckle sounded in the darkness at his left. His black eyes darted over and he saw Kramer sitting up in bed, watching him. Vince stiffened, but he kept walking. He wouldn't stop now. If Kramer tried to stop him, then Kramer would die. He kept on walking and Kramer only chuckled again as if he knew something.

Vince smiled to himself. Well, let the fool chuckle. If he only knew that Vince would be out of the place soon, he'd stop chuckling soon enough.

He looked at Harry. Harry wouldn't stop him from escaping either. No matter how strong he was. Vince thought of raking out those watching eyes and stamping on them. He'd scrape them out the way he'd scraped Jane's face that night when she tried to seduce him. The way he'd tried to do with Saul that day before the maid had come in and found them.

Harry stepped back and Vince stood nervously in the hallway. He heard the door shut behind him and the sound of it shutting away his prison was like a chord of triumph.

He padded along quietly beside Harry, controlling his urge to twist away from the moist hand that lay on his shoulder, the heavy arm pressing across his back. At his sides, his hands still ran over his legs with menacing glissandos. They hovered and waited.

Build to the climax, Vincent! Build to it!

"Did you wait long for Harry, Vincie boy?"

Vince made a sound of assent. Be quiet, he told himself. Harry mustn't suspect anything about the escape.

"That's good, boy. I like your spirit. I told you I'd take care of you. Didn't I?"

Another sound of assent.

"Speak up, Vincie boy, speak up. Nothing to be scared of. We're gonna have a nice time, you and me. A few smokes, a couple shots of whiskey and—who knows?" He jabbed his elbow into Vince's side. "Eh, Vincie, boy?"

Vince nodded. He didn't hear what Harry was saying. His eyes kept moving down to the end of the hall. There was an office there. Vince remembered when they brought him there he had sat in the office and been finger-printed. There was a guard there, too, and the guard would have a pistol.

"Whoa, there. Where you goin', Vincie boy? This is Harry's room right here. You think you're out for a stroll, boy?"

The voice was slightly menacing. Vince smiled as if he didn't hear the menace. He waited quietly while Harry pushed open the door and gestured for him to go in. He entered the small room and heard the big male nurse follow him in. He saw the dim bulb burning overhead. Then the door shut, the lock clicked and Vince's throat moved. He pressed his thin lips together. If he failed, he'd kill himself.

"Sit down, Vincie boy. Take a load off your feet."

Vince turned and looked at Harry's face, the pink, smooth skin, the fat sweat drops under his nose.

"I said, sit down, Vincie boy," the voice warned gently.

Vince sank down on the bed that had its covers thrown back. His hands flinched on the cool sheet. His eyes moved to the bedside table; to the half empty whiskey bottle on top of it, its cap off and lying beside it; to the open pack of Chesterfields. They didn't get cigarettes in the ward. Vince licked his lips.

"You want a butt, Vincie boy? You want one?

Vince swallowed. He nodded once.

"Well go ahead, boy. Have a butt on Harry. That's all right."

Vince reached for the pack. Harry's hand closed over his.

"You remember favors, don't you boy?" Harry said. "When a pal does you a favor you remember it, don't you?"

Vince looked blank. Harry patted his cheek and nodded, chuckling.

"Sure you do, Vincie boy. When a pal does you a favor, you remember it. Take one, Vincie boy. Light up. Enjoy yourself."

The fumes tickled deliciously in his throat and nostrils. *Time,* he heard a voice, *you need time.* Over the glowing tip of the cigarette, he looked around the room at the closet, the bureau, the throw rug on the floor.

Then there was a rustling sound and Vince, looking up suddenly, saw that Harry had pulled off his white, short-sleeved shirt. His face tightened.

"What's the matter, Vincie boy? Take it easy. Harry won't bite your head off. Harry is your pal, remember?"

Vince looked bleakly at the dark swirls of hair that covered Harry's chest, the fat ridges that pushed over the belt line.

"Relax, Vincie boy. You're on a picnic, a regular picnic."

Harry's voice dripped like honey. But Vince had heard the same tone in his voice the time Harry had crushed in an old Italian's nose with one blow. Vince remembered the scream. He remembered the writhing body on the floor. A shiver passed over his body. He'd have to wait. He sat there smoking and his right hand played Scriabine and didn't know.

"How about a little pick-me-up, Vincie boy? You drink, don't you? Sure you do. There's nothing like a nice little pick-me-up to get us girls acquainted."

The amber liquid gurgled into the two glasses as Harry poured. Vince watched the hands. He was thinking of how Harry had watched him for a long time. When the men took their showers and Harry stood in the doorway to see there was no trouble, Vince had seen the male nurse watching him, running his eyes over the smooth leanness of Vince's body, the small, hard muscles, the firm stomach.

Once, when McCarran had shoved Vince so he fell down on the icy wet floor, Harry had stepped quickly through the stinging sprays of water to spin McCarran around and drive his beefy fist into the Irishman's stomach. Then Harry had leaned over and helped Vince up and pretended to lose balance, pulling Vince's wet body against him.

Vince re-focused his eyes on the glass held before him. Even breath drained from his thin nostrils. *That's it,* he heard the whisper in his brain, *control your breath. That shows you're sane. No matter what happens you're going to get out of here.*

"Drink up, Vincie boy. Good for you. Puts hair on 'em."

Vince didn't take the glass. He knew he should drink to set Harry at ease. Yet he knew he mustn't touch it. Vaguely he recalled a time when that same dark liquid had stultified his brain and his reflexes.

That was the night of the big party, he remembered, the one Stan threw after the concert at Carnegie. And Jane had taken him into the bedroom with her. No, drink was bad: he mustn't drink because he had no escape.

"I said drink, Vincie boy."

Vince shook his head, smiling.

Harry's face went blank.

"You're not drinking, boy?" he said flatly.

Vince stared at him. He felt his heartbeat catch suddenly.

Then a cry broke from his thin lips as Harry grabbed him by the hair and jerked back his head. Vince clamped his teeth together before Harry could pour in the whiskey. He could smell the nicotine breath of the big nurse, and the red face blotted the ceiling from sight.

"I said *drink*, you dirty little bastard!"

Vince twisted away with a whine and Harry, strangling on a curse, flung the contents of the glass in his face. Vince gasped and blinked as the whiskey burned in his eyes. Tears sprang from beneath the lids to mingle with the drops of whiskey on his face.

Harry shoved him onto his back.

"Awright, damn it," he growled, "cut the crap. I know what you are so *cut* it!"

Vince tried to sit up, but the nurse, with one hand, pinned him down by the throat. Vince forgot his plan completely. He started to thrash violently on the bed forgetting everything but the wild need to escape. He clawed at Harry's eyes and his nails scraped across the hot forehead. Harry cursed and something hard exploded against Vince's jaw. The sound of Harry's breathing flooded away and, when he tried to open his eyes, the red face was hazy before him.

"You want to fight, huh?" the words came through a fog. "Don't you know you ain't foolin' me? You ain't foolin' Harry for one minute, *Vincie* boy. I know you like it. Don't you, boy, *don't* you?"

Vince jerked away from the whiskey-laden breath. He whimpered in fright and a voice crackled in his brain.

Dear boy, do go to the bathroom and wash off your face. You look positively bizarre.

Harry's hands started to move over him. The pain in Vince's jaw made him groan. His struggles began to weaken. Then he shuddered violently as Harry started to unbutton his shirt. The moan in his throat rose in volume.

"Aah, shut up, boy! You know you like it." The red face leaned close and the obscene breath covered Vince's mouth and nostrils.

Vince closed his eyes. All he could think of was three words. They drummed into his brain again and again.

When it's over, when it's over, when it's...

⬛ ⬛ ⬛ ⬛

He opened his eyes. The sound of bubbly snoring filled his ears. He sat up quickly and slid his bare legs over the side of the bed.

He stood looking down over Harry. On his flesh he still felt the bruises and teethmarks. As he stood there, breathing evenly, his hands moved on his stomach as if they were rubbing off something.

His mouth tightened. Well, it *was* over now and he was one step closer to freedom. His plan had worked. Harry was dead drunk. Vince had seen to that. He'd needed an advantage and now he had it. Smiles and touches had made the male nurse drink all of the whiskey, leaving Vince clear-headed and strong.

Now he reached out as if he meant to start the opening chords of the Rachmaninoff Second. But instead of music he drew an empty whiskey bottle to himself. He stood there motionless over the bed, looking down. Then, with a sharp motion, he broke the bottle in half across the table edge. Harry stirred and mumbled to himself and Vince heard someone screaming in his brain, *If you dare touch his hands, I swear to God I'll kill you!*

Vince leaned over Harry, his eyes glittering in the light of the bedside lamp. He rolled the bottle neck in his fingers. Then, abruptly, the color drained from his face and a trembling pulled back his lips. He tapped Harry on the shoulder.

"Wake up, Saul," he said.

And, when the sleep-thickened eyes fluttered open for a second, he raised his arm and drove the jagged glass edges straight down into them.

1:15 AM

Bob looked up from his work as the kitchen door swung open and Ruth came in carrying a tray with sandwiches and milk. She was wearing her pink quilted robe and her blonde hair was drawn back in a ribbon-knotted horse's tail. She smiled at him as she moved across the rug.

He put down his blue pencil.

"Honey, you should be in bed," he scolded her.

"If you can work until one o'clock Sunday morning I can stay up to feed you."

She set down the tray on the card table over the sheaf of papers he'd been working on.

"There," she said.

He smiled tiredly and stretched.

"You look cute," he said.

She leaned over and kissed him on the nose.

"That's for flattery," she said.

She got the hassock by the chair and drew it up to the table. Then she sat down on it and smiled up at him. A slight yawn parted her red lips.

"There, you *are* sleepy," he said. "You should be in bed."

"You're sleepy too," she countered. "Are you in bed?"

"I am the wage earner," he said. "The bread-winner. The proletariat."

"Eat."

He picked up a sandwich and bit into it.

"Mmmm. Good," he said.

"How's the work coming?" she asked.

"Oh, pretty good, I guess."

"Almost finished?"

"Just about," he answered. He sighed and reached for the glass of milk. He took a sip and put it down.

"I'm sorry we had to miss that dance," he said.

"Oh, don't be silly," she said. "Anyway—I guess I won't be gallivanting around much any more."

He grinned and patted her warm cheek.

"Little mother," he said.

Then he leaned over and kissed her on the mouth.

"I take mustard," she said.

167

"How romantic." He yawned again.

"I bet you say that to all the expectant mothers."

"Not all."

"All the girls then."

"Only those I love," he said.

"That would be—" she estimated, "Ava Gardner, Lana Turner…"

"Marie Dressler."

She made a tiny amused sound.

"How about Jane?" she said. "She's a hot number."

"She's an odd number," he said. "All she has is a body."

He grinned at her. Her face had fallen a little.

He knew what was bothering her. Ever since Ruth had become pregnant she would keep looking in the mirror, searching for signs that she was getting fat. It bothered her. She always liked to look her best for him.

"Well…" she said.

"Honey, you know you're the only one."

"She *is* sort of pretty," she said.

"Who, Marie Dressler?"

When she didn't answer he pulled her hair gently.

"Now cut it out," he said.

She took his right hand and pressed it to her cheek. "I'm sorry," she said quietly.

"Okay." He finished the sandwich. "Speaking of that," he said, wiping his fingers on the napkin, "when is Stan going to wise up?"

She shrugged.

"I don't know," she said. "Poor Stan."

"Well," he said, "he made his own problem. He knew what she was before he married her."

"He never should have married her."

"That is the observation of the week," he said.

"I guess he still wants her, though."

"The world is strewn with the remnants of men who wanted what they shouldn't have had."

She looked at her hands. "I suppose so," she said.

"He just ain't her speed," he said.

"Oh, he's not that old."

"Stan is forty-six and Jane is twenty-five. He's no Gregory Peck and she's a good looking woman."

She shook her head again.

"It's a shame," she said.

"Sure it's a shame. Hey, aren't you having some of this food?"

"No, I'd just get an upset stomach," she said, "You know about ladies in my condition."

He stroked her cheek once and smiled affectionately at her.

"What'll we call him?" he asked

"Him. It's decided already?"

"Sure. A son for the McCalls."

She sat there smiling to herself.

"Maybe," she said.

He leaned over and kissed her.

"Love ya," he whispered in her ear.

Then he straightened up, selected a cookie and bit into it.

"What was we talking about before we smooched?" he said. "Oh, yeah, I remember. Why Stan still hangs on the ropes."

"I don't know."

"He ought to ditch her. She's going to drive him out of his mind."

"You think it's that bad?"

"Sure it is," he said.

He smiled at the look on her face.

"I know, I know," he said. "You went to college with her and she's always been your friend. Well, you can't live in the past. Let's face it, she's a nympho. She'll sleep with anybody."

He reconsidered.

"Except maybe her husband," he amended.

"Oh, she can't be that bad. I won't believe it."

"Honey, anybody that would try to seduce Vince *must* be that bad."

Ruth looked down at her hands again. She thought about Vince for a moment. Vince, so young and so eager. And so damned.

"Poor Vince," she said. "It was a pity."

"I know," he said, "Well, Vince I can feel sorry for. That father of his."

He shook his head. Then he smiled cheerfully at her. "Come on, let's get off the subject. How about a brief discussion on a name for our seven-month-distant heir?"

"Don't you have to work?"

"Oh, I can finish up in the morning. Right now I want to relax with my wife for a while."

A look of pleasure crossed her face. He got up and helped her to her feet. They walked over to the couch and she sat down. Then he went over to the record player, put on a record and came back to the couch. As he sat down and put his arm around her the first strains of Ravel's *Daphnis and Chloe* filled the room.

Ruth cuddled close to him and lay her head against his shoulder. He reached down and patted her stomach.

"Comfy, Guiseppe?" he asked.

"Is that what we're going to call him?"

"Sure," he said. "Guiseppe McCall; that's a fine name."

"Guiseppe McCall," she said. "It has a ring."

They sat in silence awhile, listening to the music and thinking about their coming child. While she listened and dreamed, Ruth looked up at her husband's face, at his silky blonde hair, his straight nose, the strong chin line. She wanted to reach up and touch his slight beard. Emphatically, her right hand twitched in her lap and she made an amused sound to herself.

"Hmmm?" he asked.

"Nothing."

Nothing, she thought, it was a good deal more than nothing. It was rapidly coming to the point where she adored him.

Sometimes she thought that maybe it was the child, maybe it was an instinct for love and protection in a needful time. But then she knew she'd felt this way before she'd become pregnant too; pregnancy had only made it worse. Or better.

She was afraid that sometimes it was too obvious. She dreaded making a pest of herself; men never loved that kind of clinging woman, she was sure. And yet there wasn't a single detail of him that didn't fascinate her. She watched him dress, admiring his tall, muscular body, paying minute attention to each motion he made. Each morning she did that until he was dressed. Then she would rush into the kitchen and make breakfast.

She liked to watch him eat, enjoying the relish he gave each meal. She liked to watch him when he worked sometimes after office hours, bringing his briefcase full of papers to set out on the card table. She even liked to watch him shave; that's how bad it was. Watching him do everything gave her the feeling of absorbing him completely, every detail of him. It gave her a strange yet certain feeling of safety; as if she belonged to him and was protected from all bad things.

She sighed and pressed against him.

"Now what are we going to call him?" Bob asked.

"Who?" she asked.

"Our son."

"Mary?" she suggested.

"Not tough enough," he said, "What about George?"

She shook her head. "Uh-uh."

"Max?"

"Nope."

"Sam, Tom, Bill, Phil, Jim, Len, Vince—oops, sorry, slip of the tongue."

She didn't smile.

"Wonder where he is," Bob said.

"I don't know," she said.

She felt the other feeling now; the one that came whenever something was discussed that seemed to mar their happiness. It was silly to feel that way, she knew, as if she wanted to wear blinders or be like that sundial. What was the statement that went with it? *I record only the sunny hours.* Well, that was really silly. There was a lot of night in the world too.

But, at least, you didn't have to think and ponder about things that were all over with. There was only one person who could let her past with Vince hurt them and that was her. She mustn't dwell on the past, as Bob said.

"God, I'll never forget that afternoon up in the agency," he said, "It was—crazy."

"Don't," she said.

"All right." He smiled and kissed her cheek.

They sat listening to music some more. He tried to forget it but the memory of that scene stayed with him. Sometimes he would jolt up from the bed in the middle of the night, reliving it. The thunder storm, working alone in his office after a bad afternoon, and then, to top it all off...

He shook it off.

"Are we going to that party next Friday night at Stan's?" he asked.

"It's up to you, honey," she said.

"Well, there's no use lying; I don't particularly want to go. Stan's all right, but Jane gives me the creeps. I get the feeling she's going to explode sometime right in my face; a million pieces of Jane Sheldon flying all over the apartment."

"I get the same feeling," she said. "At college, Jane used to throw herself around so much I wondered how she'd ever graduate."

"Did she?"

"In the top ten per cent of the class."

"My God. Wouldn't you know it."

He looked down at her and smiled as he stroked her soft hair. He shook his head slightly without her seeing it. How in hell she and Jane ever managed to stand each other's company for three years at college, he'd never know. They were so utterly different. Jane was a hand grenade with the pin out. Ruth was...

No, you couldn't pin a pat little metaphor on Ruth; she was too atypical.

Jane you could characterize. You could put her down in words. She was more like a taut spring than a woman, made of sharp lines and angles with no contour that was smooth or soft; stiff, high breasts, hips and buttocks flat and hard, and legs like taut pistons driving her on.

That was a woman, maybe, but not the kind of woman he wanted. It wasn't that he'd been brought up so strictly; not that he was a momma's boy who always sang within himself the old refrain of *I want a girl just like the girl...*

It was just that, after a man had lived a while, loved a while, been around a lot of women, he wanted a woman he could trust and be at ease with. One he could feel sensual heat with, sure; but not a heat that was so constant it started to consume. That was Stan's trouble. You couldn't burn at a constant heat without charring after a while.

No, you needed a girl you could relax with too. A marriage took place in all the rooms of an apartment.

Bob thought about the first time he'd met Ruth. He'd been doing publicity work on one of Vince's concerts. One night Stan, Vince's business manager, had held a party. One of those endless parties that seemed always to be going around Stan's beleaguered head. It was there that he'd met Ruth.

He had liked her appearance; the neat, unaffected way she dressed; the well-scrubbed facade she presented. He liked her smile.

But the thing he'd liked most was her complete difference from Jane. Jane was tight and hard, always brittle, always dashing around the party from one person to another, cigarette in one hand, cocktail in the other; always pushing so hard to be terribly clever and terribly sophisticated. It was against the aura of pseudo-smartness that Ruth had stood out so strongly.

Was there a word that typified his Ruth? It wasn't *old-fashioned* because that had connotations of prudishness that didn't apply to Ruth. Maybe *real* was the word. She didn't try to impress anyone. And that was the secret of her impression on him. Even now, after three years of marriage, after long intimacies and discoveries, she was still something new and vital to him. And the fact that she carried within her a tangible part of him was something even more exciting and wonderful.

He tightened his arm around her and she grunted.

"Easy, strangler," she said.

He chuckled. Yes, with a wife like this he could even stomach *Hilton, Hilton, Joslyn and Ramsay: Advertising*. He thought about his office there, bright and clean, the grey wall-to-wall carpeting, the soft lights.

Then, all of a sudden, he was back to that day when Vince had come there. He hissed in disgust at not being able to rid himself of the memory.

"What's the matter, darling?" she asked.

"Nothing."

"Thinking about Vince?"

He looked at her in surprise. "How did you know?"

"Expectant woman's intuition," she said, half in amusement.

He sighed.

"He was quite a boy," he said, "I wonder what kind of a life you would have had with him."

"I don't even want to think about it. That temper..."

She slid her arms around him suddenly.

"I love you, Bob," she murmured.

Just the music undulating in the air. Bob pressed his cheek against her hair.

"I know, sweetheart," he said, "I love you too."

They sat there on the big couch and listened to the record. Ruth looked around the room at the bookshelves, at the furniture. She kept trying to put Vince out of her mind. It was a terrible memory. She had been a small town girl fascinated by his lean good looks, by his smile, by his ability to play the piano. Only when she saw his temper did she realize it could never work out. And then Bob had come along.

The music ended.

"Bed?" he said softly.

"All right."

They rose leisurely and, while Bob turned off the phonograph, Ruth looked at what he'd been working on all night.

"Will it sell cars?" she asked.

"It better," he said, "or we'll have to put Giuseppe in an orphanage."

"He wouldn't like that."

"That's why this has to sell automobiles," he said.

"It will, honey."

Arms around each other they walked slowly across the room and he flicked off the light as they went into the bedroom.

1:50 AM

Vince crouched over the body of the unconscious guard and jerked the heavy pistol out of its holster. It felt good to have it in his hands, a solid comfort. When a man was excited and nervous he needed a crutch, and a pistol could be that crutch. A gun made him strong and it would frighten people. Most important it would hurt Bob. It would leave him dead—suddenly and completely—the way Vince wanted him.

His face twitched and his finger almost tightened on the trigger, so urgent was his desire to empty the pistol into Bob. The fact that Bob was so many miles away made Vince tremble with frustrated hate.

He straightened up and moved for the office door, anxious to get to the subway.

It had been ridiculously easy to overpower the old guard. The man had been sitting at the office desk, half slumped over in sleep. Vince had only to pick up the lamp and smash it across his head. The old man had crashed back in the chair without a sound. Vince had dashed around the edge of the desk and now he was almost free.

He jerked at the heavy door that led to the outside hall. At first he couldn't believe that it wouldn't open. His eyes widened as if he was surprised. A questioning sound filled his throat. He pulled harder, but the door remained fast. Vince's breath caught and he almost lunged against the heavy metal.

Then he stopped and held himself. It was not the time for temper. He had to escape. He closed his eyes. Why didn't the door open?

Then he opened his eyes. A key.

Now wasn't that terribly difficult to deduce.

His lips trembled as he moved back for the office. Always the voice of Saul in the background like an inescapable prompter hissing his cues from behind the dark curtain. No matter where Vince went, no matter what he did, there was always some old remark of Saul's that would fit the occasion. His teeth gritted together. If only he knew where Saul was, he'd kill him too.

Vince bent over the guard again and felt through his pockets until he found the ring of keys. Then he returned to the door. He kept listening carefully while he tried one key after another. The hallway was silent, but in his mind's ear he could hear, ludicrously, an old movie house piano playing "escape" music. It taunted him while he sweated over the lock.

Then the door opened. He was free. All he had to do was get down the stairs and out of the building. No one could stop him now. He gripped the pistol tightly.

The heels of his shoes were hard leather and they clattered on the metal steps. He had to slow down and hold onto the railing to ease himself down as noiselessly as possible. He put the pistol into his side pocket. It made a comforting bulge. Vince liked the pressure against his right leg.

Third floor. He stopped suddenly and his face went blank. Quickly he leaned over the railing and looked down. A gasp cut short his breathing.

There was an old woman coming up the steps carrying a scrub pail and mop, a bandanna wrapped around her grey head. Vince stepped back hurriedly. If he went through the third floor door and waited there the old woman might go in there, too, and see him. He might even run into somebody else. But if he stayed on the steps, she might go up another flight and see him anyway.

Kill her! He clutched down at the pistol.

Once more he caught himself. *Don't be a fool.* A shot would arouse everyone. Especially in this stair well, it would echo all over the building. His head moved around as he looked for escape. A rushing of notes hung in his head like the beginning of a wild cadenza. The steps came closer—weary, trudging steps on the metal stairs. He backed against the wall and almost screamed out in hate.

It had always been that way. His temper had come over him like this. There would be a particular phrase to practice and Vince would work it over on the keys again and again, but still it wouldn't come. And his temper. like steam building up in a boiler, would keep growing, and finally, in a great roar, it would break out in a scream of frustration and he would double his fists and drive them like pistons into the keys. He would smash down clusters of black and white keys, making an endless chain of dissonances that would ring out in the penthouse apartment. He'd keep hitting even though his hands were bruised on the edges of the ivory keys and started to ooze blood. And he'd keep doing it until Saul came rushing in, screaming louder than Vince. He liked to do that, upset Saul. And the only way he could do it was to place those hands of his in some peril. It was the only thing that mattered to Saul about Vince. About anything.

And when the screaming and the pounding were done and he sat there at the piano heaving with sobs and unable to talk, Saul would make him start in again and perfect that phrase. And he always did. "Master technician." That was what the critics had called him. "The virtuosity of a Horowitz…No heart discernible but virtually unsurpassed for technique."

All of this flooded through Vince's mind as he pressed his lips together to keep the scream from flooding out. He was trapped. It was the feeling he always got. The world was closing in on him and he must kick and scream to be free of it.

Instinct drove him back up the steps to cower in the shadowed landing, half-way to the fourth floor. Instinct pressed him against the cold wall and snuffed out his breath.

Vince watched the old scrub woman push through the third floor door. He watched the door swing slowly shut and thud into its frame. A smile relaxed his features. His hands lost their rigidity.

One more bow and then we'll get home to work on that Mozart phrase you desecrated this evening.

He moved down the stairs quickly, eagerly. In a half minute he was down to the first floor. He pushed open the door cautiously but the hallway was empty. Vince hurried down the length of it and reached the door. He pushed out through it and was on the street.

At first he wanted to stand there and stretch out his arms to the moon. The air was cool and delicious to the smell. He could have sung out in joy.

But there was no time; there was a thing to be done. Bob was still alive and, as long as he was, Ruth would be waiting to be freed. Vince started walking rapidly down the block alongside of the bleak grey building. He shivered a little in the cold morning air. How cool and clean it tasted after the smell of the ward with its unclean beds and the smell of many bodies crowded together.

Poor Ruth, Poor Ruth, Poor Ruth, his feet drummed on the sidewalk. He wondered if it was possible that Bob had drugged her. There had been that harmony teacher in Cincinnati, Vince remembered, who had kept his beautiful young wife under narcotics so she'd be faithful. His hands clenched together.

Ruth, Ruth! Her beautiful face twisted with pain, her lovely body profaned and—

He stopped thinking of that. He mustn't think of Ruth that way. She was purity and thoughts like that would spoil the memory of her. She was above *that.* So was he. They would live like brother and sister. They would!

Suddenly he realized he was standing still on the street, holding himself stiffly. He hurried on. The subway, the subway, where was it? He'd only ridden it twice in his whole life. Once with Ruth just to see what it was like. Then another time when he and Saul had been stuck down in the Village somehow with no one to take them back to the penthouse and no cabs available.

Vince remembered that night as he walked along toward the corner. Saul had asked directions about ten times. And still they'd gotten lost and ended up in Columbus Circle. What a fool Saul was.

The cold began to seep through his flannel shirt. Suddenly he stopped again. What a fool he'd been not to take a raincoat! Not only was it cold, but someone might recognize the grey flannel uniform of the maid. And the pistol bulged in his pants pocket.

He looked around and saw some darkened brownstone dwellings to his right. He looked into the lighted lobby and then he found himself jumping up the steps two at a time. He had to have a raincoat.

The vestibule door was locked. He looked at the names. *Martinez—3B, Johnson—3A.* They were no good. Vince skipped the

names on the second floor too. He pushed the button under
Maxim—1A.

He waited. There was no answer. They must be in bed, he
thought. He pushed the button again, more impatiently. He *had* to
have a raincoat. Still no answer. He began to wonder how he'd feel
after he pushed the button to Ruth's apartment. He wondered just
how he'd feel as he rode up the elevator with the pistol gripped
tightly in his hand. He wanted that time to come, wanted it desperately. He felt angry frustration that he'd have to wait so long before
it came.

The buzzer sounded. Vince started nervously, but forgot to push
against the door. He tensed violently and almost kicked in the thick
glass. Then the buzzer sounded again and he lurched against the
door and pushed through it.

He moved quickly as a door down the hall opened a trifle. He ran
to it and shoved his foot into the small opening.

"Open up," he said to the young woman who stood there.

She gasped and tried to close the door. His foot prevented her
from doing it. Vince reached for his pistol with an angry motion and
almost shoved the end of the barrel into her face.

"Do you want to die?" he asked in a hoarse whisper.

The girl's face went white, her lips trembled and she backed away
from the door. He pushed his way in. The girl was cowering back
against the wall.

"Don't," she said. "Don't do anything to me. Please don't."

She winced as he turned on the hall light. In the bright light Vince
could see that her hair was disarrayed and there were red scars on
her right cheek where she'd been resting on the pillow.

"Have you got a man's raincoat here?" he asked.

"What?"

"I want a man's raincoat," he snapped at her.

Then, without thought, he looked down over her pajama covered
body. His eyes moved back to her young breasts pressing against
the yellow silk. He pinched his lips together. *No!* snapped his mind
and, mocking, in the background came the voice of Saul, *My dear
boy, if the pressure is annoying, relieve yourself. You don't need a
woman for that.*

He felt a drop of sweat run into his mouth.

"Well?" he said angrily, forgetting for the moment what he was
asking her about.

"I live alone here," she said, "I—I haven't got a man's raincoat."

His hand twitched at his side. He wanted to hit her for foiling him. He couldn't go to another apartment. He was getting that trapped feeling again. He'd always been that way. If he wanted something and couldn't get it the first time, he started to feel frustrated. That's how he felt now. He couldn't go to all the apartments when he had to get to the subway and get downtown. A fresh idea came to torture him; what if the guard regained consciousness and got the police out looking for him? Sooner or later he'd wake up and tell them. His breath grew restless, his finger trembled on the trigger.

"Get in the bedroom," he heard himself say.

He followed her in, wondering why he wasn't leaving. If there was no raincoat here, what was the point in staying? He fought against the ugly pressure in his body. He didn't like it. No, he wasn't that kind; that was insane.

"Turn on the lights," he ordered.

She stood by the rumpled bed, looking at him and shivering a little.

"What are you going to do?" Her voice was thin and afraid.

He didn't answer. Instead he went to the closet door as if he knew what he was going to do. He flung open the door and reached in, trying to avoid the sight of her slender body. She's sort of pretty, the thought rose unbidden in his mind. Blonde hair like Ruth. I'd like to—

He dug his teeth into his lower lip and turned to face the closet completely, not even looking at her. He reached in and came out with a black trenchcoat. He tried it on and it fit pretty well, and the cut wasn't too feminine. He'd have to chance it.

"Have you a telephone?" he asked, still not able to understand how he managed to think of all these details when his mind was so obsessed by the one desire to kill Bob.

"No," she said.

He wouldn't have to cut any wires then, he told himself and nodded once. Still he stood there not knowing what to do, his mind filled with a dozen questions. Should he leave the girl? Wouldn't she call the police? Should he shoot her? Wouldn't the people in the house hear the shot? Vince started to tremble nervously at all the disturbing elements that his coming in here had brought on. That was the trouble with life, no matter what you did it just made everything more confusing. *Kill Bob*, that was what he had to concentrate on. *Get to the subway and kill Bob.*

His eyes re-focused on the girl who still stood there watching him. He shouldn't kill her. She hadn't done anything to him. She was a pretty girl and she didn't mean him any harm. Only an insane man killed everybody. He only wanted to kill certain people like Harry and Bob. Harry was dirty and fat, and Bob was torturing Ruth. But that was all. There was Saul, too, but Vince didn't know where Saul was.

But he didn't kill the guard, he'd only knocked him out. Didn't that prove he wasn't crazy? His face softened without him realizing and the expression he directed at the girl was one of supplication.

"Are you sick?" said the girl.

Her tone and the words she used broke the spell.

Vince's mouth tightened, his face lost all softness.

"I'll show you how sick I am," he said and pulled the trigger of the pistol.

There was a click. And suddenly, Vince felt cold sweat break out on his body. God, was he insane to make such a loud noise in this house? He gritted his teeth.

He had to save those bullets, too. He hadn't thought to look and see how many there were, but there could be no more than five. It was lucky that chamber was empty.

He saw that the girl was wavering as if she were going to faint.

"Get in bed," he told her.

She sank down weakly on the bed, her hands shaking in her lap.

"Get under the covers," he said.

"Wh-wh-why?"

"I said get in bed!"

As she lay back the top of her pajamas slipped up and he saw an expanse of white skin. His heart pounded violently and he lowered his head an instant to hide the swallowing.

Hastily the girl drew up the blankets. She lay there watching him with glazed, frightened eyes.

"Close your eyes." he said.

She put her head down on the pillow and closed her eyes. Then a sob broke in her throat and she opened them again. Her voice shook.

"Are you g-going to hurt...me?"

"Close your eyes."

He moved closer, enjoying the feeling of power it gave him to hold life and death in his palm. He thought of killing Bob. He thought of how grateful Ruth would be when Bob was dead, how she would throw her arms around his neck and kiss him and...

"I said close your eyes!" he yelled.

He looked down at her white face. Then, abruptly, he flung back the covers and stared down at her body. His hand moved down.

Get involved and you'll regret it, my fine young fool!

His hand jerked back. He threw the covers over her again and stood there looking down sullenly.

"I ought to kill you," he said. "You're not a clean girl. But I won't because I'm not as crazy as you think. Remember that if anyone asks you."

A breathless chuckle sounded in his throat.

"They'll ask you all right," he said as casually as he could.

Then he bent over and kissed her on the cheek. Her eyes rolled up and she quietly fainted. He didn't notice.

"Cheerio," he said and walked out of the bedroom and the apartment, feeling a pleasant sense of bravura. He hadn't killed the wretched young nothing. He'd just taken her raincoat as any hero might, leaving her with a kiss on the cheek. That was heroic, it was the sort of thing a girl would remember. She wouldn't tell anyone. She'd treasure this experience because it was romantic. No, he hadn't touched a hair on her head. That's because he wasn't insane. He'd just tried to kill his father, that was all. Anyone might try to kill his father.

⬛ ⬛ ⬛ ⬛

He stopped at the head of the subway steps and looked around.

There was no one following. As he had surmised, the girl hadn't screamed for help when he left. She was probably lying there and dreaming of the handsome man who had kissed her and stolen her raincoat. He smiled a smile of tragic acceptance and moved slowly down the steps.

Halfway down he stopped, the sense of poetry gone suddenly with the realization that he had no money. He stood there looking blankly down the steps. *This is absurd!* The words exploded in his mind.

His hand tightened on the gun butt. He wasn't going to let a ridiculous thing like this stop him. He walked down past the white tiled walls. He glanced at a seal balancing rye bread on its nose on one of the posters. *Gust of the bizarre.* That's what Saul would say. Vince wondered where he was, wondered if it were possible that someday they could get together again and get Vince back into concert work. Vince didn't like to admit it to himself sometimes, but he *did* miss the piano. He could tell himself that nothing mattered but Ruth, and the piano was unimportant. But why did his hands always move over the keys even though he hadn't been near one in…how long?

Oh, what difference did it make where Saul was? Their lives were parted forever. Ever since that day in the penthouse. Vince remembered the rain; he remembered Saul backing away from him. *For the love of God, are you mad? Vincent!*

It was the only time he could ever remember his father calling him by his name.

He pushed again. Then he looked down curiously and saw that he was shoving futilely against the wooden turnstile. Red flared up in his cheeks. Then he glanced hurriedly toward the change booth and saw that the man was looking at him.

Vince drew in his breath. The man started to open the door of the booth, and suddenly, Vince ducked down and darted underneath the turnstile. What if no train comes! He ran down the sloping floor, heart beating in fright.

"Hey, come back here, you!"

Vince reached the steps and jumped down them two at a time. The shouts of the man from the change booth echoed after him in the silent station.

"Come back here!"

Vince reached the platform and his eyes raced up and down the length of it. It was empty. He looked back up the steps to see if the man was following him. Then he leaned over the edge of the platform and looked out into the blackness to see if the train was coming. There was nothing. He looked up and saw that he was looking for the train that was going uptown. He moved for the other side of the platform, glancing at the stairs again.

"You ain't gettin' away, buddy!"

Vince gasped and his head twisted suddenly. He saw the man coming down the steps. He turned around and started running along the grey concrete. He heard the clatter of the man's shoes behind him. It was an older man with white hair, wearing a black coat sweater.

"You stop or I'll use this gun!" threatened the voice behind him.

Vince looked back over his shoulder and saw that the man held a small pistol. He started to whimper under his breath. The trapped feeling was coming over him again, starting from his stomach and spreading out with hot, twisting fingers.

"You want me to shoot you?"

Vince felt the gun banging against his leg as he ran.

He saw the wall ahead of him.

"Now, you're caught!" said the man.

Something filled Vince's brain with night, because he wasn't aware of what happened then. He didn't even feel himself jerk the gun from the raincoat pocket. He hardly heard the explosions that almost coincided, that of his pistol and that of the man's. He felt someone strike him on the arm and knock him off balance. That was all.

Then he was looking at the scene as if he'd never seen it before. The man was writhing on the subway platform, blood gushing out of a great hole in his chest. Vince stared at him and then, as the man tried to raise his pistol again, Vince fired another bullet into him. The gun jolted in his hand and the sound deafened him.

The man lay dead on the platform. Vince looked down, amazed at the smoke coming from the barrel of his gun. Almost repelled, he shoved the pistol into his pocket. He could feel himself shaking his head and murmuring something.

"I'm sorry," he said. "I *mean* it, I'm sorry."

Then the pain swept over him and he twitched violently. Looking down he saw blood running down the raincoat. He tried to lift his left arm and gasped at the fiery pain. His mouth fell open and a moan of fright filled his throat.

"No," he said. "No, no."

He looked incredulously at the man.

"He—he *shot* me," he said. He couldn't believe it. The man had shot him, he'd hurt him.

Then surprise and hurt flooded together into a hard hot lump of hate. He fumbled for his gun again. But his hand caught in the lining and he couldn't get it out. Forgetting for a moment, he tried again to move his left hand.

The pain almost made him faint. He felt warm blood dribbling down over his wrist and into his palm. He stumbled around on the platform, waves of darkness lapping at his feet.

"No, no, no" he sobbed, "I don't want to."

He started sharply as a screeching whistle came from the black tunnel. The station grew more clear to his gaze. He found himself looking down at the dead man in horror. What if someone saw him? They would stop him!

"No!"

Without thinking, he grabbed the limp right hand of the man and dragged him along the platform leaving a trail of blood behind. His own left hand hung uselessly at his side. In a moment he'd dragged the body behind a refuse box. Then he hurried out and ran to the edge of the platform. He looked down and saw two white lights approaching and heard the far-off roar of the train. He shook his head to clear the mists from his eyes.

He looked down at his left hand. What if someone saw the blood dripping from the end of it? With his right hand, he hurriedly put the left into the raincoat pocket, gritting his teeth, his face white.

Then he stood there waiting nervously, his stomach throbbing spasmodically. What if they saw the man? What if they stopped him from getting to Bob? What if they saw his arm? He wanted to scream. What if he had no bullets left? What if the girl had called the police? What if the guard had regained consciousness? What if he bled to death?

He stood there shaking and whimpering in terror as the train moved past him, filling his nostrils with hot rushing air. It slowed down and the lights played on his white features.

The train stopped and he saw, with a shock, that there were several people in the train. What if they...?

He closed his eyes tight for a moment and tried to make his mind a blank. He heard the door open and he looked straight ahead as he moved into the fluorescent illuminated car.

He lurched back into the hard straw seat as the train started and couldn't stop the short cry of pain. His eyes moved nervously over the people. A man sitting across the aisle was looking at him. Vince lowered his head. He bit his lips to keep them from trembling.

He couldn't keep his eyes down. He had to know if anyone were looking at him. He glanced up cautiously. No one was paying attention. He took a deep, faltering breath. Then he leaned back and relaxed.

Maybe things weren't so bad after all. He had the raincoat and he was still on his way to kill Bob. If only—he closed his eyes and felt sweat break out on his forehead—if only the man hadn't shot him. The fool! What right had he to shoot him—all for a miserable ten cents. He kept his eyes closed and the motion of the train began to make him sick. Pain fled about his body, first localizing in his stomach, then in his head, but always coming back sharply into his arm.

The train slowed down and stopped at the next station. Vince felt the blood collecting in his palm. If it didn't stop it would start to drip on the floor of the train. No, it mustn't. He had to get to 18th Street first. He looked out of the window. They were in the 80's. He closed his eyes again.

The doors closed and the train started. Vince drew in a ragged breath of the stale air. He opened his eyes and saw that a young Negro couple had come into the train. He looked blankly at them, sitting on the other side of the train and down a little ways. They weren't talking to each other. Vince's eyes moved to the girl's sweater she wore underneath a sport jacket. He swallowed and closed his eyes again.

A rattling sound filled his throat and he shivered violently. *It hurts!* Suddenly he thought of his playing. Would his left hand be ruined?

What's the difference? he told himself. *I've only got one thing to do that matters and that's to free Ruth.*

He started to remember about her. He remembered the party at Stan's where he'd met her. He remembered how they'd sat on a couch all evening and talked about music. She'd been so lovely and clean with her red knit dress and her shiny blonde hair with the ribbon in it. He had loved her from the start. Then later they had gone into the study and he had played for her. Then—he tightened at the remembrance—Jane had come in and spoiled it all, dragged them back into the noise and the smoke.

Clean, clean, clean. The wheels seemed to say the word as the train rushed through the black tunnel. Not like *her*. He closed his eyes. It was better she died when she did. If the car hadn't gone over the embankment someone would have killed her sooner or later, the way she carried on.

Your mother was a bitch, pure and simple.

He stared at the floor dizzily. The noise of the train wavered in his ears and he had to keep blinking to keep the view before him from blurring. He swallowed. The air seemed hard to breathe.

His eyes fled across the train. He saw the Negro girl looking down at the floor beside him with a look of revulsion on her face. Quickly he looked down.

A small pool of blood was collecting near his left foot. He almost cried out.

He looked up and gasped as a man got up and started over. Vince shoved up and backed against the door. He drove his right hand into his pocket and gripped the gun. The man stopped and looked at him curiously, then his eyes moved down to the bulge in the coat and he backed away nervously. He bumped into the seat he had just vacated and fell down awkwardly.

Time seemed to stand still. Vince thought he'd scream. The train went on and on, and all the people kept staring at him. He wanted to kick his way through the door. He didn't care if he was flung into the blackness, but he couldn't stand to have all these people looking at him.

The train started to slow down. A station, he'd have to get off here. He had to have help. His teeth chattered and he felt a chill run through him. The train stopped and he almost fell out as the door slid open. He bumped into a young couple.

"Say, watch it, Mac," said the young man irritably.

Vince shoved past them with a sob. The young man said something he didn't hear and then the door closed. Vince staggered across the platform and was afraid he was going to fall. He heard the train start and saw that no one had followed him out of the car, although several of them were glued to the window looking at him with wide-eyed curiosity.

"Pigs!" he screamed, and was drowned out by the train.

He staggered further and collided with the tile wall. He leaned against it gasping for breath.

Then he saw a sign that read *Men,* and he pushed away from the wall and made his way to the doorway. He tried to push through the door. It was locked. He stood there staring at it. But he had to have some water! He started to cry and leaned his head against the cold metal while the tears ran down his cheeks.

After a while, he drew his sleeve across his face and started walking along the station, ignoring the way the walls wavered before his eyes. *I'm going to kill him,* he kept telling himself. *I'm going to kill him.*

Stan.

2:30 AM

In dark stillness, she lay starkly awake, her eyes fixed on the ceiling. Under the black silk of her nightgown her firm breasts rose and fell and her long white fingers drew in and out at her sides like the delicately pumping claws of a cat. Her red nails made a rasping, scratching sound on the sheet. Her mouth was a stark red line that did not move. Jane was twenty-five and her body lay like a taut spring, waiting for something.

Across the space between the two beds Stan groaned and rolled onto his side, complaining in his sleep. She listened to him rustling on the sheet of his bed, heard the weak thud as he hit his pillow once. Then he cleared his throat and was silent again. She did not look toward him; her eyes remained fastened on the dark ceiling.

He was probably sick again. He was always sick after a party. He drank too much and ate too much and made himself sick. Most men, when they drank too much, didn't eat at all. They filled their bodies with alcohol but took in no food to offset the breakdown of tissues. That's why drunkards died usually, she thought. That's why my dear old daddy died and left me the world he could never handle.

Her still painted lips pressed together now. She felt as if she had to have something fragile in her hands, something she could crush between her straining fingers.

For a minute she closed her eyes and tried to sleep. She remembered how easy it used to be to sleep. Just a delicious exhaustion filling your body, just a closing of eyes and there you were. Now...

How could you sleep when your mind was like one of those toffee machines you see on amusement piers with those long arms turning and twisting, turning and twisting? Her brain was the toffee. She could almost visualize the metal arms twisting the great grey lengths of her mind. Desire twisted and folded over, frustration twisted and folded over. A deep sighing breath filled her lungs. Abruptly, she turned on her stomach and pressed her body into the bed. Her teeth gritted together and the column of her throat felt as if it were petrifying. God, to have Mickey Gordon in bed with her. Right now, here, even with Stan over there, what did she care? Or Johnny Thompson. Or Bill Fraser. Or Bob McCall, yes, that she'd like. Even if Ruth was her best friend. What was a friend for anyway?

Her white hands closed into tight fists. Her nails dug into her palms and she thought she was going to scream. Anyone! Even that gaunt and crazy Vince. Yes, maybe especially that gaunt and crazy Vince. That was what happened when you became a jaded connoisseur of the flesh, a jaundiced gourmet of love's old song—no longer sweet but in need of new spices. You tired of the plain fares, you wearied of the common menu. You craved something exotic, something new. And, in consequence, you positively threw up at the thought of your husband—at best, a tasteless mush.

She dug her nails into the sheets now and writhed her hot body on the bed until the gown had worked its way past her hips. *God, I'm going crazy,* she thought. *I'll end up like Vince. One night I'll get up quite calm and secure in my maniac shell and drive something sharp and final into the worthless corpulence I married.*

A rising, whining sound filled her throat. *No, stop that,* she demanded of herself. That sort of thing made Stan raise upon an elbow and whisper into the darkness his hateful, nauseous concern.

She had always thought of Stan in terms of an old nursery rhyme. Compendium of snails and puppy-dog tails—that was Stan, Mr. Sheldon. Snails for sluggishness of mind and movement. And puppy-dog tails—those flapping, flopping, rug-thumping indications of utter devotion, of adolescent, stomach-turning love. That was Stan too.

God, can't I stop thinking about him! her mind screamed. Oh, give me the empty, useless solace of a man's body here and now and let me forget the torture of mind.

In a minute she got up and went slowly into the living room. She felt her way among the glasses and plates strewn on the floor, feeling an occasional wet patch where some unstable reveler had dropped or spilled or kicked over his glass of whiskey and soda, or gin and soda, or vodka and soda or anything and soda. Ploppo, into the carpet. After the parties they'd had here, it was a wonder there was any carpet left at all.

She turned on the small lamp on the table beside the couch. She blinked and closed her eyes for a moment, then sank down on the couch and looked around the room.

She saw the end result of social tornado. Here in this penthouse, decorated by whosis of Fifth Avenue, furnished by what's-his-name and draped by the best non-entities in town—here, in this upholstered sewer, gaiety had reigned. People mixed drinks and company, told lewd jokes, crept searching fingers over the other men's wives and other wives' husbands. Flung the mud of their minds against the walls. Stolen into darkened bedrooms for quick sensation. Let the gyroscopes of their minds be swallowed under tides of liquor. Stumbled and laughed and threw up and screamed vile laughter and let the mask fall for an instant from the face of the beast. Showed the fangs and the hatreds and the endless lusts.

Jane reached over and picked up somebody's drink. I hope it was a man's drink, she thought and placed the glass to her lips. *Cheap kiss,* she thought, kissing a glass. As the warmish, watery liquor trickled down her throat the ultimate thought came—*the party is over.*

Oh God, come and take me, someone!

She wanted to scream it out in the silence of the apartment. She wanted to rip the flimsy gown off her body and give the sweetmeats of her flesh to any and all comers. Step up, line forms on the right. Jane Sheldon, wife of Stan Sheldon, has the pleasure of announcing her availability to all and sundry. Come one, come all.

She slumped down on the couch, shivering without control. Her hungry eyes ran down over her lean body, over the two hard points of her breasts, the flat stomach, the long perfectly shaped legs. She ran one hand over her stomach and it made her shudder. She finished the drink and sat staring into the empty glass, watching the tiny amber bubble on the bottom slide back and forth as she tilted the glass from side to side; slipping and gliding like a fat pig on a frozen lake.

Kill me, someone.

The thought crept into her mind, looked around, saw no resistance and took over.

He had lain there and watched her rise. He had seen her standing in the living room in her nightgown, the dark outline of her body showing against the lamp's glow.

Now he lay there in the dark bedroom staring at her as she sat slumped on the couch. He watched her run a hand over her smooth stomach and something twisted in his guts. It had been so long, so horribly long. She never let him touch her anymore. They were married, but she never let him touch her.

She hardly even let him see her. Once in a while, maybe, if she thought he was still asleep in the morning, she would let the nightgown drop rustling off her satiny body and, while she hooked and pulled and fastened and zipped, through half-closed lids he would drink in the sight of her breasts arching out from her chest, the flat smoothness of her stomach and buttocks, the curve of her legs. His own wife made him feel like a Peeping Tom, like some sub-species of voyeur.

His throat moved. Why didn't he go in there and just demand his rights? Why didn't he take her in his arms and conquer her resistance? The situation struck him in all its insulting absurdity.

Anyone else could have her but he couldn't.

He moved on the mattress and suddenly he froze, seeing that she was looking in at him. He lay there shivering while her eyes looked into the dark bedroom. He didn't think she saw him because she didn't say anything and, in a moment, she turned her head away. But for that moment, he had seen, in her eyes, how much she despised him. It had been no novelty. He saw it all day, too. But there was something faintly hideous about seeing it on her face when she didn't even think he was looking. It showed how ingrained her hatred was, how burned into her mind.

He lay there on his side looking with bleak, unhappy eyes at his wife sitting on the couch. He saw her finish the drink she'd picked up. Now she was staring into the glass, tilting it from side to side. What did she see in the glass? What was she thinking? Once he thought he had glimmers of her mind. Now she was more a stranger with each passing day. Once he could almost say they were in love. Now all he could say was that he paid the bills for the things she bought. And there were plenty of things.

A shudder made his muscles jerk abruptly and he closed his eyes to shut away the sight of her. No, he couldn't go in there and demand her body as if it were some patronage. He couldn't even talk to her.

Like some silly robot he would host her parties, pouring drinks, laughing at bad jokes, trying to ignore the sight of her on the couch or on a chair with some man, her open mouth writhing under his, her fingers raking across the man's back, that obvious dark flush filling her cheeks. Trying to ignore the moments when she would disappear and be gone from the living room. Then he knew that in the darkness of the bedroom, maybe on his own bed...

And he was a jellyfish. He could no more have gone in the bedroom when she was there with some man and confront them than he could have broken into the bedroom of the White House and demanded, *What the hell are you doing, Mr. President!*

He would go on pouring drinks and laughing at bad jokes and, maybe, if the pain in his flesh and mind got too unbearable he would make a faltering pass at some woman that no one else would make a pass at.

He started quickly to his elbow as Jane stood up and moved for the balcony.

He pulled back the covers, his heart thudding with fear. Everything was forgotten in an instant; his hate, his frustration, his despair. He was, once again, the simple, uncomplicated man who could do nothing but adore. Quickly he ran across the living room rug, his heavy body rocking from side to side, feet thumping on the rug. "Please don't, Jane. Darling, please don't. I'll make it up to you. I'll try to be what you..."

Jane turned from the railing and looked at him coldly.

"What do you want?" she asked, her voice flat.

The way she said "you." It was a knife turning in him.

"I—I thought maybe...."

"Thought maybe I was going to jump?" she asked acidly.

"No," he said. "I mean, I just thought..."

She didn't say anything and they stood there looking at each other in silence in the early morning. She stood there on the terrace flagstones like Venus in Manhattan, like a debauched Aphrodite in a sheer Tiffany creation.

"Don't you—think you should come in?" he said falteringly, "It's a little cold for just that."

"Just what?"

"I—I—that gown. I mean it's awfully thin."

Her eyes on him were like blue ice.

"You'll catch your death of cold," he offered.

"That would be wonderful," she said in a deceptive calm.

But, after a moment, she came in and went to the bar to make herself a drink.

He closed the French doors and stood there awkwardly, watching her make a drink that was nine-tenths whiskey. He swallowed and then straightened out the wrinkled twists of his pajamas. They were silly looking pajamas. He knew that. He often thought she bought them for him because she knew he would look ridiculous in them, with their little pink elephants sporting on the cloth.

"Place looks a mess," he said.

She didn't answer. She kept pouring whiskey.

"Guess I'd better have the woman in Monday instead of Tuesday," he said.

She finished pouring her drink.

"How about another?" he said.

"Another what?" she said and sat down. Her nightgown slipped up over her knees and his throat moved. She looked up at him and pulled the gown up further, pleased at the mottled color it brought.

"You look like a cow in heat," she said idly.

"Maybe I'll have one too," he said, trying to ignore her remark.

"One what?" she asked.

She always asked questions like that. He knew very well she was aware of what he was talking about. But unless he named his object in so many words, unless he used the noun, she would impale him on a question he felt obliged to answer.

"I'll have a drink," he said in a surly voice.

"Sure, why not?" she said. "Drink up, dear one."

He didn't know how to take that sort of remark either. He rarely knew how to take her remarks. They always had the earmarks of a trap he might fall into. It made him nervous analyzing each of her remarks before he answered them. But he had to or else he wouldn't know what to say. And, anyway, he invariably stumbled and said the wrong thing and, suddenly, her scorn, or her mocking laughter, would surround him. Or, worse, her raw, nerve-taut fury would lash out at him and make him afraid. That was it. He was afraid of her.

He poured a little whiskey into a glass and squirted a lot of soda in after it. He knew he shouldn't have any. But he didn't want to go back to bed and he had to have some excuse to stay with her. That was the situation too. He had to have an excuse to stay with his own wife. As he made the drink he looked at his watch. It was nearly three o'clock.

He sat down in a chair across from her.

"Couldn't you sleep either?" he asked, trying to be amiable.

"Sure," she said. "Sure, I could sleep. I'm in there now. I'm sound asleep. This is my astral projection drinking whiskey on a Sunday morning. Astral projection of Jane Sheldon drinking whiskey. Corpus slumberi of Jane Sheldon asleep in bed, dead to sorry old world."

And what did you answer to such a remark? He insulted himself by smiling a little at her, sheepishly. He retained the smile but the muscles of his stomach knew, and they tied a knot that made him grunt and bend over in pain. A little of his drink spilled over the edge of the glass.

"Oh, for Christ's sake, go to bed," Jane snapped. "Don't subject me to your goddamn attacks!"

He straightened up and tried to blink away the tears of pain that shimmered in his eyes.

"It's nothing," he said.

She turned away with a rustle on the chair, and she stared into the dark kitchen. There, too, she thought, was the result of this so glorious party: the uneaten sandwiches, the drinks all watery with melted ice cubes, the glasses and dishes broken, the crumpled napkins smudgy with lipstick wiped from many a guilty visage.

A hardly audible chuckle sounded in her throat, a brief light of amusement took away the haggard dullness in her eyes. It never failed to amuse, if only for seconds—this spectacle of passion unleashed, snuffing about like a freed puppy, seeking out the hydrants of excitement. These parties designed and executed for the sole purpose of escape.

"What's funny?" he asked, half faithful in reaction to her smile, half afraid that she was laughing at him.

Her eyes turned to him slowly, the light gone, the flat dispassion back.

"You're funny," she said.

And how did you answer that? His throat moved. His face, for one unguarded moment, flinted and was the face of a man. But there was no mind of a man behind the mask and the old will-less convolutions returned to his face.

"Why?" he asked. "Why am I funny?"

She just looked at him.

"Nothing," she said. "Forget it. Ignore it. Cancel it."

"No, I want to know." He knew very well he was punishing himself now.

"Will you go to bed?" Jane said. "Go to bed before I insult you some more."

"Seems to me you have always insulted me," he said, surprised at his own mild courage.

She looked at him over the edge of her drink and he watched her thin throat move while she swallowed the drink. Those eyes, those cold blue eyes; detached, always inspecting.

"You ain't heard nothin' yet," she slurred. "Go to bed, will you?"

"I—"

"For Christ's sake, will you go to bed!"

There was almost an anguish in her voice; as if, in spite of her despising him, she wanted to reach out for comfort. He half started to his feet, his face lined with concern for her.

But when she saw him coming toward her, she almost recoiled into the cushion of the chair.

"Don't come near me," she said, her voice thick with loathing.

His brow furrowed with lack of understanding. He stood in the middle of the room looking at her with blank eyes.

Her voice was almost hysterical. "I swear to God I'll jump off the balcony if you don't get out of here."

He stiffened momentarily.

"Now see here, Jane."

"What are you," she asked, "a whipping post? Don't you ever know when to quit?"

"Jane, I..."

"Is it possible, is it at all possible that I can make you quit?" she said, her voice a throaty insult. "Is there anything in the world I can say to make you bristle? Is there *one* insult in the whole world that will make you fight?"

"Honey, why don't you take a sedative and—"

"A sedative!"

A breathless gasp of laughter tore back her lips.

"Dear Christ, a sedative he wants me to take!" Her head shook quickly. "No, no, I'll bet there isn't. I'll bet there isn't a single insult in the world that would make you angry. I bet I could insult your whole family down to the last person and I could call you everything in the book and it wouldn't make any difference at all."

"Jane..."

"Oh—*Jesus*, will you shut up! You fool, you dolt, you ignoramus. You jerk, you—you *fat slob!*"

He recoiled under her words.

"There!" she snapped triumphantly. "Maybe I *can* get you to fight. You pig, you revolting mass of..."

The urge left as quickly as it had come. She sank back and the fire went out of her eyes. In an instant she had fallen into complete depression again. She reached out the glass to put it on the table beside the chair, but she didn't make it and the glass went thumping to the floor. She sat there twisting on the chair.

Stan had put his drink down on the table by the couch. He was still shaking from her words, his body throbbing with the pain of them. Without a word he stumbled past her chair and into the darkened bedroom. He sank down on his bed and his head dropped forward until his chin rested on his chest. He sat looking into the living room as Jane moved into sight and lay down on the couch. She had the bottle of whiskey with her and she took a drink from it. She was going to get drunk, he knew. She was going to drive herself into a cloud of forgetfulness.

He fell back on the pillow and lay there in the silence, his eyes closed, listening to the sound of his own breathing, heavy and wheezing in the darkness. He fell into a troubled half-sleep.

He wasn't sure whether it was a dream or not. But it seemed as if he heard the doorbell ringing. The buzzing sound seemed to penetrate the thick layers of darkness. He stirred slightly on the mattress, his mouth twitching a little.

Then the cry of fright jerked him up to a sitting position, his eyes wide and staring, his heart jolting against his chest wall.

"What in God's—" he started to mutter, not even conscious of speaking.

Quickly, trembling, he dropped his legs over the edge of the bed and stood up.

"I said lock the door!" he heard someone command in the front hall.

That voice. It drove like a lance into his mind and made him shudder.

Vince.

Quickly he moved into the living room, hearing Jane say something inaudible, then Vince again.

"I'll shoot you if you don't! You think I care if I shoot you?"

With a gasp, Stan backed into the bedroom. The phone, quickly, the phone! He backed across the dark room, eyes fastened on the living room. He bumped into Jane's bed and fell onto it with a start. Hurriedly, he pushed up and moved for the phone on the bedside table. He jerked up the receiver and reached for the dial.

"Where's Stan?" Vince asked, entering the living room.

Stan's heart jolted and, with shaking fingers, he quickly put down the receiver. If Vince had a gun he mustn't be found calling for help. He knew what Vince was like. *God in heaven*, he thought, *how did he get out?*

Quickly he sank down on his bed and threw up his legs. *I'll pretend that I'm asleep*, his mind planned. *Maybe Vince won't do anything then. Maybe I'll get a chance to call the police.*

"I told you he was asleep," Jane said.

Stan's legs twitched on the sheet. Maybe it was his imagination but she didn't sound afraid. She had cried out, yes, but now there was almost that sound of disinterest in her voice again.

He kept his eyes tightly shut. There was a murmur in the living room, then Vince snarling.

"You fix it or I'll *kill* you!"

"All right, all right," she said quickly.

Stan twitched as the bedroom light was flicked on. He opened his eyes and started violently. It had been a long time since he'd seen Vince. He wasn't prepared for the gaunt wildness of his face, the madness glittering in his dark eyes.

"Vince," he said automatically. "What are you—"

"Get up," said Vince. "My arm is hurt."

Stan sat up and let his legs hang over the edge of the mattress. He saw that Vince kept his left arm stuck in the pocket of a black raincoat and he saw the strange, dark wetness of the sleeve.

Stan stood up quickly, looking at Vince, not knowing what to say or do. He saw Jane walk into the bathroom and heard her turn on the light. Then he heard her rummaging around in the medicine cabinet as his eyes moved back to Vince.

He twitched at Vince's sudden words.

"Hurry up!" There was a break in Vince's voice. He stood there weaving a little, his eyes glazed with pain and fright.

"Sit down, Vince," Stan said nervously. "Why don't—"

His voice broke off and he stood silent as Vince's eyes jerked over and peered at him. He saw Vince's teeth grit together.

"I can stand," Vince said, tensely. "Don't think I can't, either."

Stan swallowed. "Sure," he said, "sure you can stand, Vince. If you want to." He felt a tightening in his throat. He couldn't be sure how to talk to Vince. He never *had* been.

They stood looking at each other and, abruptly, a nervous, rasping laugh hovered in Vince's throat.

"Broke out," he said. "Guess you never thought I'd—"

He stopped and pressed his white lips together, then drew in a shaking breath.

"Hurry up!" he yelled at Jane. "I swear to God I'll shoot you if you don't!"

"I can't find any gauze," Jane answered quickly.

"In back, in back," Stan said.

He turned back to Vince again and stood there awkwardly looking at him. There was no sound but that of Jane in the bathroom. Stan's hands twitched at his sides. He put them behind his body and they bumped into the bedside table.

At the feel of the smooth wood, he remembered the gun in the drawer. He forced his lips together suddenly because he felt them begin to tremble. He mustn't act nervous. If he could only pull open the drawer and...

"H-how are you, Vince?" he asked in a hollow voice. Vince didn't answer right away. His thin throat moved convulsively as he swallowed. The heavy pistol in his hand slowly began to lower.

"She'll b-be right out," Stan said hurriedly, "She's getting it, isn't she?" His throat moved quickly. Behind him his fingers trembled on the knob of the drawer. Could he grab the pistol in time, could he fire before Vince? Questions muddled through his mind and made his hands shake more. His fingers twitched away from the knob as Vince looked at him.

Then Jane came into the bedroom carrying a box of gauze, a roll of tape and a bottle of iodine.

"This isn't going to do much good," she said, "not for—"

"Never mind that," Vince said, voice shaking. "Bandage my arm. And don't try anything funny or I'll shoot you."

Stan watched the big black pistol waver with Vince's nervous movements. Now Jane was between him and Vince. Stan's hands moved back again and touched the drawer knob. *I can't fire if she's in the way.* And, once again his hands jerked away from the drawer.

"You'll have to take off your raincoat," Jane told Vince.

Stan shuddered at the realization that Jane wasn't afraid. At least she didn't sound afraid. He couldn't understand that. Was she so tired of living that death no longer held any menace for her? He felt sweat break out on his forehead. He had to get the gun. What if she did something foolish? If anything happened to her it would be the end of him, too. No matter what troubles they had, she was life to him. His fingers felt back again and touched the knob.

Vince was backing away from her. His dark hair had slipped across his forehead and some of the ebony hairs had been plastered to the skin by sweat. His eyes had a wild, frenzied glow.

"Don't come close to me," he warned Jane.

"How can I bandage you if I don't come close?" Jane said.

Don't talk to him like that! Stan's mind felt the stabbing of anguished fear. He tugged with a spasmodic finger contraction and one drawer edge angled out. He heard Vince say, "I mean—while I take off my coat." He heard the anger in Vince's voice and knew that Vince was hating her for her logic.

Now Jane had stepped back and there was a clear line between him and Vince. Stan shuddered once and tried to pull out the drawer further. It was stuck.

They stood watching Vince as he put the gun on top of the bureau. *Now, now!* Stan tugged harder.

The drawer squeaked.

Vince tensed and his hand half reached for his pistol.

"What are you doing?" he asked Stan, his dark eyes suspicious.

Stan shook his head in fright. "Nothing, nothing," he said. "I just bumped into the table. I'm—still half asleep."

"Don't try anything funny," Vince said grimly, "because I can get my gun in a second if you do try anything."

It angered Vince that Jane didn't show any fright. He liked it when that other girl had been paralyzed with fear. It had given him a warm feeling of power.

Well, he'd fix Jane soon enough too. She was going to die. As he thought that, he did not let himself notice the curves of her young body pushing against sheer silk.

Eyes moving from Stan to Jane, quickly, he pulled his right arm out of the raincoat. As he did the left arm tugged a little and he couldn't stop a gasp of pain from passing his lips. Jane started forward impulsively at the sound and Vince clawed at the pistol and jerked it up.

"The next chamber has a bullet for you," he said hurriedly.

Jane stepped back, feeling as if all the warmth in her body had drained suddenly into the floor. Her arms and legs felt numbed with cold as she stood there, whitefaced, staring at Vince in paralyzed silence. She'd never been that close to death. It was one thing to drunkenly contemplate it. It was another to have someone suddenly point a big black pistol at you.

Vince waved her back with the gun and set it down, again.

Stan had started forward, his heart pounding. Now, as he stood motionless by the bed, watching Vince try to take the coat off his left arm, he was amazed to realize that, for a moment there, he had been unafraid. Without a gun, without a knife, without anything, he was going to attack Vince. Because the gun was pointed at Jane, at his wife.

It was incredible that, after all she'd done to him, he was still instantly prepared to lay down his life for her.

But the sudden loss of fright had passed too. He was back against the table, not sure whether he should try to get the pistol or not. The sudden emergence of fear that followed blind courage left him trembling.

The arm was badly hurt. Vince tried but he couldn't stop the whimpering entirely. His body shook terribly as he drew the raincoat down off his shoulder. The sleeve was sticking to his arm around the wound.

He had to put down the pistol again.

"I swear to God," he said, "don't try anything or I'll shoot you both. I've already..."

No, he mustn't tell them about Harry.

"We—" Jane started to say something but couldn't finish. She stood there shivering.

The pistol was on the bureau again. Stan felt his body edging back involuntarily. *Stop, stop,* he muttered in his brain. *The drawer*

will stick, I'll drop the pistol, the pistol will jam, Vince will fire first...
He could think of a million arguments against trying to open the
table drawer and grabbing the pistol.

Vince had clenched his teeth to stop off any cries that might come
pulsing up from his throat. Like a rigid stalk of nerves he stood
there struggling with the coat.

It wouldn't come loose. Blood had glued it to his arm. He stood
there helplessly, watching them as he struggled. Every time he tried
to pull the dark raincoat loose, the movement sent a barb of pain up
his arm and into his body, making him shudder. He felt the sobs
working up through his chest. Trapped—he was trapped again. No
matter what he did he couldn't get his arm loose. Blood dribbled
down across his wrist.

His eyes jerked up at them suddenly, his lips trembling.

"Help me!" he yelled furiously. "It *hurts!*"

They didn't move. "You said you'd shoot us," Jane said, "if we
came close to..."

Vince didn't like that. He didn't like that at all. Not to be con-
founded and presented with the flaws in his own reason.

"I said you'd help me," he muttered in a gasping voice. "If you
don't, I swear I'll—"

A groan flooded from his throat. He pulled up the pistol again. It
seemed to be getting heavier. *I'm weakening!* The thought sent a
bolt of panic through him. No, he had to keep his strength! He had
to get to Bob's apartment! He had to save Ruth.

"Come here, damn it," he told Jane in a low voice.

Jane started slowly toward him, eyes never leaving the pistol.

"Don't shoot," she said. She hated herself for begging. But she
was afraid; she didn't want to get killed.

"I'm not going to hurt you," Vince said huskily. "Not if you do
what I say."

Stan stood trembling by the bed watching his wife approach
Vince. She shouldn't go near him. What if he loses hold and shoots
her? Vince was capable of violence. Stan knew what violence Vince
was capable of. He'd seen it often. And so he reached back for the
drawer again. He began working it out minutely, eyes fixed on
Vince.

Jane stood before Vince, her eyes pale, reflecting no emotion.

"Take my coat off," he told her, "and don't try anything."

"I'm not going to try anything," she said, unable to keep the coldness from her voice because it had become the way she spoke to men.

Oh God! Stan thought, *don't talk to Vince like you talk to me!*

His fingers fumbled at the drawer. He had to save her, he had to. Now there was a space of about three-quarters of an inch. He felt his fingers sliding in. He straightened up as Vince looked over. I mustn't bend over so much. He tried to stare back at Vince. But Vince wasn't interested then. Vince's eyes were clouded with pain.

"It's going to hurt," Jane said in a flat, toneless voice. "Don't point the gun at me or it'll go off when I pull off your sleeve."

"Don't tell me what to do!"

Stan jerked spasmodically at the drawer but it still stuck.

After a moment, Vince lowered the point of the pistol. "Don't think I can't pull it up quick," he threatened.

"I don't think anything," Jane said and put her numbed fingers on the sleeve. She wondered why she didn't faint.

Stan watched with fear-stricken eyes as Jane started pulling at Vince's sleeve.

Vince started to shudder without control as the white-hot spears of pain jabbed at his arm and shoulder. He cut off one whine but a second came before he could control it. He forgot the sight of Jane's body so close to him. Everything was lost in the overwhelming pain. The room seemed to swell and contract in lurches of dark and light. *What if I black out!* his mind cried out in fear.

You'll practice 'til you collapse if need be!

He jerked away to escape and the coat came off. His mouth opened in a choking gasp of agony and he fell against the wall, his frail chest heaving. He felt a trickling of warm blood down his arm.

Jane had backed away and was looking at Vince, the black raincoat in her shaking hands. "You—you'd better go in and sit down," she heard herself say.

"Don't tell me—what to—do," he gasped.

He looked at Stan and saw Stan straighten up abruptly, a look of nervous fright on his face.

He grabbed at his pistol. "What are you trying to do?" he shouted furiously.

Stan shook his head quickly. "Nothing, nothing."

"Get in the other room!" Vince ordered furiously, *"Now!"*

Rigid with anguished frustration Stan moved away from the table.

Vince stood against the wall as the two of them moved past and entered the living room. He blinked his eyes and shook away the sweat dripping into them. He wanted to scream out in fury because the world was conspiring against him. No matter what he did, he was just driven further from his revenge. Damn it, why hadn't he killed Bob that day in the agency?

Before going into the living room he glanced over at the table where Stan had been. He didn't notice the slightly open drawer. His teeth gritted and he edged into the living room.

He started for the couch. "Come over here and fix my arm," he said, his voice hoarse and shaking. "Hurry up or I'll..."

He didn't finish. A cloud of blackness seemed to rush up from the floor like a great dark bird. He stumbled back with a gasp of fright and almost lost consciousness.

Then his calves bumped into the couch edge and he fell onto it. The flaring pain in his left arm drove knives of consciousness into his brain. He saw them both looking at him.

"Don't try anything!" he cried shrilly. "I swear to—!"

No!

But he couldn't stop it. He sat there with the tears rushing down his cheeks and his thin chest shaking with sobs. Through the quivering prisms of his tears he saw them standing there, watching him.

I'd never reach him in time, Stan was thinking. *He'd shoot me before I could reach him. There's no chance.*

Jane stood staring at Vince. Only slowly was the shock departing, the sudden driving bolt of it that struck when Vince had pointed the gun at her. But now the gun was not pointing at her. And Vince's face was the twisted, frightened face of a boy. She felt sick.

What a terrible product Vince's father had put forth into the world. What a hideous testament to his distorted ambition: to produce the mirror of himself.

She found herself remembering Saul Raden as he had been the night of Vince's debut in Carnegie Hall.

She remembered the almost hysterical ebullience of the man—the father reflecting the glory of his son. No more than that—the father taking the credit for the glory of his son. A modern Svengali—that's what Saul Raden had been that night—gaunt and fever-charged, forgetting the past in a distended present. Repressing the knowledge that his own hands were useless twists of bone and meat that could no longer produce the surging glory of a Beethoven sonata or the polished effulgence of a Chopin waltz. Forgetting the auto accident that had caught him in the middle of his rising concert career, killed his bride and snapped the bones of his future like toothpicks, driving a wedge of madness into his brain.

She remembered that as she watched the son of Saul Raden sobbing on her couch, broken and mad. And she remembered the night she had tried to get Vince in bed with her.

Once again she was in the bedroom of Saul Raden's penthouse apartment, holding Vince's lean, hungry body against hers, both of them half-clothed, her naked breasts pressing into him, the dark room swept with hot winds of forgetfulness.

Then the light had flared, blinding them. Saul Raden stood in the doorway, a supercilious twist on his lips, not the shadow of an emotion on his face. Vince started up with a gasp, his face mottled with shame. And Saul's voice fell over them like a spray of splintered ice.

"Dear boy, do go to the bathroom and wash off your face. You look positively bizarre."

She remembered the fury in her, the snapping of control. She remembered shattering the whiskey bottle over the edge of the table and lunging at Vince—knowing, even in her madness, that the only way to hurt Saul was to hurt Vince's hands.

And the whiteness, the sudden rigid pallor of Saul's face; she remembered that. Remembered his lean, white-scarred hands clamping on her wrists, the twisted wound of his mouth shouting at her, "If you dare touch his hands, I swear to God I'll kill you!"

And now that son of Saul Raden was looking up at her, brushing aside tears and swallowing.

And saying in a low, throaty voice, "Bandage my arm."

She blinked and looked down at the gauze, tape and iodine still in her hands.

Without thinking she walked to the couch and sat down beside Vince. "Put it down," she said, looking at the gun that shook in his hand. "I'm not going to take it away from you."

Vince rested the pistol in his lap. "You'd better not try," he warned. "I'll kill you if you do."

Words, words, she thought, hardly hearing what he said. She was winding gauze around his upper arm, over the wound. She didn't tear open his shirt.

"Do you want iodine on it?" she asked, suddenly conscious of the fact that Stan was standing near the bedroom door, watching.

Vince's throat moved. Why did she have to ask him? He hated to concentrate on extraneous things. He had to concentrate on one thing—making it crowd out all unimportant things. *Kill Bob, kill Bob, kill...*

"Yes," he said quickly.

"It'll hurt," she said. "A lot..."

"Then don't put it on!" he snapped in a nerve-ragged voice. "What's the matter with you?"

Jane's lips pressed together, her mind more conscious of the situation again. He's like a sullen little boy, she thought—only the little boy was wounded and he had a big gun in his hand. She wondered idly if the gun was really loaded.

Stan was standing near the bedroom door. Could he run in, lock the door and get the gun before Vince could shoot open the lock? His throat tightened. It seemed reasonable enough. But he didn't move. He kept watching the two of them on the couch. He heard Jane say "You'll have to go to a doctor."

Vince started to answer, then gritted his teeth in pain and anger. She was just trying to make things more complicated. She knew he couldn't go to a doctor. And he couldn't leave there because they'd call the police and the police would take him back and they'd kill him for stabbing Harry with the bottle.

Why did everyone conspire against him? Why did everything go wrong? He had to get to Bob McCall. He had to free Ruth. It was his duty.

Your duty is to the piano, Vincent, only to the piano.

Saul's words again filtering through the years like a poisonous gas. Liar! He had no duty to the piano. He looked down at his arm, feeling the throbbing hot pain in it. Then, in a moment of terrible shock, he wondered if he would ever play again.

He felt his stomach tighten. *To never play again.*

The world fell on him. Visions ran through his mind—he was on-stage in Carnegie Hall, one empty tuxedo sleeve in his pocket, the other hand moving futilely over the keys, trying to play both parts at once. And people in the audience, silently shaking their heads. A pity, such a pity—he might have been one of the greats.

Saul, help me!

Jane looked at him in surprise when he sobbed. There was something in her eyes he didn't want to see—something that looked too much like pity.

"Don't look at me," he gasped, "I swear to God I'll kill you if you do."

As he raised the gun to point it at her he noticed Stan moving near the bedroom door. His eyes fled over and he saw Stan's face blanch.

"What are you doing?" he asked.

"Nothing," Stan said.

"You better not try anything, Stan," Vince gasped. "I swear to God I'd just as soon…"

His throat clogged and he swallowed. He had to get rid of Stan, he didn't like Stan to stand there like that.

"Get in the kitchen," he ordered. "Make me some coffee. I want some coffee."

"All right, all right," Stan said, "I'll make some for you."

Jane heard the bare feet moving across the rug, heard Stan flicking on the kitchen light, and she silently cursed him for his cowardice. She went on bandaging.

Stan stood in the middle of the bleak kitchen looking around for a weapon. He felt his heart thudding fitfully as his eyes moved over the walls, into the partially opened cabinets, over the stove and refrigerator.

He moved to the drawer in a step. Slowly, carefully, he drew it out without making a sound. He looked down at the long, shining knives.

"What are you doing!" Vince called.

Stan twitched and hurriedly pushed in the drawer.

"Making coffee!" he answered. And in his mind the accusation came, *You're afraid, you're a coward.*

In the living room, Vince was looking at the black nightgown Jane wore. As she moved her hands around his arm, tightening and pulling snug, he saw the movement of her uncupped breasts and he felt that strange, dismaying heat in his body again. It was wrong; he knew it was wrong.

The heat had come often in his young life. Saul had mocked it. Endlessly, Vince had fought that shapeless fire in his body, trying to force down the flames and, in so doing, only fanned them higher. Until they scorched.

He lowered his eyes when he saw that she noticed him staring at her breasts.

"I—I want a cigarette," he said nervously.

"Over there," Jane said, gesturing at the table beside the chair across the room.

"Get me some," Vince said.

She got up and moved over the rug. He let his eyes run up and down her body. As she stood before the table, he could see her body outlined against the lamplight. His mouth pressed together angrily.

"Bitch," he muttered, thinking she wouldn't hear.

Her mouth tightened and her throat moved as she picked up the box of cigarettes. She knew Vince was looking at her body. She wondered, momentarily, if she could use her body as a weapon.

Forcing away the tight look, she turned and brought back the cigarettes. As she lit one for him her eyes moved over his tight, boylike face.

"How did you get out?" she asked.

"That's my business," he said, "not yours."

But, after a moment, a thin, confident smile raised his lips. The throbbing wasn't so bad, the bleeding had stopped. Why not tell her, scare her?

"I'm going to kill somebody," he said as casually as he could. He liked the sound of the words.

Her eyes were on him.

"I'm going to shoot somebody right in the head," he told her.

He didn't understand the look in her eyes. Then she bent over and it seemed that, accidentally, as she did, the nightgown fell away from her breasts. He stared with sick eyes, the hot churning starting in his stomach.

Her eyes looked up at him now, suddenly inviting. It worked exactly opposite. He didn't know why, she didn't know why. But, suddenly, rage exploded in his mind and he flailed out with his pistol.

His aim was poor and the barrel end raked across her right temple, tearing open the skin. Jane fell back in fright, one hand flung up to protect herself.

"Bitch!" Vince yelled at her.

Stan came in hurriedly, his face slack with fear.

"Get in and make me some coffee, I said!" Vince screamed. Stan backed away toward the kitchen, his eyes on Jane.

"Are you all right?" he asked. He waited. "Jane?" he said.

"Make coffee, make coffee," she said, her voice low and hating.

She sat there looking at Vince, her lips tight, feeling the thin dribble of blood on her temple. *I hope the police come and shoot him down like a dog. I hope they blow him to pieces.*

She saw him looking at her breasts again, and she turned away with a shudder.

Stan stood trembling before the stove, watching the coffee perk.

He started as Vince came far enough into the kitchen so he could watch both him and Jane.

"Just don't try anything," Vince said, bluffing a menace he didn't feel. "Make me a sandwich too. I'm hungry."

"A sandwich," Stan said weakly as Vince walked out of the kitchen. He opened up the drawer again and looked in at the knives. *I have to,* he thought, *I have to...*

Vince walked around the living room, ignoring Jane. Then he stopped and looked around the room impatiently. Why was he staying here? He had to get to Bob's apartment. He had his job, his obligation to Ruth.

But *how?* How did he get to Bob's apartment without Stan and Jane warning the police?

I'll rip out the phone, he thought. He was suddenly pleased at the invention of his mind.

But the smile faded. They could go out after he left, call from a neighbor's phone or from a phone booth in some store. And he couldn't afford to waste two bullets. He might not even have them.

He fumbled with the gun, trying to open it so he could see how many bullets there were. But he knew nothing of guns and he couldn't get it open. A hiss of anger passed his lips.

Then he found his eyes suddenly on the telephone beside the chair he was in. He looked at the black receiver and at the dial.

And the smile returned.

3:15 AM

He grunted a little and felt Ruth's legs twitch against him. Then he cleared his throat and tried to go back to sleep but the jangling wouldn't let him.

He felt her hand on his shoulder.

"Honey?" she whispered.

He woke up. "Uh?"

"Telephone."

"Oh, my God," he muttered disgustedly.

He pulled back the covers and let his legs down to the floor. As he stood, he winced at the cold of the floorboards against his feet.

"Who could it be?" he heard her murmur from the dark warmth of the bed.

"God knows," he said, yawning, and walked around the edge of the bed. In the living room the phone kept ringing.

"All right, all right," he mumbled. He picked up the receiver with sleep-numbed fingers.

"Yeah."

"Bob."

Just his name; but the way it was spoken shook away the mists around his brain.

"Yes," he answered.

"This is Stan, Bob. I—could you cover over?"

"What?" Bob's voice rose in unpleasant surprise.

"Could you—Bob, could you come over?" Stan's voice was tightly urgent.

Bob yawned. "What time is it?" he asked.

"About three-fifteen."

"My God, what are you doing, having a party?" Bob asked.

There was another pause.

"No, no—the—party is over."

And the way Stan said that. It made Bob shudder; and, suddenly awake, he thought, *My God, he's killed Jane!*

His throat moved.

"You want me to come over?" he asked, not knowing what to say.

"Y-yes, Bob. Can you?"

"I guess so." He took a deep breath. "All right, Stan, I'll be right over," he said. "Are you...?"

The receiver dropped abruptly on the other end of the line and Bob stood there a moment in the darkness holding the receiver to his ear. Then, slowly, he put down the receiver and went back into the bedroom.

"Who was it?" Ruth asked.

"Stan."

"Stan? Why did he call?"

"I don't know, hon. He wants me to come over."

"Now?"

"Yes, I think I'd better go, too."

Silence a moment; she felt her heartbeat quicken.

"All right if I turn on the light?" he asked.

"Yes, of course, honey." Her voice was soft and concerned.

He turned on the bedside lamp and saw her propped up on one elbow looking at him. As the lamp flared on, she blinked and closed her eyes a moment. Then she opened them and looked back at him.

"What's wrong, Bob?"

"He didn't say, honey," he told her. "He just wants me to come over."

"Did he sound upset?"

He started taking off his pajamas.

"Yes," he said, "he did."

She caught her breath.

"Jane," she said quickly.

He swallowed, then nodded his head.

"That's what I was thinking," he said.

"Oh, *no,*" she said. "It couldn't be. He *loves* her."

"How much can a guy take?" was his answer.

Quickly he dressed and she watched him pull on his trousers and tuck in the shirt ends with quick movements.

"Shall I go with you?" she asked.

"No, honey," he said. "Stay in bed; you need your rest. And—" He blew out a breath, "if it's what we think, I'd rather you weren't there to see it."

He sat down on the bed and started pulling on his socks.

"I wonder why he called us," he said.

"Maybe he didn't know who else to call."

"Poor guy," he said. "All those people who come to his parties— and probably not one of them he could call his friend."

She shook her head.

"I hope it's not what we think," she said.

"You probably think it's a ruse of Jane's to get me over there," he said.

He saw from the way her eyes lowered that he'd guessed right.

"Lie down, dumkopf," he murmured and pushed her head down on the pillow with a gentle movement.

"Will you be gone long?" she asked.

"I don't know, honey. I guess, if it's what we think it, it'll just be a matter of calling the police."

He looked at her for a moment. Then he pressed her back again on the pillow and kissed her warm mouth.

"Go to sleep," he said.

"Don't stay too long, " she said. "I'll worry."

"I won't," he promised. "I—well, I just hope we *are* wrong and it's something else."

"Oh, so do I."

He kissed her again and stood up. Reaching down he turned out the lamp.

She lay in the silence of the bedroom listening to his footsteps move across the living room and stop at the hall closet. She heard the hangers rattle as he took his jacket out, then the front door shut quietly and she was alone in the apartment.

She looked at the radium dialed clock and saw that it was almost three-thirty.

She made a worried sound in her throat. Was it really what Bob thought? Had Stan finally lost his mind and—done it? She rustled her head on the pillow. Not that she could blame Stan. Even if Jane was her friend, she knew as well as anyone that she had been no wife to Stan, that she kept Stan at a peak of nerves with her parties and her drive and her ceaseless, open infidelities.

And Stan was the type that would take it and take it, quietly, without a scene or a complaint until one day, one night, he would snap right down the middle, rise up and slay. It was something she and Bob had discussed often. Bob had always predicted it would end like this.

She lay there quietly and then, abruptly, she was sitting up and staring into the darkness.

Was it that? Had Stan killed her? Suddenly, and for no apparent reason, she felt her heart begin to beat in great, anxious pulses and felt her hands trembling on the sheet.

Bob had joked with her about it and she had smiled; but was it so incredible that Jane might have called and asked him over? No, no, *no*, how could she believe that? Would Bob lie to her and tell her that Stan had phoned if it were Jane?

And yet, she couldn't stop the heavy heartbeats; she couldn't check the trembling of her hands. Her breath began to quicken. She knew what Jane was like. She had seen the savage lusts she could arouse in herself at the slightest notice, knew she had no discretion at all when it came. And she knew she loved Bob too much. She loved him so much that trusting him wasn't enough. She didn't trust another woman in the world.

She shook her head, furious at herself. *This is ridiculous,* she thought. *I'm going crazy. I'm making up everything. He's gone to Stan's apartment because Stan asked him to.*

But *why* did Stan ask him to?

She felt caught up in a horrible vortex whose inner currents would not let her loose. Suddenly, from nothing, she had built up a monster of suspicions and fears. Was this the lot of the pregnant woman? No, she thought, she was just a suspicious woman. She was too possessive and possessiveness bred suspicions.

She closed her eyes. She must go to sleep and wait for him to come back. She must believe in her husband.

But she found herself reaching over and turning on the lamp. She found herself standing on the cold floor, shivering. *And now what,* she asked herself, *what do you intend to do; run after him?*

Horribly enough, that was exactly what she wanted to do.

She almost cried aloud, so miserable did it make her that doubt persisted despite all reason. Not doubt, really, she tried to amend in her own favor; not doubt, but fear. She was afraid for Bob, so terribly afraid for him. She shuddered.

What if there were something else entirely? What if Jane had told Stan she had slept with Bob? What if drunk and mean, she had taunted Stan until the breaking point had come? What if, striking out blindly, she had accused Bob too, hoping to wound Stan by firing a buckshot charge of unfaithfulness at him, a charge that included every man she knew? Ruth knew how nasty and horrible Jane could get, how she'd say anything to hurt somebody she disliked.

She couldn't sleep now. She hurried nervously to the bureau and pulled clothes from her drawer. She didn't care what the reason was, she didn't care if Bob wanted her to stay home, she had to find out why Stan had called.

The nightgown rustled to the floor and her body broke out in tiny goosebumps as the cold air covered her.

Ten minutes later she had phoned for a cab, dressed and was moving down the stairs quickly.

After he put down the phone, Stan turned away, unable to look at Jane. He felt his hands trembling at his sides.

"How *brave,*" she said, "leading him here to be killed. Your own friend."

"What did you want me to do?" he muttered, sick with shame.

"Why don't you—" she started.

"Shut up, both of you," Vince said calmly.

Vince felt peace now. He felt very pleased with himself. He'd done something very clever. He had circumvented time and space. He didn't have to leave now, didn't have to worry about Stan and Jane calling the police. He didn't have to go after his prey. His prey was coming to him.

Satisfied, very confident and pleased, he walked over and sat on the piano bench. He sat there looking at Jane on the couch in her almost transparent nightgown, then over at Stan, who was looking out the window, his body looking heavy and ridiculous in those stupid pajamas.

Spritely music tinkled in Vince's mind—Liadov's *Music Box* coupled with a Chopin *Valse Brilliante*—a dissonant but sparklingly exciting tonal companionship.

Now it was just a matter of waiting. Everything was going right for a change. His arm still hurt, but the fiery, stabbing pain was gone. It had lessened to a dull gnawing ache. He could stand that. He could stand a lot of things, as long as he knew that Bob was coming.

He held the pistol in his lap and looked at it. He tried to open it again. But there was only one hand available and his teeth gritted in irritation when the gun wouldn't open.

Stan stood looking over the sleeping city. His eyes were bleak and his body felt tight, constrained within binds of shame and aching fear. He knew he shouldn't have called Bob. He should have refused. Now it was too late. Bob was on his way. His body was tense with the knowledge.

And now he was an absolute coward in Jane's eyes That was the worst element of it. His eyes closed slowly and his chest shuddered with a convulsive breath. He had to do something. He had to get the gun away from Vince. Before Bob got there.

"I'd like to get a robe," he heard Jane say then and he looked over his shoulder. "It's cold in here," she told Vince.

Vince looked at her. He didn't want her to put on the robe. He wanted to look at her like this. It added something to the scene. It was like an exciting moment in a thriller movie and he liked the feeling it gave him.

He felt very sure of himself as he stood and walked slowly to the wall thermostat, always watching them from the corners of his eyes.

He moved the tiny, serrated wheel until the dial rested at seventy-five degrees. Then he looked over at Jane.

"There," he said. "No need to be cold. Don't bother to put on a robe now. You don't need a robe."

He felt his throat contract at the look in her eyes. He forced a smile to his lips to hide the nervousness.

"What would you do if I didn't have this gun?" he said. He felt like exchanging sharp, bitter dialogue. It was exciting now. He told himself that. Exciting and invigorating. Everything going according to plan. He was in complete charge of the moment, master of the situation. He had beaten everyone—Harry and the guard and that girl and the man in the subway—*everyone*. They had all tried to keep him from his purpose, but he had beaten them. And now he had Jane and Stan at bay, too, and he was going to have Bob in his hands soon. Yes, everything was perfect.

"What would you do?" he said again, shaking slightly.

She turned her head away and rubbed her white forearms with her palms. Vince swallowed. "I asked you a question," he said.

She heard the words before she knew she'd said them. "Oh, go to hell."

She didn't notice how Stan turned, his face tightened into a mask of fright. She felt only incredible wonder at herself.

Vince had stiffened, his hand tightening on the revolver.

"Maybe I'll kill you," he said, trying desperately to frighten her.

"Maybe you will," she said and, even as she said it, felt her stomach turning over. *I must be crazy.*

Vince turned away from her suddenly. She was trying to trick him into wasting his bullets. Well, he wouldn't waste any, he told himself and his finger twitched away from the trigger. She wasn't worth a bullet. Not yet.

Women are expendables, Vincent, women are trying bitches.

He nodded to himself, driving confidence back. Yes, if there were any bullets left after he'd killed Bob, then Jane would be the one to get them. Right in her chest. He got a pleasant distracting sense of warmth in his body at the thought of firing right into those arching breasts.

He sat down and looked at her. After a moment, he looked at the floor. Why did Bob take so long? Vince took a nervous breath. He had to come soon. They might find the guard, they might find Harry. The girl might go to the police. His lips started to shake a little. *No, no, don't get upset,* he told himself anxiously. *It's going to be all right, all right.*

He sat there looking at something red under his nails.

Stan stood by the chair looking at Jane, then at Vince. He had to do something. He couldn't leave that look in Jane's eyes. Even if he died for it, he had to take that look from her eyes.

But what was there to do?

Vince's hands twitched in his lap. He heard a clock ticking in the kitchen. He *should* have done something to that girl, he thought. He could have, too; you bet your life he could have—she was that kind of girl. You could tell by looking at them. Filthy. Something about the way they talk and dress. Like Jane—sure, Jane was one of them, too. He'd like to—

No. He held himself tensely. That was wrong, it was dirty.

"What time is it?" he suddenly asked.

Stan raised his arm nervously and looked at his watch. "Twenty-five to four," he said.

"Good," Vince said, "that's just what I want."

He didn't know what he meant by that but he liked the sound of the words. It sounded as if he had planned everything to the last detail and it was all working out perfectly. He smiled to himself and brushed back his thick hair with a casual movement of his right hand. As he did, the gun thumped down on the floor.

Stan started forward, then jerked to a stop as Vince pulled up the gun and pointed it at him.

"You wanna die?" he asked Stan, eyes glittering. "Do you?"

Stan's throat moved and he started to shake his head, then stopped.

Jane pushed up abruptly and started toward the bedroom. "I'm going to get my robe," she said.

Stan's heart leaped and he felt his body tensing.

Vince watched her moving and felt heat begin to churn up in his stomach. She couldn't do that to him! Bitch! He stood up in a quick movement, feeling his left arm start to throb. *No, no, you have to save the bullets.*

"You'd better watch out," he said.

"Jane, stay away from the—*phone,*" Stan said suddenly. He'd meant to say *gun* but then he decided there might still be a chance for him to get it, and he changed it to *phone.* All he wanted to do was alert Vince anyway so she wouldn't try anything.

Jane had stopped and was looking at Stan with hate in her eyes.

"You fool," she said bitterly.

Stan stood there helplessly, feeling a terrible heaviness in his stomach.

Vince pushed Jane aside now, his fingers twitching as he touched the smoothness of the gown over her warm hip. Then he turned on the bedroom light and his eyes moved around.

"Going to try something funny, haah?" he said.

"She wasn't going to try anything," Stan heard himself saying loudly. "Don't do anything to her. Vince, I'm begging you."

"Oh, *shut* up!" Jane snapped, her nerves frayed. "Haven't you got a scrap of manhood in you?"

Stan pressed his lips together stubbornly. "I don't want anything to happen to you," he said.

For a long moment they looked at each other while they heard Vince tearing out phone wires.

"Something *has* happened to me," Jane said in a low, trembling voice. "I know this is the end. I know I'm married to a—a—"

She turned away and brushed past Vince.

Vince stood watching her as she put on her robe. His throat moved as the backward movement of her shoulders made her taut breasts press against the silk. His tongue ran nervously over his upper lip, licking at the tiny sweat drops. *No,* he heard the voice in his mind, *no, that's dirty.*

"All right," he said, forcing the swagger back into his voice. "Now get in the living room or I'll shoot you."

Trembling, she walked past him. She moved to the bar and reached for the whiskey bottle. Bob was coming over. The thought made her stomach fall. It would kill Ruth if anything happened to Bob. Especially now. Her throat tightened. It mustn't happen. It *mustn't.*

"Make me a drink, too," Vince said slyly.

At first she tightened and was going to tell him to make his own. Then she remembered the night in the bedroom with Vince. Vince could never have done those things sober. Maybe drink plus her body could get the gun away from him.

She hid the whiskey bottle from Vince so he wouldn't see how much of it she poured in and how little soda after it. When she turned, he was sitting on the piano bench. She walked over and held out the glass to him. She made a point of taking a slow, deep breath as she stood before him. Her bosom rose and pressed against the dark silk.

"There," she said, trying hard to keep the hatred from her voice.

Vince reached out casually, holding the gun and then with a downward snap of the barrel, he smashed the glass in her hand. She recoiled at the pain of the glass splinters lancing into her palm, and streaks of red drove up her cheeks.

"You—"

Vince shoved the barrel against her chest and pushed her away from him.

"Vince, don't!" he heard Stan cry out in an agonized voice. He saw Stan move quickly to Jane and try to put his arms around her. She tore loose with a wracking sob and stumbled back to the couch, looking down at her cut palm.

"You stay away from her!" Vince ordered, and Stan backed away, face torn with conflicting emotions.

Vince looked at Jane then and smiled bitterly. "You think I'd drink that crap?" he said, voice sneering. "You think I'm dumb? Well, *you're* dumb."

She sat there trembling. And, within her taut fury, she felt something else—*alarm*. Vince was clever. Simple expedients would not topple his craftiness.

She wiped her hand on a cushion, teeth gritted. Her brow furrowed. Where was Bob now? If he took his car he'd almost be there. From 18th Street to 54th Street wasn't even two miles. And in the early morning streets there would be no traffic to contend with.

Oh, God, let him have the flat tire of his life! she prayed.

Stan was in the chair now looking over at his wife. Deep in his vitals he felt the body-wrenching shame her scorn had lashed into him. It was worse than before. Then, at least, she'd been talking of things he could accept—her unfaithfulness, her restless dissatisfaction. He allowed those things and wanted her anyway.

There were excuses for almost everything, if you looked hard enough for them. But for outright cowardice there was none. He felt his muscles tightening, feeling more than sickness now. He felt drained.

"You still managing?" he heard Vince say.

He looked up blankly. "What?"

"You still a concert manager?" Vince asked again.

For a moment Stan looked at him blankly, afraid that Vince was trying to trap him into something.

"Yes," he said. "I am."

A shaky smile flitted across Vince's lips. "You still got Dinotti?"

"Dinotti?"

"You still *manage* him?" Vince's voice was rising.

"I…yes," Stan nodded. "Dinotti's still with me." What was Vince driving at? It made Stan nervous.

"How *are* things?" Vince asked.

Stan didn't know what to make of the question. Here Vince was planning to kill Bob and yet he was asking casual questions about the concert field. It was ghoulish.

"It's all right, I guess," he answered nervously.

He glanced over at Jane but she was leaning back on the couch, her head fallen forward in mute dejection.

Vince felt his hands start to tremble. He knew he shouldn't be asking. It was crazy to ask and, anyway, what did the concert field matter to him? But…

"Got many *pianists?*" he asked in a timorous voice, as a child might ask a candy store owner if he had any chocolates to spare.

Stan suddenly realized he was trying to get him to manage him again! He *was* insane.

Abruptly, the idea came.

"Not too many," he said, acting on it impulsively. "Not of your stature, anyway."

He felt his heart begin to beat heavily. Could Vince hear the lie? He closed his hands into white fists on his knees.

Vince couldn't tell it was a lie. An anxious, half-eager smile raised his thin lips, then was gone nervously. Blood pulsed through his body making his arm ache. That wouldn't matter, he assured himself quickly. A bullet can be taken out, there's nothing fatal about a bullet in your arm.

"Would you like to get back into the—the field?" Stan asked.

Oh, God, it was such an arrant lie. How could Vince possibly swallow it? He had killed, he had escaped from an insane asylum and now he was being asked to believe it was possible for him to return to concert work.

But he didn't know how anxious Vince was; he didn't know that Vince wanted more than anything else in the world to believe just that.

"Well..." Vince's voice hesitated. He had to catch himself. He mustn't be too eager. The thought came warning, cautioning.

Jane was looking up at Stan now.

"There's a need, a very great need for good pianists," Stan was saying, fists trembling in his lap. "The field is shallow. Very shallow."

"But my—my *arm,*" Vince said, tense at the confession.

Stan's throat moved quickly, he strained forward in the chair.

"Your arm can be fixed," he said.

"You think so?" Voice shakingly eager.

"Of course, of course it can," Stan went on, afraid lest the assurance slip from his voice and unmask his stratagem. "Look at Dinotti. A broken wrist—and him a violinist. Is he any the worse for it?"

That was true. Vince knew that. Dinotti had been out on Long Island Sound in a sailboat and the swinging boom had broken his wrist. Now he was as good as ever. And his arm could be fixed too. Blood flowed faster in his veins as his heartbeat quickened. To play again, to really play.

"You really think so?" he asked, anxious to have Stan tell him the same thing again.

"I do," Stan said. "I'm sure of it." He felt his confidence growing. Vince was only an impressionable boy.

Now Jane's heart was beating quickly too as she looked over at Vince. Maybe Stan had some redeeming feature after all. If not courage then craft. It was better than nothing. Jane leaned forward on the couch.

"You want me to play?" Vince suddenly blurted out. And a hot flush crossed his face. He shouldn't have said that. But he wanted so to play, to be told he was good enough for concert work again. All right, he hated Saul, he'd hated what Saul did to him. But, in spite of every torturing hour of practice, he loved the piano.

Stan was sweating now. He felt large drops of it trickling down across his chest. He thought of the way Vince had looked at the piano before. A look of adoration, of hungry longing.

Was it possible that he could get the gun from Vince?

Maybe he could undo his failure and save Bob after all. A flood of hope covered him. He was excited and eager to save Bob, to gain Jane's respect. It could all come back in a rush, Jane would love him again, everything would be wonderful again. Swelling imagination filled him.

"Sure," he said eagerly. "Sure, Vince, play someth—"

His voice suddenly broke off and sweat broke out faster on him. *If he uses his left hand he'll know he can't play, he'll know I'm lying.* Stan raised his left hand and wiped it across his mouth nervously.

"Why don't we talk terms first?" he said awkwardly. "We could…"

"What shall I play?" Vince asked eagerly.

Like a little boy, he was now eager to do right. Quickly, getting rid of it, he put the gun on top of the piano. He wanted to play, to have Stan take out contracts and maps, plan a season for him. His hands shook at the thought.

Jane was tensing herself on the couch. How fast could she get to the piano and grab the gun?

"Well, why don't we—?" Stan started.

"Shall I play the Polonaise?" Vince asked, forgetting about his left hand completely.

Stan swallowed hard. "No, no," he said hastily then forced a smile to his lips as Vince looked suspicious. "I mean," he went on quickly, "you're out of practice, Vince. You should start out easy. You know that."

"What should I play then?" Vince asked sullenly.

Stan glanced at the piano, at the gun resting on top. He forced his eyes back to Vince. If he could get Vince so distracted with playing that he could get the gun…

"Well, I don't know," he fumbled for time. "You have to remember it's going to be a little rough but—"

His voice broke off as Vince looked at him coldly.

"Well, you know you haven't played in a long time," he said, new sweat breaking out on his face and body.

"I'm as good as ever," Vince said in a tight, hard voice. "I can play better than anybody.

"You bet you can, Vince," Stan said. "Sure. I just—"

Good God, how did you reason with a lunatic? His mind raced and tripped over itself, trying to find a piece that had no left hand.

"I said what shall I play?" Vince said, losing patience.

"How about—Chabig's *Tantivy?*" Stan lunged for a suggestion. *The left hand doesn't come in for at least twenty measures,* he exulted inwardly.

"Oh, all right," Vince said.

Jane's eyes were fastened on the heavy pistol on the piano. When Vince got into the piece, she'd try for it.

Stan was sweating again. The piece was fast, very fast. What if even Vince's *right* hand wasn't as good as it had been? What if he made mistakes and faltered, lost his temper? He dug nails fiercely into his palms. *He's got to be able to play it, he's got to...*

Vince turned from them, a smile faltering on his lips. Yes, that was a good one. He thought of the long hours of practice he'd spent memorizing this piece. In his mind, he saw the score as clearly as if the music were resting on the piano.

His right hand arched over the keys, settling like a diffident spider. The pads of his fingertips pressed into the ivory keys to get the feel of them. From the corner of his eyes he saw Stan get up. It didn't matter. He could get the gun before they could do anything.

He looked back at the keyboard, hearing the flurry of Saul's old commands like cool winds in his mind. *Never drive down the keys, never use your fingers like senseless mallets. Press. Make the note ring clear and certain. Combine. Blend. Build to the climax.*

In the quiet of the room the first notes of the *Tantivy* sprinkled.

Jane slid to the edge of the couch with a careful guarded movement. Stan saw her move and caught his breath. He suddenly realized she was going to try for the gun and he almost started running for the piano.

He caught himself. He took a slow, wary step toward the piano. It seemed as if he hardly moved at all.

The music sprayed through the room, an icy clatter of notes. No fear of his right hand, Stan noted with the back of thought. Vince's touch was, as ever, supreme. He took another step, feeling his throat tighten.

The gypsy violence discorded into his ears as he edged closer. Surely Vince could see him coming. But Vince was absorbed in his playing. Stan tightened as he saw Vince's left hand slowly raising and preparing to strike. Chabig had saved the left hand in order to make the entry one of shocking dissonance. The pianist struck with all his power a chord of five notes. Stan moved more quickly, his hands shaking. What if Vince saw him coming?

Now Jane looked up and saw Stan coming closer. But she knew the piece too and knew that any second Vince's left hand would smash down on the keys.

She stood up. She was almost behind Vince and he couldn't see her clearly. Stan couldn't get there in time, she had to get the gun.

Stan tried to catch her eye, but her attention had returned to the piano and the heavy black pistol on it. Stan stopped and began to shake. He hadn't meant it to be this way. She'd be killed!

He strained forward and as in the middle of a step as Vince's left hand drove down on the keys.

The gagging scream of agony stiffened them both. They stood there gaping at Vince as he raised his left hand in front of his eyes.

It won't play! The words were like a hot flame playing on his brain. He tried to move the fingers but they were like rotted sausages. And a shooting pain filled his arm.

His face grew taut, the vein at his right temple began to throb and suddenly, with a wrenching sob, he drove his clenched left hand down on the keys. He jerked up the bunched hand and drove it down again, smashing down a cluster of white and black keys, filling the room with thick dissonance.

Jane broke into a run for the piano.

Stan couldn't hold back the cry. *"Jane!"*

Vince leaped up at the yell and knocked back the piano bench. As he lunged for the pistol, Jane jumped on him and they both went crashing into the piano.

Stan started forward, eyes widening, hands snapping into fists.

Vince screamed into Jane's face as she drove a fist into his wounded arm. He jerked up the pistol but she shoved it aside and he couldn't get a grip on the trigger.

She struck at him again, but missed and lost her balance. Vince felt her soft body against him. From the corner of his eye he saw Stan rushing at him.

With a strangled cry he ripped the gun up and drove it across her temple. Jane reeled back with a dull cry and fell on her back.

Stan jolted back as the gun was shoved out at him. He stepped back and almost tripped.

Vince stood there breathing hoarsely.

"Trick me, haah?" he gasped.

He turned toward Jane who lay motionless on the floor. Slowly he turned the pistol on her.

"I'm going to blow your guts out," he said in a low choked voice.

Then, suddenly, his breath stopped. He stood there, stomach and chest trembling while his eyes focused on the hallway that led to the front door.

The doorbell was ringing.

3:40 AM

The cab pulled up to the curb and Ruth got in quickly.

"367 West 54th," she told the driver.

"Yes, ma'am."

The driver pulled the door shut and the cab pulled away from the curb. The street was completely silent except for the sound of the motor.

Ruth shivered as she settled back on the cold leather seat. *God, I hope he isn't angry when he sees me,* she thought. *What if he knows what I'm thinking; about Jane trying to get him there?*

Her throat moved. Maybe she should go home. Maybe it would be better. Nothing could be wrong. Maybe it was better she just went home to bed and let herself worry. That was better than Bob's knowing she hadn't trusted him.

But it wasn't a matter of trust, she told herself.

Oh, it was no use arguing with herself. She might as well clear her mind of everything. She was going and that was all there was to it. She loved him too much to lie awake at home, tossing on the bed and dying a thousand deaths of fear each second. It was no use. If she was going to make a *faux pas,* then she was going to make it. Better that than a nervous breakdown of concern.

Bob would forgive her when he knew she only did it because she was afraid.

The cab crossed Twenty-second and, at Twenty-third, turned right and headed toward Lexington.

"Could you go a little faster?" she asked.

"Beg pardon, ma'am?"

"Could—could you drive a little faster. This is rather urgent."

"Yes, ma'am."

Rather urgent. Now she really felt silly. She could just visualize all of them together and the cab driver telling them, *So she tells me to drive faster, see?* And then they'd all break into breathless laughter.

She almost smiled at herself, the scene seemed so real.

But what if it were true? What if Bob was in danger?

Time suddenly fell on her like a weight. How far had he gone? Was he at Stan's apartment yet? She'd had to dress, go downstairs and wait for the cab.

She leaned forward.

"I'm sorry to bother you but—do you have the time?"

"Quarter to four, ma'am," the driver said.

"Thank you."

"Be there in a jiffy, ma'am."

She smiled as she leaned back on the cold seat.

It was that tightness in her stomach she couldn't rid herself of. It wasn't intuition, she knew that. This business about pregnant woman's intuition was just a lark she'd made up for Bob. No, she was worried, that was all. She couldn't help it.

Anyway, she rationalized, how would any woman feel to have her husband called away at almost four o'clock in the morning? How would any woman like to be wrenched from sleep, and watch her husband dress and leave her? Especially when she wasn't sure why he was going, even *where* he was going. No, pregnancy had nothing to do with it. Any sensitive woman would worry under circumstances like that.

She took a nervous breath of the cold morning air. Why did it have to happen? She felt such a horrible foreboding. It was probably just because it had happened in the dead of the night. It was a strange time, a silent, barren time. It was a frightening time, this lonely empty shell of hours that was not night and not day. And it frightened her to be out in the streets in a cab now.

Up Lexington Avenue, past the silent store fronts, the dead faces of the restaurants, now and then past the thin, green neon of a bar still open, people in there drinking. How could they be awake and living at this hour? *Maybe they were another race that lives when all of us go to sleep.*

Then she suddenly thought, what if she got sick to her stomach? She'd had a rough time the past few weeks. But she'd really feel foolish if she came to Stan's place and had to run right to the bathroom. A sort of harried smile crossed her lips. What would Bob say?

223

No more thought, she told herself. *I'm going and that's all there is to it. No matter what he says. If he yells at me I won't mind as long as it's a nice, healthy unharmed yell. If he takes me over his knee and spanks me I won't care. As long as the hand that spanks is nice and safe and mine.*

In the darkness, in the silence of the great city, the cab sped up Lexington Avenue, its motor humming. Thirty-fifth Street, Thirty-sixth Street, Thirty-seventh, Thirty...

4:00 AM

Vince stiffened at the sound of the bell. The apartment seemed to shake with the sound. He stood tensely, his chest rising and falling with heavy breaths, his throat congested. He coughed. He didn't know what to do exactly.

He looked at Stan.

"All right," he said hoarsely, "you're going to—"

"Vince, for God's sake, don't do it!" Stan suddenly burst out. "He hasn't done anything to you."

Vince was going to shout at him to shut up, but he held it in. His dark eyes glittered as he spoke quickly, gutturally.

"Shut up," he said. "You're going to open the door and let him in."

Stan looked at him with blank eyes. He glanced toward Jane. His heart was thudding rapidly.

"Get out there," Vince said.

"Vince..."

Vince raised the gun and pointed it at Stan. "You want to die?"

Stan braced himself. *I'll let him shoot me,* he suddenly thought. It would warn Bob. He felt himself shudder. *No, no,* his mind rationalized quickly. *He'll shoot Jane then. You can't do it.*

But, deep inside, he knew he was a coward and afraid to die.

Vince moved behind Stan. He prodded the gun into Stan's back as Stan stopped by his wife.

Stan jolted nervously as the gun barrel touched him. He looked into the hall with sick eyes and started walking toward the door. *God, why am I doing what he tells me to?* His teeth ground together in impotent fury.

The doorbell rang again and kept on ringing. Vince felt a wild, surging elation. Now he was going to avenge Ruth. All right, he couldn't play the piano but at least he could save Ruth. He *would* save her.

Strangely enough though he couldn't feel much about Ruth. He knew he wanted revenge. But he didn't realize it wasn't Ruth he wanted to avenge. It was himself, on the world. The world which had crippled his left arm and made it impossible for him to play anymore.

They stopped.

"Now," Vince said in a grating voice, *"open the door."*

No. No. Stan tried to turn the word into sound. His fingers curled around the door knob. Bob was his friend and yet he had brought Bob here to die. Scream out and beat on the door and warn Bob. Turn and fight Vince until the bullets were all gone from the gun into his body. He wanted to fight for Jane.

But he couldn't. He stood there, shaking and helpless, his stomach a hot, churning knot of pain. And the words stabbed at his brain drawing the blood of his self-respect, the last few drops of it. *I am a coward.*

"Open it!"

The cloud of Vince's hot, furled whisper surrounded him.

He unlocked the door and opened it.

"Stan, what is it?"

Bob stood in the doorway looking at Stan, white and trembling.

He moved forward.

"Stan, what—"

Then, suddenly, he leaped to the side with a gasp as the door was slammed shut from behind and he saw Vince's glaring face before him.

Stan backed away, shuddering, his eyes wide and staring. Vince leaned against the door, his chattering teeth jammed together, the gun wavering in his hand.

"Vince," was all Bob could say as he stood there, paralyzed with sudden fear.

"Get inside," Vince said.

He forced a calmness through himself. Bob was here now, in his hands. There was no use ending it right away. Bob would pay; but slowly.

"Vince, you—"

"I said get inside!" Vince ordered, his thin voice ringing out shrilly in the hallway.

Bob backed into Stan as he retreated.

"Bob, I'm sorry," Stan murmured in a weak voice. "Please don't hold it against—"

"If you don't get in there," Vince's voice was low and menacing, "I swear to God, I'll…"

They backed into the living room, their eyes never leaving Vince's white, twisted face.

As they entered the living room Stan heard a groan and, turning suddenly, he saw Jane sitting up, holding her forehead with her hand, blood trickling between her white fingers.

"Jane," he muttered, brokenly.

"Leave her alone," Vince said.

But, for some reason, Stan didn't listen. Maybe it was because he felt dead already. He helped his wife up.

"Let go of me," she muttered hoarsely, in a voice that bordered on hysteria. "I don't want—"

"Be quiet," he said, quietly firm. "You haven't helped any either."

Jane sank down on the couch, wordless. She looked at Bob, then at Vince. Her teeth dug into her lower lip.

"I'm going to wash off her forehead," she heard Stan say to Vince.

Vince said nothing. He backed over to where he could watch Stan in the kitchen. Stan might try for a knife. He kept looking from Stan to Bob, the gun held tightly in his hand. *Why didn't I stop Stan from going in there?* he wondered. And then he realized that he was afraid of Stan. You couldn't trust Stan's kind, they were unpredictable. One minute they would be blubbering for pity, the next minute they would come lunging at you, eagle-clawed, eyes like fire. He had seen that at the asylum. The little man who coughed, he was like that. Cry, cry, cry and then, suddenly, with a shriek and a gibber, he would leap at you.

Bob stood in the middle of the room looking first at Jane, then at Vince.

"How did you get out?" he asked weakly.

"Never mind that," Vince said carefully. "Do you want to know *why* I came out?"

Bob stared at him, his throat moving, still numbed from the shock of seeing Vince.

"I came to kill you," Vince said.

Bob started as if someone had kicked him in the stomach. He stood there, his face petrified. Vince liked that. It gave him confidence again, confidence that he'd been losing when first Jane, then Stan, had defied him. He needed constant obedience to his words or he became unnerved.

"Ki—" Bob's voice broke off. He drew in a harsh breath. *"Kill?"* he said, his voice flat and unbelieving.

"I'm going to blow your brains out," Vince said, his voice a low, throaty sound. His eyes were like glowing coals.

"But—but I haven't done anything to—"

"Shut up!"

A bubbling chuckle filled Vince's throat and his nostrils flared in scorn.

"Yellow," he said. "You're afraid to die, aren't you?"

Bob's throat moved convulsively.

"Aren't you?"

"Vince, don't be crazy," Bob heard himself saying. "You don't want to kill anyone. You know you—"

Vince's laughter stopped him, made him shudder.

"I don't want to kill anyone," Vince mocked. Then his face flinted. "I've killed *two* men to get to you. Do you really think I'm not going to..."

He broke off suddenly and almost jerked the trigger. He wanted desperately to pull the trigger and watch Bob crumple to the floor in a hail of bullets. He wanted to stand over Bob's twitching body emptying the gun into him.

The holding back made him shudder.

No, he told himself. *Wait; enjoy yourself.* He wondered briefly if he should make Bob call up Ruth and get her over here too. How she would love him if she saw him shoot Bob right before her eyes. Then she'd give herself to him right in front of Stan and Jane.

No. No. He shouldn't think of Ruth that way. She was clean and beautiful. He wasn't insane. That proved it.

"Sit down," he told Bob.

Good. Now he was in control of himself.

Bob stared at Vince without moving. *Kill me?* The words drummed in his mind and made him shiver convulsively. He couldn't conceive of it. To suddenly have death facing you; that was impossible to understand.

"Are you going to sit down or...?"

Bob sank down on the piano bench with a faltering of leg muscles. He sat there, eyes fastened to Vince's face.

"Get out here," Vince told Stan.

He backed into the wall as Stan passed. Then he shoved Stan's back and almost made him fall over.

"Watch where you're going, stupid," he said.

Stan's breath caught and a strange, unfamiliar fury burst in him. That they should be subject to the whims of this adolescent lunatic! It made him shake with anger.

Then, as he walked past Bob, for a moment their eyes met. And there was something in Bob's eyes that made Stan's lips tighten, that made him turn away his gaze.

"Stan," Bob said and it was like a knife turning in Stan's body.

"You're going to die, you know that," Vince said.

He wanted to frighten Bob more. He liked the look Bob had gotten in the hall; that drained, terrified look, one cheek twitching; the backing away in horror. Vince liked that a lot. It made him feel good to terrify people. He thought for a moment of that girl he'd taken the raincoat from. He wished he was back there.

Bob didn't answer Vince. His heartbeats were slowing down now. The initial shock had left his muscles feeling slack and impotent. His mind began slowly to function again.

What do I answer? he wondered. Was there an answer that would satisfy Vince, prolong the time he had to live?

He glanced over to where Stan's hands moved gently over Jane's forehead. Why had Stan done this to him?

"I asked you something," Vince said, the anger coming again. "I'm not going to wait much longer. I won't be defied."

Bob looked at him.

"What do you want me to say, Vince?" he asked.

Vince stiffened. *Wrong answer!* The words exploded in Bob's mind and made him go rigid with new fright.

"Why do you want to kill me, Vince?" he asked quickly.

Vince's eyes slitted. Was he being tricked? Well, no one would trick him.

"You know why," he said slyly.

Yes, Bob thought, *I know why.* He did know. Because of Ruth, because Vince had hated Bob with a paranoid hatred since the day he'd married the girl Vince had wanted for himself.

"Listen, Vince," he said.

"Don't try to save yourself," Vince said. "You can't."

"You have no reason to kill me," Bob said desperately. "I haven't done you any harm."

Vince stood there looking at Bob without any expression on his face. *That's right,* his mind prodded silently. *Beg for your life; I'll stand here and listen.*

"Vince, I haven't *done* anything to you," Bob said.

The room was silent. It was warmer now that the heat was up. Vince's flannel shirt was getting hot and chafing him.

I haven't done anything to you.

Bob's words repeated themselves in his mind and the words made Vince's lips twitch. No, he hadn't done anything; only taken away Vince's life, only taken away the only girl Vince had ever wanted, the only thing he'd ever really asked for in his life.

Momentarily he thought of Ruth as he'd met her so long ago at the party after the first Town Hall engagement.

Ruth had been sitting on a couch, all alone. Vince had wandered over, sat beside her. Nobody was paying any attention to her then, only Vince. He was the one who had introduced her to everybody, the one who had made her laugh and taken away her strangeness and timidness.

And what did he get for it? He tightened. She had married Bob and deserted him.

He swallowed. No, that wasn't what had happened. Bob had tricked her, he had hypnotized her. Maybe even drugged her. Ruth loved *him,* not Bob. She had said it that day in the music room. Oh, maybe not in so many words, but in her eyes she had said it. She couldn't get away from Bob, that's what was wrong. She was helpless and that was why...

He refocused his eyes and realized that Bob had been talking to him all the time he'd been thinking of Ruth.

"Vince, for God's sake—" Bob said.

"Shut up," Vince told him.

Now they all sat silent, watching him; Jane and Stan next to each other on the couch, Bob on the piano bench—all their eyes on him. It made Vince a little nervous, but he liked being the center of attention. It was the way it should be. He'd always loved that last minute of the concert when he knew they were all watching him from the audience and soon he would rise and bow carefully and slowly from the waist, a thin smile on his face.

"Where's Ruth?" he asked Bob suddenly.

Bob didn't answer. He just sat there looking at Vince. And he was thinking quickly. Was Vince actually planning to go to Ruth too? His throat moved. He had to stop him.

"I'm talking to you," Vince said. "Answer me when you're—"

"Vince, put that gun away," Bob said.

"Listen!" Vince snarled. "You think I'm afraid of you? You think I'm afraid to kill? I've already killed two men and they can only get me once for—"

The words, his own, made him stiffen. He stood there staring at them, his heart pounding.

Get him? He'd never even considered it. He feared it, yes, but never for a moment did he believe they could really catch him. He was going to kill Bob and then he and Ruth would go away and have a new life.

Die? The word made him shudder. No, he wouldn't let himself think of it.

He edged over to an arm chair and sank down on it. He hadn't realized how tired he was but his muscles felt slack and dead as he relaxed. He shifted a little in the chair, rested the pistol in his lap. The pistol was getting still heavier, he realized worriedly. He shouldn't wait; he knew that. He should get it over with and go. But it was different now. Killing Harry was easy because Harry had been filthy. Killing that man in the subway had been quick, almost accidental. It was different to kill someone after you talked to them, to kill deliberately. To end a sentence, then raise your gun and fire. It was hard to kill without passion. *You see,* his mind said, *that proves I'm sane, doesn't it?*

"What are you going to do?" Jane asked, "make us *wait?*"

"You'll wait. As long as I say," Vince told her.

"What if we don't *want* to wait?" she said.

His throat moved.

"You'll wait as long as I say."

She sank back against the cushion. Was it possible it was as simple as that? Just a matter of instilling a negative reaction in his fevered mind? It did seem to work.

So long as she didn't trip, so long as she didn't fall over a block in his mind, it might work.

Bob had caught it too. At first when Jane had spoken he had stiffened and thought, *Good God, she wants him to kill me.* But then he realized it was the only way. Buying time, tricking Vince into thinking they didn't *want* to wait so he would make them wait.

But how long could it last? Bob's throat moved convulsively and his mouth felt dry and hot. How long before Vince would suddenly tire of waiting, rise up, on impulse, and fire his gun?

Bob's muscles tightened involuntarily. Did he dare make a jump at Vince? Was it possible that Vince would be so shocked by the move he couldn't fire in time?

The thought made Bob shiver. What if he *wasn't* too surprised to fire?

It seemed impossible, this moment of melodrama. Just a few hours before he'd been sitting with Ruth on the living room couch listening to Ravel, everything lethargic and peaceful. Now this.

That was the trouble, he realized with sudden alarm. Now that the first shock was over he couldn't really bring himself to believe that anything was going to happen to him. He was nervous, yes, but the very core of him revolted at the thought that, in minutes, he might be killed.

How could he make himself jump at Vince when he couldn't quite believe, in his own flesh, that Vince would really shoot him? And if that were so, then jumping would bring on the very thing he wanted to avoid.

Stan sat by his wife, never moving, tense and ready. If he had to, he was telling himself, he'd shield her body with his. He knew that life would be meaningless without Jane.

But his stomach was shaking and he had the horrible feeling that if the moment came he would be so petrified with fright he couldn't budge to save her.

The room became so silent that they could even hear the slow buzzing of the electric clock in the kitchen. Soon now, Vince told himself, I'm going to shoot him. There's no point in waiting.

Bob looked nervously at his watch.

"Never mind what time it is," Vince said. "It doesn't matter to you anymore."

And yet Vince could not repress the sensation that time *did* matter, the feeling that if he didn't shoot soon the whole thing would be impossible. As if every second were throwing up a barrier around Bob and Stan and Jane and, if he didn't fire soon, they would be encircled, inviolate.

It was as if they were all in a play and when the moment came to shoot Bob, when the cue was given, he had to shoot or the chance was over. And he felt his throat moving. What if the time had already passed?

That was stupid!

But he found himself straining forward in the chair, his heart pounding in fright. In his mind he saw the completion of the play; the men in white bursting into the apartment and grabbing him, dragging him away screaming and kicking. And Ruth was there in the last scene too, laughing as the curtain fell.

No, that *was* stupid. He threw all those thoughts away.

He stood up again restlessly. *What are you waiting for,* the voice filled his mind.

Suddenly he stopped walking and a rattling sound filled his throat.

They were all looking toward the front hall.

The doorbell was ringing again.

4:15 AM

Bob felt his muscles tighten. For some reason the sudden idea had occurred that it was Ruth at the door. But it couldn't be her, it *couldn't.*

He looked back. Now they were all looking at Vince.

Vince's throat moved and he stood there with a restless, nervous stance. What was the *matter* with the world? Why was everything so complicated? He wanted to kill the world.

"Nobody's answering it," he told them. "The first one who makes a sound ..."

He trained the gun on each of them, moving his hand in an arc from Bob to Stan to Jane and back again.

"They'll see the light under the door," Jane said.

"No," Vince said.

"What if it's the police?" Jane said. "You'd better get out the back way."

"It's not the police."

A bolt of fear had exploded in Vince's chest at Jane's words. No, it couldn't be the police! His job wasn't done yet. He needed time, *time!*

His throat moved and the gun shook as it pointed at Bob. *At least I can do this,* he thought.

The doorbell ringing, someone knocking loudly on the door now. Bob started up, then sank down nervelessly as Vince extended his right arm and the dark barrel pointed at Bob's head.

"Vince, you'd better go out the back way," Jane said. "If it's—"

"Shut up!"

"But if it's the police."

"It's not!"

"It might be, Vince," Stan had added hurriedly.

"What if it *is* the police?" Bob suddenly joined in. Scare him, he thought, drive him away.

Vince's eyes jerked from one to the other.

Now they were all suddenly still, dead still, and Bob felt his heart hammering.

For, in the front hall they could hear the pounding on the door; but above the pounding, a voice calling.

"Bob! *Bob!*"

Bob jumped to his feet.

"Ruth," he muttered, his face bone white, a hundred frightened thoughts tearing through his brain.

Vince felt his heartbeat skip and his muscles tighten. A sudden smile lit up his gaunt, sweat-greased features. *Ruth!* She'd come to him!

He started for the hall.

"No," he suddenly heard Bob gasp and, before his startled eyes, Bob broke into a run for the hall.

"Ruth!" Bob yelled, "Ruth, get away! *Get away!*"

"Stop it!" Vince screamed.

Bob didn't stop.

"Ruth, get away!" he shouted, "Ruth, get...!"

The thunder of the gun explosion drowned out his words. Bob suddenly went lurching against the wall and bounced off, landing on one knee, a surprised expression on his face.

Vince pulled the trigger again but nothing happened. Outside, in the hall, he heard Ruth scream out Bob's name. He broke into a run for the door. Bob tried to reach up and grab his leg but Vince kicked the feebly outstretched arm and Bob toppled over on his face with a rattling gasp. As Vince leaped over his body he noticed blood, slick and red across the leather of Bob's jacket.

"Vince, *don't!*" Jane screamed as she ran toward Bob. Stan stood by the couch, immobile with shock.

Vince jerked open the front door and Ruth recoiled with a breathless cry, her eyes suddenly wide with horror.

Vince grabbed at her, forgetting the gun, and the barrel cracked across her forearm, driving a numbing bolt of pain up her arm.

Vince thrust the gun into his waistband and grabbed Ruth's arm.

"Come *in* here!" he gasped.

Wordless, staring, she was dragged into the apartment and the door slammed behind her. Then, as she was spun around, she saw Bob half in the living room, half in the hallway, crumpled on the rug with Jane kneeling over him.

"Bob!"

The shock was so great she could hardly speak. Instinctively, she started forward, but Vince jerked her back. She turned for a moment and looked at him with a startled, confused expression. Then she turned again and her voice broke.

"Bob, Bob," she mumbled. "I'm—"

Vince pulled her against him and, as in a nightmare, she saw his white face loom before her and felt his cold lips brush across her cheek as she twisted away instinctively.

"Ruth, *Ruth...*" Vince's voice was husky and shaking. It was Ruth, his Ruth; she had come to him. Ruth felt his lean body press into hers and she thought she was going to scream. Over Vince's shoulder she saw Bob lying there on the rug and Jane looking up now, her face white.

Jane saw that Vince's back was turned. Abruptly she pushed up from the floor. Stan jerked out his hand and caught her wrist.

"What are you doing?" he whispered in fright.

"Let *go!*" she hissed back.

She tore from his grasp and started for the bedroom. Stan jumped up, his face slack, and ran around the couch edge. He reached the door a second before she did.

"Don't be insane!" he begged her in a hoarse whisper. "You saw what he did to Bob!"

"God *damn* you!" Her voice was a crackling mutter of hate.

Her eyes fled to the hall. Then, suddenly, she turned and ran dizzily across the living room, her head aching. Stan started toward her but she reached the phone first and jerked up the receiver.

Dead. She'd forgotten the living room phone was only an extension from the bedroom connection; the one Vince had ripped out.

Suddenly all the fury and hate exploded in a scream that tore from her lips.

"I'll *kill* him!"

With a wrenching sob she shoved aside Stan and started running for the kitchen.

In the hall, Vince heard her scream and, suddenly, he shoved Ruth aside. She crashed into the wall with a gasp and Vince grabbed his gun. He raced past Ruth into the living room, jumping over Bob's motionless body.

Ruth pushed away from the wall and moved on trembling legs toward her husband.

Jane was pulling out a kitchen drawer as Vince came in. Without a thought he jumped toward her and pushed her against a cabinet. She whirled with a sob, a carving knife clutched in her right hand.

"I'll kill you!" she screamed in his face.

The gun clattered to the floor unheeded as he grabbed for her wrist.

"Vince!" he heard Stan cry from the kitchen doorway.

Vince's mind erupted. The world was trying to trap him! For a moment he and Jane strained against each other. Then, with a vicious snarl, he drove his knee up into Jane's stomach and she doubled over with a retching gag. The knife went skidding across the cabinet top and clattered into the sink.

Then, as Vince whirled, he saw Stan on his knees grabbing at the gun.

With a grunt he brought up his knee again, this time into Stan's face. Stan went flailing back onto the linoleum, striking his head against the bottom of a cabinet door.

Vince grabbed up the gun, pointed it at Stan's chest and pulled the trigger. There was only a clicking sound as the hammer hit. Vince pulled the trigger again, again.

Empty.

With a howl of berserk fury he flung the gun with all his might at Stan; but his aim was bad and the gun bounced off the cabinet door and skidded across the linoleum.

Vince scuttled back until he banged against the sink cabinet. His left arm was pinned against the edge and he gasped at the pain.

Gritting his teeth, his shaking fingers moved into the sink and drew out the long knife.

He stood there shaking, looking down at the two of them writhing on the floor. His thin chest shuddered with breaths and he could feel warm drops of blood running down his arm again.

Jane half sat, half lay against the sink cabinet, her legs drawn up, her hands pressed into her stomach. Her face was white, her open mouth gasping for breath. Little sounds of gagging agony sounded in her throat as she writhed in pain. A cough burst through her lips, racking and dry.

Stan struggled to his knees, moaning from the pain. It had been like a spike driven into his brain. For a moment he had blacked out and thought he was going to die. Then the sounds and sights of the kitchen had flickered back to him again—Vince leaning against the sink, panting, the long knife sticking out from his right hand, Jane lying there and...

Stan started up.

"Jane," he mumbled in a thick voice.

"Get up," Vince gasped. "Get up."

As Stan stood on wobbling legs, Vince backed into the living room. He lowered the knife until he held it at his side, pointing at Stan.

Then Vince glanced over to where Ruth was kneeling by Bob, sobbing and trying to stop the bleeding with her fingers.

"Get to you in a—in a minute," Vince gasped.

He turned to Stan. Stan was trying to help Jane to her feet but she couldn't get up. Vince's head whipped around. What was he going to do? There were too many people to keep track of; he had to make them go away. He wanted to be alone with Ruth.

The bathroom.

"You..." he said, forgetting Stan's name for a moment, "you...*Stan*. Take her in the bathroom."

Stan looked at him with sick, frightened eyes.

"What?" he asked, a break in his voice.

"Get her in the *bathroom*, I said!" Vince said loudly. Why didn't anyone *listen* to him?

Stan leaned over Jane.

"Honey," he said brokenly. "Honey. We—"

Vince watched him, trembling with anger when nothing happened.

"God damn it, get her up!"

He started toward the kitchen, then looked at Ruth again. She was looking at him, her face white and drawn.

"Vince," she murmured, "help..."

He raised his right hand to let her know he'd be with her in a second. He saw the knife blade pointing at her and drew it down quickly.

"I'll, I'll, I'll—" he stuttered nervously and almost felt as if he were going to cry. Everything was so complex and nerve-wracking.

"Vince!" Ruth begged.

He didn't hear her. He was looking at Stan.

"Damn it!" he cried furiously, *"get her up!"*

Stan tried to, but Jane's legs were curled up to keep the pressure off her stomach.

"Get away," she groaned. "Get away."

Tears of pain ran down her cheeks.

"Honey, we've got to..."

He gasped and jolted to the side as he felt something cold and thin jab into his shoulder. He stood against the sink trembling, feeling blood trickle down his back and the wild sensation of pain in his right shoulder.

Vince bent over Jane and stuck the point of the knife to her throat.

"Get up, get up!" he ordered, his voice shrill in the tiny kitchen.

"Vince, don't..." Stan sobbed.

Jane looked up at Vince, her mouth still open, gasping for breath.

Suddenly Vince grabbed her hair with his left hand. A bolt of pain raged up the arm and he let go with a gasp. Still holding the knife, he grabbed Jane's dark hair with his other hand and tried to drag her to her feet. She'd get out of here if he had to drag her out himself!

A breathless cry of pain twisted Jane's lips as Vince pulled her up.

"Get up, I said!"

Vince backed away as she stumbled into the sink with a sob of pain and Stan caught her around the waist with one trembling arm. The two of them stood there shaking without control, driven and afraid. All subtleties had gone from their minds; they were two hurt, frightened animals; the eyes they watched him with were dumb and uncalculating with fright.

"Get in the bathroom," Vince said.

He backed into the living room but they still stood there as if they didn't understand him.

Hot tears flew from Vince's eyes as he leaped forward with a gagging curse.

"God damn it!" he screamed at them. "Are you—"

"Don't hurt us!" Stan begged.

Vince backed away, shivering, while they came stumbling out of the kitchen, Jane bent over clutching her stomach, Stan, eyes wide and dumb, staring at Vince.

Ruth gasped as they came out. She couldn't understand it; it was like a senseless, incredible dream. From the moment she'd seen Vince, then Bob lying on the floor, her mind wouldn't function. Thoughts jumbled one on top of the other.

"Stan," she muttered, "Jane…"

She knelt there, looking first at them, then at Bob's white face, at the blood running across the leather jacket and around his still body to the floor.

"Go on, go on," Vince snapped in a jaded voice.

Vince's mind felt numbed now. Too many things had happened. He didn't want to think; it was too painful. There was only one thing he wanted to worry about. Ruth and him going away and…

"I'll be right out," he told Ruth in what he thought was a comforting tone.

She stared at him unbelievingly.

Then, with a gasp, she stood and ran for the hall. *I have to get help!* The words burst in her brain, the first coherent thought she'd had since Vince had opened the door.

She turned in numbed surprise as Vince grabbed her coat and pulled her back.

"You're not going away?" he asked, surprise in his voice, incredulous surprise.

For a second she stared at him blankly.

"I—I have to get help," she said feebly. She didn't understand.

"No," he said as if he were reasoning with her. "No, Ruth. You and I…"

She still didn't understand. She tried to pull away but he held on to her. She stared at him, face still expressionless, eyes wide and uncomprehending.

"Ruth, you and I …" he started again.

"But I have to get help!" she suddenly burst out. "My husband is hurt!"

She recoiled as his face twisted angrily.

"You're not going anywhere!" he snapped, "I killed him for you and—"

"You!"

She backed into the wall with a shudder.

Vince's throat moved. He wouldn't let himself believe that look of horror on her face. He grabbed at her wrist.

"Get in there," he said.

She froze against the wall, staring at him.

"I said get *in* there!"

His voice broke and he almost started crying. Why wouldn't she do what he asked? What was the matter with her? It was obvious that he'd only killed Bob to help her.

Her body shuddered as Vince half dragged her into the living room. Stan and Jane were still there, Stan leaning against the bedroom door and supporting Jane, who still bent over, hands clutched over her stomach.

"I said get in the bathroom," Vince ordered.

He pulled Ruth back from Bob.

"He's hurt!" she cried out at him.

"He's dead! Leave him alone!" Vince cried back at her.

Her white hands pressed into her cheeks.

"No."

Stan moved across the bedroom staggering because he had to almost carry Jane.

Vince pulled Ruth into the bedroom.

"No," she muttered in a dead voice. "No, he isn't."

"He *is*, he *is*," Vince insisted, then looked at Stan. "Get in there!"

He pushed Ruth toward a bed.

"Sit there," he said.

She tried to rush for the living room but he stood in her path and drove his left hand across her cheek. They both gasped at the same time, she from surprise, he from pain.

She backed away with a whimper.

"Sit down, Ruth," he said.

Her brain wouldn't work. She stood there staring at him, her heart pounding in great, body-shaking beats.

"Sit down."

Vince wanted to cry because nobody would do what he asked. He wanted to be nice to her and make her happy. What was wrong with her?

Now he heard the sound of the toilet cover in the bathroom being knocked down.

Vince moved across the bedroom and flicked on the bathroom light. He saw Jane sitting down and Stan turned, blinking, his face very white.

"Close the door," Vince told him. "Lock it."

"Huh?"

Vince pulled the door shut. As he waited he looked toward Ruth.

"Don't move," he told her. "I don't want to hurt you."

He turned back.

"Lock it!" he yelled.

He heard the door being locked. Then he looked around and found a chair. He propped the back of it underneath the knob and kicked it in tight.

There. They were out of the way.

He turned for Ruth.

4 :35 AM

The two maiden ladies came marching up the steps, obdurate, thin-lipped with puritanical ire. They wore their robes up to the top of their necks, their respectability to the tops of their heads.

"I think we've had just about enough from the Sheldons," said one, her voice acid with a righteous disgust.

"It's time their *parties* were reported to the authorities," said the other.

"Parties indeed!" the other woman joined in. "More like..."

She looked over her shoulder lest someone be found trailing them. Then she looked back at her sister.

"Orgies."

Her lips framed the word; she dared not speak it aloud.

"Wouldn't be surprised." said the other, "not a bit. That *lady* he married. She's just a..."

Her eyes too moved over one shoulder.

"Hussy," she finished, satisfied that no one lurked behind, taking notes.

The two of them reached the top of the flight and moved across the hall toward the door.

"Almost five in the morning," said one of them, "and still they're at it; banging on the piano and knocking over furniture and breaking bottles and screaming at the top of their lungs. It's a disgrace, I tell you, a disgrace."

"They're probably just having a little *fun*," snapped, the other.

"Uh," was all her sister replied.

They stood before the door and one of them pushed in the door-bell button.

They stood there waiting for someone to answer.

"He'll probably be *drunk* when he comes to the door," one predicted ruthlessly.

"I hope it's not *her*," said the other. "I don't even want to *look* at her."

"Hussy," murmured the first.

No one came to the door. Inside, they thought they heard a cry, then only silence.

"I'm sure you're having a *good time*," said the one addressing the revelers she imagined within, "but we're not leaving here until you open the door."

They both nodded once, sternly in agreement.

Silence inside. The two maiden ladies shuffled blue and pink mules on the cold hall floor. Each held the same posture, each held the top of her robe shut at the throat with a clenched right hand. Each seethed with indignation.

"Well, of all the...!" one finally snapped angrily.

"I never..." said the other.

"Probably too *busy* to answer."

The first held her finger against the bell.

"Well, you'll answer," she said sharply to the sybarites she envisioned in every corner of the apartment.

"You'll answer if we have to—to *ring* your brains out!"

They both nodded once. They liked the phrase. Ring them out. Toll out the evil and the blackness, burn out the...

"Who's there?" they heard a voice inside.

The turkey throat of the first woman moved.

"Kindly open the door, Mr. Sheldon," said the woman.

"Who *is* it?"

The first looked at the second. Her lips framed the words, *"That's not Mr. Sheldon."*

"We're from apartment 7C," said the second woman. "We live in the apartment below and you're keeping us awake with your *party."*

The way she said *party* made them both nod vigorously. Whoever it was inside could not fail to recognize, they knew, the acidity in the pronunciation of the word.

"There's no party," they heard the voice inside say.

"We would like to speak to Mr. Sheldon," said the first maiden lady, "We feel—"

"He's *sick,"* interrupted the voice, "He can't see anyone."

Sick. The first framed the word with her lips and the second nodded with a bitter smile. They knew what *sick* meant.

"I'm sorry but we must demand silence," said the second woman, taking the reins in her hand. "We cannot—"

"Go away!"

"Oh!"

They stood there trembling with outrage.

"Very well," said the first. "Perhaps we'll just call the police then and—"

"Don't!" cried the voice inside.

The old ladies smiled and nodded to themselves. There, that had put the fear of God in him.

But the door stayed shut.

"Maybe he thinks he's having a great laugh on us," one muttered to the second, visualizing the man inside doubled over with scornful laughter.

The other one spoke, supposedly to her sister, but, actually, directly at the door.

"Well, come along, Nell," she said, "I guess we'll just have to call the police then."

They stood there a moment longer. Then with a firming of lips, a stiffening of backs, they moved slowly away from the door.

"Well, did you ever?" muttered the first as they reached the steps.

"No, I never," responded the other.

"Should we call the police do you think?"

"I—think we should."

But they weren't sure. They didn't want to get involved in any trouble. They lived a simple, cloistered life and they didn't want police asking them questions. Especially on the Sabbath.

As they started down the steps one of them stopped.

"Good heavens," she said, leaning over to squint at the steps, "what are those spots?"

The other one looked, gasped.

"They look like…"

▄ ▄ ▄ ▄

Vince lay against the door until the sound of their footsteps had shuffled away. Then his throat moved and he pushed away from the door. They were going to call the police! He had to get Ruth and get away!

I hope I didn't hurt her, he thought anxiously as he moved down the hallway.

When the doorbell had rung Ruth had cried out, tried to run to the door and answer it. Vince had struck her to make her quiet.

Why did he keep hurting people? All he wanted to do was live with Ruth and be happy. And all he did was hurt people. Some people didn't matter, of course. Harry didn't matter and Bob didn't matter. But he didn't mean to hurt the man in the subway station or to hurt Stan or…well, Jane, he didn't care about.

Then, as he started into the living room he gasped and stopped in his tracks.

Bob was looking at him.

Vince stood there rigidly looking down at him. *He's dead,* his mind said. *He's dead and he's staring at me.*

"V-V-Vince."

Bob groped for speech, the word thick and sticky in his throat.

"No." Vince cowered away.

"Vince."

Vince edged around Bob into the living room. He couldn't touch Bob now. It was different. Before it hadn't been so bad. Bob had tried to send Ruth away and he shouldn't have done that; Vince was forced to shoot him.

But now it was different. He didn't want to touch Bob, he didn't even want to look at him.

"Vince…h-help."

"No," Vince muttered, "no."

"Vince."

"No, leave me alone," Vince gasped. "No. I don't want to..."

He ran into the bedroom and shut the door again. He leaned, against it, shaking. Why didn't anything go right? Why wasn't Bob dead like he should be?

"I—didn't mean to..." he muttered, but he didn't know what he meant by that.

Carefully he locked the door and moved over to where Ruth lay sprawled across the bed on her back. He had to hurry; they had to go before the police came.

Quickly he felt for her pulse. His throat moved. She was all right. He straightened up. He should get a wet rag and wipe her face. But he couldn't use the bathroom because Stan and Jane were there. And, if he went to the kitchen he'd have to go past Bob again. He didn't want to do that either. Vince was afraid. Suddenly, all rage and violent hate had gone from him. He was afraid and nervous.

He sat down beside Ruth and held her hand. He looked at her still face. His eyes grew pained when he saw the bruise where he'd struck her on the jaw. He shouldn't have hit her. But if he hadn't she would have run into the hall. Why? What was the matter with her?

He stroked her hand slowly and his throat moved.

"Ruth?" he said. Timidly.

He started to bend over to kiss her but then he straightened up. No, he'd wait. Until she'd wake up and smile at him and kiss him and they'd go away together and start a new life.

"Just you and me, Ruth," he said to her as if she could hear. "We'll go somewhere—together. Some little place, somewhere. Some town, you know, maybe in Ohio. It doesn't matter, maybe Missouri. I can get a job in a bar maybe or a roadhouse. I can play the piano and we'll have our secret and we'll get a little house to live in. And maybe I'll give a concert and—well, anyway we'll have a little house. And—and we'll be happy."

He sat there looking at her as if he wanted her to answer him. He forgot about the police coming. He was content to sit there with her.

Abstractedly his eyes moved down from her face, over her chest.

He drew them back, conscious of looking. No, that wasn't right, he wasn't that way. They were going to get married and be happy together. Vince's throat moved and he drew in shaking breaths. He tried to ignore the hot feeling in his stomach, the feeling he knew so well. He shuddered.

He looked down. *She looks hot,* his mind said. *It's hot in here. I better open her coat or she'll get overheated and then she'll catch a cold when we go to the train and...*

Nervously, hands shaking, he undid the belt of her coat and lay the coat open on both sides.

"There," he muttered.

Then, guiltily, his eyes moved toward the bathroom. Could they see him through the keyhole? He swallowed and felt a sinking sensation in his stomach.

No, the chair covered the keyhole; and the bedroom door was locked. He was safe with her, alone with her. No one could get in and...

"No."

He muttered it again, defying himself, becoming frightened at the heat that was crawling along his limbs. His arm ached and he felt a hot flush moving up his cheeks. *No, no.* His hands twitched on his lap. He reached out to touch her, stopped. A tight, hot ball was forming in his stomach. No, it wasn't right.

His eyes moved down over her body. A harsh breath burst from his nostrils. She had on only a thin sweater over her brassiere. He could see the movement of her breasts as she breathed. He watched them rise and fall.

"No," he muttered.

But he couldn't stop. He stared at her body. After all, his mind reasoned weakly, we're going to get married. I'm going to be her husband and we...

His throat moved harshly. His hand reached out, he jerked it back again.

"No, I just..." he started, then broke off into a pitiful moan.

What was the matter with her? His mind went off on a new tack. She should know better than to wear such a tight sweater on her body. That wasn't nice. Any girl who did that was...

Trying bores, Vincent. Disgusting filth!

He twisted in actual pain on the bed. His arm throbbed and felt as if it were expanding.

He turned away with a hiss. He closed his eyes and shook without control as he sat there.

Abruptly then, he turned back and slapped her face. He grabbed her by the hair and shook her.

"Wake *up*," he said, almost angrily, almost resenting her being such a temptation. "Wake up. Don't you see we..."

His hand moved out and touched her breast.

He pulled it away with a whimper, a tingling sensation in his fingers. No! Wrong, dirty, *dirty!*

He clenched his fists until his left arm ached and burned. I'll punish myself! I'll cut off my hand and—

Something snapped. He turned and looked over her body, his chest rising and falling in shaking movements.

And, suddenly, with a wretched sob, he dug his fingers beneath the neck of her sweater, jerked with all his might and ripped it off her body.

"Ruth..."

His voice was a gasp, a snarl, a shuddering ache of sound.

4:40 AM

He held a cold, wet washcloth against Jane's forehead. She sat erect, her face still white, her hands still over her stomach.

"How...are you?" he asked.

She didn't answer. She took a ragged breath and didn't even look at him.

His eyes fell.

"You may as well be nice to me," he muttered. "We'll probably both be dead soon."

He'd meant that to sound cynically brave, but the words made him shudder. He stood up.

"Floor's cold," he said.

She sat there, staring at the wall.

"What should we do?" he said, just to say something. He knew very well there was nothing they could do.

"Why don't you jump out the window?" she said bitterly.

His lips pressed together. He turned away from her and looked at the window.

Jane looked up in surprise as Stan clambered into the bathtub and pushed up the window.

As he looked out, Stan could see that there was a six inch ledge that led along the building to the window that opened on the eighth floor hallway.

His stomach fell as he looked down at the street, murky grey in the early morning. What would she say if I *did* jump, he wondered.

"I could," he said, thinking aloud.

"Shut that window," she said irritably. "There's a draft."

His throat moved and he turned to face her.

"I could get out," he said. "If…"

She looked at him blankly.

"What are you talking about?"

He licked his lips.

"The window," he said. "There's a ledge."

With a grunt of pain she stood and moved for the bathtub, grimacing as she walked. He stepped aside and she lifted one leg over the edge of the tub with an indrawn breath. Stan took her arm and supported her and she didn't pull away or say anything.

She looked out.

"My God, there is," she said, suddenly excited.

She looked at him quickly and he felt his muscles tighten. There was no scorn in her face, no reviling.

"Do you think you could?" she asked.

He swallowed and stared at her. He was sorry he'd mentioned it. He'd never thought…

She turned away, her face falling into its old, bitter lines. He reached out impulsively and caught her arm.

"I could," he said, "if—if you asked me."

For a moment they looked directly at each other and something flickered between them, something that had not been a part of their relationship for years.

"Stan," she said.

He tensed himself.

"I'll go," he said.

She looked at him for another moment.

"Hurry then," she said.

Stan stepped out of his slippers and stood on the cold porcelain of the tub. Then he took a deep breath and, holding onto the window ledge, he stepped up on the side of the tub. He almost slipped, then his toes caught hold. He stood there, his heart hammering, looking down at the grey pit that was Manhattan before dawn. He swallowed hard.

Before the feeling got worse, he put one leg over the window sill. As he did they heard the doorbell ring.

Stan stopped moving and they looked at each other.

"Who's that?" Stan muttered.

She shook her head once and they listened. As Stan drew back his leg they heard a sound of feet running in the bedroom, then a muffled cry. Silence for a moment, more footsteps and the bedroom door shut.

In silence, they stood there listening.

The next thing they heard was the bedroom door opening and closing again. Then, in a moment, the sound of a muffled voice in the bedroom, Vince talking to Ruth.

A sudden coldness covered Stan. For a moment he'd hoped it was the police and that he wouldn't have to climb out the window.

"It was probably those two biddies downstairs," Jane said, "coming to complain about the noise."

"Oh, God," Stan said bitterly. "And I bet they were too stupid to realize something was wrong."

Jane's smile was as bitter as his voice.

"Noise from our place is nothing new to them," she said.

They were silent a moment. Then she said, "You'd better go. And *hurry*. When I felt Bob's heart before, he was still alive. There may still be a chance to save him. I don't think Vince will do anything to Ruth."

Stan looked at her a moment. Then he nodded and lowered his head so she wouldn't see that he was afraid.

He put his leg over the sill again, then drew up the other until he was sitting on the window sill, his legs hanging out the window. He felt a cold morning wind blowing over his legs.

He gripped the window ledge more tightly.

"Well…" he said.

But there wasn't any more to say. He turned over onto his stomach with a straining of muscles. A dull pain started in his shoulder where Vince had jabbed him with the knife. He'd forgotten about it.

The cold wind rushed over him as he lowered his feet slowly down toward the ledge, his face red and taut from the strain.

"Where's the ledge?" he muttered nervously.

His bare feet touched the cold concrete ledge and he swallowed. He raised his eyes and looked in at her.

A smile flickered over her lips. It had been so long since she'd smiled at him and meant it. It was hard.

"Be careful," she said and it made him want to cry out in joy.

"I will," he said and moved away from the window.

He held on to the window edge as long as he could. Then he stopped. *Don't look down,* he told himself. He felt his heart beating rapidly. The wind gushed around his body and tried to push him off the ledge.

He saw he would have to let go of the bathroom window and lunge for a grip on the hall window.

But what if it were locked? The thought made his heart stop for a second.

He stood there taking deep breaths of the cold air. It flooded down his throat, chilling him. He wanted to cry out. But he knew he couldn't; not now. He couldn't crawl back into the bathroom, abject and defeated, and face Jane. He just couldn't bear to lose the faith she seemed to have in him now.

He stood there on the ledge shaking and holding onto the bathroom window edge with rigid fingers.

"Are you all right?" he heard Jane ask.

His throat moved and he bit his lip.

"Yes," he answered weakly, "all right."

He looked toward the hall window. There was nothing to grab. He stood staring at the window. There had to be something!

Tentatively he stretched out his right leg. He could just touch the other window with his toes.

There was no getting away from it. He'd have to move along the ledge hugging the wall until he stood before the hall window.

He caught his breath, held it. And let go of the bathroom window.

For one horrible moment he thought he was going to fall. But it was only an illusion fostered by fear. He leaned into the building and clutched at the rough stone with his nails.

Now he moved his right foot cautiously along the edge. The cold wind still blew over him. He moved his left foot, then his right again, sliding it over the cold, rough concrete. His stomach moved and he thought maybe he was going to be sick. He swallowed the feeling, repressing it. *God help me.*

He reached the window. He stood before it and, slowly, his right hand edged up to the inside edge of the window under the lock. His fingers tensed, he tried to push up the window.

It was locked.

●　●　●　●

With a groan Bob raised himself on one elbow, a clicking sound in his throat. Blood still trickled over his jacket and he felt as if his shoulder and back were on fire. The room swam around him and he blinked. Sweat ran down into his eyes and he tried to shake his head but the movement made his shoulder and back hurt too much.

His throat moved convulsively and he gasped for breath. He had to get help.

Ruth. Where was she? She must be in the bedroom with Vince. He had to get help. Now, now…

He started to drag himself toward the front door. As he did a rushing wave of blackness dashed over him and almost drew him under. He gritted his teeth and tensed himself. *I mustn't black out. I mustn't!*

He started crawling for the door, trailing blood behind him on the rug.

He was halfway to the door when he heard Ruth's scream from the bedroom.

●　●　●　●

Jane whirled from the window when she heard the scream. As she moved toward the door she heard Vince's angry voice and then a sound of struggling in the bedroom.

He's killing her! The thought burst in her mind and she felt her heart catch.

Suddenly she found herself at the door. She turned the lock quickly and shoved. The door was blocked. She rammed her weight against the door and felt the flaring of pain in her stomach and head.

Then the chair fell over and Jane half fell into the bedroom.

Vince started up from the bed looking frightened and guilty. Ruth was pushed back against the head of the bed, one arm across her exposed breasts, the other raised up to ward off a blow.

Sex. The word jerked across Jane's mind as she saw them. And it suddenly seemed as if the answer were obvious.

With a rasping sob, Vince grabbed up the knife and turned back to Jane.

Jane calmly, slowly, as if it were something she had planned for all her life, let down the straps of her nightgown.

"Vincie," she said in a low voice.

Vince felt his stomach muscles jerk in at the sound of her voice. He stared helplessly as the soft folds of the robe dropped to the floor and Jane was naked to the waist. His throat moved convulsively and he found himself backing away a step.

"Come to me, Vincie," Jane murmured, writhing her body a little bit. "Come to me."

The hot flush on Vince's cheeks flamed into life again. He felt breath shaking in his chest. *No, no,* the voice he heard in his brain was weak and without conviction. He stared at her with sick, hungry eyes.

Then Jane moved her right hip a little and the gown rustled to the rug. She stepped out of the crumpled black folds, arms stretched out. This is my fate, she thought as she moved for Vince.

"You don't want her," she heard herself saying, "She's not the kind you like. She's no fun, Vincie. I'm fun. I'm a *lot* of fun."

"No..." muttered Vince. He felt himself raising the knife as if he were going to attack Jane.

Ruth looked at Jane with stark, frightened eyes that didn't understand. It was hard for her to breathe.

Now Jane was between the two beds. She took a deep breath and the hard points of her breasts rose. "Come here, baby," she muttered. She couldn't look at Ruth. She had the terrible feeling that she'd start to cry helplessly if she looked at Ruth.

"I'm waiting, baby," she said and edged closer to the table.

Vince moved toward her. *I don't care,* he heard a voice in him. *I'm going to...*

There was no heat in Jane's body. The tautness of her flesh was the rigidity of frozen things, of cold calculation. Her body meant nothing, it was only a tool, a means to an end. As long as she didn't look at Ruth.

Vince was too close, she suddenly realized. Too close; there was not enough time.

"Come to me, come to me," she murmured quickly. "Never mind her. Let her *watch*."

Ruth stared with stricken eyes at Jane, at her tight, ruthless face. She couldn't. *Oh, Jane, Jane...*

Jane's smooth arm slid around Vince's back. His lean body came close and she pushed against him. Her mouth opened as it closed over his. She felt the handle of the knife bruising her back as Vince embraced her.

One of her hands left Vince's back and, rapidly, gestured toward the door. Ruth caught her breath, suddenly understanding, hating herself for not understanding. As quietly as she could, her heart pounding, she edged across the bed. Jane's hand moved down to the drawer now. She eased it open while, with her other arm, she held Vince's body close, kept his face against hers with her clinging, biting lips. She hardly felt his left hand moving up her chest. She felt almost numb.

Then she jerked at the pistol.

A spear of ice impaled her as the barrel got caught on the drawer. Vince suddenly pulled away and looked down. His heart seemed to jolt in his chest. His pupils expanded suddenly and he knew that he'd been tricked again, lied to.

"No!" he screamed at her. Jane recoiled in sudden fear as he lunged with the knife. At the door, Ruth screamed.

▬ ▬ ▬ ▬

Stan pounded on the front door, his wrist still running blood from the long gash he'd gotten punching in the hall window.

He turned away with a gasp. What am I going to do? He turned back with a sudden whine and threw himself bodily against the door. No use! He felt a surge of terror and uselessness at not being able to get in and protect her.

He turned away and rushed down the hall to the door of the apartment across the way. He rang the bell and pounded on the door.

"Help!" he yelled. "Help!"

Then the door of his own apartment opened and Bob came staggering out. With a startled gasp, Stan jumped forward and raced down to where Bob had sunk to one knee, blood spattering on the hall floor.

"Bob, are you…?"

Without finishing the question he looked into the apartment. Where was she?

He started to bend over to help Bob up, but Ruth's scream and a crashing sound in the bedroom jolted him up. He dove into the apartment.

As he reached the bedroom door he heard it being locked.

"Jane!" he cried brokenly, *"Jane!"*

"Get away!" he heard Vince yell, "I'll kill you if you don't get away!"

A whining breath broke from Stan's lips and, with a berserk cry, he lunged at the door, driving his broad shoulder into it. It didn't move. He pounded his fists on the door.

"Jane!"

He backed up and ran at the door. It shuddered under the impact. He moved back again and crashed his large body into it. The lock snapped and he went rushing into the bedroom. As he did he saw the white face of Vince flash by, the figure of Ruth standing by the bed.

Then, as he stopped himself and spun around, he saw Vince run out the opened doorway and into the hall.

And, suddenly, with a gagging cry, he saw Jane lying crumpled on the floor, the lamp shattered around her.

The knife handle sticking out from her chest.

He stood there petrified for a long moment, his eyes wide and unbelieving. Then, abruptly, a clacking sob shook him and he ran to her.

"Jane…"

Ruth looked at him as he stumbled over and knelt by Jane. Then she ran from the room.

Stan put his hand on the knife handle, then his fingers twitched away. He felt a great pressure on his brain as if someone were holding huge, hot hands against his skull and pressing. The room seemed to twist and contort out of shape. He almost fainted.

"Jane," he mumbled. *"Jane."*

Like a child trying to wake its mother.

Her eyes opened, slowly, with a painful fluttering.

"Jane, you're—all right." The last word spoken feebly in the realization that all hope was gone.

Her throat moved and she made a clicking sound.

"Jane, I'll get a doctor," he suddenly gasped.

Her hand closed weakly on his pajama leg, holding him. Her lips moved as if she were trying to speak. But no sound came at first.

Then she said, "No."

"Jane, I..."

She made a tiny hushing sound as if she would silence all his fear and terror.

"You—" a gasping intake of breath, "—be better now."

"Jane!"

"Please." Her throat moved and she grimaced at the pain.

"I'll call a doctor!"

"No, no." She pressed her lips together. The lipstick was all smeared and caked.

"You..."

Again her throat moved. She could hardly breathe.

"Stan?"

He bent over, tears rolling down his cheeks.

"W-what, darling? What?"

"Kiss me."

His sob shook his body.

"Please," she whispered, then her face suddenly grew taut. *"Now,"* she said.

He bent over and placed his shaking mouth on hers. Her fingers tightened on his pajama leg. Her lips parted.

She died as he kissed her.

When Vince came rushing out of the apartment he saw Bob still on one knee in the hall. With a gasp he lunged past Bob and started racing down the hall, his black shoes clicking on the tiles.

As he passed another door, it opened and a man in a bathrobe came out.

"Now what—" he started to say, then his head snapped as Vince rushed past him.

Vince reached the stairs and started racing down. He kept sobbing and whimpering in fright as he descended. Half way down the flight he almost tripped and his right arm shot out to grab the banister. His shoes slipped on the edge of a step and he skidded down on his side, holding on to the banister with clawing fingers.

Caught!

The word knifed at his brain as he ran down the steps. No escape! Everybody was against him! Bob was alive and Ruth wasn't going away with him. Nothing was right! Hot tears of futility scalded down his cheeks as he ran and the stairs looked like gelatin through the quivering lenses of his tears. Lost, lost, lost!

"Saul," he gasped, "help me, Saul."

Then, at the fourth floor, he suddenly skidded to a halt, his breath caught.

With unbelieving eyes he looked down the stair well and saw the police officers running up toward him.

For a moment he couldn't move. He stood there dizzily, staring at them.

Then a sob broke in his throat and, whirling, he started up the steps again.

Fifth floor, around to the stairs; sixth floor, around to the stairs; seventh floor. His breath burst from open mouth now, there was a stitch jabbing a hot spear into his side; his breaths were choking wheezes.

The eighth floor. He stopped for breath and looked toward the apartment.

Bob was gone, the man was gone. He saw the door of the other apartment open and heard Ruth's voice inside.

Then he looked suddenly at Stan's apartment.

Stan was in the doorway looking at him.

"Stan?" he said.

Stan stood there and Vince started toward him suddenly.

"Stan, don't let them…"

He recoiled with a gasp as Stan came at him with the blood-stained knife in his hand.

With a sob, he whirled and started up the last flight of steps to the roof. He heard Stan break into a run, his bare feet thudding on the hall floor.

Vince fumbled at the hook on the heavy door with a sound of fury.

"Open," he told the door in a frenzied whisper.

"Open!"

Just before Stan reached him he knocked the thick hook off and shoved open the door. Stan's lunge didn't reach and Stan toppled forward on the gravel-topped roof.

Stan got to his knees, ignoring his torn pajamas, his bruised knees, the gashes he'd gotten on his wrist punching in the window. Everything in the world had disappeared but Vince; every hope, sensation, every fear. There was nothing but Vince racing across the roof, his shoes scrabbling on the gravel, his white face looking back over his shoulder as he ran.

Stan started forward. Slowly. There was no place Vince could go; no roof adjoined the apartment house. His bare feet moved and crunched over the gravel, his face stolid. His fingers tightened on the knife.

Vince reached the edge of the roof and whirled. Stan was coming toward him over the roof, the knife held at his side. Vince could see blood running down Stan's arm and dripping off the tip of the sharp blade. He could see Stan's face, white and like the mask of a dead man.

"Stan, no!" he yelled, "Stan, I didn't hurt you! Stan, don't do any—"

He leaped to the side and Stan went crashing into the side of the roof, almost toppling over the edge.

Stan turned, his face blank. He started toward Vince again.

"Stan," Vince muttered.

He ran a little ways across the roof, then turned.

"Stan, don't hurt me," he begged, tears rushing down his cheeks. "Stan, *please* don't hurt me!"

Stan raised the knife slowly.

Vince turned and ran again toward the door.

Then he recoiled and his shoes skidded on the gravel as two police officers came lunging through the doorway, pistols in their hands.

"No!" he cried.

Now he was caught between them. He ran to the side and stood with his back to the waist-high wall.

One of the officers moved toward him. The other moved toward Stan.

"Give me the knife, buddy," he said, stretching out his free hand.

"No," gagged Stan and he lunged toward Vince.

Vince shrank back against the wall.

"No," he muttered in a terrified voice. "No, it isn't fair. It isn't fair."

He pushed himself up on the wall until he was sitting on the edge. Stan tore away from the policeman's hold and jumped at Vince.

"Don't!" Vince screamed at him, screamed at the world.

Then he was gone.

And, when they reached the edge of the roof, they saw his body falling, his arms and legs kicking and flailing as he plummeted toward the sidewalk, his screams of horror echoing between the silent buildings.

5:00 AM

Ruth turned away from the stairs as the two men carried Bob down to the ambulance on a stretcher.

"Nothing fatal," the intern had assured her. "He'll be all right."

And Bob had smiled weakly at her, gripped her hand and she had told him she'd be right down to the hospital with him.

Now she walked back to the apartment.

Stan was in the bedroom. He'd put Jane on the bed and covered her up, all but her face. He was sitting beside her and staring at her.

He glanced at Ruth as she came in, his face dead and slack.

She put her hand on his shoulder.

"Stan," she said.

His throat moved.

"She was brave," was all he said.

"I—" She looked at him. "Yes," she said then, "she was."

Stan's head lowered and she stood there looking at him, feeling helpless before his sorrow.

"If there's anything..." she started.

"Thank you," he said hollowly.

She turned away and heard his tightly restrained sob.

And when she reached the street, she saw the two orderlies putting another stretcher into the ambulance, a stretcher that was completely covered.

The two officers got back in their patrol car.

"Yeah," said one, "I remember the case. The kid cracked up and killed his old man with a letter opener. Then he went to the office of this guy that was shot and he tried to kill him too. They put him away."

He made a grim sound.

"I guess he got away," he said.

"Well, he won't be killing anybody else," said the other one.

257

"No," said the first, "he won't."
And he shook his head.
"What a world," he said.
Forty minutes later the sun came up.

THE END

On Sunday

RIDE
THE
NIGHTMARE

WEDNESDAY NIGHT

CHAPTER ONE

IN THE HALL, the telephone rang.

"Now who's that at this hour?" Helen said, straightening up from the dishwasher.

"I'll bite—who?" asked Chris.

Helen made a face at him. "You," she said, "are just the funniest."

"I try."

"Sure you do."

Smiling, Helen left the kitchen and walked across the living room, her slippers making a muffled sound on the rug. In the hall, the telephone jangled stridently. They should have had it installed in the kitchen, she thought. It was an old thought; one which recurred every time the telephone rang after Connie had been put to bed.

Helen's fingers closed over the coolness of the phone and cut off its ringing. Pushing back a lock of hair with the receiver, she held it to her ear.

"Hello," she said.

"I want to talk to Chris Phillips," said a man's voice.

Helen felt herself bristle. The voice was so sharp, so demanding.

"I'm sorry," she said. "You have the wrong number."

Was that a laugh? It sounded more like a viscid clearing of the throat.

"I don't think so," said the man.

A look of irritation tightened Helen's face.

"I'm sorry but our name is Martin," she said.

"Never mind that," the man said, and Helen got a vision of teeth clenching, of lips drawn back. "Put Chris on the phone I said."

Helen shivered. "I'm afraid—" she started.

"I said put Chris on!"

Helen stared blankly at the receiver.

"You his wife?" the man asked.

"Yes. Now would you—?"

"So old Chris is married," said the man.

"You have the wrong number," said Helen.

"You just put Chris on," said the man. "You just put him on."

Impulsively, Helen dumped the receiver onto the table and headed back toward the kitchen, wondering why she hadn't hung up. Obviously, the man had a wrong number. It was just that he sounded so certain of himself. He'd intimidated her with his rude assurance.

"Who was it?" asked Chris.

"Some man," she told him, frowning. "He wants to talk to Chris."

"So what's the mystery?" he asked. "I'm Chris."

"Chris Phillips," she said before he'd finished.

He made a scoffing sound. "So what are we talking about?"

"He's—still on the line," she told him.

Chris looked surprised. "How come? Didn't you tell him he had a wrong number?"

"Yes, but—" She shrugged and looked exasperated. "He wouldn't listen. He just said—put Chris on."

He looked at her, a faint smile edging up the corners of his mouth.

"I'm sorry," she said.

"What's our name, lady?"

She shrugged. "So all right," she said. "You tell him."

"Yes, my love." Chris got up and walked out of the kitchen. Helen stood motionless beside the dishwasher listening to his stockinged feet thud across the living room. For some reason her heartbeat was unnaturally fast.

In the hall, Chris said: "Hello."

Helen found herself straining to hear the man's reply as if his voice were audible.

"I'm sorry," she heard Chris say. "You've made a mistake. My name is—"

There was a pause.

"I'm sorry," said Chris. "My name is Martin." His voice was louder now. Helen moved toward the living room.

"Now, listen," said Chris. "I'm telling you you're making a mistake."

Helen stood in the doorway looking toward the shadowy figure of her husband in the hall.

"My name is Martin, I tell you!"

Helen took an involuntary step into the living room, her heart beating even faster. She could feel it pummeling beneath her breast.

Chris shouted: *"What?!"*

When she reached him, he was trembling in the semi-darkness of the hall, staring into the receiver. She could hear the sharp buzzing of the dial tone.

"Chris, what is it?" she asked

His face was blank as he turned to her. Slowly, he lowered the receiver, feeling for its cradle. The dial tone stopped.

"Who was it? Did you know him?"

He shook his head.

"What did he *say?*"

"He said he was going to kill me," he told her.

"He said—" She couldn't finish. A vacuum of dread swept across her and, for a moment, she thought she was going to faint. "Chris," she murmured, clutching his arm.

He looked at her dazedly. "Chris, it was a wrong number."

"Of course it was," he said, hollowly.

"Well...who was he? Why should he—"

"I don't know."

"But that doesn't make—" She broke off, hearing a shrill quality in her voice. Taking in a deep breath, she tried to calm herself. "What did he say, Chris? Just that—"

"Just that he was going to kill me."

"But that doesn't make sense!"

"I know," he muttered.

"Maybe it's a joke," she said.

Chris didn't answer.

"You know how your friends at the club are always—"

"No." He shook his head. "It's not a joke."

"Call the police," she said.

"But what if—"

"What?"

"What if it is a—joke?"

"You just said it *wasn't.*"

"I know but—"

"Honey, whether it is or not—" Abruptly, she turned for the hall. "I'll call them," she said.

"No, I'll do it," he told her. "Go finish the dishes." He walked past her into the hall, then turned and looked back. "Go on," he said.

"Call them, Chris," she said.

He turned to the table and lifted the receiver from its cradle. After a moment, she heard the clicking of the dial as he spun it once. There was a pause.

"Give me the police," he said.

He glanced across his shoulder at her, then looked away. "It's all right," he said, but there was no conviction in his voice.

"Why don't they answer?" she asked.

"Hello," he said. She heard him swallow dryly. "Could you—send a patrol car to my house right away? I—I've been threatened."

He stood silent for a moment.

"Yes," he said. "My name is—Christopher Martin. I live at 1204 Twelfth Street." He repeated the address. "Yes," he said. "He threatened me and I—I need protection. Or—"

He stood quietly for several seconds, then said "Thank you" and put down the receiver.

"What did they say?" she asked.

"They'll come over."

"Why didn't you tell them what the man said?" she asked. "All you told them was that he threatened you. You didn't say he said he was going to kill you."

"Honey, they're coming," he said.

Helen walked over to him and put her hand on his arm.

"I'm sorry," she said. "It'll be all right." But, even as she spoke, she knew she was doing it more to comfort herself than him; hoping that he'd put his arms around her and verify her words, tell her: "Yes, of course it will be all right."

He didn't. He stood beside her, wordless.

"How long did they say it would take them to get here?" she asked.

"Honey, I don't know."

"All right," she said. "I'm sure it will be—"

Her voice choked off abruptly as, beneath her fingers, she felt his arm go rigid.

"What is it?" she gasped.

"What if he was phoning from the drugstore at the corner?"

He turned and hurried to the front door, locked it. He lowered the venetian blinds across the casement windows and drew them. Then, whirling, he turned off the floor lamp, a pocket of shadows enveloping him. In an instant, he emerged from it and half ran across the room to the table lamp beside the sofa.

"Lock the kitchen door," he told her.

She hesitated, watching him crank the front windows shut.

"Helen, move!" he snapped. Twitching, she turned and hurried across the rug.

"And turn out the light!" he called as she pushed at the kitchen door to make certain that the latch caught.

"All right," she answered. She turned the lock on the knob and tested the door with shaking fingers. It held. Hurriedly, she pulled the shade down over the window on the door, then, almost lurching for the wall switch, pushed it down.

The house was now completely dark. Helen stood restively in the kitchen doorway, watching Chris draw the blinds and drapes across the picture window that faced the backyard. The living room grew even darker, blocked from the faint illumination of the moon and the street light on the next block. Chris's body became a formless shadow.

"Draw the kitchen blinds," he told her. "And the shade over the sink."

Helen turned back into the kitchen and drew the blinds, wondering what she'd do if the man were to appear outside. She cranked the windows shut, wincing at the grating sound they made. That done, she turned for the sink, her slippers scuffing across the linoleum. She bumped into the dishwasher, crying out faintly at the clank of crockery and silverware inside it.

"What is it?" Chris called urgently.

"Nothing," she answered. She pulled the shade down and leaned heavily against the sink, eyes shut.

When she came back into the living room, she could hear the furtive sound of Chris cranking shut the two windows in Connie's room and pulling down the shades. She hurried across the rug and into her and Chris's room to close the windows and draw the blinds.

This part alone was a nightmare; the two of them rushing through the darkness from room to room, shutting window after window, drawing blind after blind, lowering shade after shade. What if this were a twenty room house? she thought. Before the windows were all shut and covered it would be dawn. The sob that trembled in her throat, under other circumstances, would have been a laugh.

When all the blinds were drawn in their room, Helen pulled one back and looked out at the street.

It was quiet except for a slight wind which stirred the bushes just outside the window. Under the street lamp, a pool of pale light flooded up across the curb, immersing a segment of the lawn. On the parkway, the skeletal limbs of the small Chinese elm were shaking.

Helen could see directly into Bill Albert's house across the street. In the darkness of their living room, the television flickered. She knew that Bill and his wife were in there and it gave her an eerie feeling. They knew nothing of the terror across the street from them. Engrossed, perhaps even laughing, they were completely separated.

Nearby, there was a sound and Helen whirled, her hands retracting spasmodically.

"You locked the kitchen door?" Chris asked.

She swallowed. "Yes."

"Then he can't get in."

"Chris."

"What?"

"Do you think that. maybe we should—leave? I mean, go across to Bill's house or—?"

"No, we can't."

She stared at his outline in the darkness.

"Chris, what if the police don't get here in time?" she asked.

"I don't know," he said after a moment. Helen felt a weight of terror pressing at her. Suddenly a sob forced back her lips and Chris put his arms around her. But what good were his arms if he couldn't do anything? She tried to push the thought aside but couldn't. In a moment of fear, she turned, naturally, to Chris. If he acted unafraid—seemed to know what he was doing, then she wasn't so distressed. Even if he pretended and she sensed it, it still gave her assurance.

But when he was as lost and frightened as she was...

"It's all right," he murmured. "It's all right, Helen."

"But what are we going to do?" She had the premonition that, once more, he was going to say he didn't know.

"You're going to stay in here," he told her.

"What?"

"Come here," he said. "Here. Sit down on the bed."

"Chris, what are you—?"

"I'll be right back."

"Where are you going?"

"Outside."

"No!" She lurched up from the bed and caught his arm. "Are you out of your mind?"

"Honey, I'm not going to just stand here and risk your life and Connie's," he said. "He has a gun and—"

"A *gun?*"

"Of course he has a gun. What do you—?"

"But the police will be here any second now."

"Wait here," he ordered.

"Chris, don't!"

As he moved across the hall, she caught his arm again. "Chris, you mustn't!"

"Honey, let me go," he said.

Helpless, she followed as he pulled away and walked into the kitchen. There, in the darkness, she heard him pulling out a drawer. She shivered violently at the sound of knife blades sliding against each other.

"Oh...God, why don't we have a gun?" Chris muttered savagely.

Helen shivered again; this time not from fear but from something in his voice—a tone she'd never heard before. It was as if, abruptly, he had been transformed into a man she didn't know. She drew back, staring at the dark shadow of him turning from the cupboard with something long and pointed in his right hand.

"Chris, no," she said.

Then, suddenly, both of them had stopped moving and were standing frozenly, their heads turned toward the living room as they listened to the sound of the front door knob being turned from side to side.

CHAPTER TWO

A DRY GASP tensed her throat as Chris's fingers closed on her wrist and pulled her into the kitchen.

"Don't make a sound," he told her. His voice was the stranger's voice again.

"Chris, we—"

"Shhhh!"

She bit her lower lip.

"Stay in here," he whispered. "Don't move." He pushed her against the wall, one hand pressing at her shoulder.

"What are you going to do?"

"Never mind," he said. "Just stay here."

He stepped into the living room and stood there looking toward the front porch. The man had stepped in front of the windows now, his body framed against the light of the street lamp. Helen thought that he had his face pressed against one of the windows as though he was trying to see through the blinds. She had the hideous sensation that he was watching Chris.

"Chris," she whispered.

As he stepped back into the kitchen, the shadow of the man stepped off the porch and disappeared.

"I told you to be quiet!" Chris said.

"But I have an idea."

"What?"

"If the man saw you he'd know he made a mistake."

"What?" The sharpness of his whisper made her flinch.

"Well, isn't it true?" she asked. "If we turned on the light and—"

"Helen, he has a gun!" Chris said. "He's not here to look at me!"

She bumped against the door jamb as he spoke. His voice was so harsh and alien.

"Now stay here," he said, "and—"

He stopped instantly, his right hand clamping on her wrist. Helen felt a crawling on her scalp at the sound of fingernails scraping on the back living room screens.

"Don't move," Chris said.

Outside, she heard heels clicking on the patio, moving, it seemed, quite casually. I'm going to scream, she thought, and frantically pressed her lips together.

The clicking of the heels stopped and she felt Chris's grip loosen. "Go in our bedroom," he told her.

He pushed her from the kitchen and she found herself walking across the living room. She wanted to stay with Chris. Yet, at the same time, his remoteness seemed to drive her from him. She stumbled into the hall and stopped there, looking back toward the kitchen. Chris was not in sight.

Instinctively, she started back. Then she saw a movement by the kitchen door and knew that he was still inside.

She whirled at a sound. The man was trying to open a window in Connie's room. She went in, recoiled against the wall, gaze fastening to the shadow at the back window. No, her mind begged, no, he can't get in. He can't.

On the bed, Connie muttered in her sleep. Helen dug every nail into her palms until the biting pain drove away the blackness that threatened to envelop her. Bracing herself, she pushed off from the wall and edged across the room, her eyes never leaving the window. She saw the man's arms reach up, heard him tugging at the frame. Connie started fussing again. Oh, God, don't wake up! She almost cried the words aloud. If only Chris would come, if only she could call him.

The man turned and walked away from the window.

Breath rushed from Helen's lungs and she became conscious of a cold sweat trickling down her back and sides. Hurriedly, she leaned over the bed and, drawing a Kleenex from her bathrobe pocket, patted gently at the dew of perspiration across Connie's forehead. Her trembling fingers brushed aside the soft hairs, then drew back the spread so that Connie had only a sheet and blanket over her.

Straightening up, she turned quickly toward the hall. She'd call the police again. What was the matter with them? Chris had told them he'd been threatened. Didn't that mean anything to—?

In the kitchen, a window was broken in.

There was a cry of pain, then the sound of the door banging violently against the cupboard. As Helen rushed across the living room, there was another cry, then a scuffle of shoes on the linoleum. Her left slipper flew off but she kept on running.

"God damn—!" She heard the fury of the man's voice. Another cry of pain, a rushing sound, then a loud crash as someone, colliding with the dishwasher, knocked it over. Helen lurched into the kitchen doorway and saw a figure near the doorway.

"Chris?" she gasped.

The figure recoiled a step. The man's harsh voice surrounded her. "Put on the light," he ordered.

"Don't shoot!"

"The *light!"*

Her shaking hand felt along the wall until it touched the switch, then pushed it up.

He was short, lean. Helen stared at his white face, at the tangled black hair across his forehead. She looked at the revolver he was holding in his hand. As the man leaned back against the kitchen door to close it, she saw blood running across the hand and dripping to the linoleum in bright spots.

Chris's groan made her glance over to where he was struggling up from the floor in a debris of broken dishes and silverware. She saw a red welt rising on the side of his jaw and a ragged scratch across his cheek as if he'd been struck with the pistol barrel.

She looked back at the man. He was standing by the booth now; a man dressed in a stained serge suit that had been sewn together in places; a man who had a young face yet something old and terrible in his eyes.

"So." He panted as he spoke. "I found you, Chris. I found you."

"You're making a mistake!" said Helen. "Can't you see he's not the one you're after! Our name is Martin!"

She shivered as the man's pale blue eyes turned on her. His lips flexed back from yellowish teeth in what was more a grimace than a smile.

"Martin, hanh?" he said.

The burst of hope she felt lasted only a second, vanishing as hatred returned to the man's expression. He looked over at Chris who was on his feet now, holding on to the sink.

"Thought you could change your name," he said. "Thought that was all you had to do. Just change your name and we'd never find you."

Chris caught his breath and Helen started at the shocked expression on his face.

"Yeah, that's right," said the man, still breathing hard, *"we.* You thought you saw the last of us, didn't you? Thought you really pulled a fast one."

"You've made a mistake," Helen told him. "Don't you—?"

"Shut up!"

Helen shrank back and the man forced the thin, mirthless smile back to his lips.

"Thought you'd never see us again, didn't you, Chrissie boy? Thought you were safe and sound."

"Chris—" said Helen.

Now the man leaned back against the booth. Holding the revolver loosely, he pushed himself up onto the table and let his legs swing idly above the floor.

"I been waiting a long time for this, Chrissie boy," he said. "For a long time I figured you got away from us. Then I saw that picture in *Life* magazine, you know? That was a lucky break for me, wasn't it?"

The photograph in *Life* had shown Chris with the Santa Monica Wildcats, the boy's baseball team he sponsored. In an exhibition game, they had managed to beat the Hollywood Stars 7-5. Helen recalled that Chris hadn't wanted to be in that picture.

"We're going to Mexico but I had to stop and see you first, didn't I, Chrissie boy?" said the man. "I been waiting a long time for this."

"You better go," said Helen. "The police are coming and—"

She broke off as the man's face hardened and he raised his gun.

"No!" she gasped, one hand reaching out as though to stop him.

The man relaxed and the smile returned to his lips. He didn't even look at Helen.

"Now you didn't call the police, did you, Chrissie boy?" he said. "I know you wouldn't do that because, if you did, you'd go to jail, wouldn't you? And you don't want to go to jail, do you?"

Helen looked over at Chris with sickened eyes. The room seemed to waver around her. "Chris, you *did* call the—"

All of it fell into a pattern then. Chris's strange reaction to the call, his refusal to let her telephone the police, his telling her that they couldn't go over to Bill Albert's house, his plan to go outside with a knife and stop the man before she could find out that...

Helen felt herself trembling with a sickness of despair which welled up in her before she could control it. With a body-wracking sob, she turned away, one hand thrown across her eyes.

"*Stay right here,*" the man's voice ordered and she stopped, leaning against the door jamb.

"Helen—" She heard Chris's pleading voice.

"You mean you haven't told her?" the man asked.

"Leave her alone." Chris muttered.

"But I think she should know all about it, don't you, Chrissie boy?" said the man. "I think every wife should know all about her husband. That wasn't nice of you, not telling her about your wicked past." He clucked mockingly. "Shame on you, Chrissie boy."

Helen barely heard him. It was as if the shock of discovery had drained the powers of her senses. Through a blur of tears she saw the living room stir gelatinously. The sound of the man's voice faltered, one moment fading into silence, the next, flaring in her eardrums. Of smell and taste there was nothing and her flesh seemed numb as she leaned against the door frame.

Now the man seemed to notice, for the first time, that he was bleeding.

"Stuck me in the arm, didn't you, Chrissie boy?" he said, almost amusedly. "Well, we'll make up for that, won't we?"

Abruptly, Helen turned, her heart jolting in slow, heavy beats, remembering that the man had come to kill Chris. "Maybe my husband didn't call the police," she said, "but I did."

The man glanced over. "Good try, lady," he said. "Just shut your mouth and maybe you won't get hurt."

"I tell you the police are—"

"Helen, don't." The sound of Chris's defeated voice made her stop.

Chris turned to the man.

"Listen," he said. "I'll go with you. Just leave my wife alone."

"Now what's the hurry, Chrissie boy?" asked the man. "We got plenty of time to chat—" his voice lowered. "Before I kill you."

"No."

The man turned again and looked at Helen.

"Lady, I told you to keep your mouth shut," he said.

"Why do you want to kill him?" she asked in a shaking voice. "You—"

"Hold it."

Helen stopped. Then, hearing what the man did, she began to tremble. The man looked past her into the living room.

"You know," he said, "that sounds just like a little girl."

The sound of Connie's crying seemed to fill the house.

"So you got a little girl," the man said.

Chris seemed to lean forward.

"A little girl," said the man. "Now that's real sweet."

"I said I'd go with you," said Chris.

"Yeah, that's what you said, isn't it?"

The man's amiable tone degraded in an instant, his face became a mask of animosity. "And what if I don't want you to come with me?" he said.

Helen glanced across her shoulder automatically. "Please, may I—?" she began, then broke off as the man slid off the table edge.

"Cliff, I'm warning you," said Chris.

The man seemed to snarl but there was no sound. "You're warning me," he said. "That's funny, Chrissie boy." He glanced over toward the living room. "All these years," he said, "I been trying to figure out a way to pay you back." His frail chest shuddered with breath. "But I never could till now."

"Cliff, I'm warning you—!" said Chris, his face whitening.

"Shut up!" flared the man. "You're not warning anybody!"

Helen remained in the doorway as he edged toward her. She stared at him with unbelieving eyes.

"You're not—?" she started faintly.

"Get out of my way," said the man.

Chris took a step away from the sink. "You're not going to touch my girl," he said.

"I'm not, hanh?" The man's voice broke stridently. "I'll show you whether I am or not!" He bumped against Helen and turned quickly, his dark eyes probing at her. She smelled the sweetish odor of whiskey on his breath and shrank back with a grimace.

"Look out," he muttered and tried to pass her. Helen lost her balance and fell toward him, hands clutching out for support.

"Get away—!" His voice exploded in her ear as he shoved at her.

It happened so quickly that the man had no chance to raise his gun before Chris was charging into him, clamping rigid fingers over his wrist. Helen went stumbling back into the living room, collided with the edge of the sofa and fell across its arm.

As she pushed up, she saw Chris and the man struggling in the kitchen. Chris was holding the man's wrist away from himself, the man was trying to push the barrel end against Chris's stomach. They slipped and twisted on the smooth linoleum, teeth clenched, lips drawn back in frozen grimaces. Helen stood watching them, torn between her instinct to help Chris and her need to get Connie out of the house.

Suddenly, the man's right foot kicked out and Chris lost balance. He started falling and lurched his trunk forward to regain equilibrium. The two of them went thudding against the booth. The table shifted on its pivot and Chris dropped off heavily onto the yellow booth, the man bent over him.

Helen ran at him but his left shoe, kicking out, glanced off her shoulder stunningly and she reeled back against the stove, gasping as her side rammed against one of the control knobs.

In her bedroom, Connie called, "Mommy?" in a frightened voice. Helen turned instinctively toward her, then back again.

The man was forcing down the grip that Chris still had on his wrist. He had the advantage of gravity, his right leg pinning Chris against the booth, the weight of his body adding to his strength. As Helen pushed away from the stove, she saw Chris throw a pleading look across the man's shoulder.

She rushed at the man again, catching at his suit, but he twisted way from her. The pistol was only inches from Chris's forehead now. Desperately, he tried to free himself, his body lurching spasmodically, but the man's leg held him pinned. Again, Helen grabbed the man's arm, again his left foot shot out, almost knocking her legs from under her. She staggered backward with a gasp.

"Helen, the knife!"

She stiffened, looking blankly at Chris's straining face.

Her eyes fled down across the floor and picked out the white-handled carving knife he'd held before. Mechanically, she started for it, hardly aware of the glass splinter that gouged into the sole of her bare foot.

"No, you don't!" cried the man.

Whirling, Helen was just in time to see his body flung backward from the booth as Chris, one knee raised, shoved him away. The man went flailing across the floor. He crashed against the toppled dishwasher and fell across it, the revolver flying from his fingers and sliding underneath the stove. Helen shrank against the wall as Chris came running at the man.

The man shot out his hand and grabbed the carving knife. Lunging upward, he tried to drive it into Chris's chest. Chris flung up his arm and deflected the stab. The man drew back his arm again and

Chris jumped forward, grabbing at his wrist with both hands. For a few seconds, the two of them stood immobile, trembling. Then, abruptly, the man's arm seemed to crumple, the knife was arcing downward, the blade tip turning in, and all sound had disappeared in the man's choking gasp.

For a moment he looked at Chris in dumb astonishment. Then he lowered his eyes and gaped down at his own hand still clutching the handle of the knife that was buried in his chest.

"You goddam—" he started in a dull, flat voice.

Then he twisted around and his white face came falling toward Helen. She felt his bony fingers clutching at her breasts, her stomach, sliding down her legs. She heard his chin thud on the floor, his forehead pressing on the hem of her robe.

She couldn't move. She stared down at the motionless figure, her mouth open, watching the scarlet thread that was beginning to extend itself across the floor.

Chris fell on his knees beside the man, rolling him onto his side so that one pale blue eye stared upward. His hand slid under the man's coat and held a moment. Then his face was raised to Helen, his voice faint against the crying of their child.

"Dead," he whispered.

CHAPTER THREE

THE SOUND OF his voice seemed to release her. Gagging, she stumbled toward the sink, almost falling as the weight of the man's head held back the bottom of her robe. She jerked herself free and heard the man's head thump on the door.

She lost her supper then. Chris came over and put his hand against her forehead but she twisted away. He stood beside her helplessly.

When it was over, Helen leaned against the sink panting weakly. Her hand reached automatically for the faucet and the rush of water began to clean the sink.

In the bedroom, Connie was screaming. Chris said, "I'll go to her," and turned away.

"No." Pulling down a dish towel, Helen dried herself, not even looking at him as she started for the door. Her stomach muscles tensed again as she saw the man's blood running across the linoleum. She walked past the body quickly, drying her eyes with the towel. She tried not to think. Her baby was crying, that was all that mattered.

Connie was sitting up in bed.

"What's the matter, darling?" Helen asked, hardly recognizing her voice.

"Mommy!"

As she sank down on the bed, Helen realized how exhausted she felt. She put her arms around Connie and kissed her cheek.

"It's all right, baby" she murmured. She smoothed back the hair from Connie's forehead. "It's all right. Mommy's here."

"Mommy—Mommy..."

"Yes, sweetheart."

She held her child in the darkness and whispered comfort to her even though she knew that she was living in a comfortless world.

When Connie had gone back to sleep, Helen went into the bathroom to wash. The face she saw in the mirror was not a pleasant one.

As she was drying herself, she became conscious of her bare foot and remembered the sliver of glass she'd stepped on. Sitting down on the edge of the bathtub, she looked at the bottom of her foot.

The sliver was a small one. She had to get a pair of tweezers from the medicine cabinet before she could remove it. Pressing out the blood, she cleaned the tiny gash with alcohol. She didn't bother to bandage it.

She sat there with her eyes shut, knowing that she'd have to go back to the kitchen. All she wanted to do was get into bed and stay there. She'd never felt so tired in her life.

She tried to visualize performing as a wife and mother the next day but it was impossible. The continuity of her life seemed to have ceased in that moment when she realized that, for more than seven years, she'd loved only part of a man.

Helen stood and left the bathroom. In the living room, she found her slipper and eased her foot into it. She noticed that the kitchen light was out and wondered if Chris had gone. As she did, he came in by the front door, shut it behind himself and locked it.

"No one seems to have heard anything," he said. "It's lucky Grace and Jack are gone." Grace and Jack were their neighbors on the left.

"Yes," she said. "That's lucky."

"I didn't mean it that way," he said.

Helen let herself down onto the sofa and leaned back heavily. It was so quiet in the house she could hear the humming of the electric clock in the kitchen. Chris stayed by the door, watching her.

"Well...?" she finally asked.

His shoulders slumped. "It's up to you," he said.

"Why me?"

He made no reply.

"No, it isn't up to me," she said. "I don't fit in anywhere."

"Helen, that isn't so!"

"Isn't it?"

"Do you think I enjoyed keeping it from you all these years?"

"I'm sure it doesn't matter."

"But it does!" he cried. "It made me miserable to—!"

"You'll wake up Connie."

Chris stopped.

"If it made you so miserable," she said, "why did you do it"?

He sank down on one of the arm chairs. He put a hand across his eyes. "I was afraid to tell you," he said "Afraid I might lose you. Afraid I might—"

"—have to go to prison?"

"Thank you," he murmured.

"Well, what do you expect?" Helen turned her head and looked away from him. Suddenly, it occurred to her that she'd never been married. To the world, she was Mrs. Helen Martin; but there was no such person. There was no Christopher Martin and no Connie Martin either. All of them were illusions.

"I thought I'd never have to tell you," Chris said. "I never thought he'd find me. Then that—picture had to be taken. It's fantastic," he went on. "A secret I've kept for almost fifteen years. Ended in a second because some kids won a baseball game!" His laugh was closer to a sob. "It's practically hilarious," he said.

Helen closed her eyes. Now it was as if the other end of the balance—his end—were being weighted. He had risked his life for Connie. He had planned to intercept the man. Wasn't it possible that he'd been less motivated by a desire to hide his secret than by a wish to protect his wife and child? That Chris loved them was beyond denial.

No! Helen sat back stiffly. That he was suffering was his own doing, not hers. He had lied to her. All these years, he had trusted her so little that, rather than speak a simple truth, he had constructed a world of falsehoods around himself. A world which was now at an end.

Chris got up and headed for the hall.

"Where are you going?" she asked, suddenly frightened.

He turned in the hall doorway. "To call the police," he said.

She stared at him.

"And *then?*" she asked.

"I'll be arrested."

She couldn't stop the cold knotting in her throat and upper chest. His hands closed slowly into fists.

"I'll go to prison, Helen," he said.

"No, Chris!" She didn't realize how anguished her expression had become.

He stood motionless for a few seconds. Then he walked over to the sofa and sat down beside her. "Do you mean that?" he asked.

"What?"

"That you don't want me to go to prison?"

"I—"

"That you're willing to—to consider doing something else besides call the police?"

Abruptly she was thrust back into nightmare again. Now it was a penny thriller, absurd and ghastly. A murdered man sprawled in the kitchen, her husband sitting beside her, asking her if she was willing to consider— "I don't know," she said, unable to keep her voice from breaking. "I don't know what you're talking about."

"Listen to me," he said. "If the body isn't found, there'll be no way for anyone to know what happened."

Helen stared at him blankly. She didn't understand.

Christ looked down at his clenching hands.

"I could take him into the hills," he said in a voice that sounded hideously calm to her. "I could bury him. No one would ever find out."

He looked at her.

"It's either that," he said, "or call the police."

She couldn't answer him.

"Well?"

"Chris, I—"

"Do you want me to go to prison, Helen?" he asked. "I've lived a decent life ever since it happened. You know that. I've done everything I could to atone for my past. Is that all to end because of—*him?*"

"No." She grasped his hand impulsively.

"Helen." His fingers tightened in hers. "Thank you."

"Don't."

"What?"

"I mean—" She shuddered fitfully. "Oh, God, let's get it over with," she said.

The folded newspaper page fell from the man's pocket as Chris was lifting him. Helen picked it up and was about to throw it in the wastebasket when she noticed the story outlined in pencil.

LIFERS ESCAPE PRISON!
LEAVE DEATH TRAIL!
Three convicts sentenced to life
imprisonment for a 1943 murder
escaped last night from—

Helen looked up, shocked. *"Murder?"*

When Chris saw the expression on her face, he put the body down. Helen handed him the paper and he looked at it.

"Helen, I had nothing to do with it," he said.

She stared at him.

"I had nothing to do with it."

She lowered her gaze from his. "All right, Chris."

"Helen, if you don't believe me—"

"All *right,* Chris."

He stood quietly for a moment, then put down the paper and went back to the body. Helen heard the man's heels scraping slightly on the linoleum, then the door bumping against him as Chris opened it.

She listened to the sound of the body being dragged down the alley and into the garage through the side door. When the door was closed, she lifted the dishwasher again and reloaded it. Then, turning to the sink, she opened one of the doors beneath it. Taking out the pail, she poured in a mound of soap powder, then ran hot water over it, watching it billow into cloud-like suds.

When Chris came back, she was running the mop back and forth across the puddle of blood on the linoleum, her lips pressed together, her eyes looking straight ahead.

"Here, I'll do it," Chris took the mop from her.

"What about—?"

"What, Helen?"

She cleared her throat. "The—knife," she said.

"I left it in him."

"Oh."

She heard Chris wringing out the mop and found herself imagining how the water in the pail looked. Teeth on edge, she moved past Chris and walked into the living room. She sat until she heard the pail being emptied and rinsed out.

She stood as Chris came in.

"I'll be back as soon as possible," he said.

"I'm going with you," she said.

"What about Connie?"

"We can take her."

"I'd rather you stayed," he said. "It's not going to be pretty."

"What about the other two?" she asked.

"Cliff couldn't have shown them that photograph," he said. "If he had they wouldn't have let him come. They're hunted men. They haven't got the time for vendettas."

She didn't look convinced.

"What if Connie woke up and saw him," he asked.

Helen shuddered. "All right," she said, "but what do I do?"

"Lock up, turn the lights out. I won't be long."

"All right," she said.

She watched him walk across the kitchen and move out onto the back porch. He turned to close the door.

Then, with a lunge, he regained the house and shut the door behind him as quickly as he could without slamming it.

Someone was ringing the front door bell.

CHAPTER FOUR

HELEN'S INSTINCT WAS to scream in fury at this monstrous piling of shock on shock. Then in an instant new terror had wiped her mind clean.

She glanced into the kitchen. Chris couldn't seem to get away from the door. He leaned against it heavily, looking trapped and dazed. The bell rang again with a coarse buzzing noise.

Now Chris moved away from the door and she heard him pull a drawer open. The bell rang again, a jarring burst of sound.

"*Chris,*" she said.

He appeared holding the revolver.

"Answer the door," he said. "If it's them, tell them I'm in the—the bedroom. Then go in Connie's room and lock the door."

She couldn't take her eyes off the revolver. "But you can't—" she started.

"Honey, she's going to wake up again," he said.

"Chris, no."

"Do what I say."

Turning, she headed for the door, a sense of hideous inevitability crowding away all feeling. Her fingers closed over the knob and she tried to turn it. It's broken, she thought in dull surprise and tried again. Abruptly, then, she realized that it was locked.

The bell rang again. Helen was about to unlock the door when an idea pierced her terror. Reaching over, she switched on the porch light. Then, holding her breath, she drew aside the blinds.

It was like a weight falling from her.

"It's Bill," she called out hollowly.

As she opened the door, she heard Chris moving in the kitchen, the sound of the drawer being shut again.

"Hi," she said.

"Say, I'm sorry to be a pest, Helen," Bill Albert said, "but we're all out of ice cubes."

"Of course." Helen forced a smile back to her lips. "Come on in. We have plenty." She wondered if her voice sounded as bad to Bill as it did to her.

Chris came out of the kitchen and smiled at Bill.

"Hi," he said. "What's up?"

"They're out of ice cubes," she explained.

"Oh." Chris nodded. "Come on in the kitchen and we'll get you some."

"I sure hate to bother you like this," said Bill.

"Not at all," Chris told him.

Helen followed them toward the kitchen, her mind leaping ahead to investigate: the floor mopped, the sink clean, the newspaper page in the wastebasket, the pistol in the drawer, the dishwasher standing and loaded again.

The broken window!

"I hope I didn't wake up Connie," said Bill.

"No, not her," said Chris. "She sleeps like the dead."

Helen shivered, stopping in the kitchen doorway. Chris had pulled down the door shade again so the broken window was hidden. *Like the dead,* her mind repeated.

"Naturally Mary had to pick this afternoon to defrost," said Bill. "I keep telling her to do it overnight. She keeps telling me to buy one that defrosts itself."

"Know what you mean," said Chris. He pulled open the refrigerator door and opened the freezer compartment.

Helen looked around the kitchen nervously. One of the plates in the washer had been lying in the blood. Moving to the washer, she pushed its top down quickly. As she turned, she saw Bill looking at her and smiled.

"How are you tonight?" he asked her.

"I'm fine."

Bill smiled politely and Helen turned to watch Chris tugging at the ice cube tray. It was stuck to the surface of the freezer.

"Can I help?" Bill asked.

"I'll get it," said Chris. He didn't sound very cheerful now. In a second, he'd wrenched the tray loose.

Now Bill had the tray wrapped in a towel and was apologizing once more for having disturbed them. Now Helen heard herself telling him not to worry about it and to take his time returning the tray. Now she was walking into the living room with the two men and listening to them say something about television which they decided to pretend was worth laughing at. Now they were saying good night and the front door was closing and Chris was leaning against it, breathing slowly, heavily.

"I'm going with you," she said.

"What about—?"

"I'll hold her on my lap," she said. "She'll be all right."

"But—"

"I won't stay here," she said.

He stared at her a few seconds. Then he sighed.

"All right," he said. "All right," he said again.

Chris turned the Ford onto the hill that led to the coast highway. On the floor in back, there was a sound of something shifting and Helen felt her skin crawl.

Chris braked beside the red light at the foot of the hill. He sat, wordless, his hands clenched over the rim of the steering wheel. Then the light changed and he turned the Ford around the corner, heading north. Helen closed her eyes as the car picked up speed. Maybe she could sleep, she thought.

After a while, she opened her eyes again and looked at the highway. The headbeams hurried on ahead, picking out a path of light for the car. She tried to shift Connie a little.

"She too heavy?" Chris asked. He sounded almost grateful for the excuse to speak to her.

"It's all right," Helen answered.

He stopped for the light at Santa Monica Canyon and Helen looked around the deserted intersection, at the steep hill angling off the highway, leading to the Palisades, the silent cafes and stores. The light changed and the car moved forward.

"Helen?"

"What?"

"I'd like to tell you about it."

He waited as if expecting her to answer. Helen swallowed. "If you want," she said.

"I know you think I lied to you because I was afraid of going to prison," he said. "That isn't true. It was you I was afraid of. You were so young when we married, so unprepared for anything like that."

"That was seven years ago, Chris."

"I know, I know," he said. "It's just that I never knew how to tell you."

The Ford started along the stretch of highway that led toward Sunset Boulevard. "I was living in New Mexico when it happened," he said. "I told you about it. That part wasn't a lie. I was working for a bank. I picked up deposits from the big stores and factories in the area. It wasn't much—"

He broke off as Connie made a restless noise in her throat. Then, after several moments, he began again.

"I was living with my mother," he said. "We didn't get along. I was seventeen but, to her, I was still a baby. So, more to defy her than for any other reason I started going to the skid row section of the city. I bowled there, played pool, just sat around sometimes. I didn't belong there and I knew it. I would have preferred going to a concert or reading a book. But music and books I associated with my mother. I didn't want to have anything to do with them."

He clenched his teeth and blew out breath. "That's how I met Adam and Steve," he said. "Later on, Cliff. The four of us sort of stuck together."

The thought of Chris associating with the dead man gave Helen a restless, uncomfortable sensation. It made her wonder if Chris was really what he'd always seemed to be.

"We saw a lot of each other," Chris was saying. "I don't know if they worked except for Adam. He was an accountant at the Coca-Cola Bottling Plant; a sort of pseudo-intellectual I guess you'd call him."

For a few moments, there was only the sound of the Ford pulling quickly around the dark curve of highway that ran beside the ocean-fronting restaurants and houses.

"Why we decided to do what we did I'll never know," Chris said. "I can't explain why four supposedly sane human beings should decide to commit a robbery."

Helen closed her eyes and shuddered. There it was. They'd robbed someone and, during the robbery, that someone had been killed. And Chris had been there. Her Chris.

"We decided to rob one of the bank's depositors," Chris went on. "He owned a jewelry store. I'd told them how much money he deposited and—Adam picked him."

They drove past the entrance to Topanga Canyon and Helen wondered why he didn't turn in, deciding that it was because there were too many people living there. There was no safe place for burying things.

"We were to use Adam's car," Chris was saying. "I was supposed to knock on the back door of the jewelry store the way I usually did. When the man opened it, they were going in to get the money while I waited in the car."

His fingers tightened on the steering wheel and beneath his foot, the Ford accelerated steadily.

"I was supposed to warn them if anything went wrong," he said.

He was silent for such a long time that Helen thought his story was finished. "Something went wrong, all right," he finally said. "The old man who owned the store had an alarm system. It didn't make any noise in the store itself though, only outside. I heard it. I was going to warn the others when I heard a police car coming."

His foot pressed down harder on the accelerator and the speedometer needle quivered past sixty.

"I lost my nerve," he said bitterly. "I didn't warn them. I just drove away as fast as I could, ditched the car when it ran out of gas. I hitchhiked out of the state. Later on, I read that they'd been caught and that the old man had been killed."

He sank back against the seat as if, suddenly, exhausted.

"That's it," he said. "I came to California. I changed my name. I managed to keep it all a secret. I thought I'd beaten it. Now..."

He gestured defeatedly with his right hand.

Neither one of them had noticed the red light blinking behind them. The first thing they were aware of was a harsh, metallic voice ringing out above the wind and engine noises.

"Blue Ford, pull over!"

CHAPTER FIVE

A HUNDRED YARDS back, the turning roof light of another car was just disappearing behind a curve.

"Put Connie in the back seat!" Chris told her.

"What is it?"

"A police car! Hurry!"

Breath choked in Helen's throat. She tried to lift Connie and felt a painful drawing in her back and shoulder muscles.

"She's too heavy!" she said.

"Grab the wheel then!"

Her left hand clutched at the wheel. Raising himself quickly, Chris grabbed Connie under the shoulders and legs and lifted her. For a second, Connie's leg was in front of her face and Helen couldn't see the highway. The Ford veered toward the opposite lane and she twisted the wheel sharply. Connie whimpered as she was dumped onto the plastic covering of the back seat. With desperate haste, Chris tucked the blanket around her. Before the police car had reappeared, he was steering the car again.

"Why did you do that?" Helen asked.

"They'll probably look in back," he said. "If they see Connie they may not look at the floor." He pulled the car to the side of the road and braked.

"But is he—?"

"He's covered," said Chris.

Helen sat there woodenly, staring straight ahead, as the black and white police car angled to a halt in front of them. The red light on top of the car revolved slowly, glaring into their eyes. Two policemen got out and Helen listened to their shoes crunching over the roadside gravel. They were carrying something in their hands. Helen shuddered, realizing that they had flashlights.

"I'll talk to them," said Chris.

The policemen separated now, one to each side of the car. The one on Chris's side directed the flashlight beam into his face.

"Don't you read traffic signs?" the policeman asked.

"Yes. I—"

"You were doing seventy in a thirty-five-mile zone, did you know that?" the policeman interrupted.

"I'm sorry," Chris said, "I—I wasn't looking. We were—"

"License, please," said the policeman.

Chris reached forward nervously and switched off the engine. He pulled out the key ring with the plastic-faced license holder attached to it and handed it out. The policeman took it and pointed his flashlight at it.

"You're Christopher Martin?" he asked.

Helen felt something like an electric shock in her body as the other policeman pointed his flashlight beam at the back seat.

"Who's that?" he asked.

She swallowed quickly. "My daughter," she said. She was startled at the aloofness of her voice.

"You still live at twelve-o-four, Twelfth Street?" the other policeman was asking Chris.

"Yes."

The policeman lowered the license and looked at Chris again.

"Why were you going so fast, Martin?" he asked. His voice was less stiff now.

"Well," Chris said, "we were going home and—"

Helen had stiffened even before the policeman said, "You were driving away from Santa Monica, Martin."

Chris drew in a shaky breath.

"I mean my mother-in-law's house," he said. "She lives in Malibu. To tell you the truth, we've been—arguing and I'm taking my wife to her mother's house. I'm very upset. That's why I was going so fast. I wasn't paying attention."

The policeman looked at Chris another moment, then at Helen. "Is that right?" he asked.

If I told him now, it would be over, she thought. But, even as she thought it, she was nodding. "Yes," she said.

"Well," said the policeman, "I'll have to give you a ticket, I'm afraid. You were going pretty fast. But I won't put down your actual speed. That way you won't have to appear in court."

"Thank you," said Chris.

They sat there quietly while the two policemen returned to their car. Helen sat staring at the light on the roof of the police car. It glared hypnotically into her eyes, then was gone, glared, was gone. In the back seat, Connie snored gently.

294

After a few minutes, the policeman returned and handed Chris the license and the ticket book. Chris signed his name and wrote his address. Then the policeman tore out the ticket and handed it in through the window.

"Take it slower now," he said.

Chris nodded. "I will."

The policeman cleared his throat.

"Look, it's none of my business," he said, "but—well, I'm an old married man myself. I have four kids and the missus and I have been through a lot together."

He smiled at them. "What I mean is, these things seem a lot worse at night than they really are. I'm not trying to interfere but—well, why not wait till tomorrow before you decide anything? Go home, sleep on it. You'll find it's not half so bad in the morning."

Helen braced herself.

"Thank you," she said. "We will."

The policeman smiled again. "Good," he said. "Take it easy now."

When he'd left, Chris said, "Now what are we going to do?"

"What do you mean?"

"We'll have to turn back and I was going to Latigo Canyon."

"Oh."

Chris started the engine. When the police car had pulled off the shoulder and disappeared around a bend ahead, he made a U-turn and started back toward Santa Monica. He kept looking up at the rear-view mirror to see if the police car were following.

"Where are we going to put him?" she asked.

"I guess it'll have to be Topanga," he said.

Helen twisted around and looked at Connie to see if she was all right. Then, unable to stop herself, she looked down at the floor. As the car turned into a curve, the body shifted and bumped against the seat. Helen turned back quickly.

All along the first five miles of the canyon, Chris had kept slowing down as if he meant to stop. Then his teeth had set on edge and he'd picked up speed again as he saw that the spot was unsuitable. Now he had turned onto the old Topanga Road.

Helen looked at the dashboard clock. It was twenty minutes after twelve. She drew in a long breath and let it seep out between her lips as she stared at the road ahead, glancing at the occasional houses they passed. Once they had discussed the possibility of buying a house in this area. She'd never want to live here now.

Finally they stopped and the rasping click of the hand brake made her twitch. Chris pushed in the light knob and darkness blotted away everything around them. He sat motionless for a moment, his eyes staring ahead. Then, with a brusque motion, he pulled up the door handle and slid out of the car.

"Could I have the flashlight, please?" he asked.

Reaching forward, Helen pushed in the button on the glove compartment door. After a few seconds of fumbling, she found the flashlight and held it out. Chris took it from her and pushed forward the seat back on his side. It fell on the steering wheel and they both gasped as the horn sounded once in the heavy silence. Chris grabbed the seat back and held it.

Then, abruptly, he shoved it back into place. Helen looked over at him as he sat down, his back to her.

"Oh, what's the use?" he said. He sat there turning the flashlight restlessly in his hands.

Helen swallowed.

"Chris, if you're expecting me to encourage you," she said, "I can't."

"I don't want encouragement," he answered. "I want—to *end* this, to get you out of it." Abruptly, he drew his legs in and closed the door.

"What are you doing?" she asked.

"Going to the police."

"Chris, *please.*" Helen closed her hands into rigid fists. "I love you. I don't want you to go to prison. If you think you can put him here without him being found, then do it. *Do* it! But, for God's sake, get it over with!"

"All right, Helen," he said. "I'm sorry."

Hastily, he slid out of the car and unlocked the back trunk to get the shovel he always kept inside. Helen wondered why he hadn't put the man in the trunk too, then remembered that the trunk door wouldn't open when the garage door was down. Chris would have had to open the garage, but then someone might have seen. He had done the only thing possible.

The only thing possible. That was what made it all a nightmare. Everything seemed so inevitable. The phone call, the locking of the house, the man's violent entrance and death, the placing of his body in the car, the drive along the ocean, the policemen stopping them, the burial now. Nothing could have happened in any other way. It was as if they were trapped in some inexorable plan which had determined their past and their present and would also determine their future.

Still it seemed impossible to accept. Such things did not happen really. Melodrama was confined to bad motion pictures. And now, melodrama had engulfed her so quickly and violently that it seemed beyond belief. If there had been something in the past to signal its coming she might be able to accept. But there had been nothing. She thought about it as carefully as she could. There had been nothing.

She'd met Chris at a concert—that was the start. The Santa Monica Music Guild sponsored a series of concerts every year to which she and her mother subscribed. That particular night, Helen remembered, Wallenstein had been conducting the Los Angeles Philharmonic.

During intermission, she walked downstairs with her mother to get a drink of water and stretch her legs. Her mother had gone into the ladies' room and Helen out onto the porch for some air. Only later did she realize that Chris was out there at the same time. If either of them had stayed outside until the intermission was over, they might never have met. The ironies of coincidence, however, were far from her mind that night and for years of nights to come.

When she decided that her mother had probably left the ladies' room and was wondering where she was, Helen went back inside. She didn't see her mother at first. Then, after several moments, she caught sight of her standing near the center aisle entrance, talking with Mrs. Saxton who owned the Melody Music Shop. She went over and they chatted a few minutes about how wonderfully the orchestra had played the Brahm's Third, how marvelously adept Wallenstein was in drawing such a performance from them.

Then a figure stepped up beside Helen and Chris was in her life.

"Marjorie, Helen," said Mrs. Saxton, "I'd like you to meet Mr. Martin."

There were the usual amenities, the usual small talk about the concert, about Mrs. Saxton's shop. Mrs. Saxton told them that Chris was working for her and that the way he was going at it, she'd be working for him before long. The laughter was polite, casual. Then the buzzer sounded and they were all returning to their seats.

"He seems like a nice young man," her mother commented as they went up the stairs.

"Yes, Mrs. Cupid," Helen answered.

The concert ended, they left the auditorium and, in walking to their car, were briefly joined by Chris and Mrs. Saxton. Again, the conversation was vague. There was no impression on either side, Helen felt. She experienced none in particular and, later on, Chris told her that he repressed what interest he had felt because he didn't feel he had a right to become involved. He'd said it was because he didn't have the time to spare from his work. Now, Helen knew why he had repressed it.

So the matter might have ended. Helen thought of that as she sat, her cheek pressed to Connie's head, listening to the shovel strokes outside in the darkness. It might have ended, they might not have married, Connie might never have been born. And how did one decide if their life would have been better if things had happened differently?

They happened as they did—without intention, in the normal pattern of events. Her mother's birthday was coming in a few weeks, her mother loved the Beethoven piano sonatas. Helen went to Mrs. Saxton's shop to order the record.

There were, of course, larger, more complete music stores in Santa Monica. Still, Mrs. Saxton was a friend of mother's and she could, certainly, order a record as well as anyone else. Helen was positive that a record with such a limited audience appeal would not be in stock in any of the local stores.

She was wrong—and amazed. Amazed at the change that had taken place in Mrs. Saxton's shop. As she entered, she saw how the decor had been brightened, the arrangement of counter and shelving changed to lend an air of pleasant informality to the shop rather than its previous one of rather unimaginative drabness.

And there, in the center of this impressive alteration, was Chris—a smiling, affable Chris; a well-informed and literate Chris; a charming and amusing Chris. Helen had been completely won over by him. He was far more than the man she'd shaken hands with at the concert. He seemed larger here, more imposing. It was as if, at the concert, he had been some sort of deposed monarch—polite as reared, dignified as bred but, deprived of his kingdom, without the stature of ego. The shop was his kingdom then. Within its boundaries, he ruled benevolently, imparting interest, bestowing humor and cordiality, making the experience of visiting the shop a uniquely nice one.

Not only had the sonata record been in stock, there had been three different ones to choose from. Moreover, Chris had initiated a practice which, only later, other record stores began to utilize—that of offering unplayed records to customers. Until that time, Helen had always found what she was looking for on the shelves—the records, unsheathed, inserted directly into their cardboard jackets. Chris had taken the records out of the jackets and placed them alphabetically behind the counter in plastic envelopes. He had, in addition, moved the turntable behind the counter and connected it to the one booth so that the record might be heard without the danger of a customer injuring it.

Had it been a coincidence that no customers were in the store that afternoon? Sometimes, Helen thought so. Sometimes, contrariwise, she had the feeling that, in any case, they would have seen each other again. As it was, the absence of customers enabled him to ask her if she'd like to have a cup of coffee and she'd accepted.

Only now did she wonder if he had realized what she was beginning to feel, if he knew as clearly as she did, what was starting between them. Had he fought the desire to ask her out for that cup of coffee? Or had it seemed the thing to do; had he been lulled into ignoring or forgetting his past?

There seemed no answer to that. It had been done and everything had commenced which, now, had ended in a dead man being buried in the night.

The cup of coffee had led to an invitation to dinner by Helen; ostensibly to listen to some records Chris had mentioned, actually as an excuse to see him again. Chris had been hesitant about accepting—she remembered that now. (It seemed as if, now, a hundred different incidents were clarified.) He had only accepted when he'd seen that his apparent attempt to back out was embarrassing her.

Again, who was to blame? Would it have been better if he had ignored that embarrassment and not accepted anyway? At least, then, this horror might not have occurred. Had he been kind to accept that invitation—or weak, thinking more of her opinion of him than of the pain to which he might be exposing her?

None of which she was aware of at the time, of course. There was, at the time, only that sweetly uncomfortable sensation of allowing an attraction to become fatal. That burgeoning struggle between the impulse to love and the desire to remain unharmed. Not that she bore the scars of any past romantic wounds. Far from it. Men had not existed in her life to any degree. Her mother had tried, often enough, to change this. But men seemed to Helen, if not frightening, somehow uninviting. The only man she had ever given her heart to had left her mother for another woman. This had not enhanced, for Helen, the attractions of men.

This plus an undefined fear of sex through her teen years had always kept her to herself or with a group of girls. Occasionally, there had been dates, some of them enjoyable. Still, at those moments when conversation ended and dates expected physical affection, Helen was half-frightened, half repelled by the artificiality of the moment. Love, when she thought of it, seemed to her an emotion that needed size and scope, one which should envelop and beautifully so—not a feeling which one could forcibly arouse on the back seat of a car, a beer-can cluttered blanket on the sands.

Maybe it was Chris's love and knowledge of music, Helen thought. His quiet refinement. Maybe it was his reticence bringing out what aggressiveness Helen had not completely repressed in herself. Something had to explain her asking him to dinner. More amazingly, something had to explain her anxiety for him to like her, for something more than friendship to develop between them.

Sometimes, she convinced herself that she was one of those females who never loved until the right man came along. At other times, with more logic, she decided it was probably closer to the truth that she was getting older and the desire for companionship was outdistancing timidity. It was not, she admitted to herself on those occasions, a union consummated in heaven. It was, under the circumstances of her life, simply a desirable and sensible relationship.

Whatever the explanation, her falling in love with Chris had been continuous and certain—to her, remarkably devoid of complications. Chris's holding back she accepted as faint heart; she overlooked it. She loved him and was, soon, convinced that he loved her in return. It seemed a very positive enterprise.

Still, there had been little things—things she'd chosen to ignore or, worse, to rationalize. Things like Chris's unwillingness to discuss his background. She tried, occasionally, to find out about his family but, outside of an infrequent comment about his mother, he was unwilling to talk about it.

One day, in talking with her mother about Chris, she had to admit that, not only did she not know where his relatives were, she didn't even know who they were or if they existed at all. A few nights later, at dinner, her mother tried to get Chris to answer specific questions about this. He was uncomfortably reluctant about it and said little. Strangely (it seemed now), Helen didn't question his reluctance but only felt a startled irritation with her mother. Later that night, she told her mother so. Her mother only shrugged and smiled.

"Well, if it's a mystery man you want," was all she said.

How fantastic that, until this moment, she had completely forgotten that incident. Forgotten that Chris always questioned, never answered. His past had all been unknown to her. She had accepted this lack of knowledge, feeling, in the security of her love, that she knew him just as well as if she were apprised of the statistical data of his past. These formed the surface of a man, she decided, not the core. The core, she felt, she understood. Had she been right? Did she really understand Chris? Was this revelation, for all its hideousness, only a belated filling in of really unimportant details? Was he still the man she'd believed she knew? Or had the filling in of his background revealed basic differences in him? In short, must she allow that she had been living with a stranger for all these years? This was the thought that tortured her in the dark silence of—

Silence.

She was chilled with the sudden awareness. That meant that Chris had finished digging the grave. Now he was lowering the body into it. In a moment or two, he would be…

She shuddered as the first shovelful of dirt was thrown. She sat there rigidly, listening, all the past swallowed in the black pain of the present. All she could think of now was that Helen Martin was lying in that grave too. She tried to think of something else but she couldn't. There was only the one thought.

Helen Martin was dead.

THURSDAY MORNING

CHAPTER SIX

CHRIS OPENED HIS eyes.

Overhead, a DC-7 was circling for International Airport. He listened to the burring stridency of its engines until the noise had faded. It was a dream, he told himself, but the thought did not deceive him.

Sluggishly, he turned his head and looked over at the clock on his bedside table. It was a little after eight. He stared at the second hand as it pointed at the numbers—eleven, twelve, one.

Exhaling, Chris turned his head and looked at the ceiling. He didn't have to get up yet. For that matter he didn't have to go to the store at all. Jimmy could handle it well enough without him. Maybe he wouldn't go. Maybe he'd just—

Abruptly, he realized that Helen wasn't in bed with him.

He pushed up on one elbow and looked around the room. Hastily, he threw the blankets back and dropped his legs across the edge of the mattress.

The floorboards were chilly beneath his feet. He shivered as he hurried across the room and opened the door. Stepping out into the hall, he looked into Connie's room. The tension faded instantly.

She was still asleep, lying on her back, her lips parted, a curl of hair twisted across her forehead. On any other day she'd be up by now, out with the neighborhood children.

Chris turned and walked across the living room. In the kitchen, he could hear the dishwasher operating. It clicked once and there was a sibilant rush of water from its nozzle.

He found Helen in the alley, scrubbing blood spots from the sidewalk. She didn't see him at first. He stood on the porch and watched her, twitching at the sound the wire brush made on the concrete. He remembered dragging Cliff's lifeless body down the alley. Apparently, it had bled all the way.

He remembered, too, the druglike horror of the burial, the long drive home, the painfully silent preparation for bed. The sleepless lying in darkness, wanting to move close to Helen, to put his arms around her, to feel her body pressing close. Lying there in wordless agony, filled with thoughts about the years passed by. Fearing that she lay beside him wondering how many lies there'd been in the seven years of their relationship; knowing that there had only been the one. Listening to hear if she were still awake. Lying tortured by indecision until the only sleep that could come came at last—the hollow, uncleansing sleep of exhaustion.

Helen turned her head and saw him. Chris stepped down off the porch, feeling the chill of the morning air through his pajamas.

"I'll do it," he said.

"I'm almost done."

Helen looked back at her work and he saw how her fingers tensed on the wooden handle of the brush.

"I should have done it last night," he said. "I didn't think."

He stood awkwardly, watching her scrub. Then he glanced around. There was a lot of dampness in the air. A whitish mist hovered above the rooftops of the houses.

She had finished now. Chris extended his hand to help her up but she acted as if she didn't see it. Pushing to her feet, she dropped the brush into the pail of red-tinged water. Chris picked up the pail.

"I'll empty it," he said.

Helen nodded once and went into the house. Chris watched her until she'd closed the door behind herself.

As he started for the garage, he glanced at Grace and Jack's house. What if they had come home, he thought. He swallowed nervously as he opened and shut the side garage door and edged past the bumper of the Ford, heading for the laundry tub. He hadn't felt this for years: this guilty apprehension of the criminal.

The thought sent such a wave of sickened revelation through him that he almost cried aloud. It had taken him so long to overcome his attitude of constant wariness. Now, in one night, it had returned.

"No!"

Chris spoke the word angrily as he emptied the pail and ran cold water into it. He wouldn't let it degrade him to the pettish animal he'd been in those early years. He *wouldn't*.

Chris put down the pail and opened the car door. Picking up the flashlight from the seat he searched the back floor. There were several dark stains where the blood had soaked through the blanket. He'd clean them today. Otherwise someone might see them sometime. No point in taking the risk.

Getting out of the car, Chris began checking the floor of the garage. There were blood spots all around. He gritted his teeth seeing them. There was evidence everywhere.

That was the most nightmarish aspect of killing. Even after the shock of taking life had passed and the offensive dead had been put away, there were so many details to be taken care of: spots to remove, objects to dispose of, hours to account for, movements to be explained. Lies and lies mounting like girders for some hideous skyscraper which you built in detail, then hoped no one would ever see.

He began cleaning up the blood.

Helen was in the kitchen booth staring at her hands clasped on the table.

"Why don't you go back to bed?" he asked.

She shook her head slowly. Chris stood looking down at her, wishing he could thrust their lives six months forward. When this worst part would be over and the strengths of their relationship would be returning.

Helen glanced up at him, then down at her hands again. "I've been thinking," she said, "about those men."

"What about them?"

"What if they come here?" she asked.

"They won't."

"What if they do?"

"They're wanted by the law, Helen," he told her.

"So was—he."

"He was out of his mind."

"Maybe they are too."

Chris tried to smile. "What do you want me to say, honey?" he asked.

"It's not a question of wanting you to say anything," she said. "It's a question of safety. We have Connie to think of."

"All right." He nodded. "I'm willing to do anything you say."

"I think we should go to my mother's for a while," she said.

"All right," he said. "When do you want to go?"

For a moment, he felt that she was planning to leave him and he fought the idea. This was only temporary; he'd make certain of that.

"Well," she said, "if they're going to come, it might be at any time."

"You want to go now," he said quietly.

She closed her eyes. "Chris, please," she begged.

"Have I said anything?"

"Honey, I'm doing it for Connie's sake," she said. "I'm not trying to run out on you."

"I know," he said.

"I need a little time, Chris," she said. "I'm trying to be loyal but—please don't expect too much at first."

He put his hand on her shoulder and she pressed it once.

"I'll drive you there," he said.

She nodded. Then, pushing to her feet, she walked over to the dishwasher which had stopped. She turned off the hot water and unclipped the faucet attachment, sliding the double hose into place. Unplugging the wire, she rolled the dishwasher against the wall. Chris watched her for a moment, then turned and walked out of the kitchen.

In the hall, he began dialing the store before he realized it wasn't open yet. He dumped the receiver onto its cradle and walked into the bedroom. It would be all right, he told himself. It was just a matter of time.

When he'd finished dressing, he went into the bathroom to shave.

"Daddy, can I get up?" Connie asked.

"Of course," he answered.

He heard her scramble out of bed. In a moment, she came padding into the bathroom in her striped pajamas, blond hair hanging tousled across her cheeks.

"I slept good, Daddy," she told him.

"Good." He leaned over to kiss her.

"Did you sleep good?"

"Yes, little troll. Very good."

Connie smiled at the name he gave her. "I slept good and you slept good," she said.

She watched intently as he finished shaving. "Will I shave some day?" she asked.

"I hope not," he asked.

"When I'm six and a half?" she asked.

"Girls don't shave their faces. You'd better get dressed now."

"I have to eat my breakfast first," she said.

"Oh. All right, Mommy will give it to you."

"Is she in the kitchen?"

"Yes."

"I'll see you then," said Connie, leaving.

"All right."

As he combed his hair, he heard Helen telling Connie that they were going to Grandma's house for a while.

"How long while?" Connie asked.

"I don't know, honey," Helen told her. Chris felt a tremor in his stomach muscles. Just a little while, he thought.

"You and me and Daddy?"

"Daddy has to stay and watch the store," said Helen.

"Oh, *foo,* " said Connie.

"One or two eggs?" Helen asked him as he sat down at the kitchen table.

"Just coffee, please."

"You'll get—" she began, then broke off.

He glanced at her as she turned back to the stove. *You'll get sick.* That was what she'd almost said. She always said it when he wouldn't eat breakfast. Except for today. Chris reached out and picked up his glass of orange juice.

"We're going to Grandma's house," said Connie.

"I know, baby," he answered.

"Will you visit us when we're at Grandma's house?"

He hid the convulsive movement of his throat by drinking. "I don't know, sweetheart," he said.

"Why, Daddy?"

"Eat your cereal," Helen told her. "I told you Daddy has to watch the store."

"Can't Jimmy?"

Chris got up, mumbling his excuse. As he walked across the living room he heard Connie persisting. "Can't somebody else, Mommy?"

"Connie, please eat your cereal."

In the hall, he dialed with quick, jerking movements.

"Martin Music," he heard Jimmy's amiable voice through the earpiece.

"Chris Martin, Jimmy. I won't be in till later today."

"Oh. Okay, Mr. Martin."

"Leave that case from Schirmer unpacked till tomorrow," Chris told him. "You can go on re-sorting the LP albums today."

"Yes, sir. Will do."

"And if Mrs. Anthony calls about Sunday's concert, tell her I'll phone her first thing this afternoon, will you?"

"I will, Mr. Martin."

"Fine. I'll see you later then."

"Okay. Oh, say—"

Chris had hung up before Jimmy could finish. Well, it didn't matter. If it was anything important, Jimmy could phone back. Chris stood beside the telephone table looking into the living room. He saw the pad and pencil lying on the sofa where he'd left it the night before, thinking that after he'd helped Helen load the dishwasher, he'd return to his planning for a children's creative workshop.

Creative workshop. He closed his eyes. It seemed a million years ago.

He started as the telephone rang. Picking it up, he murmured, "Yes?" thinking it was Jimmy.

"Hello, Chris."

His fingers clamped on the receiver.

"How are you, boy?" said the voice. "This is Adam."

CHAPTER SEVEN

CHRIS GLANCED ACROSS his shoulder and saw Helen in the kitchen doorway looking at him. He covered the mouthpiece.

"It's Jimmy," he said, appalled at how easily the lie was spoken.

"Oh." Helen went back into the kitchen. Quickly, Chris stepped off from the doorway and pressed against the wall.

"What do you want?" he whispered.

"To see you," said Adam.

"Why?"

"You want to meet us or shall we drop by?" asked Adam.

"Stay away from here!"

"Then meet us at Broadway and Twelfth in fifteen minutes."

"Listen—!"

"Fifteen minutes, Chris."

"How do you know I won't bring the police?" Chris asked.

Adam only snickered and then the receiver was buzzing in Chris's ear. Slowly, he put it down on its cradle.

Abruptly, he picked it up again and dialed once.

"Operator," said the voice.

Give me the police, he thought. He stared at the mouthpiece, feeling his heart beat thicken. He was this close now.

"Operator, " said the voice.

Chris put down the receiver and stood there trembling. What was the point in going on, with Steve and Adam to contend with now? What good was such a loaded freedom?

Still, as if helpless before some hideous command, he walked across the living room and into the kitchen.

"I have to go over to the store for a few minutes," he said.

Helen looked up from her coffee.

"I'll be back before you're ready," he said.

"We'll be ready in less than a half hour."

"All right, I'll be back," he said.

He turned and left the kitchen. All right, he told himself, *all right.* It's impossibly complicated now but it will clear up in time.

"G'bye, Daddy," Connie called after him.

He cleared his throat. "I'll be right back," he said. He pulled his topcoat from the front closet and left the house. The street was quiet and chilly. He'd left the Ford outside all night and it was coated with dew.

Chris walked in choppy strides toward Broadway, his heels clicking on the sidewalk. What was it they wanted? he wondered.

His stride suddenly faltered. Was it possible they, too, were after revenge? He almost stopped walking, his movement becoming slow and aimless. Maybe he should have taken the gun with him. It seemed an absurdly melodramatic idea and yet—

Or shall we drop by the house? Chris started walking again. Whatever happened they had to be kept from the house. Helen had been through enough. Besides, if revenge was what they had in mind, why would they warn him ahead of time by phoning?

He didn't notice the grime-streaked sedan moving up behind him. The first thing he was aware of was the sudden roar of its engine, the rush of its dark bulk to the curb beside him, the squeal of badly lined brakes, the shoved-out back door.

Chris stood there gaping into the car at the revolver Adam Burrik was pointing at him.

"Get in," said Adam.

Chris felt his legs shaking. He glanced over at the front seat and saw the hard, dispassionate face of Steve Coulter.

"He said get in," Steve ordered.

Chris stumbled across the parkway grass and onto the street. Numbly, he bent over and stepped into the back of the car. He sat down gingerly, looking over at Adam who was smiling at him without humor.

"You can close the door now," Adam said.

Chris extended a trembling hand and pulled the door shut. The old, unoiled lock didn't catch the first time and he had to do it again. As he did, Steve threw the car into first and gunned away from the curb. Chris fell back against the seat.

"Well, here we are," said Adam; a fleshier more coarse-looking Adam.

Chris tried to think of something to say but his brain felt clogged.

"It's been a long time," Adam said as the car was cornered onto Broadway and headed toward the ocean.

Chris stared at him, his heart beating slowly and heavily against the wall of his chest.

"What do you want?" he asked.

Adam smiled contemptuously. "A little charity," he said.

"We ought t'kill 'im," Steve broke in.

Chris glanced forward instinctively and saw Steve's dark eyes watching him in the mirror.

"Relax," said Adam.

He still sounded the same, Chris noticed—aloof and calculating. Years and prison had not changed that. It was the deep lining around his eyes and mouth that was different; a strained look of humor retained at the cost of nerves.

"We want money, Chris," said Adam.

"You—"

"No arguments," Adam interrupted. His only betrayal of tension was the tightening of his grip on the revolver. "You'll get us the money. Period."

Chris pressed his lips together to keep them from shaking.

"I need hardly remind you," said Adam, "if we're caught, you'll be dragged down with us. And now that you've killed Cliff—"

It came too unexpectedly. Chris couldn't stop the twitching of his legs. A smile loosened Adam's thick lips.

"I wasn't sure you had, till now," he said. "Forget it. It doesn't matter. Cliff always was a bungler. Too emotional."

Adam grunted amusedly. "Steve is like that too. If I wasn't here you'd have a bullet in your brain by now."

Chris labored for breath

"How much do you want?" he asked.

"How much have you got?"

"I can—"

"Never mind answering. It'll be a lie. We want two thousand in small bills."

"Two thousand—"

"You're getting off cheap," said Adam, the amusement stripped from his voice. "You're lucky we don't leave you in a ditch some-where."

Adam blew out breath.

"Banks open at ten," he said. "You'll get the money and bring it to us by eleven. You know where Latigo Canyon is?"

Chris shuddered, recalling his idea to bury Cliff in Latigo Canyon.

"Yes," he said.

"Bring it there."

"Where in Latigo Canyon?"

"You'll find us," Adam said. He looked at Chris appraisingly.

"You can send the police there of course," he said, "but I don't think you will. You have too much to lose."

Chris didn't reply.

"Let's make that three thousand," said Adam.

"Three—!"

"Shut up."

Chris's throat felt as if it were lined with dust. He coughed to ease the sensation.

"*Well?*" asked Adam.

"All right." Chris's voice was almost a whisper. "All right, damn you."

"Splendid," said Adam lightly. "If you fail you'll receive a visit either from the police or from us. Neither of which will be very pleasant."

"I said all right," said Chris.

Adam looked at him another moment. Then he said, "Pull over."

Steve drew the dark sedan to the curb.

"Remove him," said Adam.

Chris stiffened as Steve jumped from the car and ran around the front of it. He pressed back tensely as Steve jerked open the back door and reached in for him.

"I can—" he started, breaking off as Steve's fingers clamped over his wrist. He tried to pull free but was powerless against the stronger man's grip. His cheek grazed the door jamb as Steve dragged him out.

"If I had my way—" Steve snapped. As Chris stared at his beard-blackened face, he felt a violent blow to his stomach that jack-knifed him over, cutting off breath.

"*Bastard!*" he heard Steve's savage oath. Another clublike blow struck him on the side of the head and he went flailing forward onto the paving. As he fell, he heard Adam's voice through the blackening cloud around him.

"Be there."

Then he was on one knee, gagging, hands pressed against his stomach, hearing the car door slam and the roar of the engine as Steve and Adam left.

He struggled to his feet. Dazedly, he stumbled over to a palm tree and leaned against it, tears trickling down his cheeks. Breath did not seem to come. He kept gasping for it.

Across the street, an old man opened the front door of his house and looked at him curiously. Gritting his teeth, Chris pushed away from the tree and started walking. He couldn't take a chance on the man talking to him.

Abruptly, a sob broke in his throat. Dear God, was he still thinking in terms of escape? He walked more quickly, bent over to ease the pain. What kept him going? Obviously, there was to be no end to it.

He braced himself. No, it was only temporary. He'd give them the money, they'd go to Mexico—and mail a letter from there demanding more money?

Chris stopped walking and stood staring at the sidewalk. One more complication. One more turn in the maze leading to a blank wall.

At the corner, he entered a drugstore and walked to the rear. Sliding into a phone booth, he sank down on the seat and pulled the door shut, grimacing at the pain in his stomach muscles. The sound of his breathing was harsh and labored as he pushed a dime into the slot and began to dial.

"Operator," said the voice.

"Give me the police, please," he said.

"One moment."

There was a sound of dialing, a single buzz before Chris hung up.

He leaned forward, suddenly breathless, pressing his forehead against the cold metal of the telephone. He couldn't, he just couldn't. No matter what risks it entailed, he had to take them. To lose everything at his age; family, work, hopes; it wasn't worth it.

Quickly, blanking his mind, he re-inserted the coin and dialed.

"Hello?" she said.

"Honey—"

She couldn't disguise her exhalation of relief. "What?" she asked.

"I have to stay at the store a while. You'd better take the car."

"Oh?"

"I'll phone you there later," he said, "and we'll—discuss it."

She didn't answer. Chris winced as the pain in his stomach flared again.

"All right?" he asked. If only he could tell her to leave immediately without making her suspicious.

Another moment she was silent.

Then, softly, she said, "Good-bye, Chris," and hung up.

"Helen—!" He'd realized, too late, what was wrong. She thought he was avoiding her.

He put the receiver back onto its hook and sat there heavily. It's just for now, he told himself. She'll understand later. I'll make it up to her and everything will be all right.

Chris stood motionless in front of the store window looking in. It was a good display: neat, well-balanced, imaginative. He and Jimmy had worked it out between them two weeks before—Jimmy with his brief training in visual arts, Chris with his instinct for effective order.

He remembered how proud he'd felt of the display when it was completed. How he'd stood in front of the window for a long time looking at it. His store and its operation was an endless source of pleasure to him. At least it had been.

Chris looked at the wall clock inside the store. It was twenty-five minutes to ten. His eyes focused on the lettering—DENIS SCHOOL OF MUSIC—across its face. He remembered the day the head of the school had come into his store and offered the clock. Chris had taken it gladly. He'd just borrowed enough money to buy the store from Mrs. Saxton and he was in no position to turn down a free clock, advertising or no advertising.

A melancholy smile raised Chris's lips as he recalled those first days of ownership.

Mrs. Saxton was old and tired, anxious to retire. That was why she sold out so cheaply; that plus the fact that she liked and trusted Chris. He'd been with her for almost five years and, during that time, the store had expanded markedly. When he'd started, it had been a run-down place with a few racks of sheet music, outmoded record albums, a modicum of instruments for rent or sale. Nothing like what it became after Chris began working there.

After the purchase, he expanded it further. He took out a lease on the adjoining store which had been vacant for almost two years and had the wall removed. He had racks built for a complete line of records, three listening booths installed as well as a counter with stools where all kinds of music were sold, from orchestral scores to children's piano primers and including all the current sheet music. He had a new tile floor put in with a motif of bass and treble clefs and notes in the design. He enlarged his line of instruments and made an exchange agreement with the Denis School and others.

All this put him considerably into debt. He was unable, in the beginning, to afford help. He and Helen ran the store until Connie's growth made working too difficult for Helen. Then Chris managed on his own. It was exhausting but joyous work. The weariness he felt at night was a wholesome one.

Little by little, his venture paid off. People from the area began patronizing his store to the exclusion of others. It was a pleasant place and Chris was a pleasant host. His reputation as a man who understood children no less than music broadened. He was asked, by the Chamber of Commerce, to take over the operation of the Junior Orchestra; invited to join the Chamber.

As business increased, so did the scope of his work. He began to arrange neighborhood square dances, organizing the local mothers into an entertainment committee. Gradually, he helped convert the Junior Orchestra into a polished group which gave well-received concerts all over the Los Angeles area. He sponsored and coached the Santa Monica Wildcats who played baseball in spring and summer, football in fall and winter. Life became more and more rewarding. The store did more business and he did more for the community. His idea for the creative workshop had come only a few weeks before and it was, already, halfway to fruition. All this, ended by a phone call in the night.

Jimmy looked up from behind the counter as Chris entered. "Hi Mr. Martin," he said.

"Hello, Jimmy," Chris smiled at him. "How's it going?"

"Up to the B's," said Jimmy, grinning. "I just put Brahms in his place." Then he added, concerned, "Gee, Mr. Martin, you okay?"

"Sure." Chris stopped by the counter and hesitated a moment before speaking. "Oh, uh, my wife has the car this morning, Jimmy. Going to her mother's."

Jimmy nodded. "Uh-huh."

"I'll be needing a car for a while though," Chris said.

"And you wanna borrow mine?" said Jimmy. "Sure thing, Mr. Martin. Any time."

"I'd appreciate it," said Chris.

"Any time at all," said Jimmy. "Well, I'll get back to Britten and Bruckner now."

Chris managed another smile. "Has Mrs. Anthony called?" he asked.

"Yes, sir. I gave her the message."

"Good. Thanks."

Chris shut the door of his office and drew off his top coat. As he dropped it on a chair, he noticed the smudges on it. He must have gotten them when Steve knocked him down. He checked his trousers and found dirt streaks on the knees, a small rip. If he'd gone home, Helen would have seen them. He'd have had to tell her what happened.

He wondered what she'd say when she found out about the money. They'd been saving for a bigger house; this would reduce their account to almost nothing. Well, there was no help for it. It had to be done. After all these years, three thousand was a cheap enough price for continued freedom.

Suddenly, it occurred to Chris that after bringing the money he would no longer be of any value to Adam and Steve. He heard repeated in his mind what Adam had said: *You're lucky we don't leave you in a ditch somewhere.*

Chris sank down heavily before his desk. Dear God, what was he to do? If he gave Adam and Steve the money, he'd always be subject to their blackmail. If he went to the police, he'd be put in prison—and he had no romantic illusions about "getting a fresh start" after that. If he were twenty, perhaps. Not now.

It was in that moment that the idea came with a flash of hideous logic. An idea that had to do with Cliff's loaded gun and Chris's two enemies waiting in Latigo Canyon, with the hills around and the unlikelihood of anyone hearing a shot.

His fingers jerked suddenly into blood-drained fists. No! He was not that kind of man and never would be!

Abruptly, the false defenses seemed to fall away like scales. He'd been wrong. It might entail a kind of courage to go on in the face of pressure but to face the obligation of honesty was the only true courage.

Chris sighed. Strange that, after all his indecision, the solution should prove so simple. He could feel the simple rightness of it in his very flesh

He pulled the telephone across his desk and, lifting the receiver, dialed quickly

Helen's mother answered.

"This is Chris, Mom," he said.

"Yes, Chris."

"Could I speak to Helen for a moment?"

"Helen? Is she supposed to be here?"

"Yes." Chris felt a sinking of disappointment. "I guess she hasn't had time to get there yet."

"I didn't know she was coming."

"Yes. She planned to pay you a visit, with Connie."

"Well, how lovely," said Mrs. Shaw, "I'll be looking for them."

"Would you ask her to phone me when she gets there?" he asked.

"All right. At the store?"

"Yes. Please."

"I will, Chris."

"Thanks, Mom. See you soon then."

After he'd hung up, Chris sat restively, tapping on his desk. He was anxious to talk with Helen, to let her know what he was planning to do. He wanted to hear her shocked yet—he felt sure—proud reaction. He needed it before he could call the police.

For a moment, he wondered if what he really wanted was for her to talk him out of it. He thought about that, trying to decide what he'd do if she tried to dissuade him. Somehow, it seemed no problem. He couldn't believe that he'd change his mind now.

Sighing, he rotated his swivel chair and looked through the glass partition at the store. Jimmy was still hard at work relocating the LP albums. He was a good kid, Chris thought. With Helen's assistance, Jimmy could manage the store very well while he was gone.

Gone.

Chris shuddered. The store had never looked more wonderful to him; his life with Helen and Connie had never seemed more perfect. Yet he'd be throwing it all away by calling the police.

Involuntarily, he glanced at the wall clock. It was almost ten. There was still time. He could go to the bank, withdraw the money, drive to—

No. He closed his eyes, furious at the temptation. The choice was made. He wouldn't weaken now.

When he opened his eyes, Helen was just entering the store.

Chris stood without knowing it. He stared at her expressionless face as she came walking down the length of the store with slow, unbalanced strides. Faintly, he heard Jimmy say good morning to her. She didn't turn or answer. She kept walking toward the office, eyes fixed straight ahead, features tensely set. Chris stepped to the door on suddenly trembling legs and pulled it open.

"Honey, what is it?" he heard himself mutter.

Her voice was hoarse, shaking.

"She's gone," she said.

"What?"

"They took her!" she gasped, *"They took my baby!"*

CHAPTER EIGHT

BEHIND THE COUNTER, Jimmy glanced away embarrassedly. Chris looked back at Helen's stricken face. He could feel his hands twitch, feel a thickened pulsing at his temples. Still, there was no horror. Numbly, he reached for her arm.

"Come in the office," he said.

She jerked back. "Get away!" she whispered vehemently.

"Helen." He sucked in breath. "Helen, please come in the office," he begged, "Jimmy can hear us."

"Oh, that matters," she said, brokenly. "That really matters."

She stumbled past him and he followed dizzily, shutting the door behind himself.

"What happened?" he asked.

She whirled on him. "I told you!" she cried. "Are you deaf? They took Connie!" A sob tore at her throat. "They took my baby!"

Again, instinctively, he reached for her. Again, she shrank away.

"Don't touch me," she said.

"Helen, do you think I—?"

"Yes, I think it's your fault! You were so careful to protect yourself! So *careful.*"

"Helen, what happened?"

She caught herself, forcing down the rage and anguish. Chris stared at her, waiting. His heartbeat was a slow, painful jolting.

"They came to the house," she said, quietly, measuredly. "You knew they were coming, didn't you?"

"Why didn't you leave when I phoned?"

"You knew they were coming."

"Helen, for God's sake!" It was there now, the shock, the horror, all of it.

"They took her away, Chris. Just *took* her away. They said they'd—" her teeth clenched. "—they'd *kill* her if you didn't bring the money."

She stared at him balefully. "Now tell me you didn't know," she said.

"Helen, I swear—"

"Yes, swear, swear! I'm sure it'll bring her back!"

Chris glanced out at the store in time to see Jimmy look away again. He raised his eyes to the clock. It was after ten.

"I'll get the money," he said, "I'll bring her back."

"You'll bring her back." Abruptly, Helen began to cry, both hands pressed shakingly across her face. *"You'll bring her back."*

"Helen, you didn't call the police?"

She turned again, jerking down her hands, a near deranged look on her face. "The police!" she said. "Is that what you're worried about?"

He grabbed her shoulders. "Now, listen to me," he started.

"Is that all you're—?"

"Listen to me!" Her head snapped as he jerked her shoulders violently.

"Go on," she said, "Tell me your troubles."

"Did you call the police?"

"No! Are you happy now? Are you relieved?"

His voice shook as he answered her.

"Helen, if the police come into this, Connie hasn't got a chance and you know it."

"Oh God," she whimpered. She almost fell as a spasm of grief wrenched her. "I want my baby."

"Helen, I'll get her."

She pulled away from him and, stumbling to the wall, leaned against it, crying helplessly.

"My baby," she said, "I want her now. I want her."

"I'll get the money," he said.

"Yes, get the money, get the money," she echoed hollowly, "Save yourself."

He started to say something, then checked himself. There was no sense in trying to reason with her now.

"We'll never see her again," said Helen.

"Yes, we will, Helen. I'll get her back."

"No, no, no." She almost crooned the word, shaking her head.

"We *will.*"

She turned abruptly, pale with fury.

"How many kidnapped children ever live!" she cried, *"Tell* me!"

He caught her hands and held them so tightly that she winced.

"She'll be all right," he said, "They won't hurt her because they're planning to ask me for money again. Can't you see that? They figure I'll go on paying to protect myself and they're not going to—"

"And you will," she said.

He looked at her for a few moments before dropping her hands. "No," he said, "I won't."

He picked up his topcoat and put it on.

"Where are you going?" she asked.

"To the bank."

"I'm going with you."

He started to speak, then changed his mind. There was no time. "Come on then," he said.

He could remember joking about it to Bill Albert.

"You know which line in the bank moves the slowest?" he'd said. "The one I'm in."

Chris's gaze moved for the seventh time to the clock over the vault entrance. Ten twenty-one. He watched the long second-hand turning. Swallowing dryly, he turned back to the line. The man at the counter was pushing rolls of change into his cloth sack. Chris glanced at the other lines. One of them was shorter but he didn't dare take a chance on changing. He'd done it once already and lost time.

He drew in a quick breath. Come on! his mind cried. He thought of Connie being held by Adam and Steve, he thought about Adam's gun. He twitched as a drop of sweat trickled down his side. Hurry, he thought. Please hurry.

He looked around and saw Helen still sitting on the bench by the wall. She looked as if she were hypnotized the way she stared ahead with dull, blank eyes. He knew what she was feeling and it was a hideous sensation—one of incredulous terror. It was impossible to believe that they might never see Connie again, yet impossible to disbelieve it.

God, let it be true! Chris thought in sudden anguish, recalling what he'd said to Helen. Let them be planning to bleed him dry. Right now, he'd sign away everything he owned or ever would own just to hold Connie in his arms again.

"Good morning, Mr. Martin."

Chris started at the voice, jerking his head around so fast it hurt his neck.

"Did I startle you?" she asked.

"Oh Mrs. Anthony. I'm—I'm sorry. I—"

"Didn't see me coming. I apologize." Mrs. Anthony smiled. "I wanted to talk to you about the concert Sunday."

Chris stared at her. "Yes," he said. The line moved forward as the man left the counter. Chris stepped off compulsively. Mrs. Anthony, smile faltering, moved with him.

"What the committee was wondering," she said, "is if it might not be feasible to combine the concert with our Spring Fund Drive."

Chris nodded jerkily. "Uh-huh." He felt a tremor in his stomach muscles. Please get out of here, begged his mind.

"Now," said Mrs. Anthony briskly, "we discussed the possibilities at some length at our meeting last Friday afternoon and, after weighing the pros and cons, we reached the decision that it could be effected quite readily."

Chris ran a hand across his upper lip and drew it away dripping sweat. "I see," he muttered. He rubbed the hand on his coat distractedly.

"If, *before* the concert," Mrs. Anthony continued, "we could have, say, five to ten minutes for a short announcement about the opening of the Drive, we could easily..."

Her voice seemed to drift off into an unintelligible murmur as Chris watched her. The nightmare was back again, endless and insane as nightmares were. To stand here listening to Mrs. Anthony talk about the start of a Spring Fund Drive for The Ladies' Horticultural Society while, somewhere, Connie was—

"Does that aspect of it seem reasonable?" she asked.

Chris swallowed.

"I—I—what was that?" He smiled mechanically. "I'm afraid I—"

"I *said,*" said Mrs. Anthony, "does the setting up of a cake booth in back of the auditorium seem to you—"

The line moved and Chris stepped closer to the window. He felt the urge to shove away the two people in front of him, to push Mrs. Anthony away violently, to grab the money from the cashier's drawer and run to his car, drive to Latigo Canyon at a hundred miles an hour.

"Yes," he said, "Yes. I—I think that would be fine."

"Are you feeling well, Mr. Martin?"

"Hmmm?" Chris's smile was more of a grimace.

"You're perspiring quite heavily."

"Oh. No, I—it's rather..." he sucked in breath, "—hot in here."

"Yes." Mrs. Anthony cleared her throat. "Well, then, I can tell the committee that you approve?"

"Yes, yes, certainly," Chris blurted, "I—think it's a fine idea."

Mrs. Anthony nodded once, looking at him curiously. "Well, then," she said.

Chris looked over at Helen as Mrs. Anthony walked away. She was watching him fixedly. Chris turned back quickly. There was just the woman in front of him now although the cashier was gone. He glanced aside and saw Mrs. Anthony wave to Helen. God, don't talk to her! he begged silently. He blew out ragged breath as Mrs. Anthony left the bank.

"I beg your pardon," he said, impulsively.

The woman in front of him turned.

"I wonder if I could trouble you to—to let me ahead of—"

"I'm *sorry,*" she said. "I've been waiting here for a long time and I'm in just as much of a hurry as you are."

Are you? Chris thought.

She turned away. "I never," she was muttering. Chris closed his eyes a moment. Please, please, *please,* he thought.

A minute later he was sliding the pass book across the counter. The teller picked it up and opened it, looked at the withdrawal slip.

"I'd like to have it in tens and twenties," Chris said.

"Yes, sir," said the teller. He turned away and walked over to the row of file cabinets behind him. Chris watched him, his hands resting limply on the edge of the counter. He saw the teller pull out a drawer and start thumbing through the files.

"I'm in a hurry," Chris said. The man didn't hear him.

In a moment, the man pulled out a file and looked at it. Chris waited impatiently.

The man walked past the window toward the front of the bank.

"What are you—?" Chris started.

"Just a moment, sir," said the teller, politely.

Dazedly, Chris watched him walk away. What in God's name was happening? For a second, he almost believed that he *was* dreaming, that this was a nightmare. It was too incredible to be real.

He saw the teller speak to Mr. Finder in front. Mr. Finder looked over at Chris and, smiling, gestured for him to come down to his desk. Chris couldn't repress the groan. Clenching his teeth, he strode quickly along the counter and pushed at the gate with shaking fingers. It didn't open.

"It's *locked,*" he said, startled at the loudness of his voice.

The girl at a nearby desk looked up, startled; and gaped at him.

"Miss Grey," called Mr. Finder. She glanced back and Mr. Finder nodded at her. She pushed a button and Chris went through. *We'll never see her again.* Helen's words echoed terribly in his mind.

"What is it?" he asked.

"This withdrawal, Mr. Martin," said Finder, "It will leave your account with less than a hundred dollars."

"I know that." Was the man insane?

"Well—" Mr. Finder coughed embarrassedly. "You see, this note—"

"Note?"

"It states that a three thousand dollar loan extended to you last October would be made on the condition that the amount in your savings account serve as collateral."

Chris looked at him dumbly. He'd forgotten.

"You see," said Mr. Finder. "You signed it."

Chris held the paper and stared down at it without being able to read it.

"Naturally, if you withdraw three thousand dollars at this time," said Mr. Finder, "the conditions of the loan are no longer met."

Chris had difficulty keeping his voice steady.

"Mr. Finder, I've been doing business with this bank for the past seven years. My credit rating is beyond reproach. I need this money now. My mother is in financial trouble and needs it immediately. It will be replaced as soon as possible."

"Mr. Martin, please understand. It's not as if—"

"Mr. Finder, I have a good business," Chris said, agitatedly. "I pay my debts. I'm a member of the Chamber of Commerce. For God's sake, let's not haggle! I *need* the money. I've met every obligation to this bank in the past. Now, for pity's sake!" If I had a gun, he thought suddenly, I'd take the money.

Mr. Finder pursed his lips and looked at Chris dispassionately.

"Well?"

Mr. Finder sighed. "Very well, Mr. Martin," he said, "I really see no reason why we can't. It's somewhat irregular but—"

Less than a minute later, the doors of the Ford slammed behind them and Chris twisted the ignition key. He backed out of place and drove out of the parking lot so fast he almost hit another car. He headed down Wilshire as fast as he could and turned right onto

Ocean Avenue. A few minutes later the Ford was speeding along the coast highway toward Malibu.

"Chris," she said as they went past an orange caution light at Channel Road.

"Yes."

"Do you really believe what you said before?" Her voice was spent of anger now, almost lifeless.

"Yes," he said, "I'm convinced they plan to use me as long as they can."

"Oh..."

Chris looked into the rear view mirror, then pressed down on the accelerator. They should make Latigo Canyon in fifteen minutes, he calculated. Surely, Adam and Steve would wait. He cleared his throat. They'd wait. He was right, he had to be. They *were* planning to use him. Hurting Connie would end that and they knew it. At least Adam must know it.

"Before you came to the store," he said, "I phoned your mother." From the corner of his eye, he saw her looking at him. "I was going to tell you that I'd decided to call the police."

She didn't answer.

"I know it seems pointless now," he said, "but I *was* going to." His hands clenched on the rim of the wheel. "And, after we get Connie," he said, "I'll call them."

Still she said nothing. Chris felt himself tightening, wanting her to speak. Then he realized that she could think only of Connie. After Connie was safe, she'd respond. Chris pressed his lips together. After Connie was safe. He fixed that in his mind.

Eighteen and a half minutes later, he was turning the car into the entrance of Latigo Canyon.

Automatically, he reached up and pressed a hand over his inside coat pocket He could feel the rubber-banded clump of bills. Three thousand dollars. The result of almost four years' saving. Chris clenched his teeth. If only he'd phoned the police the night before, not only would Connie be safe, but Helen would have this money while he was gone. He felt a sudden stab of contempt for himself. It was true, what she'd said. For his own protection, he'd allowed this situation to occur.

There were no sounds of traffic now, only those of the Ford as he guided it up the tortuously curving road: the laboring mutter of its engine, the squeak of its constantly twisted tires. Behind them, the highway sank into the low-hanging fog. Ahead, the mountains loomed grey and green.

Somewhere among them was Connie.

"He didn't say any more about where he'd meet us?" he asked.

"No," she said, "He just said bring the money."

Chris pressed down on the accelerator as they reached a length of straight road. His gaze jumped ahead, looking for a sign of the black sedan. What if they missed each other? He fought off the terror of the thought. Adam wouldn't miss them. He needed the money too much.

The ocean had disappeared from view now. The car was surrounded by the silent mountains. Los Angeles *was* a strange city, Chris thought distractedly. Fifteen minutes from the most populated places were spots of absolute wilderness. Spots where a person could disappear within minutes of his home and never be found again.

"Chris."

He started from his thoughts and glanced at her.

"There's a car following us," she said.

His gaze jerked up to the rear view mirror.

"Is it them?"

Chris swallowed. "Yes," he said.

The sedan was about fifty yards behind them, following unhurriedly. Bracing himself, Chris guided the Ford to the side of the road and braked it. Suddenly, he wished he'd brought Cliff's gun; and, suddenly, remembered the clipping that had fallen out of Cliff's pocket. Adam and Steve had already killed during their escape. They had nothing to lose by killing again. The avoidance of capture was all that mattered now. He shuddered. Had he made another blind mistake? Was he endangering Helen's life now?

The sedan moved past them.

"What!" Chris stared at it incredulously. Adam was driving.

"What's he doing?" Helen asked, her voice shrill.

"I don't—" Chris broke off and shot his hand out for the ignition key. Twisting it, he started the motor, then, releasing the hand brake, put the transmission into drive and gunned off the shoulder so quickly that the wheels spun once before catching. Gravel rasped beneath the car, spattering off the underframe. Then the car was jolting forward onto the road, starting after the sedan which was just disappearing around a curve.

The Ford wheeled creakingly around the curve, then leveled off. Ahead, the sedan moved on leisurely. Chris blew out breath through gritting teeth. Was Adam playing with them? He shuddered with rage. So help me God, he thought, if you've done anything to Connie...

Three minutes later, Adam turned into a side road and stopped. Chris pulled up behind him and braked hard. Switching off the engine, he jerked on the hand brake.

"Stay here," he said. He got out of the car and started toward the sedan. Adam made no motion to get out. He sat with his back turned to Chris. Chris looked into the car anxiously. As he'd expected, Steve and Connie weren't in it. He stopped by the front window and looked in at Adam. The revolver was on Adam's lap, close to his right hand.

"I didn't think it was a very good idea to stop on the main road," Adam said, smiling.

"Where is she?"

Adam extended his left hand, palm up.

"Where is she, Adam?"

"The money."

Reaching into his pocket shakily, Chris jerked out the clump of bills and tossed it on Adam's lap.

"Where *is* she?" he demanded.

Adam removed the rubber band from the bills and started counting the money.

"Adam, for God's sake!"

"She's well, she's well," said Adam, casually, his eyes on the money. "Steve's taking care of her."

"Where?"

Adam wet his finger and continued counting. Chris stood watching him, his heart thudding slowly and heavily.

"It's all there," he said.

"We'll see."

"Adam—"

"Shh-shh-shh" Adam gestured impatiently.

It took another minute for him to finish. Then he nodded. "Very good," he said. He looked at Chris in amusement. "Contract fulfilled," he said, sliding the bills into his pocket.

"Now where is she?"

Adam reached out and pushed the starter button. The sedan's engine ground over twice, then caught. Chris looked at Adam, startled. "What are you—?"

Adam reached for the gear shift.

"What are you doing?"

Adam smiled at him. "We'll be seeing you," he said. The car started moving.

"No!"

CHAPTER NINE

CHRIS ACTED WITHOUT thinking. As the sedan rolled forward, he jerked open the front door and reached in.

Adam grunted in surprise, snatching downward at his gun. Before he could reach it though, Chris had grabbed his coat and started dragging him off the seat. Adam swung out wildly with his left hand and missed. Abruptly, moving with the car, Chris stumbled on a rock. As he fell, his fingers clamped on Adam's coat and, in an instant, the two men were sprawled on the road, the pistol landing near them.

The sedan kept rolling.

Chris got an instant's view of Helen pushing out of the Ford as he straightened up. Then Adam's fist was clubbing at the side of his head, Adam was pushing to his knees, a dirty scrape across his left cheek. He was looking for the pistol, seeing it, lunging for it.

Before he could reach it, Chris was on him. The two men rolled and tumbled in the dirt, dust scaling up around them. Chris's foot kicked out at the pistol and sent it bouncing away. Adam reached for it but Chris pulled him around and slammed a fist into his jaw. Adam, half standing, reeled backward, stumbled and fell down heavily on his side.

He was starting up when they heard the grating sound. Instinctively, both men looked down the road in time to see the sedan going over the edge of the canyon rim, its back end flipping up, hanging suspended for a moment, then disappearing.

"Son of a bitch!"

Chris went flailing back as Adam dove at him. They went crashing into the road again, Chris gasping as he landed on a small rock. He flung up his arms as Adam began hitting his face. He tried to roll the heavier man off but couldn't. He grabbed at Adam's right hand but the left struck on his upper cheek, driving jagged streaks of pain into his eye. Hissing, he lurched his body upward, shifting Adam to one side. He pushed at Adam violently, Adam lost his balance and had to reach to the side for support. As he did, Chris jerked in his left leg, got the foot against Adam's side and shoved as hard as he could. Adam thrashed over onto the road.

He was barely on his feet when Chris hit him. His face went blank for a second, then he was swinging back, his blow glancing off Chris's temple. Chris swung again, his left fist driving into Adam's stomach. Adam sucked in gagging breath, his swing missed Chris entirely.

Chris grabbed the pistol from the ground.

"Now," he gasped.

Adam shrank back, wincing, as he saw the pistol pointed at him. "Chris!"

Chris's finger loosened on the trigger and he drew in a long, body-shaking breath. Helen ran over to him.

"Chris, don't—" she said.

"Where is she?" he asked Adam.

Adam looked at him, one hand pressed across his stomach, the other leaning on the ground.

"Well?"

Adam spit into the dirt.

"I'll *kill* you, Adam."

"No, you won't." Adam stood up slowly, an expression of baleful contempt on his face. "You haven't got it, Chris."

Chris stepped forward and slammed the pistol barrel across Adam's forehead. With a surprised grunt, Adam stumbled back and fell.

"Where is she, I said!"

The contempt was gone from Adam's features now. Only hatred remained.

"I'll kill you for that," he said.

Before he'd finished the sentence, Chris had stepped forward and driven the barrel across his head again. Adam went crashing onto his back and pushed up, gasping, feeling at the welted scrape on his forehead.

"You don't believe me, do you?" Chris spoke in a low, trembling voice. "Well, you'd better, Adam. You'd *better.* What freedom means to you, my kid means to me. You'd kill for freedom, I'd kill for her."

"Go to hell, you son of a—"

Chris hit him again, then fell on one knee beside the dazed man. Hauling him up by his jacket, he shoved the pistol underneath his jaw, the barrel end pressing at his throat.

"You tell me now," he said, *"You tell me where she is or get your filthy head blown off."*

Adam's face went pale. "No, don't," he said.

"Where is she?"

"In the canyon. A shack."

"Where?"

"Down the road. Not far. There's a dirt lane."

"You'll take us there."

Adam swallowed with effort and pushed the pistol away from his throat. "All right," he muttered.

Chris shoved him back and stood. "Get up," he said.

Adam got up slowly.

"I guess I underestimated you," he said. There was no admiration in his voice, only self-criticism.

"Yes, I guess you did," said Chris. He gestured toward the Ford. "Go on," he said.

Adam turned and started walking unsteadily, brushing at his clothes.

"Chris." She came up beside him and took his arm.

"We'll get her now," he said.

As they started walking, Chris was conscious of her looking at him. He glanced aside and managed a smile.

"It'll be all right now," he said.

"What happened, Chris? Why did you—?"

"He was going to leave with the money."

"You mean he wasn't going to—?"

"No." He glanced at her as she caught her breath.

"It's all right, Helen. We'll get her now."

"Chris, shouldn't we get the police first?"

"There's no time. Steve is probably wondering already what happened to Adam. We have to go there right away."

She looked at him and he thought he knew what she was thinking.

"I'll call them afterward," he said.

"I didn't mean that."

As they walked past the canyon edge, Chris could see the sedan at the bottom. It was lying on its side, its upper wheels still turning slowly. It was fortunate it hadn't caught fire.

"Toss back the money," he told Adam.

Adam took the bills out of his jacket pocket and tossed it back without a word. Chris pointed at it and Helen stooped to pick it up. She slipped it into her coat pocket.

Adam was waiting by the car.

"Get in the back," Chris told him.

Adam opened the front door and pushed the seat forward. Bending over, he stepped into the back of the car and sat down. Chris waited until he was settled, then, slowly, cautiously, sat down in the front seat, half-turned around so he could watch Adam.

"You drive," he told Helen.

"All right." She got in quickly and shut the door. Leaning over, she switched on the engine.

"Well?" asked Chris when they were back to the main road.

"Keep going inland," Adam said.

Chris heard Helen draw in a quick breath. "Is she all right?" she asked in a stiffly controlled voice.

Chris looked at Adam. "She asked you a question," he said.

"She's all right."

"She'd better be," Chris told him.

Adam had regained his poise by now. He smiled thinly at Chris.

"Quite the hero, aren't we?" he said.

Chris was silent.

"Planning to turn us over to the police?" asked Adam.

Chris only looked at him.

Adam smiled. "You, of course, realize what will happen when you do."

Chris said nothing and the smile faded from Adam's face.

"You'll go to prison," he said, coldly.

"And you'll go to the gas chamber," said Chris.

Adam seemed to tense forward and Chris raised the pistol. The sight of it seemed to relax Adam rather than caution. He leaned back, smiling again.

"Don't worry," he said, casually, "I won't give you cause to shoot me. I plan to live for a long time."

"Good luck," said Chris.

"The turn is just around this bend ahead," said Adam.

They all sat quietly until the car had turned off the road onto a narrow, rutted lane.

"Stop," said Chris. Helen pushed in the brake and the Ford came to a halt.

"How far down is it?" asked Chris.

"A hundred yards or so," said Adam.

Chris looked at him a moment, then, abruptly, pulled up the door handle and pushed outside.

"We'll walk," he said.

Adam shrugged. "Up to you," he said.

"Come out slowly," Chris told him.

"Very slowly," said Adam. He sounded as if he were almost enjoying the situation now. He pushed the seat forward and leaned over to get out of the car.

"Be seeing you," he said to Helen. He sounded very confident.

Chris held the gun on him and leaned over to speak into the car.

"You stay here," he said, "I'll send Connie out to you. Then you go get the police."

"What are you—?"

"I'll stay with them," Chris interrupted. "Just get the police as fast as you can. There's a station at Malibu."

"Chris—"

"Do what I say, honey." Chris straightened up. "Let's go," he ordered.

"Chris."

He glanced at Helen.

"Darling, please be careful," she begged.

Despite the tension, Chris felt a rush of happiness at the sound in her voice.

"I will," he said.

He and Adam started walking down the road.

"Nice day," said Adam.

"Just remember what I said."

"Oh, I will, I will," said Adam.

Their shoes crunched along the hard-packed dirt. Chris glanced ahead but saw nothing. "For your sake, that shack better be there."

"For your daughter's sake," said Adam. There was mockery in his voice now. Chris stiffened.

"She'd better be all right too," he said.

Adam chuckled. "The trouble with you would-be heroes," he said, "Is you don't know what you're up against. Sooner or later, you make a mistake. You'll make yours."

"You—"

"There's the shack," said Adam.

Chris's stride faltered as he caught sight of a battered shingle roof rising above the bushes ahead.

"Hold it," he said.

Adam stopped and looked over at him.

"What now, little hero?" he asked.

Chris hesitated. This part had to be right. If Steve knew, for a moment, what was going on, he might kill Connie—of that Chris had no doubt. This part had to be exactly right.

"Well?" asked Adam.

Chris's grip tightened on the revolver.

"You're going to call him out," he said.

"Am I?"

"I'm not fooling, Adam."

"Shall I call him now?"

"Walk down further," Chris told him. "I'll be right behind you. As soon as you're in front of the shack, call him—and, by God, you'd better make it casual."

Adam looked at him a moment, a detached smile on his lips. Then he turned. "Watch your step," he said as if to a casual chess opponent. He started toward the shack.

"Remember—I'll shoot if I have to."

"Don't worry, I'll remember everything," said Adam.

Chris walked after him, the gun tightly readied in his hand. He drank in a mouthful of air and exhaled it—then shivered, realizing how cold it was, how heavily still. So still it seemed as if his footsteps must be audible inside the shack.

Up ahead, Adam stopped, glanced back. Chris nodded. He was just out of sight of the cabin doorway, a mass of bushes hiding it from him.

Adam called out. "Steve!"

Chris felt his heartbeat jolt at the loudness of it. Was he wrong to try it like this? he wondered. Was there a better way?

"Hey, Steve!" Adam called again. He sounded very casual.

Chris stiffened as he heard the cabin door squeak open.

"Where the hell have you been?" Steve asked.

Abruptly, Chris lunged out from behind the bushes, gun raised. "Hold it!" he ordered.

Steve twitched in surprise. Then, suddenly, he was grabbing for the gun in his pocket.

"Keep your—!" Chris started before reflexes, quicker than thought, had pulled the trigger and a blast of thunder surrounded him. At the top of the rise, Steve hitched around, one hand clutching at his shoulder. He fell back against the cabin, a gush of blood drenching his fingers.

Chris threw a glance at Adam, who was still standing in the same place. Then he looked toward the cabin again. Steve was writhing on the ground, teeth set in a grimace of agony.

"Don't try it again," Chris warned him.

"Sonofabitch," gasped Steve. Suddenly, he whined, biting at his lower lip.

Chris looked at the doorway.

"Connie!" he called.

The cabin was silent. Chris felt a chilling tremor in his loins. "No," he murmured.

"Connie!" he shouted again. "It's Daddy!"

"Daddy!"

Inside the cabin, there was a sound of bare feet running. Abruptly, Connie appeared in the doorway, still wearing her pajamas. When she saw Chris she cried out convulsively and ran out of the cabin. Without looking, she rushed down the steeply sloping ground toward him.

She'd almost reached him when she slipped. Instinctively, Chris jumped forward to grab her. The next instant, flailing down the slope to keep from falling, she crashed into him, knocking him off balance. He struggled to keep his footing but couldn't. His right foot twisted under him, pitching him sideways onto the road, the impact breaking his grip.

The revolver went sliding away from him.

"Honey, look out! " he gasped, lunging for it desperately.

Adam got there first. Chris saw him looming overhead, his lips pulled back in a brutal smile. Then everything was blotted out by Adam's hurtling shoe. For a split second Chris tried to fling up his hands, tried to twist away. There was no time. The shoe tip crashed against his temple, stabbing a wedge of agony into his brain. Chris toppled over backward with a cry. Somewhere Connie screamed. Chris tried to move.

The next kick sent him spinning into blackness.

THURSDAY
AFTERNOON

CHAPTER TEN

HELEN WAS STANDING by the Ford when the explosion of the shot reached her.

For an instant, she stood transfixed, the rocking waves of sound breaking over her. Then, with a gasp, she broke into a hobbling run, her sandals slapping at the dirt. She ran heedlessly, her gaze held straight ahead on the road turn where Chris had disappeared. "No, please," she kept on murmuring. "Please." As if she were entreating someone.

Up ahead, Connie screamed.

"No!" Helen tried to run faster and felt a sting of pain on her sole where the sliver of glass had gone in the night before. She winced but kept on running.

Suddenly, Connie appeared, fleeing around the bend of the road.

"Connie!"

Connie rushed across the uneven ground and flung herself against her mother's legs. She couldn't speak. She clung tightly to Helen, her body trembling. Before Helen could say a word to her, Adam came racing around the curve, the revolver in his hand. When he saw them, he skidded to a halt.

"All right," he said. He gestured toward the shack with his gun. "Go on."

His lips flared back in a grimace of fury as Helen stared at him.

"I said go on!" he ordered.

"Mommy, no," begged Connie, her face buried in Helen's skirt.

"It's all right, baby," Helen told her. She leaned over hastily and kissed the top of Connie's head. "Please. We have to go. Mommy will stay with you. I promise."

"*No,* Mommy."

Helen shuddered at the look on Adam's face. "So help me God, lady," he muttered, pointing the revolver at Connie's head.

"*Baby, walk with me,*" Helen said. She tightened her arm around Connie's shoulders. "You have to come with Mommy now. You have to, Connie."

"No." Connie stumbled beside her, her face still pressed against Helen's body.

"It's all right, sweetie," Helen said in a hollow, shaking voice, "Just walk with Mommy. That's a good girl." She held Connie's head against her side with rigid fingers as they walked past Adam.

"Don't hurt her," she whispered.

Adam said nothing. He gestured jerkily with his head and Helen tried to quicken her step. Connie stumbled and had to be pulled erect. She started to whimper again.

"It's all right, baby." Helen felt a spill of tears down her cheeks. "It's all right," she said, faintly. She glanced across her shoulder and saw Adam getting the keys out of the Ford.

When she saw Chris lying in the road, she stiffened in her tracks, eyes widening. She stared at his body, a thin wavering sound starting in her throat. She could barely feel Connie against herself.

"Come on."

She twitched as Adam pushed the barrel end against her back. Involuntarily, she started forward, drawing Connie with her. She couldn't take her eyes off Chris. He was so still, his body sprawled on the rutted ground, one leg twisted beneath the other, his hands above his shoulders as if, in falling, he had flung them up to ward off the blow that had put him there.

"Chris," she murmured.

"In the shack." Adam's hand was clamping suddenly on her right arm, redirecting her instinctive move toward Chris. Helen gasped, twisting around so quickly that it sent a prickling shock along the muscles of her neck. Connie cried out and she had to pull her close again, stopping to hold her. Adam cursed and shoved her back, almost knocking her over.

"Get in the shack!" he ordered.

She started up the steep incline; drawing Connie beside her, conscious of her own voice soft and trembling as she comforted Connie, not hearing a single word of it. She kept glancing back across her shoulder at Chris and saw Adam lean over, reach under Chris's coat.

He straightened up angrily. "You have the money?" he called up after her.

She turned and stared at him.

"The *money!*"

She remembered then and reached into her coat pocket It was empty.

"I—I can't—" she started, standing there awkwardly on the steep, rutted ground. Abruptly, she recalled that the clump of bills was in her other pocket. She tried to ease Connie away, but Connie held on with talon-like fingers.

"Baby, let me get—" Helen bit her lip and tried not to cry. She forced her left hand in between her own and Connie's body and slipped it into the pocket of her coat.

"Come on!" snarled Adam.

Her fingers closed over the money and started to pull it out. As she did, the rubber band slipped off and several of the bills went fluttering to the ground. She tried to stoop and pick them up but couldn't because Connie was holding on to her so tightly. She heard Adam curse again, then shrank back as he clambered up the rise and snatched the pack of money from her shaking hand.

"Get in the shack," he told her.

"Don't hurt her," she said instinctively.

He jerked her around and shoved her toward the door. Helen felt a rush of dizzying shock as she found herself looking at the other man who was leaning against the shack, his left hand pressed against his shoulder, blood running between his fingers and down his wrist.

"*Shut her up,*" she heard Adam order from behind her and she was suddenly conscious of Connie's terrified crying.

"Connie, don't—" she pleaded. She pulled her daughter against her, shielding Connie's eyes from the sight of the bleeding man. She almost carried her past him into the fetid chill of the shack. Pulling her to a chair, she sat down and lifted Connie onto her lap, pressing her close, brushing at her hair with short, trembling strokes. "Shhh, baby, shhh. It's all right."

Outside, she heard the two men talking and she raised her face from where she'd had it buried in Connie's hair.

"—doctor," she heard the wounded man finish.

"Use your head," Adam answered stiffly and the wounded man said something she didn't hear except for the curse of pain.

Suddenly, there was a sliding, scraping sound.

Unaware of it, Helen pressed back slowly against the chair, the old wood creaking in the silence of the shack. She hardly heard Connie's sobbing. All she could hear was the raking noise outside that was drawing closer and closer. She felt a chilling tingle up the back of her neck and her gaze, unblinking, held on the doorway.

Abruptly, Adam appeared dragging Chris into the cabin, one hand twisted around the collar of Chris's jacket. Her mouth opened as if to breathe but there was no breath in her. Air seemed to stifle in her lungs and in the heavy length of her body it seemed the only thing that lived was her heart.

"Is he dead?" she heard the other man ask as he stumbled into the shack after Adam.

"I don't know," Adam answered carelessly. He released his fingers and Chris's head and shoulders thumped down on the floor. Helen couldn't restrain the faint gagging sound in her throat. Adam glanced over at her, then turned to the wounded man.

"Let's see," he said, drawing Steve's hand off the wound. Helen twisted her gaze from the sight of the man's blood-pulsing shoulder. She pressed her eyes to Connie's head again, her arms tightening convulsively around her daughter's body.

"I gotta have a doctor," she heard Steve insist.

"And end up in the gas chamber?" Adam snapped.

"I'm bleeding, damn it!"

"Hold still."

There was a moment's silence, then the sound of cloth being torn. Blotted out, in an instant, by Steve's hoarse cry of pain. Helen glanced up instinctively and saw the torn, blood-pumping hole in his shoulder.

"I need a doctor," said Steve. There was a shakiness beneath the hard sound of his voice. Helen looked at Chris again. He didn't move.

"Come here. Sit down while I bandage it," said Adam.

Helen looked up, startled, and saw him leading Steve toward her. She shuddered as his eyes met hers and, hastily, she struggled to her feet, holding Connie against her. Connie started to look around but Helen pressed her head down to keep her from seeing.

"It's all right, baby," she said. She edged away, watching Steve sink down heavily onto the chair, his face ashen, his teeth clenched together so rabidly she could see the bulge of his jawbone beneath his ears.

"For Christ's sake, hurry up," he said.

Turning, Helen moved over to where Chris was lying. She felt numb, almost dreamlike. The entire situation had such an air of unreality about it that, somehow, the dread in her could rise no higher. Simply, the mind would not accept more.

She looked down intently at Chris's pain-twisted face. There was an ugly, purplish welt across his forehead. She bit her lip and looked at his chest. At first she couldn't see any movement and the horror she had repressed seemed to flood through her body like a cold slime.

Then she saw a hitching rise to his chest and heard a faint, liquid groaning in his throat. Catching her breath, she put Connie down.

"Mommy."

"I have to help Daddy, sweetheart."

Connie turned and looked down at her father. Her breath seemed to stop. She stood motionless, lips parted, staring at him. Helen kneeled beside him quickly and ran a trembling hand over his cheek.

"Chris?" she murmured.

He didn't move. Helen looked around and saw a bottle of water on the table. She pushed up and started for it. Connie caught onto her.

"I have to get some water," Helen told her, "Daddy needs—"

"Mommy, don't—"

"*Stand by Daddy,*" Helen told her. "Be my brave girl now." She backed off slowly, raising her hand as Connie started after her. "Just stay there," she said. She glanced across her shoulder at Adam who was pressing a handkerchief against Steve's shoulder.

"Your slip," he said.

Helen twitched and stared at him.

"Your *slip,*" he repeated. He started to turn and she drew back. Connie made a frightened sound.

"All right, all right," Helen said. Shivering, she turned away and bent over. Drawing up her skirt, she pulled quickly at her half slip until it fell around her ankles. She stepped out of it and picked it up. Adam grabbed it from her outstretched fingers and, turning back, started tearing it into strips. Quickly, Helen moved to the table and picked up the bottle of water. She carried it back to Chris and kneeled beside him again. Opening the bottle, she pulled a handkerchief from her skirt pocket and poured some water over it. She began patting it against Chris's temples and cheeks.

"That'll hold it," she heard Adam say behind her.

"No, it's still bleeding too much." Steve sounded a little frightened. "I gotta have a doctor, Adam."

"Damn it, use your head!" snapped Adam, "We've wasted enough time. We have money now. We've got to clear out."

"You wouldn't be so damn sure if it was you," said Steve. There was almost a whining in his voice now.

"Look you want a doctor, go get one. I'm going to Mexico."

Helen glanced across her shoulder and saw the two men looking at each other.

"What about—?" She saw Steve's head jerk slightly toward her and she felt a sudden, cold depression in her stomach.

"There's no room," said Adam, flatly.

Helen stared at him, her heartbeat suddenly jolting. She couldn't take her eyes off Adam's expressionless face. When he turned to look at her, she kept gaping at him.

"No," she whispered. She couldn't hear herself. She reached out and pulled Connie against her. "No, please." Her fingers clamped on Connie's arm. *"Please."*

Steve groaned. "I've gotta have a doctor," he muttered.

"Later," said Adam, his eyes on Helen. He reached into his coat pocket. Helen felt a scream rising in her throat. The room seemed to wheel around her.

CHAPTER ELEVEN

"NO, NOT LATER!"

It was as if Steve's voice came from miles away. Cringing back, Connie tight against her, Helen looked dumbly at him, at the pistol he was pointing at Adam's back.

Adam looked around. "What are you—?" He stared at Steve incredulously.

"Get your hand out of your pocket," Steve told him.

"Are you out of your mind?"

"I'm getting a doctor."

"Sure you'll get a doctor—but later!" said Adam, "We have to get out of here! Don't you understand? We've been—"

"I want him now!" Steve's chest rose and fell unsteadily. He blinked and leaned back dizzily against the chair. "Don't move," he ordered, "Don't move or I'll—"

"You're a fool," Adam said.

Steve pressed his lips together and tried to push himself up. His legs vibrated beneath the weight and he fell back with a muffled grunt.

He glanced at Helen. "Get over here," he said.

"What do you want?"

"Get over here."

Helen stood up and pushed Connie away from herself. "Stay by Daddy," she said. Connie started to object but Helen cut her off sharply. *"You have to stay by Daddy,"* she said.

"Get over here, lady." There was a half-mindless drone in Steve's voice now.

Helen moved toward him. He swallowed and grunted.

"Take the rod out of his pocket."

"You're out of your mind!" Adam shouted at him.

"Take his rod."

"His—?"

"Gun, gun! Take it!"

"Yes." Helen edged over slowly until she was standing behind Adam. Carefully, her hand trembling, she reached toward his side coat pocket.

"Hurry up!"

Her hand twitched and bumped against Adam's side. Swallowing, she pressed her lips together and slid her hand into the pocket. He stirred a little and Steve muttered, *"Watch* it."

Helen's fingers touched the cool, oily surface of the revolver. A sudden tension filled her. Did she dare try to shoot at Steve? She inhaled quickly, raggedly. What if she missed? She'd never fired a gun in her life. Was it possible that she could fire it while it was still inside the pocket? Otherwise, in trying to jerk it free, it might catch on the pocket lining.

"Get it out, damn it!"

There was no time, no time! With a faint, hopeless sob, Helen drew the revolver out of the pocket and stepped back. For a moment, Adam's body stood between her and Steve. *Now!* cried her mind—but her muscles would not obey. Nervously, she moved over to the table and put down the gun. She couldn't take the chance. If she missed, Connie would be killed in seconds, Chris would be killed.

"You're gonna get me a doctor," Steve said.

At first she didn't realize he was talking to her and she started back toward Connie.

"I said you're getting me a doctor!"

She stopped and looked back at him. *"Me?"*

"Get in your car and—"

"For Christ's sake, will you—?" Adam started.

"Shut up!" Steve shrilled. "I'm not dyin' on the road for you!"

"You won't die on the road, damn it! We'll stop as soon as—"

"I said shut up!" The gun shook in his grip as he pointed it at Adam.

"Oh...*Christ,*" said Adam, tightly.

"Go, get a doctor," Steve said to Helen.

Helen backed off toward Connie. She felt her daughter move up into the shelter of her arm.

"How?" she asked, "I can't—"

"I don't care how!" Steve interrupted, "Just get him here!"

As Helen stared at him, his lips flared back abruptly from yellowish teeth and he extended the pistol shakily.

"Go on!" he said.

She nodded jerkily and began leading Connie toward the doorway.

"She stays," said Steve.

Helen looked at him with unbelieving eyes. "No," she murmured.

"Let go of her."

Helen found herself shaking her head fitfully. "No," she said, "I won't."

"Maybe you'd like her killed right now!" he threatened.

Helen pushed Connie behind her. "I won't leave her," she said in a low, shaking voice, "If you're going to kill us you'll have to do it now." She drew in a rasping breath. *"I won't leave her,"* she said.

Steve's fingers tensed on the trigger, then eased. He stared at Helen with a dull, almost animal-like confusion.

"Kill her!" snapped Adam. "You're wasting time! She'll never get you a doctor!"

"By God, then *he* will," muttered Steve. He pushed up with a groan and stumbled away from the table. Abruptly, he whirled and pulled Adam's revolver off the table, sliding it into his trouser pocket. He walked erratically across the room, eyes almost slitted from the pain, his lips drawn back, breath hissing from his mouth. He brushed by Helen and staggered over to Chris. He jabbed the tip of his right shoe against Chris's side.

"Get up," he said.

"You're wasting time," said Adam, tensely.

"Then I'll waste it!" snapped Steve. He rammed his shoe tip against Chris's side. "Get up!" he said. Helen winced and closed her eyes a moment.

"Get up, damn you!" With a rasping whine, he bent over and picked up the water bottle. He tilted it over and the water poured down heavily, splattering off Chris's face. Chris twitched and grunted, his arms and legs retracting spasmodically.

"Look, we'll stop at a doctor's, then," Adam said.

"Sure," sneered Steve. "We'll just walk into his waiting room and sit down with the other patients."

Adam's face tightened angrily. He looked around as if seeking some escape. When he saw that there wasn't any, his expression grew angrier yet, color pulsed into his cheeks.

Now Chris was breathing more rapidly. His eyes still closed, he reached up one hand and pressed it to the bruise on his head.

"Get up!" Steve told him.

Chris opened his eyes. They closed a moment, then fluttered open once more. He stared up dazedly at Steve. Then he pushed up on one elbow and looked around. *"Honey..."* he mumbled.

"Chris." Helen spoke his name automatically as their eyes met. He looked, with alarm, at her and Connie.

"Get up, get up." Steve nudged him fiercely with his shoe. Chris gasped and his gaze jumped around. He sat up dizzily, then pulled his legs in slowly and stood. He wavered there, blinking his eyes, trying to focus them properly He started to move toward Helen but Steve pushed the gun against his side and stopped him.

"By God, you better move right or I'll blow you guts out," he said, thickly.

Chris looked at him without expression, still not fully conscious.

"You're gonna get me a doctor," Steve told him.

"Doctor?"

Steve glanced at Adam. "Where are the car keys?" he asked.

"At the bottom of the canyon with the car."

"Their car," growled Steve.

Adam stared at him coldly for several seconds. Then he reached into his trouser pocket and pulled out the ring of keys. He tossed it so they fell on the floor at Steve's feet. "You're going to regret this," he said.

Steve ignored him and stepped back from the keys.

"Pick 'em up," he told Chris.

Chris bent over slowly and picked them up, almost falling as he did.

"Now listen to me," Steve told him, wheezingly, "I killed two men already, see? And I'd kill your wife and kid in a minute too. You understand me?"

Chris glanced over at Helen involuntarily. Connie was shivering against her.

"You bring the cops and you don't have a wife and kid anymore," said Steve, "You have a couple o' corpses. *Understand?"*

"How—how do I—?" Chris began.

"How do ya know I won't kill 'em anyway?" Steve broke in. "You don't know. But if ya don't get me that doctor, you're all dead right now. Understand?"

Steve suddenly closed his eyes and there was clicking sound in his throat. Adam tensed and seemed to lean forward. Then Steve's eyes opened again, his body twitching as if he were starting out of a doze.

"Go on," he told Chris.

Helen braced herself. "Let him take my girl," she said.

Steve looked at her as if he were drugged.

"Sure. why not?" said Adam, "Let 'em all go. We'll just sit here and wait for the cops to—"

"He goes alone," said Steve, stumbling back toward the chair.

"Isn't it enough I stay?" Helen asked, "Please. I'll be—"

"He goes alone." Steve waved Adam back and sank down on the chair with a groan. He rubbed the back of his hand across his mouth and looked at Chris who was still standing in the same place, looking at his wife and child.

"Get out o' here," he said, "You have 45 minutes."

Chris's face tightened. Then, slowly, he moved over to Helen and Connie and put his arms around them.

"I'll come back," he murmured.

Helen shook her head. "They won't let us go," she said, "Not now."

His fingers tightened convulsively on her arm. "Please don't give up," he begged, "For Connie's sake—"

"You'd better go," she interrupted.

Chris swallowed and looked at her helplessly. Then he leaned over and kissed Connie's forehead.

"I'll be back for you," he whispered to her, "Don't be afraid, baby. Daddy will come for you. Do what Mommy says and—"

"Get out!" raged Steve.

"Please let him take her!" Helen begged.

"I said get out!"

Chris turned hurriedly and headed for the door.

"Steve, for Christ's sake, don't do it! " said Adam. "We can stop at a doctor's place but if you let him go we'll never get out of here!"

Steve looked at him unsteadily.

"I'm not goin' anywhere like this," he said.

"He's the one that shot you! Are you going to—?"

"Shut up!"

"I'll get you a doctor then!"

Steve laughed breathlessly. "Sure, I'll let you leave me here," he said.

"Damn it!" Adam clenched his teeth and started forward, then stopped as Steve pointed the gun at his chest.

"You're putting us right in the gas chamber," he said.

"He'll be back," said Steve. He looked at Helen and Connie and his grip tightened slowly on the pistol.

"He'll be back," he said again.

Chapter Twelve

CHRIS STOPPED WALKING and looked back at the cabin, a wave of premonition passing over him. Suddenly, there seemed no escape, no answer. Go back, he thought; stay with them. Nothing he did could change the situation now except that one more human being might die if he brought a doctor.

He shuddered violently. And it was his doing. Because of him, Connie was in there facing death, because of him Helen was in there. And he was free. The irony was perfect. He drove nails into his palms until the pain made him wince. *His doing.*

He looked around desperately, somewhere, deep in his mind, a wild idea gathering. He saw himself brandishing a heavy stick charging into the cabin, swinging wildly, getting Steve before he could fire his revolver, getting Adam. Before the thought had reached even the periphery of decision, he had discarded it bitterly. Anything like that would only destroy his wife and child that much sooner. There was only one thing he could do. What he'd been told.

Forty-five minutes.

Chris whirled and started running toward the car. How much time had elapsed? Five minutes, six? How could he possibly get to a doctor and bring him back in a little over half an hour? Again, he stopped and looked back, his head throbbing painfully. Could he call back, plead for more time? No, Steve would never give it to him. He should be in the car now, speeding off. Chris turned and sprinted around the curve, every jolting stride like a spiked club against his brain.

He jerked open the door of the Ford and slid in, pulled the door shut again. Hastily, he slid the key into its socket and twisted it. The motor coughed, failed. Chris turned the key again, jerking out the choke, then shoving it in as the engine turned over. He pumped at the gas pedal until the engine sound flared. Quickly, he knocked the shift into *Drive* and the car jolted forward.

He glanced up into the rear-view mirror. He couldn't see the shack; it was beyond that clump of trees. He felt an uncontrollable tensing in his stomach and chest—as if invisible elastic cords were binding him to his wife and child and, as he drove, the cords were growing more and more taut until they threatened to tear his insides loose, leaving the better part of him behind. It seemed impossible to drive away like this knowing where they were—to leave them alone with men who would kill without hesitation. Yet there was nothing else to do—or, if there were, his tortured mind could not discover it. Rescue was beyond his means; he knew that. He was just a fallible man. Only blinding fury had enabled him to fight successfully with Adam before. There was no such life-giving strength in the fear that gripped him now.

He turned the car onto the canyon road and accelerated as much as he could. Thirty-five miles an hour was the limit because of the sharply narrow curves. Chris glanced at the dashboard clock. It was twenty after twelve. How much time was left?

His mind raced ahead. There was no chance at all of getting to their own doctor in Santa Monica. He'd have to stop at the first one he came to. That would be in Malibu; far enough as it was. Chris pressed down instinctively on the gas pedal and the Ford tilted squeakingly around a curve. To his left was only space, far below, a rock-strewn valley. Chris tried to go faster but it was not possible. On the next curve the wheels of the car left the concrete and skidded onto the shoulder, casting up gouts of sandy earth.

Nine minutes later he was braking at the canyon entrance, waiting for a truck to pass on the highway, then shooting across to the southbound lane and turning in. He drove the pedal to the floor and the Ford started gaining speed, the dashboard needle quivering past forty, fifty, sixty. Wind hissed and whistled past the windows as he drove. If I'm stopped, he thought, it's over.

You don't have a wife and kid, Steve's words echoed in his mind. *You have a couple o' corpses.*

Chris looked up at the mirror automatically—and suddenly tightened.

Behind, in the distance, a motorcyclist was following him. Chris pressed his lips together and eased his foot from the pedal. If it was a state patrolman, there was no chance of slowing down enough to fool him.

Chris couldn't take his eyes from the mirror as the figure came closer and closer. He felt his heartbeat like a piston at his chest wall. The figure on motorcycle was dressed in black, he stayed in the same lane, coming closer. Chris felt a heavy sinking in his stomach. I'll have to tell him, he thought. The officer would call in, the police would come, they'd surround the cabin and Connie and Helen would be shot to death. A vision of the entire sequence flashed across Chris's mind. He sat frozenly, waiting for it to begin.

Abruptly, the motorcyclist roared out into the outside lane and put on speed. In another few seconds, he was pulling by the Ford and Chris could see the expression on his face. He was a teen-ager wearing a black jacket and a black, goggled helmet.

With an indrawn hiss, Chris jammed down the pedal and the Ford surged forward again. Lost: one precious minute.

He was just speeding into the Malibu area when he remembered the doctor Helen's mother went to. They'd taken her to him once when she'd cut herself badly on a piece of glass. The doctor was close by. Chris's gaze leaped ahead, searching for the turn-off. Just a little way now.

It was almost twenty-five minutes to one as he pulled into the small parking lot beside Dr. Arthur Willoughby's office. He was out of the car before the fan blades had stopped turning. He raced across the lot, jumped onto the one-step porch and pulled open the door, lunged inside.

The waiting room was at the end of a short hallway. Chris's footsteps sounded muffled on the carpeting as he half ran along it. Steve had to wait. He *had* to.

There were four people in the waiting room: an old lady, a workman in overalls, a mother and her small boy. They were sitting around the walls of the small room, the old lady on a couch, looking at a *National Geographic Magazine*, the workman playing with the cap in his hands, the little boy sitting on the edge of a chair swinging his feet back and forth, kicking the metal legs. When Chris came in, the boy looked up and stared. He watched Chris move across the room toward the partition of opaque glass that opened on the nurse's anteroom.

"Stop kicking," said the boy's mother. She did not look up from her movie magazine.

Chris tapped on the partition with the nail of a forefinger. From the corner of his eye, he saw the old lady glance up at him. He drew in a quick breath and looked intently at the moving patch of shadow behind the glass. Come on, he thought. *Come on!* He bit his teeth together, reached forward to tap the glass again.

The shadow darkened, the partition was drawn aside.

"Yes?" asked the nurse. She was young, bleached blonde, her face so darkly tanned it made her lipstick color dull.

"Could I see Dr. Willoughby?" Chris asked her.

"About your head?" she asked.

"What?" Chris started. He'd forgotten. "No," he said, "No."

"Did you phone for an appointment?" asked the nurse.

"There was no time. I have to see him right away. Please...can I—?"

"I'm afraid there are several people ahead of you," she told him.

"You don't understand." Chris was suddenly conscious of the fact that every patient in the waiting room was looking at him. He leaned in close, not noticing the way the nurse edged back a little.

"This is an emergency," he said, "I've got to see him immediately."

"I'm afraid I can't—" the nurse began.

"Now," he said, his voice flaring strickenly. "Look. Tell him that Mrs. Shaw's son-in-law wants to see him."

"Oh. Are you—?"

"Please! There's no time!"

The nurse looked at him blankly, her lips twitching. Then, with a brief nod, she turned away. Abruptly, she turned back and reached forward to slide shut the partition. Chris stood there watching it move until it had thumped shut. He closed his eyes for a second. Helen. Connie. He thought about them in the shack with Steve. *Forty-five minutes.* He looked around the room with panicked eyes but there was no clock on the wall.

"What time is it?" he blurted to the man in overalls.

"What?" The man started, blinked up at Chris. "I—I don't have a watch," he said.

The old lady put down the *National Geographic Magazine* and, slowly, drew out the extending chain of her lapel watch. She picked at the face until she had opened the tiny round door on it. She squinted down. "It is just past twenty minutes until two o'clock," she told him.

Chris felt a sudden traction in his stomach muscles. He made a faint, dazed sound.

"I beg your pardon," said the old lady, "It is just past twenty minutes until *one* o'clock."

"Thank you," muttered Chris. He glanced at the little boy who was staring at him with a vacant expression, his shoes still thumping on the legs of the chair.

"Stop kicking," said his mother, reading. There was no inflection in her voice.

Chris turned back and stared at the glass partition again. Inside, he heard a faint murmuring of voices. He recognized Dr. Willoughby's voice. Oh, God, hurry up! he thought. He looked over at the door, his hand twitching empathically with his need to grab the knob, turn it, push inside. He rubbed a hand across his forehead, hissing a little as he touched the bruise. What was he going to tell the doctor, how could he get him away from the office? It was true, there *was* no answer. Everything was insanely impossible. And yet he had to make it possible—and in twenty minutes.

Twenty minutes!

He couldn't help the indrawn sob in his breath. He stiffened reactively, then, on an impulse, grabbed the knob of the door and turned it.

Dr. Willoughby was just coming down the hall when Chris entered. He jerked up his head abruptly, an expression of stern surprise on his face.

"What is it Mr.—?"

"Martin. I'm—I'm Mrs. Shaw's son-in-law if you—"

"Yes. Yes. I recall," said Willoughby, "What's the trouble. Your head?"

Chris swallowed quickly and glanced across Willoughby's shoulder at the nurse. She was staring at him.

"No," he said, "It's my wife."

"Helen?"

"Yes." For a second, Chris was startled that Willoughby knew her name. Then, he realized, Willoughby had been Helen's doctor too before they were married.

"What's wrong with her?" asked the doctor.

"She—fell," said Chris, "We were out hiking in Latigo Canyon. And she fell."

"Where is she?" asked Willoughby, quickly.

Chris cleared his throat. "She's still out there," he said.

"What?"

Chris felt the waves of dizziness coming over him again, the sense of nightmarish unreality. How could he possibly be standing here lying to this man, attempting to lure him to his possible death? Was he insane?

"She—I couldn't move her," Chris heard himself going on despite the horror he felt, "I was afraid to. She had a bad fall."

Willoughby turned abruptly to the nurse's desk and grabbed the telephone. He picked up the receiver and started to dial.

"Who are you calling?" asked Chris, unaware of the frightened thinness of his voice.

"Hospital," said Willoughby. "We'll get an ambulance out there right away." He finished dialing and listened. "You should have done this," he said grimly.

"No, you can't," Chris said. Everything was going wrong. Every second brought Helen and Connie closer to death.

Willoughby looked at him in surprise.

"You have to come with me," said Chris.

"My dear man—"

"I said you—" Chris broke off as there was a clicking on the telephone, a faint voice.

"Emergency, please," said Willoughby.

"No." Chris hand shot out and depressed the cradle He held it down frozenly as if he were afraid that, if he released it, the connection would be re-established.

"What in God's name are you doing?" Willoughby stared at him incredulously.

"She doesn't want an ambulance," said Chris in a trembling voice. "She wants you. You have to come with me."

Willoughby looked at the welted, blood-caked bruise on Chris's temple, then met Chris's gaze again.

"Come in my office, Mr. Martin," he said.

"It's not my head!" Chris snapped.

He glanced up at the wall clock and saw that it was almost quarter to one. A sob broke in his chest and, suddenly his right hand was clutching at the doctor's wrist.

"You're coming with me," he said. He tried to sound authoritative but his voice was too ridden with terror.

Willoughby pulled back. "Let go of me, Mr. Martin," he said.

The nurse caught at Chris's arm and held him. "You'd better sit down," she said, sounding coolly, maddeningly unruffled.

"No!" Chris jerked free of her and grabbed at Willoughby's white jacket. "You've got to come with me!" he said.

"Mr. Martin!"

With a violent effort, Chris forced himself quiet. He clenched his teeth and let go of Willoughby's jacket.

"Please," he said, "Will you come with me? It's a matter of life and death."

Willoughby took his arm with a strength surprising for his age and build.

"Now, sit down," he said, firmly, "We'll take care of this. But there's no time to—"

"Are you coming with me?"

"Your wife will be taken care of," said Willoughby, "Just sit down and—"

"You've got to come with me now!" All the terror billowed up in Chris as he visualized Steve pointing the revolver at Helen, pulling the trigger, pointing it at Connie—

"Give me your gun," he demanded, "Quickly."

Willoughby and the nurse gaped at him.

"Oh, *God!*" With a sobbing cry, Chris whirled and jerked open the door. He lunged across the waiting room without seeing any of the patients. Behind him, Willoughby shouted, "Mr. Martin!" Then Chris was skidding to a halt at the end of the hall, pulling the door open, racing out into the parking lot.

Willoughby came running out and raised his arm.

"Mr. Martin!" he shouted, "Wait!"

Chris gunned the Ford across the parking lot and roared onto the street, only one thought left in his fear-crazed mind.

The gun at home.

Chapter Thirteen

STEVE'S SOUNDS OF pain came regularly now. Every few seconds, he would make a throaty noise which was partially a grunt, more an involuntary whine. He slumped tensely in the chair, shoulders forward, eyes staring, apparently sightlessly, across the dim room of the shack. Whenever Adam made any kind of movement, however, the eyes shifted instantly, Steve's fingers flexed on the revolver stock. Adam leaned against the opposite wall, watching him—waiting.

Helen and Connie were against another wall, sitting on the floor. Connie, her head in Helen's lap, had fallen into a heavy, emotion-spent sleep. Helen kept stroking gently at her hair, her eyes fixed on Steve. If he lost consciousness, Adam would grab his gun, kill them and leave—probably steal a car or stop one on the road, kill the motorist, then head for Mexico.

She kept telling herself that she should be on her feet, ready to rush for Steve's revolver in the event he fainted. She felt so tired though, so strengthless. If only she could rest; it seemed as if days had passed without rest. Her eyelids felt weighted.

Worse, it was impossible to retain specific dread any longer. It was so quiet in the shack except for the faint sounds Steve was making, the occasional squeak of the chair. Her mind could not hold on to tension, could not keep her muscles prepared to act in defense of her life and Connie's. She was exhausted by fear, depleted by the savage pattern of shocks she'd been exposed to since the telephone first rang not even sixteen hours before. The realization of how little time had passed was startling.

Where was Chris now? she wondered almost with a sensation of not caring. Had he reached a doctor yet? Which doctor would he go to? Somehow, she could not believe that what he did was important any more. No matter what it was she felt that nothing could be changed. Finally, it appeared, she had accepted the nightmare. She had given up resisting it.

Then, suddenly, she looked up, her heartbeat jolting, as Steve's body twitched, his shoes thumping on the floor. She felt her body go taut, readying itself to jump up. She stared at him intently. He was looking around the room in the manner of a man who has just started from unwanted sleep. The revolver was raised from his lap, the barrel of it wavering uncertainly in his grip.

"You're going to die if you stay here," Adam told him. After the long period of silence, his voice sounded unnaturally loud.

"Shut up." Steve spoke without emphasis, slurring the words together. He swallowed and grimaced, licked his lips. Breath faltered in him. "Damn..." he muttered.

Abruptly, he made a half-angered, half-agonized sound. Helen couldn't take her eyes off him. She sat woodenly, her gaze unmoving on his pain-twisted features. He looked over at her and her eyes fell, closed momentarily. *God, please help us,* she thought, the words flaring in her mind without volition.

She knew then that she hadn't given up, that she couldn't give up as long as Connie was alive. There had to be a way out. It was too impossibly monstrous that Connie should die in this horrible place, in this horrible way. There were sudden words in Helen's mind again—terrible, heart-chilling words.

The sins of the fathers, they began.

No! Helen sat rigidly, her lips trembling in the midst of fear, a great outraged fury. Connie would not die. She would not!

She glanced up and saw Steve trying to look at the watch on his wrist. He couldn't seem to focus his eyes properly. He kept blinking them, his teeth clenched. He was close to the edge now, she realized.

"Do you want me to read it for you?" she asked, almost awed by the brittle presence of her voice.

Steve looked up at her. From the corner of her eye, Helen noticed Adam watching her.

"Do you want me to tell you what time it is?" she asked. This time there was a little bass tremble to her voice. She spoke more consciously now, more aware of what instinct had driven her to speak.

"Do you?" she asked.

"It's ten minutes to one," said Adam.

Helen felt a sudden coiling in her stomach, part of it hatred. Adam knew what she'd had in mind—to get beside Steve, try to wrest the revolver from him.

"If we don't leave now," Adam said, coldly, "You're going to die."

"I said—"

"All right, die!" Adam interrupted, "What the hell do I care?"

"That's right, you don't care," mumbled Steve, "Nobody cares."

Helen realized, then, that, within the sight of death, what small sensitivity remained in Steve was piercing his shell of brutality. He was frightened, terrified and he had so long repressed these feelings that he was incapable of responding to them, of even recognizing them.

"He's got ten minutes," said Adam, scornfully, "Think he'll make it?"

There was a dry clicking sound in Steve's throat. "He'll be back," he said; but there was more desperate hope in his voice than assurance.

"Wrong," said Adam, "He won't. He's probably out of the county by now."

Helen started and looked over at Adam's malign face. It isn't true, she thought.

"He won't be back," said Adam, "Why should he? For *them?*" he asked, gesturing toward Helen with his head. "Don't be a fool. He never told her what he'd done. Even after he murdered Cliff, he talked her into not telling the cops. Was he worrying about them then?" Adam snickered contemptuously. "The hell he was," he said.

"Shut up," said Steve; but it was closer to a request than a demand.

Helen felt a cold tremor pass through her body. *No,* she thought but there was no conviction in her. She didn't know whether Adam was right or not. She really wasn't sure—and, in a way, it was a more terrible feeling than the fear of death.

"And you gave him the car," said Adam, "You let him go." He shook his head slowly. "I always knew I should have left you and Cliff. Well I'll be rid of you soon."

"Will ya?" Steve shoved his arm out and pointed the revolver at him.

"Go on!" snapped Adam, "Shoot me! Then you're *all* alone. Then you *really* haven't got a prayer, you ignorant bastard."

Steve drew in a harsh, shaking breath. "He's coming back," he said.

"Sure, sure, he's coming back," said Adam, "He's bringing Florence Nightingale and your sainted mother and the first girl you ever kissed and a box of candy with a ribbon on it. *You—moron. I* should—"

He broke off suddenly as Steve pressed back against the chair, his mouth yawning in a sucking gasp of pain, *"Oh, God,"* he whimpered, *"Don't, don't…"*

In an instant, Adam was alert, his body straightened from the wall, his legs slightly bent as if he were getting ready to rush across the room at Steve who was twisting his head from side to side, tiny noises of fear and agony and disbelief hovering in his throat. Helen's fingers tensed on Connie, she began to shift her to the side so she could put her on the floor and stand—get ready to rush for the gun.

"Get over here," said Steve, hoarsely. He looked at Helen with glazed, watering eyes. He said something else but it was too garbled for her to understand. Hastily, she lowered Connie's head to the floor and stood up.

"You let her over there, she'll grab your gun!" Adam warned.

"And you won't?" muttered Steve. There was a glitter in his eyes now. He spoke through teeth continually on edge. Helen moved toward him very slowly.

"Come on!" he snapped.

Bracing herself, she walked over to where he sat. He looked up at her groggily.

"You wanna die?" he asked.

Helen bit her lower lip and shook her head. "No," she said.

"Then keep me awake."

Up close, she could see the waxy pallor of his skin, hear the laboring of his breath. The bandage on his shoulder was dripping with blood.

"How?" she murmured.

"I don't—" He broke off suddenly and pressed his teeth together so hard that she could hear them grinding. The whine in his throat was like the high note of a song. It would have sounded funny under other circumstances.

"Just keep me awake!" he told her, "Your kid'll be the first one to get it if I feel myself—"

He gritted his teeth and stared at Adam with baleful eyes.

"And if I don't kill her," he said, *"He* will. So you better keep me—"

Steve shut his eyes, his head slumped forward.

Helen caught her breath and glanced over at Adam. He wasn't moving. She looked back at Steve and saw that his head was raised again, his feverish eyes were open. He said something to her.

"What did you—?"

"Don't try t' get my gun," he warned.

"I won't." Helen looked down at the revolver with a revulsive fascination. It looked huge. She saw how Steve's index finger kept twitching against the curved edge of the trigger. Her insides seemed to turn to stone as she watched. She could never get it away from him, she knew. Even if he began to lose consciousness, his hand would still grip the stock. In trying to get it away from him, she would only arouse him.

She shuddered and looked over at Connie. She was lying motionless, still asleep. Adam was leaning against the wall again, motionless. The only thing that moved was time.

"Five minutes," Adam said.

Chapter Fourteen

FIVE MINUTES!

Chris twisted the wheel sharply and the Ford spun onto Wilshire Boulevard with a grating of tire rubber. He straightened it and drove to Twelfth Street trying not to think. If he thought, it would be about the hopelessness of getting the gun and returning to Latigo Canyon in five minutes. Resolution would fail him then, nerves would desert him. Steve would wait; he had made up his mind to that. He wouldn't let himself consider anything else.

Still, braking in front of the house, his eyes moving instinctively to the dashboard clock and seeing that it was one o'clock, he couldn't check the sob that broke in his chest. All he could do was cut it off and push out of the car. He raced across the lawn and jumped onto the porch.

The door was still open. Chris pushed inside and hurried across the living room, skidded around the corner of the doorway and entered the kitchen. Charging to the drawer, he jerked it open.

The gun was gone.

"No!" A spasm of demented anguish drove through him and he pulled the drawer out all the way, shoved his fingers wildly through its contents. Pads, pencils, tacks, rubber bands, stamps, envelopes, pennies, clips—no gun. A wave of dizziness flooded across him and he fell against the edge of the cupboard, gasping for breath.

Clenching his teeth then, he lunged for the other drawers and pulled them out one by one, plunging his hand into each, clattering berserkly through silverware, pulling out dishtowels, knocking over jars and cups and boxes. *"Oh, God—Oh, God—Oh,* God." The horror was back again, he couldn't stop it. Helen and Connie were going to die.

"No." Chris spoke the word softly, as a man speaks just before the end—with one last surge of resisting will. Whirling, he ran out of the kitchen and across the living room rug. Helen could have put in their room, fearing that Connie might come across it in the kitchen drawer.

Skidding into their room, Chris ran to the bureau and hauled out the top drawer. He rummaged frantically through Helen's things, a shearing pain in his heart as he touched the smoothness of her lingerie, the crackling sheerness of her stockings.

The gun wasn't there.

On an impulse, Chris dropped to one knee and pulled out the bottom drawer. He drove his hand beneath the neat pile of skirts and sweaters. At first, his fingers only rubbed along the lining of the drawer. Then, abruptly, they were bumping against the barrel of the gun. He jerked it out and stood, breaking into a run for the door. As he rushed across the living room, he shoved the pistol into his jacket. He pulled open the front door.

"Oh!" Helen's mother twitched back, startled, on the porch.

Chris couldn't speak. He stood, petrified in the doorway, staring at her, feeling as if his body were rocking with the violence of his heartbeats.

"Chris, where have you been?" asked Mrs. Shaw, "I've been phoning you all morning. Where are Helen and Connie?"

Chris shivered. "I'm going to them now," he said.

"I thought she was coming to the house. I've been frantic, Chris! Why didn't you phone?"

"I'm sorry, Mom. I have to go now. I'll—I'll be back in a while."

"Where *are* they?"

"In...downtown."

"Downtown?"

"She had to go shopping. I'm going to get her now."

"But you said she was going to—"

"I know!" He couldn't keep the sharpness from his voice. "I'll get her, I'll bring her over. Now—" He started past her.

"Chris, what's wrong?"

He had to press his lips together they shook so badly. "Nothing," he muttered.

Mrs. Shaw looked at him, frightened. "Chris, don't lie to me!" she said, She gasped and caught at his sleeve. "Has something happened to them? Are they hurt?"

"No, Mom. I—"

"Your head..."

"Mom, I have to go!" He started across the porch but she held on.

"There's been an accident," she said in a forcibly calm voice. "You can tell me, Chris. Are they—?"

"They're all right!" Chris tried to jerk free and the movement jarred the pistol from his pocket. He caught it as it fell.

Helen's mother shrank away from him. *"Chris,"* she whispered.

"Mom...Mom, please," he begged. "They're all right. Just let me go. Wait here. I'll bring them back."

"Where are they?" Mrs. Shaw's voice was barely audible.

"Mom, they're all right! Just stay here!" Abruptly, Chris jumped off the porch and sprinted for the car. Steve would wait. He was badly hurt, he had to take the chance that Chris would return with a doctor. Chris pulled open the car door and slid onto the seat, glancing toward the porch. Helen's mother had gone inside. With a quick movement, Chris turned the ignition key and started the motor.

He was just pulling away from the curb when it struck him. Jamming in the brake pedal, he slapped the gear shift into neutral and pushed out of the car. He ran around the front of it and across the lawn. The door flew open before the impact of his body.

In the hallway, he heard Helen's mother gasp; then suddenly, cry out, "Give me the police! Quickly!"

Chris ran across the room and into the hall. Helen's mother caught her breath and pressed back against the wall, the telephone receiver clenched in her hand. Without a word, Chris grabbed it.

"No!" Mrs. Shaw raised her arm as if he were about to strike her.

"Mom, for—!" Chris pulled the receiver from her and slammed it back on the cradle.

"Don't..." she pleaded.

"Mom..." Chris stared at her in anguish, trying to decide what to do. If he left her, she'd only call police again.

"Come with me," he said.

"No."

"I'll take you to them, for God's sake!"

"Chris, what have you done with them?"

"I haven't done anything! Come on!" He grabbed her wrist. *"Please,* Mom!"

"You killed them!"

"Oh, *God...*" Chris pulled her toward the living room. "They're all right," he heard himself telling her, "They're all right, Mom. Just come with me. I'll take you to them."

She stopped and pulled free.

"Chris, we've got to tell the police," she said in trembling voice.

Rage billowed up in Chris. Even though he sensed that it was only subverted guilt, he couldn't stop it. With a gasp, he pulled the gun out of his pocket.

"You're coming with me," he ordered.

Helen's mother stared at him as if she'd never seen him before. Then, without a word, she turned and walked through the doorway.

"Mom, I..." He couldn't finish. He followed her across the lawn and opened the door of the car for her. He hurried around it and got in beside her, gunned the engine. He made a quick U turn and headed back toward Wilshire Boulevard.

As he drove, he began to tell her exactly what had happened.

CHAPTER FIFTEEN

"Look out!"

Steve's head jerked up, the revolver bucked explodingly in his hand. Across the room, Adam dove to one side as a jagged hole appeared in the wall beside him. Helen stood frozen, her ears ringing. Steve looked around as if trying to remember where he was. His gaze fell on Adam, who was scrambling to his feet.

Then they were all looking over at Connie as she sat up with a shrill cry. The sound seemed to free Helen. Ignoring the gun, she ran across the room and knelt by her daughter, embraced her tightly.

"What the hell are you waiting for?" she heard Adam raging. "It's quarter after one! You gave him till one!"

"Son of a bitch," muttered Steve.

"All right, listen, damn it!" Adam said, hastily, "We can still get out of here. We'll flag a car, get started for Mexico. On the way, we'll stop at a doctor's. What do you say? Let's get *out* of here! We're pushing our luck. He could have called the cops a dozen times over since he left."

"Bastard," mumbled Steve.

"For Christ's sake, use your head! Do you *want to* die?"

Steve didn't speak. He looked at Adam with glazed, unblinking eyes. "Sonofabitch," he muttered.

Adam stared at him.

"Steve?" he said.

Steve coughed. He made a gagging sound and tried to speak. The saliva rolled across his chin. *"Bastard,"* he said under his breath as if it weren't even a word. He raised the pistol shakily and rubbed the barrel end across his chin. Adam kept staring at him. Helen glanced across her shoulder and saw how Steve was weaving on the chair, his head wobbling as if imperfectly attached. He's *going,* she thought. She started to get up but Connie clung to her desperately.

Steve muttered something. Helen didn't hear him. She held on to Connie. It's all right, baby, prompted her mind but she couldn't speak the words aloud.

"Coffee, damn you!" snarled Steve, hoarsely.

Helen looked around. He was staring at her vacantly, his mouth hanging open.

"Coffee," he muttered.

Helen swallowed. "Wh-where?" she asked.

His head hitched around slowly and he looked across the room toward a small alcove. Helen followed his gaze and saw a rusty kerosene stove standing on a shelf, a coffee pot on top of it.

"All right," she said. She straightened up, pulling Connie with her. "Come with Mommy," she said.

Connie walked beside her shakily, silent except for the gasping sobs that shook her body. They moved between the two men and entered the alcove. Helen glanced back. Now she was twice as far from the wounded man as Adam was. If Steve fell there was no possible way she could reach the gun in time.

Biting her lip, she turned back to the stove. She had to heat the coffee quickly, get it to Steve before it was too late. He'd lost so much blood though. There was a dark patch of it on the floor around him; the cloth of his shirt and trousers was saturated with it.

Hastily, she picked up the book of matches beside the stove, then froze as Steve gasped with pain. Stooping hurriedly, she looked over and saw him gaping at Adam, his mouth almost wide open. She glanced at Adam. He was almost coiled against the wall, ready to leap. Helen stood with the matches, one arm still tensed around Connie.

"Mommy, let's go," said Connie.

"Yes, yes." Hands shaking, Helen tore one of the matches loose and struck it. It didn't light. She dropped it quickly, tore another one free, glancing toward Steve.

He was leaning to one side; it seemed as if he had to fall from the chair at any second. His eyes were almost closed, the revolver was in his lap as if he hadn't the strength to lift it anymore. With a faint, shaking murmur, Helen struck the match once, twice. A tiny flame seared up, she leaned forward and touched it to the burner. It wouldn't light.

Helen made a frightened sound and looked back once again at Steve. His eyes were almost shut. He sagged off balance. She started to turn, the match still in her hand. He grunted and sat up a little, a look of dread on his face. He looked over at her and she turned back to the stove, dropping the match with a hiss as it burned her fingers.

Shaking helplessly, she lit a third match, then noticed that the tiny cock hadn't been opened on the stove. She twisted it, touched the match flame to the burner. In a moment, it ignited with a faint, puffing sound, burning blue. Helen leaned over automatically and looked into the pot. She had to—

There was a crashing sound behind her. Helen whirled. Across the room, Steve was sprawled on his side, trying to struggle up. Helen saw him raise the gun to fire at Adam who was rushing at him. Before he could pull the trigger, Adam's shoe was kicking the revolver from his hand, it was clattering across the floor. Adam started for it but Steve, with a final effort, lunged out and grabbed at his ankle. Adam lost balance and went crashing down heavily on his chest.

Helen didn't wait to see anymore. In an instant, her fingers had clamped down on Connie's wrist and she was rushing for the doorway, half dragging her daughter with her. Running, she glanced over at the two men and saw Adam kick his right foot against Steve's bandaged shoulder. The wounded man fell back, screaming.

Then she and Connie were out the doorway. *Which way?* Muscles seemed to answer before her mind, driving her along the front of the shack and around its side. There could be no doubt about the result inside. In a matter of moments, Adam would be coming after them with the gun. His first instinct, she sensed, would be to go toward the road, assuming that it had, also, been her first instinct. There was not enough time to make the road though. Their only chance was to hide in the brush until—

Reason ended there. There was no until. She pulled Connie across the dry, eroded ground, past the back edge of the shack and toward a tangle of bushes. Suddenly, in the shack, there was a shot, another. It was over!

"Hurry, baby!" she gasped. Her grip tightened on Connie's wrist as her daughter started to fall. She pulled Connie up almost brutally. "Run!" she said, *"Run fast!"*

Then the only sound was that of their feet and of their straining breath. Helen looked back across her shoulder. No sign of Adam yet.

Abruptly, they were in the bushes, their bodies thrashing past the dry-leaved branches. Connie cried out as one of the branches whipped across her forehead. Helen glanced down at her and saw a long, red scratch across her brow.

"Keep your head down!" she ordered, "I'll lead you!"

She grunted as a razor-edged twig sliced across her arm. She glanced back again. Had he heard them yet? They were making so much noise! She tried to run faster but Connie tripped and fell and, for several yards, Helen was almost dragging her. She stopped an instant to haul her erect, then started running again.

"Hurry, baby!" she whispered.

Now they were out of the bushes, struggling through long, brownish grass. Helen felt the dry blades scourging at her legs and skirt. Connie started to fall again and she pulled her up, a painful shooting in her back and shoulder. Breath was hot and stinging now, burning her throat. Abruptly, a stitch needled at her side. She bit her lip to cut off the gasp of pain. They couldn't stop! With a lunge, she started up the hill, her sandals slipping on the hard, flaking ground. Again, she looked behind. Where was he now?

"Mommy, I can't!"

"You can!" She dug her fingers into Connie's wrist. "You have to!"

Once more, Connie, unable to match her mother's stride, was pulled from her feet. Once more, Helen jerked her forward and up. The slope was so steep now that she was unable to run. She could only climb with short, desperate strides, pulling Connie with her.

They reached the top of the hill. The heat which had clung to the hollows was gone now, replaced by a damp coldness. Helen looked back, for an instant, her eyes catching sight of the broad hills in the distance, the curving ribbon of the Latigo Canyon Road. Then her gaze had dropped, she saw the shack below, the dirt lane, the—

Breath caught. Adam was just charging from the bushes. He was stopping, looking around.

"No." Helen spun around and lunged over the crest of the hill, dragging Connie with her.

Suddenly, they were plunging down a grass-thick slope, their legs pumping frantically to keep themselves from falling. Helen felt herself losing balance and, twisting, pressed the sides of her sandals against the ground, leaning in heavily toward the slope. She fell on her hip and slid on the ground, wincing as it raked skin from her calf, then from her thigh as her skirt pulled up. Connie cried out faintly and fell against her. They were skidding downward, jolting violently against the bottom of the narrow draw. Pain lanced along Helen's right ankle as it twisted beneath her.

They stayed there for a second, gasping at the warm, heavy air. Helen tried to hold her breath and listen. It seemed as if she heard, in the distance, a thrashing noise, a sound of thudding shoes.

"Hurry!" she said, and suddenly, they were running again, rushing along the foot of the draw, unable to climb because the wall on its other side was too steep.

Helen clenched her teeth against the shooting pains in her ankle, her side. She mustn't stop! Eyes straight ahead, her face a mask of dread, she kept on running. In front of them, the draw turned gradually toward the east.

"I can't, Mommy!" Connie cried out shrilly.

"You can!" Helen almost sobbed the words. She pulled Connie up again, then, hastily, lifted her. She thudded along the rock-strewn base of the draw. Something exploded up above. There was a piercing whistle and earth erupted nearby. Connie shrieked. Dirt specks stung into Helen's cheek and she jerked her head around.

Adam was running along the crest of the draw, pointing the revolver at them. With a desperate lunge, Helen ran around the beetling wall. They were out of sight of Adam now. Helen dropped Connie to her feet.

"Run!" she commanded.

Ahead, the draw widened into a grass-covered slope. The two of them ran onto it, frightening off a flock of birds which scattered darkly into the air. Helen's gaze kept jumping around as they fled, searching for a place to hide. They couldn't go much farther. Connie was dragging at her arm so much that she was virtually carrying her. Her own legs were exhausted, her ankle threatened to give at any second. Still there was no place to stop, to hide. There was nothing in sight but open space and knee-high grasses.

"Mommy—" It was a weak, breathless plea.

"Little further!" Helen gasped, looking back.

In the distance, Adam was scuffing down the wall of the draw, raising a cloud of dust. Helen turned back with a faint sob. They had to go on!

Ahead, the open slope was closing in again to form another draw. Helen headed for the entrance to it, lips pressed together bloodlessly as she fought the burning pains in her ankle. She looked back once more. Adam was just emerging from the draw, running hard, the revolver lowered in his hand. He wouldn't fire until he caught them, Helen realized. He'd already used three of six bullets. He wouldn't waste the three remaining.

"You've got to *run!*" she cried frantically.

"I *can't.*"

Impulsively, Helen snatched her daughter up and kept on running, almost blindly now, as if she ran on some fantastic treadmill in limbo, unable to stop, her body afire with pain, wanting to collapse, unable to collapse. She had to save Connie!

What if she stopped, the thought burst wildly in her mind—stopped, put Connie down and ran back? Could she force him to use all three bullets on her?

No! She sobbed and bit her lip, unable to meet Connie's panic-dazed look. Even if she made him use the three bullets, Connie still wasn't safe. Adam could kill her with his hands. He could—

She was so involved in terrified thought that she almost ran into the canyon wall in front of her. She staggered to a halt, put Connie down and looked with stark, uncomprehending eyes at the steep walls rising on three sides.

The only exit was in back of them.

Helen turned on shaking legs. A hundred and twenty yards away, Burrik was coming at them. She stood trembling, watching him approach. No, her mind protested; No, it can't be. She stumbled back slowly, against the canyon wall, Connie half-behind, little arms clamped desperately around Helen's thigh.

"It's all right, baby," she whispered hoarsely, "Mommy's with you."

Suddenly, Helen was conscious of something hard and thin pressing against the pain of her thigh where the small hands clutched. Instinctively, she reached down. In her pocket was the book of matches, thrust there by habit, and forgotten.

She pushed the child away and, ignoring her cries, knelt on the grass. Fingers trembling, she pulled open the cover and struck a match, held it to the grass. For a moment, nothing happened. It's too wet! she thought in horror. Then there was a faint crackle and, abruptly, the grass was burning, the bright flame rising, smoking whitely. Helen lurched back from it and looked up.

Adam was less than seventy yards away.

Desperately, Helen lunged to the right, fell to one knee and struck another match. More grass ignited, crackling. She pulled away from it, ran to the left and set fire to more.

This time when she straightened up and looked toward Adam, she could barely see him through the mounting barrier of flame. She set fire to another patch, another—then ran to Connie and pulled her to the canyon wall. She stood there numbly, waiting, expecting to see Adam come charging through the fire. There were open patches in it wide enough to pass a running man. She held Connie to herself and waited, staring.

Seconds passed, a minute finally and Helen realized that Adam wasn't going to come through. She glanced up. He might climb the walls and fire down at them but there wasn't too much chance of hitting them from such a height. They were—

Helen froze. *Safe?* She shrank back, flinching, against the hard, rocky face of the canyon wall and almost stupidly, watched the bright flames moving at them.

Chapter Sixteen

CHRIS JERKED OUT the hand brake and straightened up.

"Take the car back to the canyon road," he said quickly, "If we're not back in ten minutes, drive to the nearest phone and call the police."

"Chris—!"

Without waiting to hear what she was going to say, Chris pushed out of the car and started running down the dirt lane, blanking his mind to the fact that he was thirty minutes late. He sprinted around the curve, drawing the gun from his pocket. There was a broken window on the west side of the shack, he remembered. He'd fire through it at Steve, then at Adam if he had to.

He left the lane and clambered up the slope as quietly as he could, eyes on the doorway to the shack. It was so still. *It's over,* his mind persisted but Chris wouldn't listen. He gritted his teeth and edged over to the window, looked in.

Steve was lying on the floor, his face in a pool of blood. Chris's startled gaze fled around the shadowy interior. There was no one else.

He whirled from the window and looked around. Where were they? Had Adam taken them with him? Were they in some stolen car, headed for Mexico? It had a frightening logic.

He was just turning back toward the road when he heard the screaming. Twisting around, he looked up at the hill behind the shack. It was up there! Abruptly, he broke into a run, plunging into the clump of bushes that barred his way, tearing through it, then lurching up the steep rise. The screaming was closer now, so highly pitched that it was impossible for him to tell whether it was a man or woman. Chris lunged the rest of the way to the top of the hill and looked around.

He gasped.

Running across the hilltop, a torch on legs, was Adam Burrik. Chris felt his muscles clamping in as he stared at the burning man. Adam's shrill, brainless screaming pierced the air. He saw Chris and started rushing toward him, the flames whipping backward from his clothes like bright pennants. Chris stood impotently a moment longer, then, with a shudder, dashed forward to help Adam put out the flames, to find out where Helen and Connie were.

Before he could reach the burning man, however, Adam had tripped and fallen, he was rolling down the hillside, screaming with agony. Chris started after him as he bounced and slithered down the slope but, at the bottom, Adam plunged into a thick patch of grass which, immediately, caught fire. In a second, he was swallowed by the rising flames. The last Chris saw of him was a waving arm, the last he heard was one long shriek of horror. Then there was only the spreading fire.

Chris whirled and headed for the top of the hill again, escaping the flames. There was no time to try and put out the fire. He had to find Helen and Connie. Where were they? How had they escaped Adam? How had he caught fire? Questions pounded through his mind as he ran.

Then he saw the scaling pall of smoke in the distance and started running toward it, throwing down the heavy gun. It was of no use any longer.

Seconds later, he heard Connie's scream.

With a frightened grunt, he jolted forward, running as fast as he could. Below, the fire was contained within an open draw, Chris's gaze leaped around the blazing hollow of it, searching for them.

"Helen!" he shouted.

There was no answer. He rushed along the edge, looking downward but the smoke was too thick to see through. He stopped near the foot of the draw and squinted down, the smoke burning his eyes, making them water. He moved again, edging restlessly along the cliff-like drop. He shouted, "Helen!"

There was another scream—almost directly below, it seemed.

"Helen!" he called.

"Chris!"

He fell to his knees and looked down into the smoke-obscured draw.

"Where are you?" he cried.

"Here! Help us!"

Sucking in breath, Chris looked around and saw a narrow ledge about four feet below. Hastily, he lowered himself across the edge and slid down onto it. For a second, losing balance, he almost pitched backward into the smoke, only at the last second catching hold of a bush that grew on the ledge. Turning around, he looked down, brushing the tears out of his eyes, blinking hard.

"Helen!"

"Chris, hurry!"

"Where are you?"

"Here! *Here!*"

Suddenly, Chris caught sight of them through a rift in the heavy smoke. They were about twelve feet below on a wider ledge, pressed against the wall of the draw, ringed in by leaping flame. He saw Helen looking up frantically, trying to see him.

"Hold on!" he shouted. He looked around desperately. Four feet down and to the right was another bush. Quickly, Chris lowered himself over the side of the ledge and put his feet down until they settled on the bush. Holding on to the ledge with talon-like fingers, he put more and more weight on the bush until he was standing on it. Then he let go and ducked downward, grabbing hold of the bush.

"I'm almost there!" he called. He looked down and saw Helen gazing up at him with frightened eyes.

"Hurry, Chris!" she begged.

Chris jumped the rest of the way, sprawling down beside them on the ledge.

"Daddy!"

"Yes, baby." He held her for a moment, turning to Helen.

"Get on my shoulders," he said, "I'll hold you while you climb to that bush up there."

"All right." As Chris leaned against the wall, she clambered shakily to his shoulders. He held onto her calves while she reached up gingerly and caught onto the bush.

"Can you pull yourself up?"

"I'll try…"

In a few moments, her weight had left his shoulders and he heard the scrambling noise her sandals made as she climbed.

"Are you there?" he called up.

"Yes!"

"All right, I'm passing up Connie!"

Chris grabbed his shaking daughter and raised her to his shoulders.

"Grab her!" he said.

"I can't reach her!"

"Connie, stand up!" he ordered.

"I can't!"

"Yes!"

Her clutching hands left his head, he felt her trying to stand on his shoulders.

"Daddy, I'm falling!"

"You're not! I've got you. Reach up and take Mommy's hands!" A wave of dizziness passed over him. The heat seemed about to swallow him. He heard Connie's labored gasping above, heard Helen telling her to reach up a little further.

"Hurry, baby!" he shouted hoarsely.

Abruptly, Connie was off his shoulders, being drawn up. Chris fell, gasping, against the wall. Suddenly, he threw his arm up as a wind-driven burst of flame flashed toward him. He felt the searing heat on his flesh. Then the wind had sucked it back. Turning, he looked up. He could just make out their forms clinging to the side of the wall, their feet on the bush.

"Can't you reach the ledge?" he called.

"I can't, Chris! Not holding her!"

Gritting his teeth, Chris leaped up and caught onto the bush. For a moment it seemed as if he hadn't the strength to pull himself up. Teeth clenched, he strained upward inch by inch. He couldn't break now, not when they were so close to safety.

Another few seconds and he was on the bush beside them. He pulled himself up onto the narrow ledge, drew Connie up, then Helen. Then, too easily it seemed after all these horrible hours, all of them were on the rim of the draw and he was holding Connie, they were running from the fire and, though it seemed impossible to believe, he knew they were safe and that the nightmare was ended.

CHAPTER SEVENTEEN

CHRIS STOOD BY the living room window, staring out at the surf. In the back bedroom, Connie had just fallen asleep in Helen's arms. In the kitchen, Helen's mother was preparing some lunch. It was almost two-thirty.

None of them had spoken since the first few moments of hysterical relief that followed their escape. They had gotten into the car and Chris had driven them out of the canyon, stopping at a telephone booth to report the fire. Helen's mother had suggested that they go to her house for a while and, without comment, Chris had driven them there.

He glanced down at his left arm. There was a slow crawling of pain on it. He drew up his sleeve and saw that the skin was red. He let the sleeve fall. He'd take care of it later.

"Are you hungry?"

Chris looked around and saw Helen's mother standing in the kitchen doorway, looking at him. There was no expression on her face.

He shook his head a little. "No, thank you," he said. For a second, he tried to remember when it was he'd last eaten. Then, turning back to the window, he forgot about it. It didn't matter.

A few minutes later, Helen came out of the bedroom. Chris turned at the sound of her footsteps.

"How is she?" he asked.

"All right."

He swallowed dryly. "Is she—burned?" he asked.

"A little on her hands," she answered. "I put some salve on them."

He nodded and watched her move into the kitchen. He saw her mother embrace her and he turned back to the window.

In a minute, Helen came back in with two steaming cups. "Coffee?" she asked.

"Thank you." He took one of the cups and sat down on the sofa. It wasn't until his weight had settled on the cushion that he realized how tired he was.

Helen sat across from him on an armchair. She didn't meet his eyes.

"Does your head hurt?" she asked.

"No." It did hurt but he didn't want to talk about it.

"Helen?"

She looked up.

"Are you—?" He swallowed. "Do you want to know what I'm—going to do?"

Her lips flexed together tensely and Chris felt a flare of pain in his head. *She doesn't care,* he thought.

"Yes," she said, quietly.

"I'm going to the police."

"I see."

Is that all? asked his mind. Then he realized that it seemed a small thing now after what had happened.

He put down the cup and stared at his hands for several moments. Then, with a sigh, he got up.

"I'll go now," he said.

They looked at each other in silence. Her lips moved as if she couldn't find the proper words to speak.

"It—can't be the same," she said.

"I know." He kept looking at her, hoping that something could be said or done to end this pain. "I—know," he repeated, turning away.

"Do you—?"

He turned back. "What?"

"Do you want me to go with you?"

"If you want to."

She nodded slowly. "You're still my husband," she said. It sounded more like a reluctant admission than a statement, though.

You don't have to, bristled his mind. Then he knew that he had no privileges of resentment any more.

"Let's go then," he said.

"I'll tell Mom."

Chris stood by the front door while Helen spoke to her mother in the kitchen. He couldn't hear what they said. In several minutes, Helen came out and they left the house. They got into the car and Chris started driving toward Santa Monica.

"What do you—?" she started after they'd been driving for a while in silence. "What do you think will happen?"

"I don't know," he said.

"Oh..."

Helen glanced over at him. He had never looked so grave. She felt an urge to touch his hand, to comfort him. She repressed it. Things could *not* be the same. Thoughtless emotion had no point now.

Still, she thought, Connie was safe. She would not be if it hadn't been for Chris. Nor would she have ever been exposed to such horrible danger if it hadn't been for Chris, her mind reacted.

Nor would she have ever been born if it hadn't been for Chris, it reacted once again.

Things whirled in a circle. Every moment was the result of those before it, the foundation of those that followed. You could not divorce one from the other and find separate meaning in the parts. It existed as one flow—good and bad together—which you accepted or did not. Chris was in her life. She had accepted the good of that for many years. Now she was being asked to accept the bad of it. Right or wrong, could she turn her back on him?

Impulsively, Helen reached out and laid her hand on his arm. Don't! cried her mind but it was still a relief to be committed.

Chris was looking at her now. She had to speak and what she said had to be just right—not cruel yet not unquestioning.

"Just—give me a chance, Chris," she said.

He caught at her hand and held it tightly. And they said no more.

THE END